KT-131-844

Under Attack

By Edward Marston

THE HOME FRONT DETECTIVE SERIES

A Bespoke Murder • Instrument of Slaughter • Five Dead Canaries
Deeds of Darkness • Dance of Death • The Enemy Within • Under Attack

THE RAILWAY DETECTIVE SERIES

The Railway Detective • The Excursion Train • The Railway Viaduct
The Iron Horse • Murder on the Brighton Express
The Silver Locomotive Mystery • Railway to the Grave • Blood on the Line
The Stationmaster's Farewell • Peril on the Royal Train
A Ticket to Oblivion • Timetable of Death
Signal for Vengeance • The Circus Train Conspiracy
A Christmas Railway Mystery • Points of Danger

Inspector Colbeck's Casebook

THE BOW STREET RIVALS SERIES

Shadow of the Hangman • Steps to the Gallows
Date with the Executioner • Fugitive from the Grave

THE RESTORATION SERIES

The King's Evil • The Amorous Nightingale • The Repentant Rake
The Frost Fair • The Parliament House • The Painted Lady

THE BRACEWELL MYSTERIES

The Queen's Head • The Merry Devils • The Trip to Jerusalem
The Nine Giants • The Mad Courtesan • The Silent Woman
The Roaring Boy • The Laughing Hangman • The Fair Maid of Bohemia
The Wanton Angel • The Devil's Apprentice • The Bawdy Basket
The Vagabond Clown • The Counterfeit Crank
The Malevolent Comedy • The Princess of Denmark

THE CAPTAIN RAWSON SERIES

Soldier of Fortune • Drums of War • Fire and Sword
Under Siege • A Very Murdering Battle

a&b

Under Attack

EDWARD MARSTON

Allison & Busby Limited
12 Fitzroy Mews
London W1T 6DW
allisonandbusby.com

First published in Great Britain by Allison & Busby in 2017.
This paperback edition published by Allison & Busby in 2018.

Copyright © 2017 by EDWARD MARSTON

The moral right of the author is hereby asserted in accordance with
the Copyright, Designs and Patents Act 1988.

All characters and events in this publication,
other than those clearly in the public domain,
are fictitious and any resemblance to actual persons,
living or dead, is purely coincidental.

All rights reserved. No part of this publication may be reproduced,
stored in a retrieval system, or transmitted, in any form or by
any means without the prior written permission of the publisher,
nor be otherwise circulated in any form of binding or cover
other than that in which it is published and without a similar
condition being imposed on the subsequent buyer.

A CIP catalogue record for this book is available from
the British Library.

10 9 8 7 6 5 4 3 2 1

ISBN 978-0-7490-2200-6

Typeset in 11/16 pt Adobe Garamond Pro by
Allison & Busby Ltd.

The paper used for this Allison & Busby publication
has been produced from trees that have been legally sourced
from well-managed and credibly certified forests.

Printed and bound by
CPI Group (UK) Ltd, Croydon, CR0 4YY

CHAPTER ONE

Everitt White had spent most of his life afloat. Born on a narrowboat in Staffordshire, he'd devoted his early years to helping his father in the unremitting work of hauling cargo up and down canals in the Midlands and beyond. To broaden his horizons, he'd joined the merchant navy and learnt to cope with rough seas and gale force winds. When he felt that he'd seen enough of the world, he applied for a job in the Thames River Police and found his true métier. It was hard, gruelling labour but White was ideally suited for it. He made light of long days heaving on his oars and mastering the capricious tides. He didn't blench when he had to retrieve the bloated corpse of a human being or of an animal from the water. Nor did he recoil from the distinctive reek of the Thames. It was his whole world now and he relished it.

The police galley was a clinker-built open boat less than thirty feet in length. It had three thwarts for oarsmen and a seat in the stern from which Inspector White could steer with rudder strings. He commanded a crew of three men, two of whom had only a single oar while the third, on the centre thwart, pulled on a pair of sculls. It was the position that White himself had held for many years so he knew how much skill and effort it took. He'd learnt how to read the river and, having seen colleagues swept helplessly into it over the years, he always respected its power. Though it seemed relatively placid that morning, White remained alert.

In the normal course of events, he rarely looked up. He was too busy scanning the surface of the Thames with a well-trained eye. For once, however, his attention was diverted and he stared up at the sky. Emitting an odd clanking noise from their whirring propellers, a fleet of fourteen big biplanes was cruising above him. His men also lifted their gaze upward. All of them thought at first that they were witnessing a display of British air power, visual proof that the city was well defended. It was a common mistake. They could hear people on both banks yelling in admiration or breaking into applause. Tragically, celebrations were soon cut short. When the bombs began to fall, everyone realised that they'd been cruelly deceived. London was under direct attack. Gotha bombers had reached the nation's capital in broad daylight and they showed no mercy.

Their bombs caused deafening explosions and spread

disaster. White was horrified at the sheer audacity of the attack. Cold, systematic and unchallenged, the planes were wreaking havoc. The main targets seemed to be the docks and the area around Liverpool Street Station. Poplar, in particular, was taking real punishment. Since they were close to the docks, the river police were right in the middle of the action. Fire sprung up among the warehouses around them. Moored vessels sustained direct hits. Dock workers were sent scurrying for cover. The Gothas kept up their barrage relentlessly until all their bombs had been dropped then, content with their work, they turned in a wide circle and headed for the south coast. Behind them they left chaos and confusion. Everitt White summed the attack up in one word.

'Bastards!'

When he looked down at the river once more, he saw that they had company. A dead body was bobbing up and down only yards away.

CHAPTER TWO

It was not the best way to return to work. Harvey Marmion had had to force himself to go back to Scotland Yard that morning. He'd taken ten days' leave in order to search for his son, Paul, who had run away from home months earlier, but it had been a fruitless venture. For all his efforts, Marmion had found no sign whatsoever of him. He couldn't even come back with the reassuring news that Paul was still alive because he had no evidence of it. All that he could tell his wife was that they would find their son one day. It was cold comfort. Arriving at his office usually gave him an instant stimulus. Instead of being primed for action now, however,

Marmion simply wanted to curl up in a corner and hide away. As a detective, he had an excellent record of success behind him. Yet when it came to tracing his only son, he'd failed abysmally.

Joe Keedy tried to cheer him up.

'Paul can look after himself,' he said.

'Why doesn't he just tell us where he is?'

'He has his reasons.'

'I'm one of them,' admitted Marmion. 'We were never close. Other fathers get to spend time with their children but shift work stopped me from doing that. I let him down, Joe. I'm afraid that Paul left home because of me.'

'That's nonsense.'

'I was so proud of him when he joined the army. Life in uniform brought out the best in him at first. He blossomed. Then came the Somme and that ruined him. It wasn't so much the physical wounds. He got over most of those in time. It was his mind.' He heaved a sigh. 'Paul couldn't even be civil with us any more.'

'That was *his* fault, Harv, not yours.'

'We were all at fault – me, Ellen, Alice and even you, to some extent.'

Keedy bridled. 'You can't blame me because he hopped it.'

'You're part of the family, Joe, and that's what he's turned his back on.'

'Since he got back from the army, I hardly ever saw him.'

'Neither did I. That's why I feel so guilty.'

Marmion made a conscious effort to shake off his lethargy and dispel his gloom. Forgetting his son, he asked to be

9

brought up to date with the investigation on which Keedy had been working during his absence. The sergeant pulled out his notebook. He was concise yet comprehensive. His report provided a good basis for discussion and they traded ideas freely. Time slipped more easily past and Marmion began to feel at home once more. They were just about to go off to the canteen when the door was flung open to reveal the tall, slim figure of Superintendent Claude Chatfield.

'Ah,' he said, seeing Marmion, 'you're back at last.'

'I tried to report to you, sir, but you were busy with the commissioner.'

'We had a lot to discuss – until the air raid interrupted us, that is.'

'What air raid?' asked Keedy.

'Are you deaf, man? German aircraft have been pounding the docks this morning. There's been significant damage and many fatalities.'

Marmion was surprised. 'Zeppelins don't usually attack in daylight, sir.'

'This was a raid by Gothas, apparently,' explained Chatfield. 'How they got this far, I shall never know, but it's given us a nasty shock. The war is no longer something that's happening on the other side of the English Channel. It's right here.'

'You mentioned fatalities, sir.'

'I can't give you a number but it will be a distressingly high one. The latest information I have is that there was a direct hit on a school in Poplar. The bomb detonated in the basement where the youngest children were being taught. You can imagine the disaster it must have caused. It's inhuman,' said

Chatfield with sudden passion, 'and it's happened right here in London. None of us is safe any longer.'

It was a grim prediction. With its recurring defeats and setbacks, 1916 had been a dreadful year for the Allies. Its few victories were bought at enormous cost. There seemed to be little visible progress in the succeeding year. Trench warfare had moved the conflict close to a stalemate. British tanks had been lauded as the weapons to change the face of the war but it had simply not happened to the degree imagined. The latest outrage would tilt the advantage in favour of Germany once more. The sight of bombers flying at will over the capital was a far more powerful image than a photograph of tanks stuck in the mud on the Western Front.

'However,' said Chatfield, fussily, 'let's concentrate on our own work. We can leave the emergency services to deal with the aftermath of the air raid.'

'The sergeant has been telling me what I've missed,' said Marmion. 'I'm well prepared to continue with the investigation now.'

Chatfield was peremptory. 'I'm assigning it elsewhere.'

'Why?'

'Because something more important has come up,' explained the other. 'Trying to solve a spate of burglaries is not the ideal use of your time. You and the sergeant are at your best when you have something to get your teeth into.'

'That's true,' agreed Keedy.

'A corpse has been hauled out of the Thames. It's not another case of suicide this time. We've had our fair share of those. There's clear evidence of foul play. I want you to handle the case, Inspector,' he went on with a shrewd glance at him. 'I take it that you're up to it?'

'Yes, sir,' replied Marmion, firmly.

'If you need more time to settle in . . .'

'I'm fine, Superintendent. All we need are the details.'

Chatfield handed him a sheet of paper. Marmion was annoyed at the suggestion he might need time before he was functioning properly in his role at Scotland Yard. He showed no irritation, however, because Chatfield had been very accommodating. The two men had never liked each other and there was always a residual unease between them. When he'd applied for leave, Marmion had expected some opposition from the superintendent but it never came. A father himself, Chatfield encouraged him to go in search of his missing son. Marmion was very grateful for the unconditional support.

'Did you make any headway?' asked Chatfield, softly.

'No, sir,' replied Marmion. 'To be honest, I made none at all.'

'I'm sorry to hear that.'

'We won't give up the search until we find him.'

'How is Mrs Marmion?'

'My wife is . . . doing her best to remain hopeful, sir.'

Ellen Marmion was struck by the paradox every single day. Having wanted her son to go, she was in despair at his disappearance. When Paul was there, she'd found his presence both intrusive and worrying. He'd been so rude to any friends she'd invited into the house that she stopped asking them to come there. He showed his mother no respect, still less any affection. It was like having a stranger living with them. Since

12

her husband worked such long hours, the burden of dealing with their brusque and uncommunicative son fell on her. It had been a struggle for Ellen simply to get a few words out of him. Paul had treated her with something approaching contempt. And yet she wanted him back. She longed to be reconciled with him.

Pain, anxiety and guilt had combined to take its toll on her. Ellen had been a plump, attractive, middle-aged woman until her son had been invalided out of the army. All of her old vivacity had now drained away. Her eyes were dull, her brow wrinkled, her shoulders hunched and her whole body seemed to have shrunk in size. Alice was all too aware of the physical changes in her mother. It was one of the reasons she tried to spend more time at home. She wanted to offer love and companionship. What she was unable to do, however, was to still the demons in Ellen's mind.

'I thought that your father would find him somehow.'

'So did I,' said Alice.

'That's his job, after all – searching for people.'

'Tracking down criminals is a different matter, Mummy. There's usually a trail of evidence to follow. Paul didn't leave that. We had no clue as to where he might have gone. When he first set out, he probably had no clue himself. He just wanted to get away from us.'

'Away from *me*, you mean.'

'Away from the situation he was in,' corrected Alice. 'He felt trapped and worthless while he was here – and you mustn't think that it was because of you. The blame lies with this terrible war. That's what destroyed him.'

'Other young men had worse injuries and learnt to live with them.'

'Paul couldn't manage to do that.'

'We were ready to help him in every possible way, Alice.'

'He spurned our help. There was an element of cruelty in that.'

'I know,' confessed Ellen. 'He wanted to *hurt* us.'

She hugged her daughter impulsively. Alice was in the Women's Police Service but, because her shift didn't begin until that afternoon, she'd spent the morning at home again. Her mother had been distressed when she'd first moved out to enjoy a degree of independence. Looking back, Alice was glad that she'd done so. Being stuck at home when her brother was there would have created an even more fractious household. Though she sympathised with her mother's plight, Alice felt that she'd made the right decision.

When she broke away, Ellen's eyes were moist with tears.

'My biggest fear is that Paul will . . . end it all.'

'No, Mummy, I don't think that's likely somehow.'

'But he said in effect that his life was not worth living.'

'That doesn't mean he's been thinking of suicide,' said Alice. 'If he'd reached that stage, he'd have done something about it long before now.'

'You read such awful stories in the newspapers. There was one only yesterday about a disabled soldier who slit his throat because he'd lost both legs and no longer felt like a proper man. And there have been lots of others.'

'Those are the exceptions, Mummy. As you said earlier, most victims have found a way of pulling through. Paul will survive somehow. He's got far too much sense to want to do anything desperate.'

'Running away from us was an act of desperation.'

'He might have thought he was *helping* us, Mummy.'

'*Helping* us,' echoed Ellen. 'He frightened me to death.'

'I'm trying to see it from Paul's point of view.'

'I did that when he was here. It was a waste of time.'

Alice glanced at the clock on the mantelpiece. 'I must be going.'

'Thank you so much,' said Ellen, squeezing her daughter's hands.

'I'll come again as soon as I can.'

'Don't go yet. There's something I must tell you. I haven't had the courage to tell your father yet. I'm not sure that I ever will. But . . .' Ellen was clearly wrestling with mixed emotions. She took a deep breath before plunging in. 'When he spent all that time searching and came back empty-handed, I was very upset at first. Then I remembered what I had to go through when Paul was here and . . . well, part of me was glad he wasn't found. Isn't that a dreadful thing for a mother to admit?' she said, biting her lip. 'But it's true. I'm not sure that I ever want him back, Alice.'

The detectives were familiar visitors to the police morgue. Since they dealt almost exclusively with murder investigations, their work often began there. While he was not squeamish, Marmion never enjoyed being obliged to view cadavers, especially if they'd been butchered in some perverse way. Keedy, by contrast, took it all in his stride. Having worked

15

in the family undertaking business, he'd been cheek by jowl with death on a daily basis and was accustomed to the hideous distortions it could inflict on the human body. The information that had taken them there was scant. All they knew was that an unidentified, middle-aged white male had been pulled out of the Thames earlier that morning.

Entering the building with his usual flutter of trepidation, Marmion was delighted to see someone he recognised. The burly frame of Everitt White was seated on a bench. He got to his feet instantly and extended a gnarled hand.

'How are you, Harvey?' he said, pumping away. 'It's good to see you again.'

'It's good to see *you*, Everitt,' said Marmion, noting the strength of the handshake. 'You've found us another customer, I see.'

'I like to keep you busy.'

'You remember Sergeant Keedy, don't you?'

'Yes, I do.' He shook hands with Keedy. 'You're looking spick and span.'

'Someone has to set standards,' said Keedy with a grin.

It was a gibe at Marmion who always looked shabby even in his best suit. Keedy, by contrast, took great pains to look smart. White was in uniform and manifestly proud of his rank. Marmion showed him the sheet of paper he'd been given. When he'd glanced through it, White handed it back.

'I can add a few things to that,' he said. 'For a start, I can tell you exactly where the poor devil was found. We were too busy watching the air raid to spot him at first.' He waited until Keedy had his notebook out. 'Ready, Sergeant?'

'Yes, I am,' said the other. 'Fire away, Inspector.'

'This chap is unusual. Bodies usually stay underwater for one or two weeks. My guess is that he was only dumped in the river three days ago at most. Don't ask me why or I'll talk for the whole afternoon. My judgement is based on years of pulling corpses out of the Thames. Trust me.'

'How was he killed?' asked Marmion.

'He was strangled. The marks around his neck tell their own story.'

'Is there anything else of interest?'

'Before he made a big splash,' said White, 'he was robbed. His wallet, watch and cufflinks were taken. His shoes are missing as well, but they could just have been eased off by an undercurrent.'

'What kind of man was he, Everitt?'

'Oh, he's not short of a few pennies, I can tell you that. His suit has real quality and his shirt probably cost more than I earn in a month. When we'd hauled him aboard, my immediate impression was that we had a wealthy businessman in the galley.'

'Are you still using those old things?' said Keedy. 'You should have gone beyond rowing boats by now. Why not use a steam-powered vessel?'

'We tried a couple of them,' replied White, 'and they just weren't up to it. Three strong men in a galley are much more reliable. That's why you've had a steady supply of bodies from us over the years.'

'This latest one takes priority now,' said Marmion. 'One of us has to go in and take a close look at him. I'm volunteering you,

Joe.' Keedy gave a hollow laugh. 'If there's no identification on him, we'll need some of his effects. Since he's so well dressed, he may have an expensive London tailor.'

'I'll ask him,' said Keedy.

After an exchange of farewells with White, he went off and left the two old friends alone. White narrowed his eyelids as he peered at Marmion.

'You look tired, Harvey.'

'I feel exhausted.'

'Has that swine of a superintendent been making a nuisance of himself?'

'No,' said Marmion, 'he hasn't. In fact, Chat has been very understanding. Our son decided to run away from home and I was granted ten days' leave to find him. Chat urged me to go.' He shook his head sadly. 'It was a wild goose chase. I only came back to work today.'

'I'm sorry to hear about your son.'

'We all have our crosses to bear, Everitt.' He forced a smile. 'Let's go back to the murder victim. When you first saw him, did you draw any other conclusion?'

'Yes, I did.'

'Go on.'

'It's based on instinct rather than on any evidence.'

'I'd still like to hear it.'

White ran a contemplative hand across the lower part of his bulbous features.

'I think he was killed as a warning to others,' he said. 'That's why he was allowed to bob back up to the surface. If his killer had wanted him to disappear altogether, he'd have attached weights to keep him underwater indefinitely. But he deliberately let him pop up for us to find.'

'It's an interesting theory, Everitt. I'm not sure that I'm convinced by it.'

'There's something I haven't mentioned.'

'Oh?'

'His tongue has been cut out.'

CHAPTER THREE

When the war broke out in 1914, Sir Edward Henry was well past the age of sixty and on the brink of retirement. A sense of duty impelled him to stay on in his taxing role as commissioner of the Metropolitan Police Force. A distinguished career in the civil service and the police lay behind him but he felt that he still had more to offer. He was a tall, elegant, impeccably attired man with curling grey hair counterpointed by a curling grey moustache. Everyone in the force respected him, though those in the lower ranks found him rather aloof, resenting his habit of dealing primarily with those at superintendent level or above it.

True to type, he summoned a group of his senior colleagues to his office to pass on the latest news.

'I can't give you chapter and verse,' he apologised, 'but I do have some numbers to pass on. They are demoralising. As a result of today's air raid, 162 people were killed and somewhere in the region of 400 were wounded.'

There was a general murmur of sympathy and disgust.

'All of these victims, please note, were civilians.'

'It's intolerable,' said Chatfield. 'War should be fought between soldiers. Due consideration should be given to non-combatants.'

'I couldn't agree more, Superintendent.'

'Do those figures include the victims at that school?'

'Unhappily, they do,' replied the commissioner. 'On the top floor, a class of girls was having a singing lesson. When the bomb came through the roof, one of them was killed outright. On the floor below, a boy was killed by flying rubble but the real carnage was in the basement. That was where the bomb exploded. It took away the lives of eighteen children and left thirty or so horribly maimed. Such are the monsters we are up against, gentlemen. They make no distinction whatsoever between soldiers and civilians. Women and children are equally attractive targets to them.'

'It's revolting!' exclaimed someone. 'It must be stopped.'

'That task falls to our armed forces. All that we can do is to protect the people of London and give them a sense of safety, however tenuous it may be. In view of today's raid, that will be even more difficult. When the war started,' he reminded them, 'the government imposed censorship on the press and controlled the flow of information that was released. They rightly suppressed some of the horrors at the front to prevent such news from spreading panic. But it's impossible to hide what happened in the skies above London today. It was a perfect example of German ruthlessness. Our citizens will go to bed in fear tonight.'

'Where was the Royal Flying Corps?' demanded Chatfield. 'Why weren't our planes taking on the Gothas?'

'You may well ask, Inspector.'

'We had no defence at all.'

'I'm sure that the newspapers will make that point,' said the commissioner. 'At least, they'll have a story to tell tomorrow. When they're starved of news, they make it up for themselves. Who will forget those nonsensical claims earlier this year that the bodies of soldiers killed in action were taken to a factory where they were boiled down to provide material for pig feed, fertiliser and soap? That's what the British public were being asked to believe.'

'I believed it myself at first,' murmured someone. 'The Huns are bestial.'

'Even they have their limits,' added Chatfield.

'I've called you here this afternoon,' said Sir Edward, 'to issue two warnings. The first is to handle the press with care. There has been a lot of sniping at us recently. Naturally, I've had to bear the brunt of it but that's my job. What I object to is the routine attacks on our operational efficiency. Newspaper editors seem to forget that we've taken on an increased range of duties with depleted manpower. I suppose that the pendulum was bound to swing the other way,' he continued. 'We all enjoyed the praise we garnered from the way we dealt with cases like those of Dr Crippen and Steinie Morrison. Our triumphs were well and truly trumpeted then. Open a newspaper today, however, and it's our perceived failings that get the publicity.'

There was general agreement that Scotland Yard had come in for sustained criticism of late. Instead of praise for their success, they were being called to account for their failures. Rising crime figures were attacked and those involved in unsolved murders were castigated. Pressure on the police was increasing all the time. Several people in the room had felt the painful lash of a newspaper's whip.

'To conclude,' said the commissioner, bringing the debate to a halt, 'we must get the press back on our side. The best way to do that is to redouble our efforts to solve outstanding cases and to project ourselves in a better light. And though we need to impress crime reporters, don't get too close to them. Don't leak information to them about a particular investigation. In a word – beware.'

As he let his words sink in, he looked around at every face in the room.

'You said that there were two warnings, Sir Edward,' recalled Chatfield. 'What's the second one?'

'It's linked to the first. I'm talking about juvenile gangs. Reports of their antics are getting more and more publicity. It's another stick with which the press can beat us. Unfortunately,' said the commissioner, 'it's another consequence of the war. The fathers and elder brothers who could control these delinquents have either joined the army or died in action. There's no strong voice in such families.'

'It's the same everywhere,' someone interjected. 'Glasgow has an appalling problem with young hooligans. Manchester, Birmingham and other cities have similar headaches. Feral gangs are terrorising the poorer districts. They're running riot.'

'Well, they're not going to do that here,' said the commissioner. 'The rule of law must be obeyed. When we lost a sizeable number of our men to the army, we appointed 20,000 constables in their wake. They're all good, public-spirited men but they're predominantly elderly. They can't chase hooligans as fast as they'd like. So let me issue this warning,' he went on, raising his voice, 'I intend to divert resources to take a more robust stance against juvenile crime. As of today, I'm appointing a special unit to coordinate our response.' Everyone voiced their approval. 'London has enough to put up with already. I'm not having this city plagued by gang warfare.'

There were eight of them in all and they walked along the street with the arrogant strut of conquering soldiers. All of them carried knives and some had additional weapons. Most of them bore scars from earlier encounters or from initiation ceremonies. Huddled in the doorways, old men, women and small children looked at them with mingled respect and fear. Nobody dared to get in their way. This was their territory and they were untouchable. The oldest of them was fifteen but he had the build of a full-grown man. As he led them into a long, dark tunnel, they yelled out obscenities for the sheer pleasure of hearing the echo. When they came out into the light again, they were laughing. Fatally, they were off guard. Before they knew it, they were ambushed by well over a dozen rival gang members, armed with broken bottles, hammers and knives. With the advantage of surprise, they struck with ferocity. The clash was over in a minute. When the attackers fled, they left wounded bodies strewn across the ground in pools of blood.

'This is getting us nowhere,' complained Keedy. 'He may not even have had the suit made here in London. We could wear out our shoe leather for nothing.'

'I thought you'd enjoy calling on some of the cream of our men's outfitters, Joe. Every time you look in a window, you drool.'

'I could never afford a suit like those.'

'Staring at them costs nothing,' said Marmion.

'Well, I've had enough goggling for one afternoon.'

They'd just come out of their third shop in Bond Street and it had been as unhelpful as the previous two. None of them had recognised the suit that had been removed from the corpse and – after most of the water was squeezed out of it – put into a sack. Managers of all three shops had recoiled when the soggy mass had been hauled out for their inspection.

'This is ridiculous, Harv,' said Keedy.

'Why?'

'We're keeping dogs yet barking ourselves. This is not *our* job. We've got detective constables at our beck and call. Let one of them do the legwork.'

'Do you really want to miss the fun?'

'I haven't noticed any so far.'

Marmion laughed. 'See it as your reward, Joe,' he said. 'Because you took on the sordid job of viewing the body on the slab, the least I could do was to let you be there when we discover who the deceased really is.'

'We may never find out. The killer cut the tailor's name out of the suit.'

'He was just trying to make it difficult for us. I'm relying on Everitt White's judgement. He knows a good suit when he sees one. Only last year, he fished a member of the House of Lords out of the river. And he was right about the latest victim, wasn't he?'

'Yes,' conceded Keedy, grumpily. 'The pathologist agreed that he'd only been in the water two or three days.'

'The post-mortem may tell us why.'

'Meanwhile, I have to carry this sack around London. It stinks.'

'My sympathies lie with the man who used to wear it.'

Keedy lowered his head. 'And so should mine.'

'Remember that, Joe.'

'I'm sorry to moan. *He's* the victim, not me. Oh, I hate this stage of an investigation,' he said. 'It's tiresome. I joined the police for action.'

'That begins when we have his identity.'

'If we ever do, that is.'

Marmion nudged him playfully. 'Your optimism is an inspiration to us all.'

By the time that the two middle-aged special constables got there, most of the gang had got to their feet and were threatening reprisals against their attackers. Some were badly wounded. The policemen could see the discarded broken bottles in the gutter and imagine what had happened. When they took out their notebooks, however, they were met by a wall of silence. None of the gang was prepared to give his name or to describe what had happened. Ignoring dire warnings, they vowed to get their revenge very soon.

'We'll kill them!' boasted their leader.

'Then you'll finish up behind bars,' said one of the policemen.

'It'd be worth it.'

The other policeman had been examining wounds. 'Five of you at least need to go to hospital. Those gashes should be stitched up.' He looked around at the members of the gang. 'All of you need to be examined by a doctor. Some of you might have broken ribs or other wounds that are not visible.'

'We'll manage,' said the leader.

'You need help, lad.'

'That's our business.'

'When there's been a brawl in the street, it's *our* business as well.'

The gang sniggered with contempt and, though they were in obvious pain, they began to slink away. When one of the policemen tried to go after them, his companion put a restraining hand on his shoulder.

'Let them go, Dave,' he advised.

'We should at least search them for weapons.'

'And do you think they'd stand there meekly while we did so? Let them go. If they want to bleed to death, they'll be doing us a favour.'

* * *

At their fifth port of call, they finally had success. The manager wrinkled his nose in disgust when he first saw the suit, then he did something that none of his predecessors had done. They'd dismissed it instantly because it was not in their individual styles. Having laid out the jacket and trousers on the counter, the latest man extracted a tape from a drawer and took a series of measurements. Their hopes were raised.

'Was it made here?' asked Keedy.

'I'm fairly certain that it was, sir,' said the manager.

'What are you doing?'

'I'm trying to bring its owner back to life for you. We keep a detailed record of our clients' measurements. You'd be surprised how they change over the years.' He lowered his voice. 'This gentleman, for instance, had a substantial paunch.'

'I know. I saw it.'

'You can see how the tailoring accommodated it so skilfully.'

When he'd taken a complete set of measurements, the manager disappeared into the back room. In the plush surroundings, the suit looked both repulsive and incongruous. Marmion pointed to the model in the shop window.

'How would you like to wear something like that, Joe?'

'I'd love it,' replied the other, eyeing the suit covetously. 'But there's the small problem of paying for it. I'd need to be promoted to the rank of commissioner before I could afford that.'

'You'd have to leapfrog *me* to do that. And I'd have to leapfrog Chat.'

'The chain of command above us is endless.'

'I agree. We have to resign ourselves to staying where we are.'

'You had a good chance to move up in the world, Harv.'

'That was a mistake. When the job was within my grasp, I realised I didn't really want it.'

When the post of superintendent had become vacant, Marmion had applied for it along with Claude Chatfield. Both were equally well qualified to take on extra responsibility. Most onlookers felt that Marmion would be the better choice. At the last moment, however, he'd deliberately failed the interview so that he could keep a job that he prized. Knowing nothing of his change of mind, Chatfield had been promoted on the grounds of what he believed was his clear superiority and he was never slow to remind Marmion of that.

They were still admiring the suit in the window when the manager returned with a small, round-shouldered man in his fifties, his face clouded with grief. The detectives were introduced to Mr Vickery.

'Is it true that he's dead?' he asked, querulously.

'That depends who you mean,' said Marmion.

'He's been a client for years. I made all of his suits.' He looked wistfully down at the jacket and fingered the lapel. 'Including this one.'

'Then who the devil is he?'

'I thought it might be Mr Vickery's work when I first saw the suit,' said the manager. 'The measurements confirmed who bought it.'

'What was his name?'

'Mr Gilbert Donohoe.'

'Do you have an address? We need to inform his next of kin.'

'Of course, sir,' said the other, reaching under the counter to produce a ledger. 'Mr Donohoe lived in Birmingham.'

CHAPTER FOUR

Back on duty, Alice Marmion walked along the pavement with her beat partner, Iris Goodliffe. Of the two, Alice was by far the slighter, smarter and prettier. Iris was always bemoaning the fact that, while her friend was engaged to a handsome detective sergeant, she aroused no interest at all in the opposite sex. It consigned her to a lot of lonely evenings.

'I don't know what to do, Alice,' she said.

'Someone will come along eventually.'

'I've been saying that to myself for years.'

'It's one of the legacies of the war, Iris. It's obvious why. Young men are in very short supply. Hundreds of thousands of them joined up. Many of those left behind are either married or not available for some reason.'

'How did you manage to get your hands on someone like Joe Keedy?'

'Oh, we'd known each other for ages,' said Alice, 'ever since he and my father started working together, in fact. Joe was simply a friend at first. Nothing developed between us for years, then one day . . .'

'If only that sort of thing could happen to me!'

'It will, I'm sure.'

Alice spoke with false confidence. It was easy to see why Iris was not popular with men. She was a big, rather plain young woman with an over-eagerness that would deter most potential suitors. Worryingly, she'd started to copy Alice in the hope of improving her appearance. She had the same hairstyle and used the same cosmetics. Iris had even started to pick up her friend's catchphrases and speech rhythms. In aping Alice, however, she was making herself even less appealing.

'I wish I'd had the chance to meet him,' she said.

'Who are you talking about?'

'Paul, of course – I'd like to have known your brother.'

'He wasn't very sociable, Iris.'

'I'd have been happy to make allowances.'

'He could be quite coarse sometimes.'

'Beggars can't be choosers,' said Iris with a wan smile.

Though she enjoyed working with her, Alice had always protected her private life. She didn't want to let Iris get too close and she certainly hadn't been ready to introduce her to the members of her family. The one time she'd gone out for the night with Iris had been unnerving. Pleasant and easy-going at first, Iris had become a different woman when she had a drink inside her. It had released all her inhibitions and she'd made a scene in public. Alice had had to hustle her quickly out of the bar into which they'd gone after an evening at the cinema. From that time on, she'd kept the other woman at arm's length when off duty.

'Do you think that Paul will ever come back?'

'We don't know, Iris.'

'But you're sure that he's still alive.'

'Oh, yes, there's no doubt. Daddy feels strongly about that.'

'You have such a happy family. Why did your brother run away?'

'We don't know. He felt he didn't belong with us any more, perhaps.'

'Since he had shell shock, you'd have thought he'd be even more dependent on you all. He was virtually blind at first, wasn't he?'

'His eyesight steadily improved. Unfortunately, his behaviour didn't.'

'Didn't he have any friends from the army?'

'He did at first,' replied Alice. 'He used to meet a group of them from time to time. They'd all been invalided home. Paul soon got bored with them. He used to be so tolerant in the old days, but not any more.'

'It must be so upsetting for you.'

'It is.'

'Do you think the army did enough for him?'

'They did what they could, Iris. Paul is only one of

33

thousands, many of whom are in a far worse state. There was only so much time the doctor could give him.'

'Is he bitter about the war?'

'Who wouldn't be in his position?'

'We had a taste of war ourselves earlier on. That air raid really scared me.'

'I was visiting my mother when I heard the explosions. Those incendiary bombs can cause so much damage.'

When they turned a corner, the road widened. Coming towards them on the opposite pavement were two policemen on their beat. Alice acknowledged them with a smile but Iris gave them a cheery wave. Both men grinned. Iris was despondent.

'I don't know why I bothered,' she said. 'They only looked at *you*.'

Marmion and Keedy caught a train to Birmingham and managed to find an empty compartment where they could talk freely. They reviewed what they'd learnt from the visit to the tailor's shop.

'They both said the same thing,' observed Marmion. 'Mr Donohoe was very refined. When he came to London, he often went to the theatre or a concert.'

'I wish I had the time and money to do that.'

'The likes of us have to make do with the cinema, Joe.'

'We haven't seen a film for months,' said Keedy. 'Alice is always complaining about it.'

'Inspector White summed him up correctly. Donohoe was a rich businessman. Knowing his politics, I'm surprised that Everitt didn't call him a bloated capitalist.'

'That's what he was – in both senses. He was very flabby. It takes a lot of four-course meals to make a body look as repellent as that. It's a pity that neither the manager nor Vickery knew where he stayed when he was in London. Donohoe had a secretive streak, by all accounts.'

'Refined, prosperous, overweight, secretive,' mused Marmion. 'He lived in a very different world to us, Joe.'

'How well do you know Birmingham?'

'I know enough to recognise that Edgbaston is one of the posh parts of the city. Since he lives there, he must have money to burn. What surprises me is that nobody's reported him as a missing person.'

'He'd only been in London for a few days, Harv. Maybe his family was used to him being away that long. After all, he had business to transact in the City.'

'Not any more, he doesn't.'

'There'll be partners and associates to talk to,' said Keedy, uneasily. 'We're on foreign soil there. That suit Donohoe was wearing cost over a hundred pounds,' he added in disbelief. 'We're going to be dealing with people who have the same expensive tastes.'

'They may have the money,' said Marmion, hand to his chest, 'but our job brings us rewards of the heart. Besides, it's not impossible that the killer was a business rival. He won't have much use for a hundred-pound suit when we secure a conviction. He'll be shivering in prison garb as he waits for the hangman to come calling.'

'Do you think Donohoe *was* murdered by a business rival?'

'It's an obvious assumption. On the other hand, it may be

that he was simply killed for his money. Wallet, watch and cufflinks were taken. They're the kind of things a thief would be after.'

'Why did he remove the tailor's name out of the coat?'

'He wanted to delay identification of the victim.'

'Most thieves wouldn't have bothered. As soon as they'd got what they wanted, they'd simply drop their victim in the river and run for it.'

'Everitt White thought he might have been murdered as a warning.'

'Who was the warning aimed at?'

'Some associates of his, I suppose. Don't forget his tongue.'

'Yes,' said Keedy, 'why was that cut out?'

'Perhaps he spoke out of turn and someone objected to what he said. We can but speculate. The main thing is that we have a name and address. Once the family has been informed, details can be passed on to the press. If Donohoe was a regular visitor to London, a lot of people will have known him. We just have to hope that they'll come forward to help us.'

Though often derided by those in the lower ranks, Claude Chatfield had his virtues. Indeed, in some ways, he did certain things better than Marmion. He had a good grasp of detail, a readiness to take on the burden of administration and a gift for deploying the right people to the various cases that landed on his desk. His ability to work long hours impressed his colleagues. They found him less admirable when Chatfield, a devout Roman Catholic, lapsed into homiletic mode. Most of them felt that finger-wagging Christianity was out of place in Scotland Yard.

Chatfield was leafing through some documents when there was a tap on the door and the commissioner entered. The superintendent stood politely to his feet.

'Sit down, sit down,' said the visitor, flapping a hand. 'I just wanted you to see this report. It's so relevant to what I was saying to you all earlier on.'

Handing a sheet of paper to Chatfield, he waited while the other man resumed his seat and started reading. It was a report of the brawl between two gangs. The superintendent was shocked by the details.

'This is deplorable,' he said. 'It's open warfare on the streets of London.'

'That's what it's come to, Superintendent, and it's why I'm giving it priority.'

'They're nothing but adolescent ruffians.'

'As you can see, the ones who were viciously attacked call themselves the Stepney Warriors. They're a law unto themselves. We don't know their individual names. They refused to give them. When they staggered off, some of them had the sense to go to the hospital for attention but they gave false names there.'

'Were there no witnesses?'

'There were several,' said the commissioner, 'but they stayed in their houses and watched from behind the curtains. Needless to say, they didn't rush to come forward when our officers asked for statements.'

'They're afraid, Sir Edward. These gangs always threaten revenge.'

'Oh, I think we know where they'll try to get that – from the vile thugs who laid that ambush. They rejoice in the name of the Evil Spirits. Well, they can't be allowed to do so for long. I want the whole area exorcised.'

'I couldn't agree with you more, Sir Edward.'

'The East End can do without any more upheaval. It's been in the eye of the hurricane for far too long. Don't these hooligans realise that there's a war on? Heavens!' exclaimed the commissioner. 'Poplar was hit by German bombs only this morning and so was part of Stepney. Those gangs should have been helping to rescue people from the rubble, not doing their damnedest to kill each other.'

'Thank you for showing me this,' said Chatfield, returning the report. 'It's a timely reminder of a growing problem.'

'I came to you for advice. When I discussed it with the new unit, we were of one mind. The most effective way to deal with this problem is to infiltrate the gangs in some way.' He raised a palm. 'I don't mean that we should hire some fifteen-year-old to take his life in his hands and join the Stepney Warriors or the Evil Spirits. That would be impossible. But we need someone who knows the East End well and who can get close enough to these young blackguards to find out their names and anticipate where they'll strike next.'

Chatfield scratched his head. 'That's a tall order, Sir Edward.'

'I'm asking a number of senior officers to suggest names.'

'The detective chosen would be taking huge risks.'

'That's why we need someone who does that routinely.'

'Ordinarily, I'd have put forward Sergeant Keedy,' said Chatfield. 'He's fearless to the point of being foolhardy at times.

But he's a first-rate detective. The main strike against him is that he's not an East Ender. He wouldn't blend in so easily. Also, he and Inspector Marmion are already busy elsewhere.'

'Can you think of anyone else?'

Chatfield pondered. 'There *is* someone,' he said at length.

'What's his name?'

'Constable Burge.'

'How long has he been with us?'

'He came to Scotland Yard five years ago, Sir Edward, and I've heard nothing but good of him. In fact, I believe that Clifford Burge is sergeant material in due course. His record is exemplary.'

'Does he know the area?'

'He was born and brought up in Limehouse. When you first meet him, you think he ought to be selling fruit from a stall in the local market but you'd be mistaken. He's got a keen intelligence and a talent for making significant arrests.'

'I like the sound of this fellow already.'

'Interview others, if you must, but I do recommend that you also take a look at Constable Burge.'

'I most certainly will.'

About to leave, the commissioner remembered something. 'You mentioned Inspector Marmion a moment ago.'

'He and Sergeant Keedy are on their way to Birmingham.'

'What are they doing there?'

'They have to break the bad news to a family of a murder victim.'

'Is this the man who was hauled out of the Thames earlier on?'

'It is, Sir Edward. His name is Gilbert Donohoe. He was a businessman of sorts and a very successful one, it seems.'

'Perhaps someone resented his success,' said Sir Edward. 'At all events, you put the right person in charge of the investigation. Inspector Marmion never lets us down, does he?'

With some difficulty, Chatfield manufactured a semblance of a smile.

The house was even bigger than they'd anticipated. Sitting on two acres of land, it was a Victorian construction with three storeys. Standing apart from it was a large garage with living accommodation above it. When the taxi dropped them off there, Keedy stood and marvelled.

'It's enormous,' he said. 'It's big enough to have a snooker room.'

Marmion laughed. 'Is that your idea of luxury, Joe – to play snooker whenever you fancy?'

'Don't mock. You enjoy a game as much as I do. If you keep at it, you might actually beat me one day.'

'Your luck won't last for ever.' As they walked towards the house, Marmion pricked up his ears. 'Can you hear something?'

'It's only the sound of money being counted.'

'No, *listen*. It's quite clear. Someone is playing the piano.'

Keedy concentrated. 'You're right, Harv, and they're playing it very well.'

'It's a shame to interrupt the music – especially with the news that we bring.'

He tugged the bell pull and there was a tinkling sound deep inside the house. The door was soon opened by a maidservant.

Marmion performed the introductions and both men produced their warrant cards. Young and pale-faced, the woman was clearly alarmed.

'Mr Donohoe is not here,' she stuttered.

'We know that,' said Marmion. 'We came to speak to other members of the family. How many of them are here?'

'Mrs Donohoe is in the music room. That's her, playing the piano. Her son is here as well. He's not long come back from the factory.'

'We'd like to speak to both of them together, please.'

After inviting them into the hall, she went off down the corridor. The first person she alerted was Adrian Donohoe who came at once. When he reached the detectives, he appraised them with an almost patrician air. He was a tall, lean, assertive individual in his thirties. Keedy recognised the facial similarities with the father. Before they could explain the reason for their visit, they saw Clara Donohoe coming towards them. Middle-aged and of middle height, she was a woman with natural poise who'd kept both her figure and her beauty. After names had been exchanged, she invited the detectives into the spacious and tastefully furnished living room. While she sat on the sofa with her son, Marmion and Keedy settled into armchairs opposite them. Keedy had been more than happy to take the lead at the morgue. In a situation like the present one, however, he was glad to let Marmion do most of the talking. The inspector had many years' experience of passing on bad news gently and tactfully.

'Is this about my father?' asked Adrian, bluntly.

'I'm afraid that it is, sir,' replied Marmion.

'Has there been some kind of accident?'

'It's rather more serious than that.'

Clara tensed. 'What's happened?'

'A body was retrieved from the Thames earlier today, Mrs Donohoe. We have reason to believe that it might be that of your husband. To be absolutely certain,' said Marmion, softly, 'we'll need a formal identification by next of kin, of course.'

Clara was numbed. Significantly, Adrian made no attempt to comfort his mother. He fumed in silence for several seconds then blurted out an accusation.

'You must be mistaken, Inspector,' he said. 'Father had a regular schedule whenever he went to London. He'd never go anywhere near the river. You've given us an unnecessary fright. I think you should be more certain of your facts before you barge into someone's house like this.'

'We spoke to his tailor, sir. He recognised the suit that Mr Donohoe had been wearing. Your father has been a client for some years, I gather.'

Adrian was scornful. 'Is that all you're going on – the word of a tailor?'

'Keep your voice down,' advised his mother, quietly.

'I refuse to believe that Father would either have fallen in the river when he'd drunk too much or – an even more ridiculous idea – that he committed suicide. Both suggestions are palpably absurd.'

'I haven't made either of them, sir,' said Marmion, levelly.

'Then how is he supposed to have ended up there?'

The inspector looked from mother to son before speaking. 'He was murdered, sir,' he told them, almost whispering. 'Valuables were taken from him and there were no means of identification on the body. We had to resort to a trawl around a series of men's outfitters. One of them eventually recognised the suit.'

'It was at Langley, Hope and Catto in Bond Street,' interjected Keedy.

'Does that name ring a bell?'

Adrian glared at them. 'Yes, it does,' he said through gritted teeth.

Before he could say anything else, his mother put a firm hand on his arm.

'Let the inspector speak, dear,' she said. 'I want to hear every single detail he can tell us. Then we can go to London in due course to . . . identify the body ourselves. I'll need you with me to do that.'

'Your son could go in your stead, Mrs Donohoe,' suggested Keedy.

'He was my husband, Sergeant. I won't shrink from my duty.'

'You must do as you wish.'

'We'd be grateful for all the information you can give us,' said Marmion. 'We'd like, for instance, to know where he stayed when he was in London and whom he was going to see on this latest visit.'

'Before that,' she said, mastering her emotions, 'I'd like to know exactly what happened. However disagreeable the truth, I must hear it.'

Marmion was astonished at the control and dignity she was showing. It was at variance with the glowering resentment exhibited by her son. Adrian Donohoe was still not ready to accept their version of events. He kept looking for ways to challenge the account that Marmion went on to give. Having viewed the corpse, Keedy gave them a succinct report of what he found, mentioning the bruising around the neck caused by strangulation but omitting any reference to the missing tongue. Clara listened intently throughout. When the detectives had told her everything they intended to, she thanked them for their straightforwardness.

'You must have heard the piano when you first arrived,' she said.

'We did,' said Marmion. 'You play beautifully, Mrs Donohoe.'

'Did you recognise the music?'

'I'm afraid not.'

'It was a Chopin nocturne – my husband's favourite, as it happens.'

'His tailor mentioned that Mr Donohoe was fond of music.'

'We often went to concerts together, here and in London. My daughters took after us. They both play an instrument. Adrian is the odd one out. He doesn't have a musical bone in his body.'

'I have many compensating skills, Mother,' he said, acidly.

'You're obsessed with business.'

'I regard that as a virtue.'

Marmion was hoping to press her for details of her domestic life and for a description of her husband's normal activities during his visits to London, but she suddenly stood up abruptly and, without excusing herself, marched out of the room. The detectives looked at Adrian Donohoe who, it seemed, had finally come to accept that the body found in the Thames had indeed been his father. Face puckered, he was trying to gauge the enormous repercussions that would follow. Since his mother was not there, Marmion decided to question him about his father's business activities. Before he could do so, however, he was interrupted by the sound of the piano. Clara Donohoe was playing the same Chopin nocturne they'd heard before, though it was subtly different now. It had become a requiem.

CHAPTER FIVE

When he was off duty, Everitt White didn't stand on ceremony. At work and in uniform, it was a different matter. He let everyone know that his status as an inspector entitled him to obedience and respect. His preferred drinking hole was the Mermaid Tavern, a small, stuffy but welcoming pub in the East End within easy walking distance of his house. The moment he walked in, boundaries ceased to exist. If he saw lowly members of the river police there, he'd greet them as equals and they admired him for that. One of the regular denizens was Leslie Burge, the man who handled two oars in White's galley. The fact that the inspector had done the same in his younger days gave them a special bond.

On his way home from work that evening, he called in the pub for his usual pint of beer. Expecting to see Burge, he instead met his brother, Clifford, a detective constable at Scotland Yard. Though he lacked Leslie's muscularity, Clifford Burge was a strong, thickset man in his early thirties with a pleasantly ugly face. They exchanged greetings.

'Where's my bruvver?'

'He'll be along sooner or later.'

'Got some news for him,' said Burge. He sipped his beer and grimaced. 'This stuff gets worse and worse. They're watering it far too much.'

'It's starting to taste like horse piss,' said White.

'Can I buy you a pint?'

'Thanks, Cliff. I know how well you get paid at the Yard.'

Burge's laugh was mirthless. 'Barely enough to keep us alive.'

'You look healthy enough to me.'

'I survive.'

He ordered the drink then the two men adjourned to a table in the corner.

'What sort of a day have you had, Ev?' asked Burge.

'Oh, it's been fairly typical,' said the other, airily. 'We hauled a murder victim out of the Thames, we caught two men trying to steal from a cargo boat, we saved a child from drowning, then a German submarine surfaced near London Bridge and we arrested the entire crew.'

'You're pulling my leg!'

'The bit about the submarine was made up, perhaps, but the rest is true. Oh,' he added, 'and we watched those bombers doing their best to flatten the docks and kill as many people as they could.'

'Yeah, saw that from a distance,' said Burge. 'Diabolical! Flew all the way here and nobody tried to stop the bleeders.' He sampled some more beer. 'What's this about a murder victim?'

'It will be in all the papers tomorrow.'

'Love to be involved in a murder case.'

White chuckled. 'All you have to do is kill someone.'

'You know what I mean. Spend all my time on break-ins. Gets boring after a while.' He brightened. 'That could change.'

'What do you mean?'

'Told you I had some news,' said Burge. 'That's why I called in here. Wanted to crow over my bruvver for once.'

'Have you had a promotion?'

'Not exactly – but I've been asked to go for an interview. They've set up a unit to tackle juvenile crime – chaired by the commissioner himself.'

'You *are* going up in the world, Cliff.'

'Haven't got the job yet – be other geezers up for it.'

'What are your chances?'

'Pretty good, I fancy. Turns out I was recommended by Chat – Superintendent Chatfield, that is. Vinegary old sod but he knows a good copper when he sees one. Put my name forward, so the rest is up to me.'

White raised his glass. 'Good luck!'

'Thanks.'

'It's a feather in your cap, Cliff.'

'Not counting my chickens but I'm hopeful. Interesting

work, by the sound of it. Won't have to go on dealing with loopy old women who forget to keep their doors and windows locked.' Burge emptied his glass in a few noisy gulps. 'Get some real action for a change.'

Gregory Wain was the leader of the Stepney Warriors but he was a fallen hero now. A blow from a lump hammer had knocked him almost senseless and left him with a pounding headache and a simmering anger. His chief lieutenant was Bruce Kerry, a thin, lanky, rat-faced boy with six stitches in the knife wound in his arm that he'd collected during the ambush. Wain was bigger, chunkier and had a permanent scowl on his face. Both were fifteen. They were in the tiny front room of Wain's house used as the meeting place for the gang.

'Wor we gonna do?' asked Kerry.

'We'll wait.'

'We gotta strike back 'ard, Greg, or the Spirits'll think they killed us off.'

'Thass wor I wan 'em to fink.'

'Bur there's more of us than them.'

'Duzzen matta. We need time to ger betta.'

'I say we goes for 'em straight away.'

Wain grabbed him by the neck. 'You the new leader, are ya?' he demanded, tightening his grip until Kerry spluttered. 'No? Then shut yer gob and do as you're told.'

Kerry nodded eagerly and was released. He rubbed his neck ruefully.

'Sorry, Greg. You knows best.'

'Doan worry. The Spirits will ger wot they deserves – only it'll be when I say it is. Okay?' Kerry nodded again. 'Right – piss off and spread the word.'

Clara Donohoe suffered a delayed reaction to the news of her husband's murder. She'd been remarkably self-possessed at first and had even gone off to play the piano. The full horror of the revelation then hit her and she retired to the bedroom in tears. Her son reacted with a speed and concern that surprised the detectives. He not only summoned both of his sisters by telephone and urged them to come at once, he sent a message to Father Hanley, the parish priest at the nearby Catholic Church and a man to whom Clara had turned before at a tragic moment in her life.

'It was wise of you not to explain the reason why they're needed here,' said Marmion. 'Such news should only be imparted face-to-face.'

'I know that,' said Adrian, crisply.

'While we're waiting for them to arrive, perhaps you'd be kind enough to tell us something about your father's business affairs. We know very little about him beyond the fact that he was very successful at whatever it was that he did.'

'My father was a King Midas, Inspector. Whatever he touched turned to gold. When he bought the glass factory in Stourbridge, he had stiff competition but it didn't take him long to swallow up his main rivals.'

'Is that the factory where you were earlier on?' asked Keedy.

'No, Sergeant. I manage our engineering works. It turned in a record profit last year. I promised my father that it would.'

As Adrian talked on, it was clear Donohoe had a sizeable empire. He was a great believer in diversity of products, covering a wide spectrum instead of merely specialising. His son's attitude towards him was ambivalent. Adrian was, by turns, proud, critical, envious and almost aggressive. What was missing was any real sign of sorrow at the death of his father. The detectives soaked up all the information like sponges. Keedy worked through page after page of his notebook. The recitation of commercial success was only stopped when other members of the family arrived. Marmion and Keedy had fleeting introductions to Adrian's two sisters and to Father Hanley, a white-haired old man with wire-framed spectacles through which a pair of searching blue eyes stared. The women were shocked by the news about their father and needed time to absorb its full impact. Father Hanley, however, adapted to the situation at once, comforted the sisters in turn, then told them that their mother was in need of consolation.

While everyone trooped off to see Clara, the detectives had time to compare thoughts. Keedy referred to his notes.

'What he said about his own position was interesting. There he is, running a profit-making factory yet he sounded so aggrieved.'

'I think he wants an even bigger slice of the empire, Joe.'

'He'll have the whole lot now.'

'Not necessarily,' warned Marmion. 'There must be a reason why his father kept him where he is. Donohoe went to London so often that he and a partner started a property development company. That's where the real money was rolling in. I think the son is piqued that he's been kept out of that side of the business. He's stuck in his factory in Northfield, listening to the deafening clatter of industry all day long. Going to London must have a lot more appeal for him.'

'Do you think he actually *liked* his father?'

'Now and again, maybe, but I didn't sense any deep affection.'

'What about his mother?'

'Oh, I think he just tolerates her.'

'Why isn't he married? He must be in his thirties.'

'So are you, Joe,' said Marmion with a smile. 'Why are *you* still single?'

It was a painful question. Keedy winced.

Alice Marmion was wrestling with the same question. When two people loved each other as much as they did, why didn't they find a way to be together? Time alone with Keedy was always very limited. As soon as he embarked on a new murder investigation, her chances of seeing him dwindled dramatically. If a case took him outside London, it could be a week or more before he was within reach. On the rare occasions when they did spend more than a few snatched hours together, Alice pressed him to agree to a date for the wedding. Every time she did so, he came back with a different excuse for delaying the event. It had now reached a point where she was about to accuse him of not intending to marry her at all.

As she made her way back to her lodging, she decided to write a letter to him, listing all the reasons why the wedding should be sooner rather than later. Even if she decided not to send it, she felt, the act of writing it would clarify her mind. It would also remind her why she'd fallen in love with him in the first place. Alice had had boyfriends before but they had never been serious attachments. For his part, Keedy had been seen with so many different young women that he'd built up a reputation among his colleagues as a kind of Lothario. It was the reason why Marmion disapproved of his friendship with Alice at first. He didn't want his daughter to be the latest in a succession of discarded girlfriends. Slowly, Keedy had won him over and shown himself capable of becoming both a good husband and an acceptable son-in-law. Then the trouble started.

In the first whirl of excitement, Alice had been ready to forgive and forget about his rumoured conquests. He was hers now and that was all that mattered. As time passed, however, she realised that she was making a far greater effort on his behalf than he needed to make on hers. There was an imbalance that irked her and she'd mentioned it to Keedy whenever one of their arguments got out of hand. The only way the tensions between them could be resolved was by their being joined together in holy matrimony. Their respective pasts would be wiped clean then. Their lives could start afresh with the sound of church bells ringing in their ears.

The whole journey was taken up with the composition of the letter. When the bus dropped her off, she'd already decided on the opening paragraph. The important thing, she believed, was to strike the right note. Alice had to be loving, reasonable, uncomplaining, firm yet not demanding and, above all else, willing to compromise. The moment she entered her room, she sat down at the little table, reached for some stationery and began to write.

* * *

The trip to Birmingham had told them a great deal about the business and domestic life of the Donohoe family. The deceased was clearly a person of consequence. His murder would cause huge ripples of shock and regret to spread out in every direction. Once they'd adjusted to the terrible news, Donohoe's two married daughters questioned Marmion and Keedy in the vain hope that the detectives might at least be able to name possible suspects. While they insisted that their father had no enemies, they conceded that he might have aroused a degree of annoyance among his rivals. His daughters were keen to stress that he'd won a number of prestigious awards in the business community, testifying to his pre-eminence and popularity. They claimed that he was on the verge of being named in the next Honours List.

Hazel, the elder of the two, was a striking woman with a rather garish taste in clothing. Her sister, Doreen, was altogether more subdued in every way. What both Marmion and Keedy noticed was that neither of them mentioned their brother or showed any interest when his name was introduced into the conversation. When they'd garnered all the answers they could, the two women went back up to their mother who was still being comforted by Father Hanley. Moments later, Adrian came into the living room again. He was carrying a small bag.

'Right,' he said, as if addressing menials, 'it's been decided. Mother is not well enough to travel to London. I will identify the body, then spend the night there. Since you'll need to return yourselves, I can offer you a lift to the station. Even as we speak, the chauffeur is getting the car out of the garage.' A series of mechanical noises confirmed the statement. 'I'd prefer it if you don't try to get me into conversation.'

'If that's what you want, sir,' said Marmion.

'I prefer to be alone with my thoughts.'

'We respect that.'

The three of them headed for the door, which was being held open by the maidservant. Keedy saw the nervous look that she gave Adrian Donohoe. The chauffeur stood in readiness beside the car. Adrian got in the front seat and left the others to clamber into the rear of the vehicle. The plush upholstery made it a far more comfortable ride than the one they'd had in the taxi to get there. When they reached New Street Station, Adrian ignored them completely. He bought a first-class ticket and walked away. Keeping to a strict budget, they had second-class return tickets. As they waited on the platform, they were a long way apart from the man with whom they were supposed to be travelling.

'He likes to give himself airs and graces, doesn't he?' said Keedy.

'Yes, Joe, but he's not exactly behaving like someone who's about to inherit a fortune.'

'Why is that?'

'Perhaps he has some idea what's in his father's will.'

'As the only son, he's the obvious beneficiary. Talking of which,' he went on, grinning, 'I reckon that he's the obvious beneficiary of that pretty servant's favours as well.'

'Then I feel sorry for her.'

'What do we do when we reach Euston?'

'We divide and rule,' said Marmion. 'You can take him to

the morgue to view his father's body while I call on the hotel where Donohoe always stayed.'

'The Devonian – never heard of it.'

'I have, Joe. It's tucked away off St James Street, one of those places that is very discreet and highly expensive.'

'That's two good reasons why *I've* never been there.'

'It was on my beat when I was in uniform but I never actually went in.'

'What about that partner of his in property development?'

'We'll both tackle him. When you have a positive identification from the son, tell Chat immediately and he can inform the press. He'll have the sense to say nothing about the absent tongue. We don't want to spark ghoulish speculation.'

'It's bound to come out in the end, Harv.'

'Agreed, but it won't have the same impact on Mrs Donohoe and her two daughters, will it? They'll have started to recover from the blow we dealt them today. As time passes, it will be easier for them to cope with an additional shock.'

'What's your feeling?' asked Keedy, seriously. 'Do you think the killer is from somewhere in the Midlands or is he based in London?'

'Oh, I'd opt for a metropolitan villain.'

'Why do you say that?'

'It's an educated guess.' The thunder of the approaching train made him look down the line. 'Here it is at last. Make sure you don't trespass in first class, Joe, or Donohoe's son will have you thrown back where you belong.'

Sharing a laugh, they stood back from the edge of the platform.

* * *

When he put his head into the superintendent's office, Sir Edward Henry looked tired. Chatfield glanced up from his desk.

'Good evening, Sir Edward.'

'Time to go home,' said the other. 'I just wanted to see if there was any news.'

'Marmion and Keedy have returned from Birmingham with the murder victim's son. He's made a positive identification so I've released a statement to the press. It was vital to have the word of a family member. My greatest nightmare is that we announce that someone is dead when he's still alive and kicking.'

'It almost happened in that Salvation Army murder,' recalled the commissioner. 'The victim had been using someone else's name as a cover. Had Marmion not stepped in quickly to expose the deception, we could all have had red faces.' He gasped as he felt a stab of pain and grunted. 'I do apologise.'

'The person who should apologise is the demented man who shot you in the chest,' said Chatfield, sympathetically. 'Most people in your position might have considered retirement but you soldiered on bravely.'

'When it comes, the pain is sharp but I get long periods of remission.'

'I'm glad to hear it.'

Five years earlier, Sir Edward had opened his front door to be confronted by a wild-eyed man who fired three shots at him. Albert Bowes had no personal animus against the commissioner. He simply saw him as the personification of law and order. Bowes had recently been refused a licence to drive a mechanical carriage because of an earlier conviction

57

for being drunk and disorderly. By way of protest against the decision, Bowes had tried to kill the commissioner. It was only because of Sir Edward's personal plea for mercy that the man's life sentence was reduced to fifteen years. Every time he felt the searing pain, it was as if a bullet was piercing his chest.

'You showed real compassion,' said Chatfield.

'The man was not in his right mind.'

'That's no excuse in my book, Sir Edward.'

'The moment has passed now,' said the commissioner, taking his hand away from his chest and breathing more easily. 'What else did Marmion and Keedy report?'

'They're still gathering information. Keedy called in here after taking Mr Donohoe's son to the morgue.'

'Where's Marmion?'

'He's currently talking to the manager of the Devonian Hotel.'

'I hope he doesn't try to stay there,' said the other with a dry laugh. 'An inspector's salary is woefully inadequate at a place like the Devonian. I'll be interested to hear what he makes of it.'

Patrick Armitage was a short, sleek, compact man in his forties with an air of self-importance tempered by the need to serve others. As manager of the Devonian Hotel, he occupied a privileged position, meeting some of the wealthiest and most important people in the city and seeing to their needs with smiling readiness. He was a very handsome man and, Marmion suspected, would take advantage of the fact when off duty. Alone with him in an office that was uniquely tidy, the inspector listened to the manager's description of Gilbert Donohoe.

'He was a model guest in every way, Inspector, and we'll

miss him sorely. It was always a pleasure to have him staying here. He was exceptionally kind to my staff. That's not always the case, alas. And you tell me that he's been *killed*?' He brought both hands to his face in a gesture of despair. 'Why? What possible reason could anyone have to do such a thing to a gentleman like Mr Donohoe?'

'It's one of many mysteries.'

'He was such a generous person.'

'His wife stayed here occasionally, I gather,' said Marmion.

'Yes, it was a joy to have them both here. Music was their mutual passion. We have a grand piano in the dining room and Mrs Donohoe sometimes asked for permission to play it. She has real talent.'

'I know, Mr Armitage. We've heard her.'

'As a couple, they seemed so happy together.'

'How long was he intending to stay here this time?'

'Oh,' said the manager, 'for a week at least.'

'Then why didn't you report him missing? He disappeared from here for three days. Your housekeeping staff would have noticed that his room had not been used.'

Piqued by the implied criticism, Armitage drew himself up to his full height.

'It was not unusual,' he explained. 'When Mr Donohoe made a reservation, he didn't always stay here for the entire duration. He often disappeared for a day or so, asking for his room to be kept. We simply complied with his wishes.'

'Why pay for a hotel room that he didn't use?'

'It wasn't my place to ask such a question, Inspector.'

'But you must have been curious.'

'My job is to manage the hotel, not to pry into the lives of our guests.'

'I'd like to see the room, if I may.'

'Yes, of course,' said Armitage, moving to the door. 'I have a master key.'

He conducted Marmion to the lift near the reception desk, passing several members of the staff as they did so. They ascended to the third floor. When they reached the room, the manager first unlocked it then stood back so that the inspector could step into it first. Marmion was taken aback by the size and opulence of the suite. The room comprised a writing desk, a sofa, two armchairs and a low table. Off it was the bedroom, an equally luxurious area with a large bed, two substantial wardrobes and a dressing table. The bathroom was next door. To stay the night in such a suite, any guest would incur a substantial charge, so leaving it unoccupied for days seemed perverse.

'If he expected to be here for a week,' said Marmion, 'he'd surely have brought some luggage.'

'Mr Donohoe always travelled with a large suitcase and an attaché case.'

After looking around the room, Marmion opened the wardrobes in turn. Both were empty. He even glanced into the bathroom but saw nothing left behind by the man who'd reserved the room. It was as if Donohoe had never been there.

'I'd like to know the exact time and day that he left here,' said Marmion.

'We can easily establish the day, Inspector, but the exact time will be more elusive. Mr Donohoe didn't check out at reception because, technically, he was still paying for this room. He liked to come and go as he wished.'

'That's rather odd, isn't it?'

Armitage's smile was almost saturnine.

'If truth be told, sir,' he said, 'Mr Donohoe was a rather odd person.'

CHAPTER SIX

War had made Ellen Marmion an even more assiduous reader. She had always liked to borrow library books but, forced to spend so much time alone, she tried to avoid boredom by taking out a succession of romantic novels in an attempt to fend off reality. She was deep into a poignant story of forbidden love between a young nun and a Roman Catholic priest when she heard a key being inserted in the front door. Seconds later, her daughter walked into the room. Ellen leapt up.

'I wasn't expecting you, Alice,' she said before noticing the bag she was carrying. 'Are you going to stay the night?'

'Yes, Mummy, if that's all right with you.'

'It's an absolute treat. I thought I'd be all alone this evening.'

'Have you heard from Daddy?'

'He rang a while ago to warn me not to wait up for him. He and Joe have had to go to Richmond for some reason. Anyway,' she went on, embracing Alice warmly, 'put your bag down and I'll make a pot of tea.'

'Thanks. I've had nothing to eat or drink since I left work.'

'You must be famished. Let's see what I can rustle up in the kitchen.'

They went off together and traded gossip until the tea was made and they were sitting down with a plate of sandwiches each. As Alice ate away gratefully, her mother kept a close eye on her.

'Has something happened with Joe?' she asked, tentatively.

'No, Mummy.'

'You're different – that's why I ask.'

'Different in what way?'

'Well, you've been coming here regularly to spend time with me because you know how much I'm worrying about Paul. And you've been a tower of strength. But I don't think that's why you came this evening, is it?' Alice shook her head. 'When you're good and ready, tell me what it is.'

There was a lengthy wait. Alice got through two sandwiches and most of the tea before she was ready to confide in her mother, and even then she needed to be prompted.

'When did you last see him?'

'It was almost a week ago. We had less than half an hour together.'

'When did you see him *properly*?'

'It must be the best part of a fortnight, Mummy. He's so busy – though I don't need to tell you that because Daddy's the same. I went out for a meal with Joe. That's getting to be a very rare event.'

'Is that the problem – not seeing him when you want to?'

Alice was resigned. 'That's *always* going to be a problem,' she said. 'He has a job that demands him to be very flexible with his time. I accept that. Emergencies happen at all times of the day and someone has to respond to them. No, Mummy,' she continued, pouring herself more tea, 'I can't complain about something that's not really Joe's fault. What upset me is something that *is* his fault. To save time, you'd better read this.'

Taking a letter from her handbag, she handed it to her mother. Pursing her lips, Ellen unfolded the two pages and read them slowly. She was clearly distressed by what Alice had written. When she looked up, her eyes were pools of sympathy.

'You're right,' she said. 'It *is* Joe's fault.'

'Did you ever have this trouble with Daddy?'

'No, dear, the problem I had was getting my parents to accept him. When they finally did, there was no chance for him to drag his feet. My father insisted that he agreed to a date for the wedding. He was terribly old-fashioned,' said Ellen. 'When your father first asked for my hand in marriage, Daddy actually demanded to know if his intentions were honourable. Your father would feel embarrassed to do something like that. Apart from anything else, he's known Joe for years.'

'Does he ever talk about him?'

'What do you mean?'

'Does Daddy ever wonder when Joe is going to commit himself fully?'

'It's on his mind, Alice. He never says anything but I can tell he worries about it. I've told you before about that promise he made when we got married. If ever we had a daughter, he vowed, he'd never be as strict with her as my father had been with me. That's why we've never interfered in your private life.'

'He'd *like* to have interfered, Mummy. When Joe and I first got together, Daddy didn't approve at all. It was so obvious. Yet he didn't say anything and I'm very thankful for that.'

After glancing at the letter again, Ellen handed it back to her daughter.

'Are you going to send it to Joe?'

'I don't know. It's one of the reasons I came here, to be honest. Would reading that letter make things *better* between us or would it . . . do the opposite? I just don't know. What would *you* do in my position?'

It was late evening and all the light had been sucked out of the sky. As they sat in the rear of the police car, Marmion and Keedy were in darkness. The vehicle couldn't compete with the Rolls-Royce in which they'd travelled with Adrian Donohoe but it was vastly preferable to another jolting train journey. Keedy described his second visit that day to the morgue.

'It was weird,' he said. 'He hardly looked at his father's body.'

'Was that out of indifference or queasiness?'

'Oh, he wasn't queasy. Adrian Donohoe showed no discomfort at all. His face was motionless. It was all over in seconds. After a mere glance, he gave a nod then walked out. It was so . . . what's the word?'

'Perfunctory?'

'That might be it. He didn't speak until we were well clear of the place. Then he asked about his father's effects and when the inquest will be.'

'Where did he go after that?'

'He took a taxi to the Devonian Hotel – like father, like son.'

'He must have arrived just after I'd left.'

'How did you get on there, Harv?'

'It was a real eye-opener.'

He described what he'd learnt from the manager and drew a gasp of disbelief from Keedy. To a man like him with a limited income, the notion of someone reserving a room in an exclusive hotel then not actually sleeping in it was an act of madness. He was interested in Marmion's assessment of the manager.

'I found him too smarmy and self-regarding. He's one of those men who enjoy keeping secrets. I fancy that he knew far more about Donohoe's time in London than he was prepared to say.'

'How did he respond to the news?'

'Armitage behaved as if he was hearing about the murder of a close friend. He was either deeply moved or a very good actor. A minute later, he was talking calmly about Donohoe as if he'd already known about his death.'

'Do you think he could be party to it in some way?'

'It's far too early to say that. He puzzles me. It's your turn to tackle him next time. I'd like to know what *you* make of Armitage.' He smiled. 'I thought he looked a bit like a penguin in that frock coat of his but he's obviously adored by the female members of his staff. Every time we walked past one of them, she beamed at him.'

'We could do with more of that kind of thing at the Yard.'

'You always get an adoring smile from Chat,' teased Marmion. 'Isn't that enough for you?'

'No, it isn't. Even when he's happy, Chat scowls at you. That's all he did when I saw him earlier on. Oh, by the way,' he went on, 'I did pick up one snippet of information. The commissioner is giving a higher priority to juvenile crime.'

'And so he should. It's on the increase.'

'He's looking for someone who knows the area and can get close to the gangs. Do you know who Chat suggested?'

'Tell me.'

'Constable Burge.'

'I've heard of him. He's full of promise, they say.'

'Yes,' said Keedy, 'he's bright, hard-working and ambitious. I had a natter with him over a pint once. All that Cliff Burge could talk about was investigating homicides. I told him he had to earn his spurs first. If he gets this new job, he may well have the chance to do just that.'

Clifford Burge stayed in the Mermaid Tavern longer than he'd intended. Everitt White had drifted off eventually but Leslie Burge had insisted on celebrating what he viewed as a signal success.

'Keep telling you, Les,' said his brother. 'Haven't got the job yet and I may never get it. Hate to tempt fate like this.'

'One more pint, Cliff – go on.'

Though he raised his hands in protest, Burge succumbed in the end. It was half an hour before the two of them rolled out of the pub. Since their parents had died years ago, Leslie, as the elder brother, had inherited their little terraced house and lived there with his wife and children. Burge had lodgings in Shoreditch but – lulled into a feeling of certainty by the drink – he decided to familiarise himself with the streets of Stepney in readiness for his forthcoming work there. Before they split up, Leslie was dismissive.

'Kids will be kids,' he said, tolerantly. 'We were the same, Cliff.'

'We didn't throw bricks through people's windows or stab each other. That's what some of these gangs are doing.'

'They'll grow out of it.'

'But they'll do far too much damage before they do so,' said Burge. 'When the gangs have a scrap, they don't use fists like we did. They got knives, hammers and other weapons. Big problem, Les.'

His brother slapped him on the back. 'Then you go and sort 'em out.'

After shaking hands, they went off in opposite directions. Burge walked along narrow, dimly lit streets that he'd known during his childhood. Most of the families there were far too large for the cramped, malodorous tenements and overcrowding led to all kinds of tensions. Having grown up amid poverty and desperation, Burge felt sad that, in the last twenty years, there'd been no visible improvement in the lives of the local people. The same evils still existed. In removing so many men of fighting age from the area, the government had added greatly to its problems. Despite the hour, the place was full of noise. Apart from the many blazing rows Burge could hear behind closed doors, or glimpse through windows with tattered curtains, there was the sound of revelry from the pubs he passed. Lost in a drunken stupor, a man was clinging to a lamp post and singing the national anthem. Somebody was shovelling gravel off a handcart and into a wheelbarrow. A busker was trying to play a violin under a gas lamp. Dogs were barking and cats were hissing at each other. It was a normal night in Stepney. Hardly a street was silent and empty.

When he turned a corner, Burge could see a dim outline of someone at the far end. Halfway along, he heard a yell behind him and swung round to see a diminutive figure waving his arms. The distraction was successful. Before Burge realised what was happening, a boy sprinted up behind him, grabbed his hat and ran off. He and his friend laughed derisively at him. Burge was not sure whether the theft or the mockery hurt the more. Taking to his heels, he charged after the two boys and ordered them to stop. They immediately bolted. Handicapped by the amount of beer he'd consumed, he nevertheless kept up a fast enough pace to close the gap. What he didn't know was that the thieves had been hoping he would chase them. It was all part of their plan.

Reaching a lane, they sped off down it with Burge on their heels. The more he shouted at them, the more they laughed and sneered. Making a final effort to catch them, Burge got within yards of them but his progress then came to a halt. As he came level with a rickety garden shed, the boy perched on top of it poured a large bucket of water over him and soaked him to the skin. The sheer surprise of it made him stop dead and shake himself. The boy on the shed, meanwhile, hopped nimbly to the ground and ran off to join his two friends. Ridicule echoed the length of the lane.

Sodden and enraged, Burge had learnt a lesson. The gangs didn't indulge in horseplay as he and his brother had once done. They sought victims to humiliate. He was one of them.

Seen in ghostly silhouette, the mansion was daunting. It stood in its own grounds and commanded a view of Richmond Park. Thanks to Adrian Donohoe, who'd supplied the name and the telephone number, Marmion had rung Norris Sprake to pass on the news that his former business partner had been murdered. Sprake had immediately volunteered to come to Scotland Yard but Marmion preferred to see him in his home to get a fuller picture of the sort of life he lived. Getting out of the car, Keedy stared at the looming edifice in front of him.

'I could have *three* snooker rooms in a place that big.'

'Are you thinking of putting in a bid, Joe?'

'Why not?' asked Keedy. 'It'd be ideal for me and Alice.'

Two large lamps illumined the portico. The door opened before they even reached it and they were beckoned into the hall by a maidservant. She escorted them to the library where they found Sprake ensconced in a high-backed leather chair with a blanket over his legs. Putting aside the book he'd been reading, he indicated the walking sticks beside him.

'Forgive me if I don't get up,' he said, looking at Marmion. 'You, I take it, must be the inspector to whom I spoke.'

'Yes,' replied the other, gesturing at his companion. 'And this is Sergeant Keedy. I'm sorry that we had to call on you so late, sir. Given your condition, it was very brave of you to offer to come to us in Scotland Yard.'

'Gilbert Donohoe was my partner and best friend. I'd have been ready to crawl to you, if need be.'

Sprake was quite unlike the person Marmion had envisaged. What the inspector had heard on the telephone was the strong, compassionate, educated voice of a middle-aged man. What he was actually looking at was a wizened old character with sagging shoulders and wavy grey hair. The company he ran with his partner had been hugely profitable but it was clear that Donohoe had supplied the dynamism needed. Sprake's abilities lay elsewhere.

'May I offer you a drink of some sort?' he said.

Marmion shook his head. 'No, thank you, sir.'

'Not even a glass of the finest malt whisky?'

'I'm afraid not.'

'I'd have loved a whisky,' said Keedy under his breath.

Waved to seats, the detectives settled down and glanced around the room. Shelves covered two of the walls and there were various photographs separating the books into neat rows. On a table beneath a silver-framed mirror was a large model yacht. Above the mantelpiece, occupying pride of place, was a map of the British Isles with a series of tiny flags stuck in it. Sprake saw them looking at it.

'That's not the full extent of our empire,' he said. 'We own property abroad as well but, unfortunately, the German army is currently preventing us from getting anywhere near it.'

'How long has the company been in existence?' asked Marmion.

'Ten years, Inspector – we were about to celebrate our first decade. Somebody, it appears, was determined to stop us in our tracks.'

'Have you any idea who that person might be, sir?'

'I wish I did. When you told me what had happened, my mind went blank. I'd be grateful for more detail before I make any comment.'

Keedy already had his notebook out. Marmion gave him his cue and the sergeant delivered a concise report that covered the previous ten hours. Sprake was duly impressed.

'My word!' he exclaimed. 'Bond Street tailors, a trip to Birmingham and back, a visit to the Devonian Hotel, then a drive in the dark out here – your feet can hardly have touched the ground.'

'Speed is of the essence in a murder investigation,' said Marmion. 'The first day is always the most important because it may be your only chance of gathering evidence that will otherwise disappear.'

'And have you found such evidence, Inspector?'

'We're not entirely sure.'

'If there's any way in which I can help, please tell me.'

'There are some questions we'd like to put to you, sir. Principally, they're about the day-to-day operation of the property company. Before we get on to that, what really intrigues me is this: since you and Mr Donohoe were so close, why did he stay at a hotel in central London when you could have offered him accommodation here? That seems strange to us.'

'Very strange,' said Keedy.

Sprake smiled wearily. 'It was a necessity,' he said. 'All work and no play is a very sensible adage. I've abided by it all my life. If Gilbert had stayed here, work and play would have overlapped dangerously. He simply couldn't stop formulating new ideas for the expansion of our portfolio. This is not a criticism of him, mark you,' he emphasised, 'but the fact is that work had taken over his whole life. I, on the other hand, have preserved my leisure. I'm a keen sailor, for instance, or at least I was. On that table over there is a scale version of my yacht, *Gloriana*. My wife and I used to spend three or four weeks every year sailing around the Greek islands. It was wonderfully refreshing.'

'What sort of holidays did your partner have?' asked Marmion.

'He didn't believe in them, Inspector. He and his wife did sometimes go to music festivals on the Continent but Gilbert never viewed those as holidays. He used the trips to befriend other businessmen. That was his goal in life.'

'We're curious about his arrangement with the Devonian Hotel.'

'It suited him perfectly.'

'Then why didn't he spend more time there?'

'He had other fish to fry in Birmingham. Gilbert never lost sight of his many commitments there.'

'I was talking about his habit of reserving his room at the hotel without actually staying there. According to the manager, he was supposed to stay for a week this time but disappeared for three days.'

'Can you explain why, sir?' asked Keedy.

Sprake looked mystified. 'Frankly, I can't.'

'He didn't, for example, come here?'

'No, Sergeant, we never transacted any business in this

house. We have offices in Barnes. That's where we always met.'

'Does that mean you didn't know about his disappearances?' asked Marmion.

'It means exactly that.'

'Yet you worked so closely together for ten years.'

'We didn't live in each other's pockets, Inspector.'

'Can you suggest where he might have gone?'

'No,' said Sprake with a shrug. 'Your guess is as good as mine.'

'What about his attitude to money?'

'He liked making it – and so do I, for that matter.'

'Would you pay for a room at a luxury hotel then not use it?'

'I certainly wouldn't.'

'Would you expect your former partner to do so?'

'No, it's quite out of character.'

Keedy changed tack. 'Did you ever visit him in Birmingham?'

'Yes, I did, Sergeant. My wife and I stayed with them a couple of times. It was very pleasant. Clara played the piano for us.'

'Was her son there at the time?'

'Yes, of course – Adrian lives with his parents.'

'But he's not involved with the property company, is he?'

'He has other responsibilities, Sergeant.'

'What did you think of him?' asked Marmion.

'He has his father's capacity for hard work,' said Sprake, guardedly, 'though he hasn't dedicated his whole life to it. We found him . . . pleasant enough. Adrian didn't have a chance to say much with his father around.'

'How did they get on?'

'Very well, in the main, I suspect. I daresay there were a few strains and stresses but that's the case in all families. I speak as the father of three daughters.'

'But they're not involved in the business, are they?'

'No, they're not.'

'Adrian Donohoe is. We formed the impression that he wasn't entirely happy with the role he was asked to play.'

'I don't know anything about that.'

'We sensed an underlying anger,' said Keedy.

'None of us is immune to feelings of anger and frustration at that age, Sergeant. You must belong to the same generation as Adrian. Both of you are still trying to make your way in the world and hate any obstruction put in your way.'

'That's true.'

'Then I'm sure that *you* get restive at times.'

'I've a lot to get restive about,' said Keedy, thinking of Chatfield. 'But there's a big difference between Adrian Donohoe and me. I had to compete every inch of the way for what I've achieved. He's had everything handed to him on a plate. Anybody else in his position would feel grateful. It's obvious that he doesn't.'

There was a taut silence. Sprake refused to be drawn on the subject of the Donohoe family. Since there was no point in pressing him, Marmion changed the topic completely. He glanced at the book on the table beside the old man.

'May I ask what you were reading when we came in, sir?'

'Of course,' said Sprake, picking the book up. 'It's my favourite novel and has been since I first read it. It's *Treasure*

Island by Robert Louis Stevenson.' He saw their amazement. 'You don't like the book?'

'It's not a question of liking or disliking it, sir,' said Marmion. 'It just seems peculiar that, when you hear about the murder of your business partner, the first thing you do is read a novel.'

'Each of us copes with tragedy in his own way, Inspector. I reached for this book when my parents died and it brought me great succour when the doctor told me that I'd never be able to walk properly again. It's so beautifully written,' he went on, holding it up, 'and it's defined my working life. It was the same for Gilbert Donohoe. Whatever dangers lay in the way, we were both in pursuit of a hidden treasure.' He gave them a cold smile. 'Does that answer your question?'

CHAPTER SEVEN

When he finally got back to his lodging, Clifford Burge was still wondering if he'd been attacked by the Stepney Warriors or the Evil Spirits. His pride had been hurt and he wanted retribution. Looking in the mirror, he saw that his hair was plastered to his head and that his coat was still glistening with moisture. He was wearing the suit he intended to put on for the interview the following morning. If he turned up in that state, he knew, he'd be summarily dismissed as a candidate. Burge had to look his smartest to impress the commissioner. The loss of his hat rankled. He'd bought it for himself as a present to celebrate an important arrest he'd recently made.

By his standards, it had been expensive. It suddenly dawned on him that wearing it in Stepney along with his suit had not been the wisest thing to do. He didn't fit in. Even in the patchy light, he'd have been seen as an interloper and that made him a target. Burge made a mental note that, if he was given the new role, he'd dress in old clothes and wear a flat cap so that he didn't stand out. He needed camouflage.

After taking off his things, he hung them carefully on clothes hangers and hoped his only other suit wouldn't look too wrinkled when he faced the interviewing panel. Unlike his brother, he wasn't taking anything for granted. Other people would be competing with him. Some of them might have better qualifications. On the other hand, he remembered, Claude Chatfield had singled him out and that was something that made him optimistic. The superintendent was a difficult man to please, always more inclined to dispense criticism than praise. To be favoured by him was a positive sign. Though he might not get this particular assignment, Burge had put down a marker. It was a definite step towards the promotion for which he yearned.

Putting on his dressing gown, he picked up a towel and went along to the bathroom he shared with the others in the house. Burge dried himself off completely then combed his hair. He then realised that he had a problem. When he met the interviewing panel, did he tell them about the incident or say nothing whatsoever about it? It was a dilemma. If he admitted that he'd had a preparatory stroll around Stepney, they might applaud his initiative. They'd be less enthusiastic, however, when he recounted how easily he'd been tricked by three young lads who robbed him of his hat then lured him into a trap. On balance, he decided, drawing a veil over the whole episode might be the best plan.

That didn't mean he'd forget it. As soon as he got back to his room, he reached a dog-eared map book of London from its shelf and leafed through it until he came to the appropriate page. He then traced his journey from the Mermaid Tavern to the street where he was ambushed. Burge jabbed his finger at the lane where he'd been given an unexpected shower. If he was successful at the interview, he promised himself, it would be the first place he'd visit.

'Where can he be?'

'I've asked myself that until I'm blue in the face,' said Alice.

'And why doesn't Paul get in touch?'

'It's because he doesn't want to, Mummy.'

'He wrote us such lovely letters when he first joined the army. He was keen to let us know how he was getting on.'

'It's different now.'

'Do you think he's deliberately *hiding* from us?' asked Ellen.

'I just hope that he's . . . found whatever he was looking for.'

'We've no way of knowing. It's cruel of him not to get in touch.'

'I'm not sure about that. You saw that message he left in the bin. That was where he belonged, he said. He believed he was nothing but rubbish. Paul didn't feel he had a right to stay here.'

'He's part of the family, Alice. He has *every* right.'

'He has every right to go in search of another life as well,' said the other, gently. 'He's an adult. He's old enough to fight for his country. And he's under no obligation to tell us where he is.'

It was late and they were both tired but they kept asking the same questions over and over again. Alice turned the conversation back in her direction.

'So you believe that I shouldn't show my letter to Joe?'

'It would be a mistake.'

'I meant every word I said in it, Mummy.'

'Tell him to his face. It's the only way.'

'But I can hardly ever get to see him. I feel very strongly about this. If the only way to reach him is by letter, I'll post this first thing tomorrow.'

'And what will that do?'

'To start with, it will remind him that we're engaged.'

'I don't think Joe will forget that for a second.'

'He's forgotten that it brings obligations and he needs to be told that.'

'Then wait until you can tell him in person,' said Ellen, worriedly. 'If he reads that letter, he's not going to agree to a date for the wedding there and then. I think he's more likely to be annoyed.'

'I'm the one who's annoyed,' asserted Alice.

'And it shows. Yes, I know you've tried to be as restrained as you can but you'll still make Joe feel as if you're holding a gun to his head.'

'I've been forced into giving him an ultimatum. It's my last resort.'

Though she sympathised with her daughter, Ellen was

afraid that her letter might have the opposite effect to the one intended. Instead of bringing Alice and Keedy together, it might actually sour the relationship. Even though it was couched in the most reasonable language, it had the potential to cause damage. For that reason, Ellen wanted to stop it ever being sent. For her part, Alice felt let down. In coming to the house, she'd expected to get the usual loving and uncritical support from her mother but it was not forthcoming. That had shocked her.

'You don't understand the pressure I'm under,' she protested.

'Yes, I do, Alice. It must be unbearable or you wouldn't have written that letter.'

'Iris Goodliffe keeps badgering me about Joe. She can't believe that we aren't married already. It gets on my nerves sometimes.'

'Have you told her that?'

'Yes, but it makes no difference. Because she has no boyfriend herself, she's got this fascination about me and Joe. She's desperate for someone like him. At one point, she even asked me if she could meet Paul.'

'Thank heavens you kept her away from him!'

'Iris has her heart in the right place but she can be so irritating at times.'

'I shudder at the thought of what might have happened.'

'So do I.'

'Paul just doesn't know how to *be* with women any more. He terrorised Sally Redwood and ruined my friendship with her mother. Then there was that girl in Gillingham he used to sneak off to see. What he tried to do with her was . . . well, it was

81

disgusting. And it happened in a *church*,' said Ellen, tearfully. 'It made me feel so ashamed of my son. I used to take such pride in both of you but that's changed. Whatever's got into Paul?'

It was past midnight when they finally left the house and they had to wake up the driver who'd dozed off at the wheel. When they clambered into the rear seats, the car set off for Scotland Yard.

'I feel guilty,' confessed Marmion.

'Why?'

'We kept that old man up so late. He's disabled. He should have been tucked up in bed hours ago.'

'I don't agree,' said Keedy. 'We were the ones who were yawning. He may have looked as if he was at death's door but, in fact, he was quite spry. Those glasses of whisky helped him to keep going. I was so envious.'

'We don't drink on duty, Joe.'

'You sound like Chat.'

'We have to keep a clear head.'

'Sprake had three or four tots and he was as sober as any of us. He certainly made me work. I wasn't just taking notes. It was like writing a novel.'

'What kind of novel?'

'A tale of mystery.'

'And who's the villain in your story?'

'Big business.'

'Good answer.'

They'd learnt a great deal from the visit. Gilbert Donohoe had taken on much more definition now. Sprake had explained how his friend operated in the partnership and what drove the man on so relentlessly. At the start, they seemed a rather unlikely couple and the detectives wondered what they talked about when they were alone together. Sprake was urbane, cultured and devoted to sailing. Though he had a passion for music, Donohoe's only real interest was in expanding his empire and increasing his power. For most people, war was nothing short of a disaster, shattering lives and creating endless bereaved families. For Gilbert Donohoe, it was simply a commercial opportunity to be exploited. He'd somehow contrived to get a contract to supply some of the army's food. Crouching in their trenches and listening to enemy bombs and bullets whizzing past, Britain's soldiers on the Western Front were routinely being served with tinned meat from one of Donohoe's factories.

'He's got fingers in every pie!' complained Keedy.

'And they'll be freshly baked pies. Donohoe would never eat anything out of a tin. Nor, for that matter, would Sprake.'

'I almost got to like him.'

'Oh, I liked him as well,' said Marmion. 'I just wouldn't trust him an inch. His partner went out searching for new properties to buy but I bet that Sprake was the one who negotiated most of the deals. He was so fiendishly plausible.'

'I wonder why he wouldn't talk about the Donohoe family.'

'Force of habit – his kind always keep their cards close to their chest. We were supposed to be there to gather information but I fancy that he learnt far more about us in the process. That takes skill and cunning.'

'Why didn't you tell him the truth about Donohoe?'

'The man was murdered. That's all he needs to know.'

'The killer sliced off his tongue.'

'So?'

'Sprake might have been interested in that detail. It could, possibly, have contained a message for him.'

'His partner was silenced. That's enough of a message, isn't it?'

Keedy patted his notebook. 'He gave us lots of names but he wouldn't say if any of them were potential suspects. Why was that, do you think?'

'He might have been taking out life insurance,' said Marmion, cynically. 'I fancy that there were names he was careful *not* to mention. If he'd pointed one of them out, and if we'd descended on that person, there might have been repercussions.'

'He didn't look like a man who scares easily.'

'We're all frightened if our lives are in danger, Joe. He's just better at hiding it than the rest of us. Don't forget that, if you or I were attacked, we could defend ourselves. Sprake can't do that. He's reminded of it every time he tries to get up out of his chair.'

'What about that book he was reading?'

'*Treasure Island*?'

'It was written for children. Our teacher used to read bits out of it.'

'It's a classic adventure story, Joe, and it's got elements that most pupils are too young to understand properly.'

'What sort of elements?'

'Greed, deception, revenge, trust, camaraderie – they're all there below the surface. All that most kids want is the excitement.'

'My chief memory is of Ben Gunn, marooned on the island for years and dreaming of eating cheese again.' He sat up abruptly. 'Hey, I've just realised. Sprake reminded me of him somehow.'

'I saw no resemblance at all. Ben Gunn is poor, ignorant and pathetic. Sprake is none of those things, especially being poor. In fact, he's going to become even wealthier. You heard what he told us. Adrian Donohoe has no link whatsoever with the property company. At his father's death,' said Marmion, 'the whole thing is bequeathed to Norris Sprake. He's the outright winner here.'

'So?'

'Put two and two together, Joe.'

Keedy gaped. 'Are you seriously suggesting that he was party to the murder?'

'It wouldn't surprise me in the least.'

Clifford Burge hated interviews. He never shone in them and his Cockney vowels usually worked against him. He preferred to be judged on his deeds rather than his words. As a result, he was hoping that Chatfield had spoken up for him in the report he'd given to the panel. Three of them were up for interview but he didn't know either of his rivals. One of them was even more nervous than Burge but the other had an air of brash confidence about him. It was the nervous candidate who was first called in. Burge tried to chat to the other detective but all that the latter did was to boast about the successes in his career.

'Do you know Stepney?' asked Burge.

'It's a real shithole. What else is there to know?'

'Lots of good, decent families live there.'

'And so do bloodthirsty gangs that'll stop at nothing.'

'Done this kind of work before?'

'No,' said the other, 'but I'll soon get the hang of it.'

Burge made no comment. White-faced and dithering, the first candidate came out after less than five minutes. Defeat was written all over him. Without saying a word, he dashed out of the room. Burge's companion grinned.

'It looks like it's between me and you,' he said.

'Good luck!'

'I won't need it.'

He was the next person to be summoned, leaving Burge to wait alone in the anteroom. He was already resigned to rejection. The other man looked smarter and sounded more intelligent. Of the three of them, he would definitely be the best candidate. When ten minutes had passed, Burge abandoned all hope of getting the assignment and rued the fact that he'd told both his brother and Everitt White about his nomination. He was not looking forward to admitting to them that he'd failed. Still bristling with confidence, the other candidate came out and pointed to the door.

'They asked me to send you in.'

'Oh,' said Burge, rising from his seat.

The man curled his upper lip. 'Not that there's much point.'

Doing his best to ignore the sneer, Burge went into the room to be met by the sight of four people seated behind a table. In response to a gesture from Sir Edward Henry, he sat down on the chair in front of them, feeling isolated and defenceless. The panel consisted of two superintendents and a chief inspector but the only person who mattered to Burge was the commissioner. As chairman, he had the privilege of asking the opening question.

'What appeals to you about this post, Constable?'

'Problem needs sorting out, Sir Edward.'

'You know the East End well, I gather.'

'Born and brought up in Lime'ouse. Bruvver still lives there. Leslie's in the river police.'

'So you belong to a family of law enforcers. That's good to hear. Juvenile crime is getting out of hand, Burge. You know that as well as us. In fact, you probably have more anecdotal evidence.'

'My bruvver's always on about it, Sir Edward.'

'How should we tackle it?'

'Well . . .'

'Come on – we're listening. What are your suggestions?'

It was the question he'd anticipated and he'd already rehearsed his answer but somehow it refused to come out in the way he'd planned. Burge was halting and confused. He could see that his Cockney vowels were grating on the ears of some of the panel but he pressed on regardless. Slowly, he became more coherent and the frowns behind the table began to disappear. Eventually, he hit his stride, talking with real passion about an area he knew and – with all its faults – loved. When he'd finished, questions were fired at him from all four of them in turn but he fielded them without the slightest difficulty. The commissioner looked at his fellow members of the panel and gauged their reaction. It was uniformly favourable. He turned to Burge.

'What did your father do?'

'Dock labour'r, Sir Edward.'

'And *his* father?'

'Worked in a ware'ouse.'

'So you've had a straitened upbringing.'

Burge smiled fondly. 'Didn't seem like it at the time.'

'The East End, as you know, is one of London's largest industrial suburbs with a population upwards of three hundred thousand. To make things more difficult, it's the most cosmopolitan borough in the city. The only way to tackle the problem we face is with someone who knows the area intimately. In an ideal world, that person should have a large team at his disposal but manpower is at full stretch coping with the effects of this terrible war. In short, Burge,' he went on, 'you'll be on your own, feeding information back to the unit we've set up here. There'll be support from uniformed officers, of course, but this will be largely a solo venture.'

'Suits me, Sir Edward.'

'There are vicious gangs everywhere. One of them, for instance, has a distinctive trademark. They snip off the pigtails of unwary girls and run away laughing. Mind you,' continued Sir Edward, 'they did overstep the mark recently. One of them tried to cut the pigtail off someone from a Chinese laundry and got a hiding for his pains.'

'Serves him right,' said the chief inspector.

'The worst gangs are the Evil Spirits and the Stepney Warriors. They have pitched battles with each other. The Spirits are the nastier of the two, I'm told. One of their tricks is to steal people's hats – and that includes policemen's helmets. They're also guilty of random violence, burglary, causing an affray and large scale vandalism.'

Burge recoiled from the news about the hats and hoped his blushes didn't show.

'It's only fair that you know the size of the problem and the dangers involved. These gangs don't take prisoners. Are you willing to tackle them?' There was a long pause as Burge took time to realise that he was the chosen candidate. 'We'd like an answer.'

'When do I start?' he asked.

Marmion's life followed its familiar pattern. Getting home long after his wife had gone to bed, he left early the next morning. Though he was pleased to see his daughter, he barely had time to exchange more than a few words with her. His priority was to get to Scotland Yard in order to prepare his report of the previous day's events. Having done so, he delivered it to the superintendent and awaited his response. Seated behind his desk, Claude Chatfield skimmed through it with a searching eye before looking up at his visitor.

'I find this very hard to believe,' he said, tapping the final page. 'Sprake and Donohoe have been partners for ten years yet the former has no idea where the latter goes when he slips away from the Devonian Hotel.'

'It may be that he doesn't *want* to know, sir.'

'Do you mean he's deliberately turning a blind eye?'

'What links the two men is a mutual desire to enlarge their property empire. There's very little socialising involved. They lead separate lives.'

'Sprake's is separate from Donohoe's and Donohoe's sounds to me as if it's very separate from his wife.'

'That's one possibility,' agreed Marmion.

'It's an avenue that must be explored.'

They went on to discuss other theories about the murder victim's occasional disappearances during his stays in the capital. All were feasible but none, as yet, had any hard evidence to back it up. When they'd exhausted the possibilities, Chatfield remembered that he had something to show the inspector. He handed him some sheets of paper and sat back in his chair.

'That's the post-mortem report.'

'Thank you, sir – any surprises?'

'I don't think so,' said the other as Marmion read the report. 'Donohoe was garrotted. Someone attacked him from behind. There's a large bruise in the middle of his back to suggest that the killer put his knee against it to exert more power. That means he must have had him on the ground.'

'This tells us how he was murdered but not *where*.'

'I doubt if it was far from the Thames. He was very heavy. His weight is given on the last page. Nobody would want to lug the corpse very far.'

'There might have been an accomplice.'

'There might indeed, Inspector.'

When Marmion had finished reading it, he handed it back. 'How much of that detail have you released to the press, sir?' he asked.

'I've been very selective and, of course, I've made the usual appeal for help from the public. *Somebody* must know what he was doing when he sneaked away now and again from his hotel. The trouble is that they may be too frightened to come forward, terrified that the same thing could happen to them.'

'You never know, sir – we could get lucky.'

'It's foolish to trust to luck, Inspector. We have to dig out the truth.'

'I accept that. It's the reason I've arranged to call on Mr Sprake at his office. It was shared by his partner so Donohoe will have left his imprint there.'

'What about the sergeant?'

'He's on his way to the Devonian Hotel, sir. Adrian Donohoe spent the night there. Sergeant Keedy is going to ask him about his father's movements when he was in London. In addition to that,' said Marmion, 'I'd value the sergeant's opinion of Mr Armitage, the manager.'

'In your report, you describe him as evasive.'

'I was tempted to use another adjective.'

'What was it?'

'Obstructive.'

They might have had breakfast together, but Alice Marmion had no hope of raising the subject that was causing her so much heartache. Her father was too preoccupied with his latest investigation and was, in any case, unlikely to offer an opinion on the letter she'd written. All she could do was settle for asking him to pass on her love to Keedy. Then he was gone. On the bus journey into central London, she took one last look at what she'd written before thrusting the letter back into her handbag. Alice was still brooding on the problem when she joined her colleagues for the daily briefing. It was given by Inspector

Gale in her usual brusque manner, her eagle eye checking the uniforms of everyone there to make sure that all her officers were presentable before being sent out into the streets.

Lost in thought about her personal problems, Alice hadn't even noticed that Iris Goodliffe wasn't there. She soon became aware of the fact because the door was suddenly flung open and Iris came in, issuing a stream of abject apologies. They were swept contemptuously aside by the inspector. Unleashing a series of stinging rebukes, she showed why her nickname was Gale Force. In the face of such a hurricane, any of them would have buckled but Iris stood there without flinching. She even dared to smile at one point, earning a secondary blast of vituperation. When she was ordered to sit down, Iris did so but there was no sign of contrition. It was almost as if she'd gloried in being dressed down in front of everyone else. Alice was baffled.

It was only when the two of them left the building to go on patrol that she had a chance to question her partner.

'What kept you, Iris?' she asked. 'You must have known that Gale Force would bite your head off. She's a stickler for punctuality.'

'I couldn't help it,' said Iris, grinning excitedly.

'Why?'

'Somebody was waiting for me when I got here. He kept me talking.'

'Who was it?'

'PC Beckett.'

'What did he want?'

'He wanted *me*. He's asked me to go out with him.'

Alice was startled. 'PC Beckett? He's years older than you, Iris.'

'So what – he's a *man*. And he likes me.'

As they walked off side by side, Iris was bubbling with sheer joy. Someone had finally taken notice of her. Their conversation had made her late but she didn't mind in the least. She'd been happy to withstand the inspector's tirade because she was armoured against it. Alice should have felt pleased on her friend's behalf, not least because a romance of her own would distract Iris from poking obsessively into Alice's private life, but that was not the case. Iris's delight only served to depress her colleague. For the whole of the day, Alice knew, Iris would engage in fevered speculation about her relationship with the man who'd asked her out. Being forced to listen to it would be an ordeal. Alice felt her heart sink.

CHAPTER EIGHT

Joe Keedy always revelled in his position as the smartest detective at Scotland Yard. When he walked into the Devonian Hotel, however, he realised that he was outclassed in every sense. He saw that every male guest was wearing a suit that made his own look cheap and poorly cut. Sartorially, he was reduced to insignificance. Gliding across to him, the manager sized him up and guessed who he might be.

'Good morning, sir – Sergeant Keedy, I believe?'

'That's right.'

'I'm pleased to meet you,' said the other, hands clasped behind his back. 'I'm Patrick Armitage, the manager, and I'm sure you've heard all about me from the inspector. He did say he might send you here to have a word with Mr Donohoe – Mr Adrian Donohoe, that is.'

'Is he still here?'

'He's enjoying his breakfast. Like his father, he has a healthy appetite.'

Keedy could see at a glance why the manager was so attractive to women. He had almost flashy good looks and exuded a sense of authority. Keedy decided that he could probably have his pick of the female staff. In spite of himself, he felt a slight twinge of envy.

'Everybody here has been saddened by the news,' said Armitage, gravely. 'Mr Donohoe was a very popular guest. What's happened is a terrible shock. It's frightening that he should end his life in such a gruesome way.'

'It was not by choice.'

'That goes without saying. Have you made any progress yet?'

'We believe that we have,' said Keedy, 'but there's still a very long way to go. We had a lot of help from Mr Sprake. I daresay you saw him here, now and then?'

'As a matter of fact, we didn't. I know who you mean, of course. Mr Sprake was Mr Donohoe's partner. In all the time I've been here, I can't recall Mr Sprake gracing us with his presence more than – what – two or three times at most.'

'I expected partners to be joined together like Siamese twins.'

'Obviously, they were not.'

Keedy felt that he'd already got Armitage's measure so he didn't spend long talking to him. Breaking away with a token apology, he headed for the dining room and was just in time to see Adrian Donohoe leaving it. The latter made no attempt to disguise the fact that he wasn't pleased to meet the detective again. When asked for a few minutes of his time, he agreed reluctantly. The two of them adjourned to the lounge and were soon sinking into leather armchairs. Keedy began by asking about his father's habit of booking a room at the hotel without always using it.

'That's news to me, Sergeant,' said the other.

'Does it surprise you?'

'Yes, it does.'

'It seems so cavalier to me. Why pay for accommodation then walk away from it? Businessmen surely expect their money's worth. In this case, the cost of the room was just thrown away without a second thought.'

'I doubt that. My father was very scrupulous about money.'

'Have you any idea where he might have gone?'

'No, but I'm sure he had a good reason for going there. The simplest explanation is that he was at the offices in Barnes he shared with Norris Sprake. Time didn't exist for my father. He worked all hours – occasionally, for days on end. If he was engaged on a particular project, he'd have been in Barnes.'

'Then why didn't Mr Sprake suggest the same thing?' asked Keedy. 'When we pressed him on the subject, he had no idea of your father's whereabouts away from this hotel. Had his partner been using their office overnight, Mr Sprake would surely have been aware of it.'

'You would have thought so.'

'Then why wasn't he?'

'Only Mr Sprake could answer that.'

'Do you intend to contact him while you're in London?'

'I've already telephoned him, Sergeant,' replied the other. 'I'm seeing him this afternoon. We need to discuss my father's business affairs.'

'Have you ever been to Mr Sprake's mansion?'

'No, I haven't.'

'It's quite palatial.'

'Then it reflects the success of the company.'

'Are you interested in property development, sir?'

'I'm interested in any enterprise with a good return on one's investment.'

'Does that mean you'd like to take your father's place in Barnes?'

'That's irrelevant,' said Adrian, sharply. 'My major concern is to sweep up the unholy mess left behind after my father's sudden death. It will involve a huge amount of time and effort. Before that, of course, there's the funeral to arrange.'

'As soon as the body can be released, we'll let you know, sir.'

'Thank you.'

Keedy regarded him with mingled curiosity and dislike. There was still no sign of regret or suffering in the other man. Had his own father been murdered, Keedy knew that he'd be devastated and would devote his time to consoling his mother. Adrian Donohoe was different. Instead of being distraught, he was irritated by the mountain of work and reorganisation that loomed in front of him. If it ever took place, mourning his father was a reaction that had been postponed. Keedy glanced across the lounge and saw one of the guests opening a newspaper. The detective's haze flicked back to his companion.

'What did you think of the press coverage, sir?'

'I haven't looked at any newspapers,' said Adrian.

'But your father's untimely death is the main story in most of them,' said Keedy. 'I should have thought you'd be interested to see how they described him.'

'Why?' asked the other with disdain. 'I've been reading newspaper articles about my father all my life. In my younger days, I used to cut them out and put them in a scrapbook. Then I had a career of my own to worry about. There's nothing anyone can tell me about my father that I don't know from personal experience. The only time I'll pick up a newspaper is when the killer has been identified and caught.'

'We hope that you won't have too long to wait, sir.'

'Why are you here, Sergeant?' demanded the other, bluntly. 'Pestering me will get you nowhere. Shouldn't you be out looking for the killer?'

'This visit is all part of that process, sir.'

'I fail to see how.'

'Well, to start with,' said Keedy, fixing him with a stare, 'I didn't come simply to meet *you* again. The fact that you stayed here last night was an incidental bonus. What really brought me was the need to interview the Devonian Hotel itself. When he was not in Birmingham,' said Keedy, 'this was your father's alternative home. He was a familiar figure. The hotel staff is discreet but watchful. Without realising it, they'll have seen things that may have had a bearing on the crime. Whoever killed your father probably knew – and may even have frequented – this hotel. That's why I'm not leaving until I've spoken to almost everyone who works here. Their collective memories of your father's visits here will be interesting and may yield some vital facts. I'm sorry that you feel pestered, sir,' he went on. 'If you think that a quiet chat in this lounge is a case of harassment, wait until the press descend on you – and they certainly will. You'll feel absolutely beleaguered then.'

Rising to his feet, Keedy swept out of the room. He didn't see the look of dismay he'd just put on Adrian Donohoe's face nor hear the angry expletive that dropped from the man's lips.

Clifford Burge took up his post immediately. Having been briefed by the head of the new department, he went back to his lodging, changed into more appropriate clothing and headed for Stepney. He wore a cap pulled down over his forehead and, though it was creased and dirtied by age, he resolved that nobody would snatch it away from him. Burge first went to the spot where he'd been given an unexpected shower. It was in a narrow lane cluttered with refuse of all sorts. He located the house he was after. One of the few that actually had a decent garden attached to it, it also boasted a small shed. It was from the top of it that he'd been soaked to the skin. Though he doubted if his attacker actually lived in the house, he walked around to the front of it and knocked at the door. It was owned by an elderly couple. Hearing that he was a detective, they asked for help from the persecution they suffered from local gangs. Children trespassed with impunity on their garden, they moaned, and trampled down anything they tried to grow. All items of value had long ago been stolen from the shed.

Promising to address their concerns, Burge warned them that it might take time. He then went off to find the two policemen who'd arrived on the scene of the fight between the Stepney Warriors and the Evil Spirits. Having read their report of the incident, he asked for more detail. They were unhappy at being supplanted, as they saw it, by a single detective and sceptical about his chances of success. He slowly broke down their resistance to him. When Burge admitted that he'd had his hat stolen, they guffawed.

'You were lucky,' said one of them. 'If it was only your hat they took, it must have been the Warriors. If it had been the Spirits, they'd have cut off your bollocks and kept them in a jar of pickled onions.'

'How often are you here?' asked Marmion.

'Five days a week, at least, and the occasional Saturday.'

'So you kept the company functioning while Mr Donohoe was away.'

'We were in constant touch by letter or telephone,' said Sprake. 'I'd never make a major decision without first consulting him.'

'Did you ever disagree over a contract?'

The other man smiled. 'We did little else. It's the essence of partnership.'

When he'd first heard about the office in Barnes, Marmion had envisaged something on the scale of his own – small, stuffy and without enough natural light. What he was now standing in was an office with the kind of space and facilities well beyond those he had at Scotland Yard. Norris Sprake occupied the largest of the rooms on the ground floor of a rambling Victorian house. As the inspector had arrived, he saw the old man being helped out of the car by his chauffeur and put into a wheelchair. He was then taken into the building and manoeuvred into the high-backed seat behind the desk. The chauffeur discharged his duties with an almost filial care, moving his employer from one chair to another as if handling a fragile vase. He was a tall, elegant, lithe man in his forties with a swarthy complexion. His movements were graceful and unhurried.

'Your chauffeur would make an excellent nurse,' observed Marmion.

'Oh, he's much more than a chauffeur, believe me. He looks after me in every way. I don't know what I'd do without Jean-Louis.'

'Is he French?'

'French mother, English father. He was born in Marseilles but brought up in Scotland. When the war broke out, he was tempted to join up but he felt that his first loyalty was to me. Jean-Louis has become my legs.'

'What does he do while he's waiting until you need him?'

'He works in the office next door. His secretarial skills are more than adequate and, of course, when we purchased property in France, his fluency in the language was a boon. Gilbert always preferred a female secretary,' explained Sprake, 'but I could never find one strong enough to manhandle me.'

'Mr Donohoe, presumably, worked upstairs.'

'Yes, feel free to look at his office, Inspector. Hattie – Miss Kane, that is – will get you tea or coffee, if you wish. She's been his secretary ever since we moved in here. Gilbert enticed her all the way from Birmingham.'

'Then I'd certainly like to meet her, sir. Who else is up there?'

'Roy Vernon, one of our associates. Another one, Malcolm Brant, is down here with us. They had a great admiration for Gilbert. He was their icon,' said Sprake with a laugh, 'whereas I don't even qualify as a statuette.'

'I'll speak to them all, if I may – the chauffeur included.'

'I was told that you had a reputation for thoroughness.'

'Oh,' said Marmion, 'where did you hear that?'

'It pays to have spies in my game, Inspector.'

'Do those spies of yours know who killed your partner?'

'Alas, no – they have their limitations.'

The office was a merger between the functional and the decorative. Wooden filing cabinets stood against one wall but there were framed seascapes above each of them. The bookshelves in the opposite wall were well stocked and punctuated by photographs and examples of exotic glassware. The largest photograph was on the desk itself, angled so that Sprake could always see it when he looked up. Standing behind the old man, Marmion could see that a younger version of his host was on the deck of a yacht in broad sunshine. Clearly able to stand without difficulty, he had his arm around a plump middle-aged woman.

'That's my wife,' he told Marmion, 'on the *Gloriana*.'

But the inspector paid no attention to her. His interest was directed at a man in the background. Looking as if he was a member of the crew was the distinctive figure of Jean-Louis Peebles, the chauffeur.

The ordeal of walking the beat with her had to be endured. Though she feared the worst, Alice was pleasantly surprised. Instead of crowing all over her, Iris Goodliffe was nervous and tentative. Thrilled to be invited out at last, she began to have doubts.

'I don't know what to wear, Alice,' she said.

'Whatever you put on, you'll always look smart.'

'Yes, but is that what he wants? Look at it from Douglas's point of view. Will he want me to put on what I usually do of an evening or does he want something more . . . well, interesting?'

'He's not expecting a fashion show, Iris.'

'All my dresses are so dull and *ordinary*.'

'He likes you for what you *are* rather than what you wear.'

'Do you really believe that?'

'Yes, I do,' said Alice, encouragingly. 'PC Beckett has only ever seen you in police uniform and that's hardly the most flattering outfit for a woman.' She tugged her jacket. 'Anything is an improvement on this.'

'I suppose so.'

'Cheer up, Iris. You're going to have a treat.'

'I feel so unprepared.'

'Don't be ridiculous. You've been waiting for this moment ever since I met you. Make the most of it.'

'It's true,' said Iris, rallying. 'I'm fed up with being a wallflower. Whenever I went to a dance, it was the pretty girls who always got asked on to the floor. I was left high and dry . . .' Her voice trailed away.

'That's not the case here,' said Alice, firmly. 'PC Beckett likes you and that's all that you need to worry about. Just don't expect too much, that would be my advice. These are early days. You need to find out what sort of person he really is.'

'Douglas is a man – that's all I want.'

'Yes, but what sort of man?'

Iris was hurt. 'Don't you like him?'

'I don't know him well enough to like or dislike. We've never even had a conversation. He seems friendly enough and I'm sure that the two of you will have an enjoyable time together.'

'Do you think he'll notice?'

'Notice what?'

'Well, that I'm very . . . inexperienced.'

'He just wants the pleasure of your company, Iris.'

'I don't want to scare him away.'

Before she could ask for more advice, she saw a car draw up at the kerb just ahead of them. Keedy leapt out of the passenger seat and came across to Alice, planting a kiss on her cheek. Iris immediately strode on a dozen paces so that they had a brief moment alone together.

'I can't stop,' said Keedy. 'I knew which beat you were on so I asked my driver to make a slight detour in the hope that we'd see you.'

'It's a lovely surprise, Joe. I'm just grateful that Gale Force isn't here. If she saw you kissing me in public, she'd haul me over the coals.'

'Sorry I haven't been in touch.'

'I understand, Joe.'

'I'd hoped we might have a moment together last night but you weren't there.'

Alice was taken aback. 'You went to the house?'

'Yes, I threw a couple of stones up at your window as usual. When I saw the light go on in the landlady's bedroom, I made myself scarce.'

'I went home for the night.'

'So your father told me. Still having to comfort your mother?'

Alice nodded. Instead of telling him that she'd been the one in need of solace, she let him think that she'd been there solely to talk about the disappearance of her brother. Her mind was in turmoil. Desperate to raise the issue that had been plaguing her so much, she knew that it was neither the time nor place. Alice was about to make a suggestion when he made it for her.

'Let's try again tonight.'

'I'll be there,' she said, 'and you won't need to throw anything up at my window. I'll be sitting beside it.'

'Good. See you later.'

He kissed her again, ran back to the car and got in. As it sped away, Iris walked back to her friend with a sentimental smile on her face.

'That was so romantic, Alice. He'd obviously gone out of his way to snatch a few seconds with you.' She put a hand to her throat. 'Do you think that Douglas would do that kind of thing for *me*?'

Marmion first talked to the two associate members of the company. Roy Vernon was a solemn, sturdy man in his thirties who spoke of Gilbert Donohoe in hushed tones. He claimed to have learnt far more from the Birmingham entrepreneur than he had from Sprake. He was unable to suggest why Donohoe had paid for a hotel room that he didn't actually use. Malcolm Brant was a short, thin, intense man in his late twenties with a nervous twitch that made his spectacles slide down his nose and need readjustment. He spoke with great admiration for the dead man, insisting that Donohoe had no enemies in the business world.

'The murder was a random attack by someone after his wallet,' he argued.

'He didn't need to kill Mr Donohoe in order to rob him. A threat of violence would have been enough. Also, thieves are not in the habit of carrying a leather strap with them in order to garrotte their victims. That's what this one did, according to the post-mortem report,' said Marmion, levelly. 'He deliberately went out with murder on his mind.'

Brant gasped. 'I didn't realise it was premeditated.'

'Somebody must have had Mr Donohoe under observation during his visits to London. Having bided his time, he chose the moment to strike.'

'Yes, yes, Inspector. I can see now that I was wrong.'

Marmion's third visit was to the office occupied by Harriet Kane. Given the fact that her employer had been murdered, the inspector was surprised that she was even there. After such a close working relationship with the man, he expected that the secretary would be overcome by grief. His supposition was partially correct. When he tapped on the door, there was no invitation for him to enter. As he discovered, the door was locked. Certain that she was inside the room, he knocked harder.

'One moment,' said a quavering voice.

In fact, it was over a minute before the door was opened. Harriet Kane had obviously been crying. She was a big, bosomy, ungainly woman in her forties with unprepossessing features and grey hair brushed back fiercely into a bun. Patently, she scorned the use of cosmetics. When he introduced himself, there was a momentary look of alarm as if she thought she was somehow in trouble. Before questioning her, Marmion took time to put her at ease. She slowly relaxed. Harriet sat down behind her desk and he took the only other chair. The office was spacious and meticulously tidy, if too soulless for his taste.

'I'm surprised to see you here, Miss Kane,' he began.

'I didn't want to come. I've worked for Mr Donohoe for many years. When I heard what happened to him, I was appalled. I couldn't stop crying. I just wanted to be left alone to . . . think about him.'

'What changed your mind?'

'Mr Donohoe's son got in touch with me. He's coming here this afternoon and wants me to help him. I have keys to everything in the office next door, including the safe. There's also a combination, of course. I memorised that.'

'Mr Donohoe must have placed great faith in you.'

'I did my best to repay that faith.'

'Do you spend all your time in London?'

'I try to go home at weekends, if it's possible,' she replied. 'My parents are both still alive. They live in a small village called Moseley, not far from Birmingham. There were times when Mr Donohoe needed me here on Saturday and Sunday. His demands always came first.'

'Was he a demanding sort of man?'

She gave a first smile. 'No, far from it – he always used polite requests when he wanted me to do something. And if I did work overtime, I was well paid.'

'Did you *want* to move to London?'

'To be honest, I didn't. I'm a Birmingham girl through and through.'

'What changed your mind?'

'Well, it was a promotion, after all. I'm allowed to do things that most secretaries never get a chance to do. Instead of taking dictation and typing letters all day, I have more important duties. Mr Donohoe said I had a good business instinct and Mr Sprake agrees.'

'Do you live nearby?'

'Yes, I rent a room less than ten minutes' walk away.'

'So you never get to stay at the Devonian Hotel, I suppose?'

'Oh, I'd be a fish out of water there, Inspector,' she said, tittering. 'The one time I did go, I felt I was intruding. I know my place.'

'Describe a typical working day with Mr Donohoe.'

Her eyes bulged. 'Why?'

'It might help me understand a few things.'

Harriet needed several seconds before she felt able to go on. Marmion sat back and listened. The secretary was such an unappealing woman that any notion of an intimate relationship between her and her employer was unthinkable. She'd earned her promotion on merit. At a time when few women were given any real status and responsibility at work, she was entrusted with insights into the complexities of the Donohoe empire. So dedicated had she been to him that she was prepared to uproot herself from the city she loved and move away from the family with whom she'd lived for her entire life.

As she talked about her duties, she shuttled between humility and pride, stressing that she did nothing without her employer's permission, then recalling times when he'd actually sought her advice. Harriet Kane had been both tea-maker and putative associate. Realising that the heady days when she'd enjoyed a whiff of power had gone for ever, she lowered her head to her chest. Marmion felt that it would be too cruel to ask her what she did with her leisure time.

'You were a woman here among men,' he pointed out. 'Didn't that trouble you in any way?'

'No, Inspector,' she said. 'They all accepted me – in time, that is.'

'Mr Sprake told me that you were indispensable.'

'That's going too far.'

'He also said the same about his chauffeur.'

'Jean-Louis really *is* indispensable. He looks after Mr Sprake then does valuable secretarial work for him. Whenever they went on holiday, he usually took charge of the yacht.'

'He's an experienced sailor, then?'

'There's nothing he can't do, Inspector.'

'Both partners were very fortunate,' said Marmion, thoughtfully. 'Each of them found someone on whom they could rely completely. Mr Donohoe had you to turn to and Mr Sprake had Jean-Louis. They were blessed.'

'Yes,' she said, 'I suppose they were.'

'How do you get on with Jean-Louis?'

'Very well, I think.'

'You only *think*?'

'We're friends. He's kind to me.'

'He isn't envious of you, then?'

'Why should he be?'

'Well,' said Marmion, 'he's more or less confined to secretarial work when he's here, whereas you have attended meetings between the partners and their associates. In short, you're senior to Jean-Louis. Doesn't that worry him?'

'Not in the slightest,' she said, briskly.

It was the first time that he knew she was lying.

CHAPTER NINE

Clifford Burge enjoyed walking through his old haunts so much that he had to remind himself that he was there in the line of duty. He paid a courtesy call on his sister-in-law, Annie, and found her trying to control two small, noisy, truculent sons while doing the washing in the tin bath in the scullery. Drying the foam off her forearms, she offered to make him a cup of tea but he told her he couldn't stay. He just wanted her to know that he'd been given the job for which he'd been interviewed.

'Les told me about that. Well done, Cliff!'

'Good to be back again.'

'I bet.'

'Bit more dangerous out there than in my days.'

'Don't we know it!'

Annie Burge was a plump woman with a fading prettiness spoilt by her protruding front teeth. He'd noticed the bulging midriff as soon as he arrived.

'When is it due?'

'Not for months yet but it feels like lead.'

'Les said you wanted a girl.'

'I couldn't cope with another boy,' she said, pausing to slap one of her sons across the back of his head. 'It's like being in the middle of the Battle of the Somme with these two. They fight all day long.'

'Did the same with my bruvver.'

'When did you grow out of it?'

'Not sure we ever did.' She laughed grimly. 'Be around for some time from now on so I'll call in another day.' There was a yell of pain from one boy as his brother punched him in the stomach. Burge lifted each of them up by the scruff of his neck. 'You're in the same family,' he told them, jocularly. 'Be friends and let your mother have a rest for once. Otherwise, she'll set Uncle Cliff on you.' He put them back on the floor and kissed his sister-in-law. 'Bye, Annie.'

'Look after yourself, Cliff.'

Letting himself out of the house, he walked along the street and reflected on the two occasions when he'd come close to marriage. In both cases, he'd had a lucky escape. He might have ended up like his brother, with a harassed wife trying to cope with two energetic children while waiting for a third to arrive. That would make five mouths to feed. Marriage had its advantages – he was the first to admit that – but it brought too many restrictions and Burge had always relished his freedom. Spurning fatherhood, he could enjoy its pleasures at a distance, so to speak, by spending time with his brother's family. He found himself asking a question that troubled him. How many years would it be before his two nephews were part of a gang? How long before their futures were shaped by a war of attrition against their enemies?

It was only a matter of minutes before he came to the market. He loved its bustle, its ceaseless banter, its pungent smells and its sheer variety. People of all nationalities mingled there. Arguments were being conducted in different languages. Most people were still talking about the air raid. Everyone seemed to have friends who were either killed, wounded or had their homes destroyed. Burge inhaled the compound of aromas and listened to the tales of woe about the raid. Rubbing shoulders with local people made him feel part of the vibrant area once again. All around him were assertive women, haggling over prices as they strove to spend their meagre resources wisely. They railed against food shortages and the bane of rationing, seen as an unwarranted intrusion into their lives. They wondered, as on every other day, when the war would end.

When he came out of the market, he walked down a long street until he reached a corner, pausing to look in the window of a junk shop. Most of the items were sad relics with little appeal. Surrounded by stuffed animals, discarded ironware, mottled vases, battered suitcases and useless trinkets, an old mangle occupied much of the space. It was ancient and rust-covered. A birdcage hung from its handle. Burge was about to walk away when he thought he saw something he recognised. He stared with more concentration this time and was startled. He was right. Something of his was indeed on sale. Perched on the top of the mangle was his stolen hat.

He was mortified.

Keedy had worked assiduously at the Devonian Hotel. Arriving back at Scotland Yard, he made use of Marmion's office to collate all the information he'd gathered. His guess about the manager had been on target. When he'd spoken to the younger female members of staff, he produced a few blushes and a lot of smiles. Patrick Armitage had something akin to a harem. The head of housekeeping had been the most helpful person. As a redoubtable middle-aged woman of fearsome appearance, she'd not been one of the manager's conquests and seemed like the only person able to stand up to him. To Keedy's delight, she had an extremely good memory and could recall the exact times over the previous year when Gilbert Donohoe had vanished for a night or two while still paying for his room at the hotel.

'Didn't you think that was eccentric?' Keedy had asked.

She was stony-faced. 'I'm not paid to think, Sergeant.'

'Did Mr Donohoe ever say *where* he was going?'

'We didn't know he'd left the hotel until the following day.'

Though the manager hovered disapprovingly in the background, Keedy had pressed on, even interviewing the lift boy and some of the kitchen staff. On his way back to Scotland

Yard, he'd prevailed on his driver to see if they could somehow intercept Alice on her beat. Their moment together sent him off with raised spirits and, he liked to think, it had cheered her up as well. Like Alice, he was acutely aware of how little time they'd spent together recently. In arranging to meet her later on, he had something to help him through the tedium of reading the endless statements he'd collected at the hotel.

Claude Chatfield burst into the room with characteristic suddenness.

'Ah, I thought the inspector was back.'

'He's still down in Barnes, sir.'

'You've been to the hotel, I hear.'

'That's right, Superintendent. I've just been going through the material I gathered there. The Devonian is a misnomer. It should be called the Iceberg.'

'Why do you say that?'

'What you see on the surface is only a small part of the whole. The real activity goes on below the waterline. It opened my eyes.'

'Really?'

He demanded to know what Keedy had learnt and was treated to quotations from a variety of sources. The woman in charge of housekeeping was most often mentioned. The superintendent became tetchy.

'So you haven't unearthed any suspects, is that it?'

'Mr Armitage might qualify,' said Keedy. 'Though he pretends to help, he's as slippery as an eel. I agree with the inspector. We should keep him in mind.'

'Why should a hotel manager want to kill one of his guests?'

'I'm not suggesting that he actually committed the murder, sir. To begin with, he's far too fastidious to get his hands dirty. If we do discover a conspiracy, however, he could belong to it.'

'Did you talk to Donohoe's son?'

'Yes, sir, I did. Trying to get information out of Adrian Donohoe is like trying to get blood from a stone. It's almost as if he doesn't want us to find the killer.'

'The inspector felt that there could have been friction between father and son.'

'It may have gone beyond friction,' said Keedy.

'Should he be treated as a potential suspect?'

'He's like the manager, sir – worthy of close attention.'

'That's too nebulous for me. I like cast-iron certainties to emerge early in an investigation. So far, we've got nothing and the press is already baying at our heels. If you've seen the coverage this morning,' said Chatfield, ruefully, 'you'll know that we've come in for a good kicking because, allegedly, we can't keep the streets of London safe. Donohoe's is only the latest unsolved murder.'

'Most killers are brought to book, Superintendent.'

'That's not good enough for crime reporters. They expect recurring success.'

'Then they should try *doing* our job,' said Keedy, angrily, 'instead of writing snide articles about it. They might realise how difficult it is then.' He looked down at the sheets of paper he'd filled. 'I've interviewed well over thirty people at that hotel and I plan to go back this evening to talk to some more.'

'What's the rationale behind that?'

'Inspector Marmion and I both agree that the Devonian is

the key location in this case. Adrian Donohoe admitted that his father had been spending more and more time there. If someone had designs on his life, they'd certainly have kept an eye on the hotel; they may even have stayed there in order to wait for the moment to strike. That being the case, the killer's name may well be among the lists of recent guests. I'll take a look at their records.'

'Couldn't you have done that this morning?'

'Yes, sir, but I'd have had the manager looking over my shoulder. He goes off duty at eight.' Keedy grinned. 'I'll get a lot more cooperation from the staff when Armitage is not around.'

'Good thinking.' He pointed to the desk. 'When you've completed the report, bring it straight to me.' Chatfield was about to leave when something jogged his memory. 'How is the inspector coping with the disappearance of his son?'

'He's coping very well, sir.'

'I just hope the press doesn't catch wind of it.'

'So do I.'

'They'd have a field day. When the inspector can't even find his own son, they'd argue, how can we expect him to track down the vicious killer who ended Donohoe's life? His competence would be called into question and that would be monstrously unfair.'

Of the three people he'd spoken to, Harriet Kane was both the most interesting and intelligent. Having none of the educational advantages enjoyed by Roy Vernon and Malcolm Brant, she'd slowly clawed her way up the ladder to become

Donohoe's personal secretary in Birmingham. So reliant had he become on her discretion and conscientiousness that he'd even taken her to London with him. Over the years, her role had been enlarged and she handled the extra responsibility with aplomb. Marmion spent far longer with her than with Vernon and Brant together. They were mere ciphers of Donohoe. She was integral to his whole life.

Marmion called next on the man who intrigued him, tapping on his door before entering the office.

'I'm sorry to interrupt you, sir.'

'No, no, do come on in. Mr Sprake said you wished to talk to me.'

'I won't take up too much of your time.'

'Take up as much as you wish, Inspector.'

Marmion had saved Jean-Louis Peebles until the very end, partly because he was the least important employee but mainly because he was the most unlikely person to find there. Vernon and Brant were exactly what one would expect of businessmen trying to advance themselves, and Harriet – now that she'd explained what she did – also seemed to fit into the company. Peebles stood out. He looked altogether too dignified to act as a manservant and to fulfil basic secretarial duties. Instead of helping Sprake into a wheelchair, Marmion thought, he should be pursuing a career of his own that was entirely free of menial chores.

The inspector soon changed his mind. Sensing what Marmion was thinking, Peebles explained that, when his parents died, he wanted to see more of the world. He therefore drifted around Europe and ended up working in a restaurant on the coast of Crete. Disarmingly honest, he admitted that it was a rather aimless life involving too much drink and too many brushes with bad company. Norris Sprake had been his saviour. While moored in the harbour one summer, Sprake and his wife came ashore to patronise the restaurant. They took an interest in Peebles and felt that he deserved something better.

'Mr Sprake had two good legs in those days,' explained Peebles. 'He was mad about sailing and delighted when I told him I'd worked on a couple of yachts in my time. I was born within sight of the Mediterranean,' he went on. 'The sea was in my nostrils. When my parents moved to Scotland, I used to go boating on the lochs.'

Peebles made no bones about the fact that he'd dodged all attempts to get him a good education even to the point of absconding from one school. As a result, he had no formal qualifications, just a readiness to work hard at whatever came his way.

'So you were, in effect, adopted by Mr and Mrs Sprake?'

'That's what it amounted to in the end, I suppose. Their three daughters treated me like a sort of pet at first then, one by one, they went off to get married and start families of their own.'

'Did you never wish to do that?'

Peebles hunched his shoulders. 'I don't have anything to offer a wife.'

'A lot of women would disagree,' said Marmion, producing a dazzling smile. 'Mr Sprake told me that you considered joining up when the war broke out.'

'It's true – I did.'

'Which army would you have chosen – British or French?'

'I'd have picked a Scots Regiment in the British Army.'

'What prevented you from signing up?'

'I couldn't leave Mr Sprake. He depends on me.'

Peebles went on to explain exactly what he did on a normal day and how he fitted into the household. It was clear that he had nothing like the business experience of Harriet Kane and had no intention of trying to acquire it. He seemed happy to carry on exactly as he was. His one complaint was that the war had prevented them from sailing around the Mediterranean again. Peebles had an engaging manner and an easy smile. He was doing his best to charm the inspector but the latter was not taken in. Though the chauffeur was careful to present himself in the best possible light, what Marmion saw was an adventurer who lived off his wits and who'd wormed his way into the Sprake family.

'What happened to his legs?' asked Marmion.

'He damaged both knees badly in an accident. The operations on them failed. Mr Sprake has been unable to walk properly ever since.'

'It doesn't seem to have made him bitter.'

'He's very philosophical about it. I wouldn't be.'

Marmion glanced around the room. It was smaller, less comfortable and far more cluttered than the others. Peebles had none of Harriet's gift for organising her office. The inspector recalled what she'd said about him.

'I've just spoken to Miss Kane.'

'She's our secret weapon. Hattie more or less runs the place.'

'Don't you mind?'

'Why should I?'

'Well, she's senior to you.'

'So?'

'Most men would feel resentful that a woman had the whip hand over them.'

Peebles smirked. 'Hattie is not what I'd call a real woman.'

'That's a bit unkind.'

'She does her job very well. I don't deny it. And it may be that she's paid more than I get for my work in this office. But that's not the point. Now that Mr Donohoe is dead,' he said, harshly, 'she'll have to go back to Birmingham. *I'll* still be here. Mr Sprake is going to move me into her office.'

When he saw his hat in the window, his first instinct was to storm into the shop, demand to have it returned and insist on being told how it came to be there. Burge realised that that would be a mistake. Instead of easing himself into the community, he'd be revealing himself as an outsider and, in the heat of the moment, might even let slip that he was an undercover detective. Holding himself in check, therefore, he walked away and pounded the streets in the vicinity until he'd calmed down enough to think clearly. By the time he returned to the shop, he'd come to see that, if he wanted his hat back, he might have to pay for it.

Burge stood in front of the window with its accumulated filth and its piece of brown paper stuck over a large crack but now peeling back at the edges. Pretending to look at the mangle, he was instead appraising the owner, a big, slovenly old man wearing dungarees and shuffling around in a pair of moth-eaten slippers. Stepney shopkeepers were canny. Burge knew that of old. While he might be able to retrieve his hat, the chances of getting the name of the boys who'd sold it to the shop were non-existent. As a result, he had to proceed with caution.

When he entered the shop, he was hit by a stench that made him cough. It was difficult to see where it came from, though the owner was making his contribution to it. His clothing stank and his matted hair looked as if it hadn't been washed for years. Wearing a shirt with no collar, he had on a gravy-stained waistcoat with missing buttons. Cigarette ash was scattered liberally over him. The most unpleasant smell seemed to come from the kitchen, making Burge wonder what on earth was being cooked there. Careful not to appear too eager, he looked around the incongruous assortment of items on display. Clothing of all kinds was there in abundance as were dog-eared books and back issues of magazines. Bentwood chairs jostled with a sagging mattress and there was a grandfather clock standing at a rakish angle. When he saw an array of gardening implements, it occurred to him that they might have come from the shed belonging to the elderly couple he'd visited earlier.

'Wot you arfter?' asked the old man, gruffly.

'Need a hat.'

'They're on the 'ooks over there.'

Burge looked in the direction indicated and saw well over a dozen hats hanging in a row. Most of them were caps like the one he was wearing.

'Need something better,' he said.

'Is it for you?'

'Naw – for my bruvver. It's his birfday soon.'

'Wot size does he wear?'

'Same as me.'

Burge crossed over to the hats and ran his eye along them. All had seen better days. There was a top hat, two bowlers, a Homburg and a straw hat almost falling apart. He shook his head.

'Need summat in better condition.'

'Got just wot you needs,' said the other, walking to the mangle and picking up Burge's trilby. 'Not long come in, this 'at – brand new.'

Taking it from him, Burge tried it on and looked at himself in the mirror behind the counter. He adjusted it slightly and murmured his approval. Then the old man told him how much it cost and Burge recoiled. It was even more than he'd originally paid for it.

'Can't afford that.'

'Why not? You said it was a present for your bruvver.'

'It is – but I don't like him *that* much.'

Handing the trilby back to him, Burge walked quickly out of the shop. He was confident that nobody would pay that amount for his hat so it was safe to leave it there. When he later returned, he was certain, he'd get it at a much cheaper price.

The brief interlude with Keedy had been just the fillip that she needed. Alice's walk was almost jaunty now. Her worries about their relationship had not been eliminated but at least they'd set a date when they could discuss them. Feeling invigorated, she was more well disposed to Iris's anxieties.

'If only that would happen to me,' said her friend. 'You're doing your job and walking your beat when the man of your dreams leaps out of a car to give you a kiss. I'd love to have been in your shoes, Alice.'

'Joe would have found that very confusing.'

Iris giggled. 'I was talking about Douglas. I'd love to have been strolling along when he suddenly appeared in a puff of smoke.'

'You make him sound like a pantomime demon.'

'Well, I'm hoping there may be *something* of a demon in him. There is in Sergeant Keedy. He's got that wicked gleam in his eyes. It must be wonderful to have that effect on a man.'

'I suppose that it is.'

'Do you think it will be the same for me and Douglas?'

'How can I possibly tell?'

'You're so much more . . . at ease with men. You know what to say.'

'I'm sure that you and Douglas won't have any trouble talking to each other. I just think it's important for you to find out certain things about him.'

'I will,' promised Iris, 'don't worry. I know you think he might be married and you want to protect me from being taken advantage of, but he's not that kind of man. Douglas is honest and open. He won't try to trick me.'

'Then you'll have an amazing time together.'

'He wants to take me to the cinema.'

'Which film are you going to see?'

'Douglas said that I could choose. That shows how considerate he is.'

'Yes, it does.'

'Who chooses the films *you* go to see – you or Joe?'

'We haven't been to the cinema for months and months, Iris.'

'Oh, you poor thing!' said Iris, touching her partner's shoulder. 'It's a warning to us. I'll tell Douglas that he's far better off where he is. If he gets to be a detective sergeant, I'd be in your position, hardly ever seeing him. Well, that's not going to happen,' she went on with conviction. 'Now that we've found each other, I'm not going to let go of him. This could be my one chance of happiness and it won't slip through my fingers.'

All of a sudden, Alice began to feel sorry for Douglas Beckett.

Harvey Marmion had a rather hasty meal at Scotland Yard with Keedy. They were able to trade details of their respective interviews that morning. The inspector was interested to hear about the exchange with Patrick Armitage and pleased that Keedy's estimate of the man chimed in perfectly with his own. He approved of the decision to return to the hotel when the manager was no longer on duty.

'Armitage has an aura about him, Joe. It will be good to see what happens when he's not there. Did you speak to Adrian Donohoe?'

'Yes – not that it did me any good. He refuses to talk at length about his father or, to be more exact, about his relationship with him. He was quite spiky.'

'Miss Kane implied as much. She was Donohoe's secretary in Barnes and probably got closer to him than anyone. I had the feeling that she was quite hostile to the son and he, in

125

turn, was no admirer of hers. They're seeing each other this afternoon. I sensed that she was dreading his arrival.'

Marmion went on to describe his conversations with Sprake and with his two associates but it was when he talked about Jean-Louis Peebles that he aroused most curiosity. Keedy was intrigued.

'So he's a servant, chauffeur, auxiliary nurse and part-time secretary. Most men would find that kind of life demeaning.'

'Sprake treats him like one of the family.'

'But he's not a real member,' said Keedy. 'It sounds to me as if he's sponging off them. They've got three children of their own so where does Peebles fit in? And what other inducements did Sprake have to offer to keep him?'

'I wondered that.'

'You saw him lifting the old man out of the car, you say?'

'That's right, Joe. He did it as if he'd had plenty of practice. Peebles is a strong man. If he'd wanted to, he could have picked him up bodily and carried him into the office block.'

'Would he be strong enough to carry someone as heavy as Donohoe?'

'Yes, no question about it.'

'Was there any hint that he might have done just that?'

'He'd do anything that Sprake asked of him.'

'Do you really mean *everything*?'

'Yes, I do.'

Keedy's appetite was whetted. He was keen to meet Peebles and make his own appraisal of the man. Meanwhile, he had other duties. After further discussion, Marmion got up to leave.

'I'd better report to Chat.'

'He asked me earlier how you were dealing with Paul's disappearance.'

'Oh? What did you tell him?'

'I just said you were coping. He was worried about the press finding out that the famous Inspector Marmion could capture the most elusive killers yet he hasn't a clue where his son is. It could be embarrassing for you.'

'I can live with that, Joe.'

Marmion took his leave and made his way to the superintendent's office. Invited in, he handed over the report he'd written on his return to the building. After studying it for a couple of minutes, Chatfield heaved a sigh.

'I can't detect any sign of real progress here, Inspector.'

'Read between the lines, sir.'

'What is that supposed to mean?'

'Everyone at those offices in Barnes knows far more than they're prepared to admit – and that goes for Harriet Kane as well. What were they holding back and why were they doing it?'

'It's your job to find the answers.'

Before the inspector could make a comment, there was a tap on the door and a uniformed policeman put his head in to say that someone was desperate to see the superintendent in response to his plea in the newspapers.

'Send him in, Constable.'

The man disappeared for a while but soon returned. He ushered in a stout, striking, immaculately dressed individual of middle years with a bald head.

'Which one of you is Superintendent Chatfield?' he asked.

'I am,' said the other, 'and this is Inspector Marmion who is leading the investigation into the murder of Gilbert Donohoe.'

'That's why I'm here. It was late morning by the time I read the newspapers. I was horrified. I caught the next available train from Kent. My name is Jonathan Ulverton,' he told them. 'I was one of Gilbert's closest friends.'

CHAPTER TEN

In the short time he'd been there, Clifford Burge had learnt a great deal. War had inflicted big changes on Stepney. There was a distinct shortage of younger men on the streets and those he did see were often on crutches, missing an arm or with hideous facial disfigurement. Bomb damage had scarred some neighbourhoods. Small children played among the ruins as if they'd been provided solely for their entertainment. It was the older generation who worried most about the lack of safety. Women, in particular, hurried along and looked fearfully over their shoulders. If they saw youths idling on a corner, they deliberately crossed the road.

Gang members popped up everywhere, showing off their strength by blocking pavements or tormenting passers-by. When policemen came into view on their beat, the groups quickly scattered, leaving a sense of menace in the air. Stepney was theirs.

It was in the market and the shops that the effects of war were at their starkest. Everything was in desperately short supply. Potatoes, the staple diet for most people, were particularly scarce. Bread had almost doubled in price since 1914. Cheese, butter and meat were also more expensive. Those with even a tiny garden tried to grow carrots, swedes, onions, potatoes or other vegetables and then had the problem of protecting their miniature harvests from nocturnal thieves. For many people, soup became the only option. Burge knew that the navy was slowly winning the battle against German submarines but that fact was not evident on stalls or in shop windows. The British public was palpably suffering.

Thanks to the policemen who'd reported on the affray between the Stepney Warriors and the Evil Spirits, Burge had been told exactly where the disputed territory lay. He made a point of walking down all the streets involved. What pleased him most was that nobody seemed to give him a second look. He was an anonymous figure who blended with the local population. When he saw children loitering in doorways, he fought off the temptation to ask them why they weren't at school because he didn't wish to draw attention to himself.

Burge soon came upon another all too common sight. As

he turned a corner, he saw a tiny coffin being brought out of a house and loaded on to the back of a cart. He joined a knot of people who were watching sadly from the other side of the street.

'That's the third one Mrs Harrity has lost,' said the old woman next to him. 'None of them reached their first birthday.'

'What did the baby die of?' he asked.

'Whooping cough. The first two had diphtheria. Mrs Harrity couldn't afford to go to the doctor. All she could give this last one was a raw onion.'

Burge knew that the traditional cure rarely worked. Infant deaths were at a depressingly high level. Overcrowding and bed-sharing meant that killer diseases spread more quickly. When he was at school, he'd lost more than several of his friends to tuberculosis or scarlet fever. It brought back searing memories. Breaking away from the cluster of people, he went on his way. Feeling hungry after his hours on foot, he headed back in the direction of the market to pick up a cheap meal. On his way, he came to the junk shop where he'd spotted his stolen hat. It was still there, balanced on the top of the mangle. If he haggled with the owner, he felt, he might get the asking price down by a half but that was still too much in his view. Burge decided to leave it where it was and return the following day. If no interest had been shown in the hat by then, the owner might be more amenable to a lower offer.

He was still looking in the window when he heard running footsteps behind him. Burge turned to see a boy coming towards him with a bulge under his coat as if he was hiding something. He darted past the detective and went into the shop. The old man clearly recognised him and held out both hands. From under his coat, the boy took out a pair of large black shoes that gleamed as if just brushed. After examining them carefully, the owner put the shoes on the counter, opened his till and took out some coins. Taking the money from him, the boy was obviously pleased with the transaction. He ran out of the shop with a broad grin on his face.

Burge was astonished. Stealing hats off the heads of unsuspecting pedestrians was relatively easy. Had the gangs now moved on to collecting shoes as well?

'I couldn't believe it at first,' said Ulverton, spreading his arms. 'I thought that it was a grotesque misprint. So I rang Scotland Yard for confirmation. Gilbert Donohoe *was* murdered, after all. I was so angry with myself.'

'Why was that, sir?' asked Marmion.

'Well, I saw him at the start of the week before I had to go back to Rochester. I'd thought of telephoning him at the hotel but I never got round to it somehow. That's what's so galling. If I'd rung the Devonian yesterday, I'd have learnt then what had happened to him. Instead of which, I only found out a couple of hours ago.'

'You said that you were a close friend, Mr Ulverton.'

'I like to think I was one of the closest.'

'Perhaps you could explain.'

Ulverton was quick to do so. It transpired that he was a man

132

of independent means who liked, in his own words, to dabble in the arts. He'd met Donohoe years earlier when the two of them had sat next to each other at a performance of Wagner's *Lohengrin* at the Covent Garden Opera House. There'd been an immediate kinship between them and it had developed into a warm friendship.

'I was different, you see,' said Ulverton, tapping his chest. 'I was quite unlike any of the people Gilbert dealt with on a day-to-day basis. They were all blinkered businessmen in search of profit. I, on the other hand, rhapsodised about music, opera, theatre, ballet, art and literature. He said I was an oasis of culture in a desert of philistinism. Gilbert had a nice turn of phrase at times.'

'How often did you meet?' asked Chatfield.

'I usually saw him whenever he was in town. Apart from anything else, there was the club to discuss. We were joint owners, you see. The Club Apollo was our brainchild. It filled a yawning gap.'

'I'm not sure that I follow, sir.'

'Are you a music-lover, Superintendent?'

'I don't have time for leisure pursuits, Mr Ulverton.'

'Then you're starving your soul of nourishment. There are many London clubs and, by and large, they offer the same facilities to their members. The Club Apollo is unique. Since it took its name from the god of music, we created a haven of beautiful sound with a resident quartet playing a classical repertoire. From time to time,' said Ulverton with a grand gesture, 'we invite well-known musicians to entertain us. Where else in this city could like-minded gentlemen enjoy

133

comfort, companionship, a well-stocked library, an excellent restaurant and some of the finest music available?'

'Like most clubs,' said Marmion, 'I daresay that it has an exclusively male membership?'

'That's true, but we have a Ladies' Night every three months when wives and women friends are invited. Those are invariably well attended. My dear wife is always there.'

'What about Mrs Donohoe?'

'She, too, is a regular visitor.'

'It sounds like an expensive place, Mr Ulverton.'

'If you want the best, Inspector, you have to pay for it. The annual fee might seem high, but we've had no complaints. Our members are very happy. They abide by our one strict rule, which is that they're forbidden to talk business. Club Apollo is for relaxation. But enough of that,' said Ulverton, face crumpling. 'I came here to talk about Gilbert, not about the club. Who could have killed him? Do you have any ideas? The newspaper article only gave scant details. What else can you tell me?'

Measuring his words, Chatfield gave him an edited account of the murder and of the investigation set up in its wake. Ulverton was anxious to hear more so Marmion eventually took over from the superintendent.

'Are you aware that Mr Donohoe sometimes left the Devonian for a night or two even though he still had a room at the hotel?'

'Yes, he used to stay at the club. We offer limited accommodation for country members. As my partner, of course, Gilbert had the use of the main suite.'

'If it's not a rude question, sir,' said Marmion, 'what did he do all day?'

'In essence, he hid away from the world. He read voraciously, he ate heartily and he listened to his favourite music. That was heaven to him.'

'Did he ever introduce Mr Sprake to the club?'

'No,' replied Ulverton with a shake of his head. 'He deliberately kept him away. Sprake was not uncultured, by all accounts, but he was not our type. We have to be very selective.'

A completely new side to Donohoe had now been revealed to them. While he knew about the man's love of music, Marmion never expected that he'd take it to such lengths and invest so much money in the venture. Norris Sprake had told him that Donohoe was so committed to the business world that it took over his whole life. It could only mean he was unaware of the existence of the Club Apollo.

'I'm so annoyed with myself,' said Ulverton, slapping his thigh. 'Instead of making contact with Gilbert, I was caught up in endless meetings about the festival.'

'What festival is that?' asked Chatfield.

'Can't you guess, Superintendent? I live in Rochester.'

'Then it must be something to do with Charles Dickens.'

'You're quite right. I'm not just the patron of the Dickens Festival, I take an active part in it. We have all kinds of events but the real joy is to dress up as your favourite Dickensian character.' Patting his stomach, he smiled. 'I'm sure you can guess the character I choose.'

'Well, it certainly won't be Scrooge,' said Marmion. 'He

could never afford the membership fees for the Club Apollo.'

'I'd plump for Mr Pickwick,' said Chatfield.

Ulverton nodded. 'Nature intended me for the role.' His ire flared up again. 'But who cares about a festival at a time like this? It's a complete irrelevance. I should have been here with Gilbert. That way, I might even have saved his life.'

Ellen Marmion did all she could to keep herself busy. When she'd finished the chores, she did the shopping, dropped everything off at the house then joined the circle of women who were making gloves, scarves and other items to be sent to soldiers at the front. Since it was now summer, it seemed unlikely that there'd be any demand but the gifts could always be kept in readiness for winter. Paul had told her how viciously cold it could get in the trenches and how any source of warmth was seized on. It was good to be back with her women friends again, some of whom had sons in the army. Understanding her situation, they were uniformly kind to Ellen and didn't ask her about Paul, knowing full well that, when she had new information, she'd be quick to pass it around the group.

On the way home from the sewing circle, she usually started worrying about her son all over again but this time it was her daughter who occupied her mind. Alice was close to despair. That was clear from the letter she'd been compelled to write. Unaware that she and Keedy had arranged to meet later, Ellen feared that a chasm would open between them. If it continued to grow, it would, in time, be impossible to bridge. When the couple had first fallen in love, Ellen's delight had been counterbalanced by her husband's disapproval. Now that Marmion was reconciled to having Keedy as a son-in-law, it was his wife who was beginning to have doubts. It was now two years since Alice and Keedy had got together. To be so close that long and still not talk seriously about marriage was worrying. She blamed Keedy.

Much as she loved her daughter, Ellen was ready to acknowledge her failings. Alice had a temper. It paled beside the fury shown by her brother but it needed to be kept in check. If Alice lost her control and hurled some of the accusations in her letter at Keedy, there was no telling what would happen. For a few seconds, Ellen thought about the consequences of their splitting up. It would leave her with an inconsolable daughter and her husband would spend every day with a rueful partner. Everybody would lose. It was a frightening thought. All that Ellen could hope was that, when they did next meet, Alice and Keedy would be so pleased to see each other again that their differences would fade away.

Realistically, however, she thought it unlikely.

Marmion was excited by the new line of enquiry that had unexpectedly opened up. Since it revealed an important element in the private life of Gilbert Donohoe, he was keen to visit Club Apollo. He therefore collected Keedy and introduced him to the ebullient Jonathan Ulverton. All three of them then set off in a police car. On the journey to Belgravia, the detectives hardly said a word because Ulverton delivered a lively commentary on the club that he and his former partner had founded. When he heard what the annual membership fee was, Keedy gaped. He couldn't believe that anyone had that amount of money to spend on occasional visits to a gentlemen's club. During a rare pause in the recitation, he managed to get in a question.

'Adrian Donohoe was a member, I suppose?'

'Your supposition is quite wrong, Sergeant,' said Ulverton, seriously. 'Gilbert would never have allowed it. His son had no interest in any of the arts.'

'What qualification does anyone need to become a member?'

'He has to be the right sort of person.'

'And who decides that?'

'It's left to the committee.'

When they reached their destination, they got out of the car and found themselves staring at a large Regency building that had once acted as a foreign embassy. Ulverton led the way in and introduced them to the club steward, Saul Rockwell, a stocky man in his forties with an impassive face and a searching gaze. Nobody, it was clear, would get past Rockwell unless he was a legitimate member. The club was cavernous with room opening out after room. As soon as they entered the lounge, they heard the strains of a string quartet playing in the adjacent restaurant.

'Haydn,' said Ulverton, recognising it. 'He wrote dozens of string quartets. This one is called "The Lark". And before you tell me that we shouldn't be playing Austrian music when we're at war with Austria-Hungary, I have to point out that music transcends national boundaries.'

'Does the quartet always play at this time of day?'

'Our members like to hear music while they're enjoying luncheon. The quartet is here three days a week and most evenings. The music is sublime, isn't it?'

'It's not what *I'd* like to hear while I'm eating,' admitted Marmion.

'Nor me,' said Keedy. 'It's distracting.'

Ulverton beamed. 'We find it utterly inspiring.'

There were only half a dozen members in the lounge. Two were engaged in some sort of discussion while the others read newspapers or, in one case, followed the score of 'The Lark'. All of them were middle-aged and oozing prosperity in a way that offended Keedy. Designed for maximum comfort and with an essentially masculine air to it, the lounge had the thickest carpet either of the detectives had ever seen. Their shoes sank into it.

'I'll show you around,' said Ulverton, proudly. 'There's much to see.'

'Then I'll be happy to come with you, sir,' said Marmion. 'The sergeant can have a few words with your steward. We'll be interested in any comments *he* has to make about Mr Donohoe.'

Taking his cue, Keedy went back to the entrance hall. Thankfully, he discovered, he was out of reach of Haydn there. Rockwell got up from his desk with routine cordiality.

'Can I help you, Sergeant?' he asked.

'Don't worry,' said Keedy, palms raised. 'I'm not applying for membership. I can tell you now that I'm not the right sort of person.'

* * *

Every day was different in the Women's Police Service. When they walked their beat, Alice Marmion and Iris Goodliffe never had a quiet and uneventful time. Problems always turned up at some point and they were often complete novelties. They'd been asked to retrieve pet cats from trees before now but they'd never had to coax a dog down from a high branch before. How the animal got up there in the first place was a mystery. It was now frozen with fear and clinging on desperately. Its owner, a tiny woman on the verge of hysteria, was terrified that her beloved West Highland terrier would fall to its death unless rescued. She pleaded with the policewomen to help.

Iris was too heavy and frightened of heights to attempt the feat so it fell to Alice to bring the animal to safety. It was a perilous enterprise. The branch on which the terrier stood would never bear a woman's weight. Somehow she had to entice the dog down to a lower branch that was within easier reach. Gritting her teeth, Alice began to ascend the tree. A small crowd quickly gathered. While some people encouraged her, Alice was at the same time berated by the owner for making the tree shake in a way that endangered her pet. She was tempted to drop to the ground again and tell the woman to get the animal down herself. Having got so far up the tree, however, she felt that she had to go on.

The dog had enough intelligence to realise that Alice was trying to help. It began to yelp piteously. She tried to beckon it towards her but to no avail. Climbing a little higher, she held out one hand.

'Come on,' she said. 'I'll take you down to the ground.'

'Be careful!' yelled the owner. 'You'll make Sidney fall!'

'Stop interfering,' ordered Iris. 'You're putting my colleague off.'

'He's my dog.'

'Then you shouldn't have let him climb up that tree.'

'Be quiet down there!' shouted Alice.

Inching closer all the time, she kept using the dog's name in order to win its trust. It seemed to work. Sidney actually wagged his tail at one point and dared to move a little way along the branch towards Alice.

'Keep going,' said Alice, stretching an arm to its fullest extent. 'Come on, Sidney. You can do it. I can't help you until I can reach you.'

Eyes rolling in terror and tongue hanging out, the dog made a brave effort to claw its way along the branch. Not far below him was Alice, one arm securely around the trunk of the tree, the other ready to grab hold of him. Iris was no mere onlooker. Foreseeing the possibility of a mishap, she undid her jacket and peeled it off. Then she got a man in the crowd to hold it open with her so that it could break the dog's fall. They were just in time. As the animal got within a foot of Alice's hand, it suddenly lost its balance, let out another yelp and fell through the air. The panic-stricken owner screamed and the crowd stood back. Iris and the man moved swiftly to get directly beneath Sidney and caught him in the jacket.

There was a round of applause from the crowd but the owner didn't join in. She simply snatched up the dog, thrust him under her arm and stalked off. Iris looked after her with disgust.

'That's all the thanks you get!' she protested.

Alice called plaintively from above. 'How do *I* get down?'

Saul Rockwell was a mine of information about the operation of Club Apollo. Having been employed there since it first opened, he knew all the members by name and could list each individual's musical preferences. Keedy was glad that they'd finally found the sanctuary to which Donohoe retired when the mood took him.

'We expected him days ago,' said Rockwell, 'but he never came.'

'Now you know why.'

'He was such a pleasant man and he went out of his way to make friends. He and Mr Ulverton were brothers under the skin. They created the perfect atmosphere here.'

'So we were told.'

'It'll never be quite the same without Mr Donohoe.'

'Who first employed you?'

'He did.'

'And where were you before you came here?'

'I worked at a club in Pall Mall. Mr Donohoe was a member there as well.'

'Did he lure you away?'

'He took a chance on me, Sergeant, and I made sure I never let him down. Club Apollo is my life now. The hours are long and irregular but I don't mind that. Luckily, I have a very understanding wife.'

'I'm hoping to have one of those in due course,' said Keedy, 'though I fancy she'd draw the line at me sneaking off here to listen to a string quartet instead of painting the kitchen or repapering the living room.'

'Mr Donohoe had no problem coming here whenever he wished. In fact, his wife encouraged him to do so. Mrs Donohoe attended most of our Ladies' Nights.'

'That's because she loved music – posh music, that is. We never had the chance to appreciate that, as kids. It was beyond us. The only kind of music *we* like is the kind you can dance to.'

'Then this is not the place for you, Sergeant.'

Rockwell was well spoken, well mannered and clearly good at his job, yet Keedy sensed there was a rough-and-ready element to the man, now carefully subdued.

'Were you ever in the army?' he asked.

'No,' replied Rockwell, 'I served in the navy.'

'Why did you give it up?'

'I met the woman I wanted to marry. The one thing she wouldn't accept was the idea of having a husband sailing the seven seas while she was stuck at home. We came to an agreement.'

Keedy nodded. 'Yes, I suppose we'll have to do that sooner or later.'

'The captain on my last ship was a member of the club in Pall Mall. He got me a job there. Within a couple of years I was the steward. I have Captain Giltrap to thank for that.'

'Did you repay the favour by getting him accepted here?'

'I'm in no position to do that, Sergeant, and there was no need in any case. This club had no attraction for him.'

'What about the other members?'

'They're all professional men from different walks of life. We have doctors, lawyers, barristers, civil servants, bankers, businessmen and so on.'

'I didn't see any younger members in the lounge.'

'You need money and leisure time to make the most of Club Apollo.'

'Are people ever turned away?'

'Oh, yes,' said Rockwell, seriously. 'It happens all the time. We set high standards here. Some people have been extremely angry when they're rejected by the committee. They've even threatened legal action.'

Keedy perked up. 'Was Mr Donohoe a member of that committee?'

'He was the chairman.'

Marmion, meanwhile, was being given a tour of the building. Since his guide talked effusively throughout, the inspector had little opportunity to ask questions. He didn't mind. The Club Apollo was a reflection of the personalities of its founders. It was a glimpse into a new and unappealing world for Marmion. He kept thinking that, while the country's younger generation was being mown down ruthlessly in the war, members of the elite club were indulging themselves with rich food, plentiful drink and exquisite music. It seemed wrong to him. The whole country was suffering from the ill effects of the war yet a privileged group of men contrived to remain untouched and unbothered by it. That struck Marmion as grotesque selfishness. At the end of their tour, Ulverton looked at him shrewdly.

'I'm sorry you disapprove of us so much, Inspector.'

'My opinion is irrelevant, sir. I'm just grateful to you for revealing things about Mr Donohoe that we'd never have suspected.'

'Businessmen are not all hard, uncaring, money-grubbing capitalists. Some have a softer side and Gilbert was one of them.'

'I didn't see any evidence of a softer side in his son.'

'Adrian was a disappointment to him,' said Ulverton, 'but that's all in the past now. Our main task is to find the man who killed his father in such a brutal fashion. It was unforgivable. I'll get in touch with Clara immediately.'

'What did Mrs Donohoe make of this place?'

'I think she was rather jealous of her husband.'

'There are no clubs of this kind for women.'

'There certainly aren't,' said Ulverton with a half-smile. 'Well, you know Gilbert's secret now, Inspector. He needed a place of escape and this was it. He made so many friends here.'

'What about enemies?'

'He had none at the Club Apollo and neither, I hope, do I. We both have a benevolent streak, you see. We like other people to be happy. That's why we tried to create all the right preconditions here.'

He was clearly fishing for compliments but Marmion had none to give.

'What happens now?' he asked.

'We carry on as before. It's what Gilbert would have wanted us to do.'

'You misunderstood my question, sir. Since your partner is

dead, will his stake in the club revert to his family? Will Adrian Donohoe replace his father?'

'Certainly not,' snapped the other, eyes blazing. 'He won't be allowed anywhere near the club.'

CHAPTER ELEVEN

When they reached the end of their shift, they were in high spirits because each of them had something to look forward to that evening. Iris Goodliffe had her night out with Douglas Beckett and Alice Marmion would at last get to spend some time with Joe Keedy. Their excitement was soon terminated. The moment they reappeared, they were pounced on by Inspector Gale who took them straight to her office. Neither of them could understand why they were in trouble.

'Mrs Hellier called here earlier,' said the inspector. 'She came to lodge a complaint against you.'

'Why?' asked Iris. 'We don't even know who she is.'

'She owns a dog and claims that you almost killed it.'

'That's not true at all, Inspector. We tried to save the animal. Alice was brave enough to climb the tree and might have been injured as a result.'

'It's Iris who deserves the real credit,' said Alice. 'When the dog fell, she was able to catch it in her jacket. It was completely unharmed.'

Thelma Gale scowled. 'That's not what Mrs Hellier says.'

'There were witnesses. We've taken some of their names.'

'I'm pleased to hear that you did *something* sensible.'

'What were we supposed to do?' asked Iris. 'Leave it up the tree?'

'Don't you dare take that tone with me,' said the inspector, administering a verbal slap in the face. 'Now, then, I've had one version of events. Let me hear yours in turn.' She looked at Alice. 'You go first.'

Alice gave a straightforward account of what had happened but failed to remove the frown from the older woman's face. Iris's report was altogether more dramatic and portrayed Alice as the heroine of the hour. Having delivered their versions, the least they expected was an apology but it was not forthcoming.

'When each of you joined the Women's Police Service,' said the inspector, officiously, 'I impressed upon you the need to present the right image to the public. They are not used to seeing women in such a role and many of them still object to us. We must not give them an excuse for criticism. That's what happened in this instance. Both of you were at fault.'

'Someone had to rescue the dog,' argued Alice.

'I agree but it was not your job. You should have summoned

148

a policeman. Did it never occur to you that, in climbing up that tree, you made it possible for someone to look up your skirt? Certain men would take advantage of that.'

'It never crossed my mind, Inspector. Besides,' she went on, touching her ankle-length skirt, 'this covered everything decently. My one thought was to rescue the dog before it fell.'

'But you didn't rescue it, did you? According to the owner, you actually precipitated the fall.'

'That's so unfair!' protested Iris.

'Be quiet!'

'Mrs Hellier was begging us to save him. In the end, we did.'

'Yes,' said the other, voice rising in volume, 'but you took off your jacket in the process. One of my officers is letting men look up her skirt while the other is removing another part of her uniform. Have you looked *inside* that jacket?' she demanded. 'It's probably covered in dog hairs. You're charged with safeguarding that uniform.'

'I wish we hadn't bothered,' muttered Iris.

'Inspector Gale makes a valid point,' said Alice, stepping in to appease her superior. 'Instead of weighing up the situation, we acted on instinct. It seemed like the right thing to do at the time but, on reflection, perhaps it wasn't.'

Thelma Gale sniffed. 'I'm glad that, in hindsight, one of you realises that.'

About to speak, Iris felt Alice's hand squeeze her arm. It was a signal for her to remain silent. All they could do was to stand there while the inspector upbraided them. Feeling that they deserved praise rather than censure, they both fumed at the injustice of it all. When the reprimand was over, they were sent out with their ears stinging. Iris was livid.

'I wish I'd let that hateful little dog hit the ground,' she said, vengefully.

'Don't listen to Gale Force. We did what was right, Iris.'

'And look what we got in return.'

'Forget about the inspector and forget about that dreadful Mrs Hellier. Yes,' said Alice, 'it was very unpleasant being yelled at like that but we came through it and we still have a treat to come this evening. You're going to the cinema with Constable Beckett and I'll be seeing Joe.'

Iris brightened. 'I was forgetting that,' she said. 'Wait until I tell Douglas what happened – he's bound to take our side.'

'In your position, I wouldn't even mention it. He's taking you out because he likes you. Enjoy the evening. Don't start off by moaning about what happened on our shift. I'm certainly not going to tell Joe about it,' said Alice. 'We have much more important things to discuss than a dog up a tree.'

On their drive back to Scotland Yard, Marmion and Keedy were able to pool information and speculate on what the latest development meant for the investigation. Marmion was interested to find out more about Jonathan Ulverton and the source of his wealth.

'He's a very different person from Sprake,' he said. 'They wouldn't get on at all. Ulverton is far too ostentatious.'

'They do have something in common.'

'I didn't spot it, Joe.'

'They both love books. Ulverton is devoted to Charles Dickens while Sprake prefers Robert Louis Stevenson. It's a choice between Mr Pickwick and Long John Silver. Which one would you pick?'

'I think Allan Quatermain is better than both of them, to be honest. My vote goes to *King Solomon's Mines*. It's a great yarn.'

'Ulverton puzzled me,' said Keedy.

'Why?'

'He was too helpful. I found him a bit overwhelming. Why did he have to keep boasting to us about the Club Apollo?'

'It's very dear to his heart – and, of course, it meant a great deal to Donohoe as well. It was only a matter of time before we found out about the place because someone in Donohoe's family would have told us. I think that Ulverton wanted to make sure that we only saw what he wanted us to see.'

'Do you think he's hiding something?'

'I always think that about people with money.'

Keedy laughed. 'So do I.'

'How did you get on with the steward?'

'Oh, we had a pleasant chat but he was too clever to give anything away. Rockwell was Donohoe's choice for the job. He's fiercely loyal to the club. I did get something useful out of him, though.'

'What was it?'

'Some people find it hard to take rejection, it seems,' said Keedy. 'When they're refused membership, they turn nasty. One of them was so upset, apparently, that he came back at night and smashed a few windows.'

'Did they have him arrested?'

'Rockwell said they had no proof and Donohoe told him to

forget the whole incident. But it shows you how far someone will go if his pride has been hurt.'

Marmion turned to him. 'Are you thinking what I am?'

'Donohoe was chairman of the committee that discussed any membership applications. He had the final say in every case. Anyone who was turned down would know that he was the man to blame. Is that what happened?' suggested Keedy. 'Did someone feel so upset that he took his revenge on Donohoe?' He waited for a reply that never came. 'You didn't answer my question.'

'I was thinking about a related question,' said Marmion. 'What is so special about the Club Apollo that it makes wealthy men so eager to join?'

It was Burge's turn to buy a pint for someone else this time. Shortly after he got to the Mermaid Tavern that evening, he saw Everitt White walk in. He immediately ordered a beer for him. Still in uniform, White raised his tankard in acknowledgment.

'How did the interview go?'

'Got the job and started work this morning.'

'Well done, Cliff!' He lifted the tankard again.

'Can see why the commissioner wants the gangs off the streets – bleeding dangerous out there.'

'Nobody would be stupid enough to tackle you.'

'Yet the little devils did.'

Burge told him about the loss of his hat, producing a barrage of jeers and a firm pat on his back. White was amused at first but he became more serious when he heard what had happened to the hat. He was amazed that Burge had been so passive.

'I'd have gone in there and demanded it back,' he said. 'If the shopkeeper had refused, I'd have arrested him on the spot.'

'I couldn't do that, Ev. I'd give the game away.'

'If your hat was on sale, he was receiving stolen goods.'

'Most of the items in there could be described that way. I know how the system works. Old man's the local Fagin. Kids steal items of value for a small fee then he sells them for a profit.'

'Are you certain?'

'Saw it with my own eyes.'

Burge went on to describe the way that a boy had arrived with a pair of shoes and sold them to the shopkeeper. White's interest increased at once.

'What sort of shoes?'

'Good ones, by the look of it – black and well polished.'

'And what size were they?'

'Too far away to see.'

'Were they small, medium, large?'

'Large, I'd say.'

White quaffed most of his beer at speed, then asked for directions to the junk shop. He told Burge to stay at the tavern until he returned.

'Where you going, Ev?'

'I'm going to get your hat back.'

'Shop'll be closed.'

'Then it'll have to be reopened for me, won't it?'

Guzzling down the remains of his drink, he put the tankard back on the counter and headed purposefully for the door.

* * *

Having got there before the designated time, Iris Goodliffe had been standing on the corner for almost fifteen minutes before doubts started to set in. What if Beckett didn't turn up? What if he'd had second thoughts about the arrangement and changed his mind? What if – and this was her greatest fear – he'd only invited her out in order to win a bet with some of the other policemen? Iris was hurt. She'd gone to such trouble to improve her appearance and her efforts had been wasted. Instead of coming to take her out, Beckett was probably in the pub with his friends, laughing at her expense. After another ten minutes, she gave up and moved swiftly away.

'Hey!' yelled Beckett. 'Don't go, Iris.'

She turned and saw him hurrying towards her. 'You came, after all.'

'I've been thinking about it all day. Nothing would've stopped me.'

'That's so kind of you, Douglas.'

'Everybody calls me Doug.'

'Then I'll do the same.'

Iris looked at him properly. Never having seen him out of uniform before, she was impressed by the sight of him in a suit and hat. He'd gone to some lengths to look smart. Admittedly, Beckett was several years older than her but their respective ages were irrelevant. She had an admirer. That was enough.

'Which film do you want to see, Iris?' he asked, politely.

'You choose, Doug. Whatever it is, I'll enjoy it.'

After trying the door and finding it locked, White banged on it hard with his fist. Above his head, a sash window creaked as it was opened. The old man's head popped out. His voice was an uncouth rasp.

'We're closed.'

'Good,' said White. 'It means we won't be interrupted.'

'What d'you want?'

'Let me in and I'll tell you. Keep me waiting and I'll get angry.'

'I've done nothing wrong, have I?'

'That depends – now open up.'

The shopkeeper vanished and the sash window was closed. White, meanwhile, stared through the glass. The mangle stood where he'd been told it did and Burge's hat was still on top of it. After a while, the old man came into the shop and unlocked the door. White barged his way in.

'I don't have any trouble with the police,' said the shopkeeper.

'I'm glad to hear it.'

'We keep to the letter of the law.'

'I doubt that very much.' White looked around. 'I want some black shoes.'

'I can't sell you anything out of hours.'

'I'm not buying them. I'm repossessing them.'

The old man was wary. 'What do you mean?'

'Fetch me the shoes that came in earlier today.' He snapped his fingers. 'Don't waste my time. You bought a pair of shoes from a boy. Where are they?'

'I don't know what you're talking about.'

'Then let's have this discussion when I put you under arrest, shall we?'

'No, no,' cried the old man, 'there's no need for that. The

155

police know me around here. We have . . . an arrangement. That's why they never bother me.'

'Ah, so you have a deal with the bobbies on the beat, do you?' said White with a knowing chuckle. 'Is that how it works? They look the other way. I've got bad news for you, sir. I don't take bribes.'

'I've done nothing wrong.'

'You're starting to make me angry. Where are those damn shoes?'

Scuttling behind the counter, the shopkeeper reached down and brought up the shoes he'd bought earlier. White snatched them from him and inspected them. They were of the highest quality.

'You were about to sell stolen goods,' he said, menacingly. 'My guess is that that's how you make your living. You buy cheap from young thieves, then sell dear. Who brought you these?'

'I don't know his name.'

'Ah, so you admit a boy *did* bring them here.'

'He found them down by the river. That's his patch.'

'Does he belong to the Warriors or the Spirits?'

'I can't tell you that,' said the old man in alarm. 'They'd kill me.'

Grabbing him by the arm, White put his face inches away from him.

'Would you like to hear what *I'd* do?' he said with a malevolent smile.

Marmion was in his office when the superintendent suddenly walked in with a grim expression on his face. Chatfield had just endured hostile questions from the press and it had been more harrowing than he'd expected. Without invitation, he sat in a chair.

'How did you get on, sir?' asked Marmion.

'They treated me as if I was the killer instead of being the person hunting him. Reporters have no respect for reputation. I had to be very severe with them and put them in their places.'

'I'm sure you did it very effectively.'

'Where's Sergeant Keedy?'

'I've sent him back to the Devonian Hotel to see what he can find out when the manager is not on duty. There's also the possibility – a faint one, maybe – that Adrian Donohoe is still there.'

'Yes,' said Chatfield, 'that was something I noticed in your report. What sort of man would open a London club then forbid his son to join? It's inexplicable. And why did Mr Ulverton show such animosity towards Adrian Donohoe?'

'That's one of many conundrums, sir.'

'It's high time we started solving some of them.'

'We're doing our best, Superintendent.'

'Try standing up in front of the press and saying that. I felt as if I was facing a firing squad today. They're supposed to *help* us not to shoot us.'

It was not often that Chatfield admitted being under pressure. Dealing with the press was something he flattered himself he could do better than anyone. His skills had failed him this time. He looked weary and out of sorts.

'Perhaps an early night might be in order,' said Marmion, helpfully.

His visitor jumped up like a startled hare. 'I'm not deserting my post because of a spat with the press. That would be a dereliction of duty.'

'You've been here for well over twelve hours, Superintendent.'

'I'll stay here around the clock, if necessary. My stamina is legendary, as you well know. It has to be in this job.'

He went on to talk about occasions when he'd worked all night on difficult cases and, as a result, earned the success he deserved. All that Marmion could do was to nod in agreement and hope that his visitor's fatigue would eventually get the better of him. As it was, they were interrupted by a knock on the door.

'Come in,' called Marmion.

'This came for you, Inspector,' said the policeman who entered the room.

Putting down a parcel and an envelope, he went out again.

'Whatever have you got there?' asked Chatfield.

'I'll be intrigued to find out, sir,' said Marmion, opening the envelope and taking out a letter. 'It's from Inspector White of the River Police,' he went on, reading the message. 'He's the man who found Donohoe's body for us. He thinks he may have found something else as well.'

'Oh? What is it?'

Using a pair of scissors to cut the string on the brown-paper parcel, Marmion took out a pair of black shoes. He held them up for examination.

'White believes these may have come from the murder victim, sir.'

Clifford Burge was so pleased to get his hat back without having to pay for it that he bought White another pint of beer.

Leslie Burge was also at the Mermaid now so all three of them celebrated what was a minor triumph. White had frightened the truth out of the shopkeeper and learnt that the boy who'd brought in the shoes belonged to the Evil Spirits. The ones who specialised in keeping the shop well stocked with hats were members of the Stepney Warriors. By dint of putting the fear of death into the shopkeeper, White had even got some names to pass on to his friend.

'There you are, Cliff. That should make your job easier.'

'I could never have found all that out so soon,' said Burge, gratefully. 'It would have taken days and days. How did you do it?'

White winked at him. 'It's called old-fashioned policing.'

Keedy noticed the difference as soon as he entered the hotel. Patrick Armitage wasn't there. Without the manager on patrol, there was a more relaxed air to the place. It was a bonus. Set against it, however, was a disappointment. When he enquired, Keedy learnt that Adrian Donohoe had left the hotel earlier that evening. There would be no chance of talking to him again. The receptionist was a short, neat, bespectacled man in his fifties with lank hair combed over a spreading bald patch. He'd just come on duty for the night shift. Like most of the staff, he remembered and spoke well of Donohoe. Eager to assist the investigation, he allowed Keedy to study the ledger in which all guests' names and addresses were listed. There was no manager to hamper him this time. He had a free hand. The ledger repaid close examination. Convinced that the killer might have stayed at the Devonian in order to stalk his victim, he looked for men who'd had single rooms on the two days before Donohoe's disappearance. It was possible that the killer might have shared a double room with an accomplice but he thought it unlikely. He therefore concentrated his search on a lone man.

He was undaunted by the fact that the killer would not have used his real name, hoping that he could learn something about him by other means. Excluding Donohoe, eight men stayed in single rooms at the hotel on the night before the murder. By flipping back through the pages, he discovered that five of them were regular patrons of the Devonian and could therefore be discounted. He was after newcomers, so his interest shifted to the three remaining names. Keedy tested the receptionist's memory.

'Were you on duty throughout the week?'

'Yes, Sergeant, I was.'

'Do you recall a Mr Jonah Jenkins from Cardiff?'

'I remember speaking to a gentleman with a strong Welsh accent but I'm not sure of his name. He wished me goodnight as he went upstairs.'

'What age would he be?'

'Oh, he was quite elderly.'

Keedy looked down at the second name. 'What about a Mr Michael Sloman?'

'He stayed on Monday, the same night as Mr Jenkins. I remember Mr Sloman because he asked if we had anything for a headache. As it happens, we do. Mr Armitage keeps a small pharmacy for emergencies. He thinks of everything.'

'Can you describe Mr Sloman?'

'He was about my height but a lot heavier. I'd say he was in his fifties.'

Keedy put the ledger back on the counter and pointed to the third name.

'That leaves this chap – Thomas Day from Birmingham.'

'I only got a glimpse of him,' said the receptionist. 'He left very early in the morning. I was just about to go off duty when he walked past and slapped his room key down. Mr Day was in a hurry to go somewhere.'

'What did he look like?'

'He was as tall as you but somewhat older. I suppose you'd call him handsome but he didn't really stay long enough for me to judge. The one thing I did notice was that he was well built.' He smiled. 'They obviously feed them well in Birmingham. That's where he came from. Mr Day was very sleek.'

'I doubt if Thomas Day was his real name.'

'Then who was he?'

Keedy thought that he had the answer. After his visit to Barnes, Marmion had given him a detailed description of Norris Sprake's chauffeur. Keedy felt that he was hearing it all over again. Could it be that Jean-Louis Peebles and Thomas Day were one and the same person? It was an intriguing possibility.

Harvey Marmion didn't believe in coincidences that worked to his benefit. They rarely occurred. Malign acts of fate were more common in his life. He was so resigned to being buffeted by them that he'd given up all hope of an occasional slice of luck. Having spent the whole day brooding on the murder, he allowed himself a few minutes to think about his son once more. On the desk in front of him was the map he'd used when trying to find Paul, going from place to place in a futile search. Every city, town and village he'd visited was clearly marked. None had yielded him reliable information about his son's whereabouts. Folding up the map, he slipped it into a drawer. The next moment, he was forced to revise his view about coincidences.

There was a knock on the door, then it opened to allow Adrian Donohoe to walk in. He was carrying a bag and looking as unfriendly as ever.

'The superintendent told me you'd be here,' he said, coldly. 'I'm catching a train back home. Before I do that, however, I'd like to know if there've been any developments.'

'Do sit down, sir,' invited Marmion, 'and I'll bring you up to date.'

'Thank you.'

Putting down his bag, he lowered himself into a chair. Many relatives of murder victims had sat there over the years and they'd all been tense and grieving. Adrian Donohoe was neither. He looked impatient and disengaged. Marmion told him about the two visits to Norris Sprake, watching carefully for his reaction. When there was no visible response, he prodded his visitor with questions.

'Did you spend time with Mr Sprake yourself?'

'We had a few minutes together. That was ample. I was there to speak to Miss Kane. She was able to tell me much more about my father's activities in the property market. Hitherto, she's been rather evasive but those days are over.' He gave a thin-lipped smile. 'Miss Kane works for me now.'

'Will she be going back to Birmingham?'

'She'll do whatever I decide.'

Marmion wanted to ask his opinion of Jean-Louis Peebles but thought better of it. In Donohoe's eyes, the man was an irrelevance, a minor functionary in the company with no power whatsoever. Marmion turned to his other visit.

'What do you know of the Club Apollo?'

Donohoe jerked as if he'd been stung. 'Why do you ask me that?'

'Sergeant Keedy and I paid it a visit earlier on. The facilities are very impressive – but you'll have been there yourself.'

'As a matter of fact, I haven't. It holds no interest for me.'

'Do you dislike music that much?'

'I'm far too busy to listen to it.'

'Nobody was busier than your father yet he found time to incorporate music into his life.'

'That's immaterial.'

'Club Apollo seems to have been the fulfilment of a dream for him.'

'How did you come to hear about it?'

'Mr Ulverton walked in here and told us he was your father's closest friend.'

'That's debatable.'

'He praised the club so much that we were keen to see the place for ourselves. It really does offer a unique service. By the time we'd finished, we felt that we'd got to know your father much better.'

'Don't flatter yourself, Inspector. You'd need a lifetime to plumb the depths of his character. All you've done is scratch the surface.'

'Have you ever met Mr Ulverton?'

Donohoe wrinkled his nose. 'I don't *need* to meet him.'

'There seems to be a mutual antagonism between the two of you.'

'Ulverton doesn't exist in my world.'

'Why is that?'

'It's no concern of yours.' He got to his feet. 'Well, if you've nothing else to tell me, I'll be on my way. You can reach me at home by telephone.'

'One moment, sir,' said Marmion, rising himself. 'You came at an opportune time. Something has been recovered that may belong to your father. I've been wondering how best to get confirmation of that when, miraculously, you walk into my office. It's the one piece of good fortune we've had in this case.'

'What is it that you wish me to confirm?'

Marmion opened a drawer and took out the pair of shoes. When he put them on his desk, the other man picked up one of them, glanced inside it then replaced it. He gave a slight nod.

'They *did* belong to your father?'

'Of course, they did,' said Donohoe, almost derisively. 'They were made in our factory. He'd wear nothing else.'

'But they must make endless thousands of shoes. How do you know that that particular pair belonged to your father?'

'They bear his initials, Inspector.'

'Do they?' Marmion was astonished. 'I didn't see any initials.'

'That's because you don't know where to look. They're inside the factory imprint. Right in the middle are the initials of my father's name – Gilbert Oliver Donohoe. That proves the shoes are his.'

Picking one up, Marmion looked inside and saw the factory name and emblem clearly. Bang in the middle of it were three tiny initials.

'I can see them now,' he said. 'They spell God.'

CHAPTER TWELVE

Alice Marmion had waited until past midnight more than once in order to see Keedy. She was spared such a protracted vigil this time. As she sat beside the window in her room, there was still enough light for her to pick out the shape of anyone approaching the house where she lived. She had agonised for hours over the problem of whether or not to confront him about their wedding and she was still undecided. Keedy would have had a much longer working day than her and would be tired. It might not be the ideal time to talk about something so important. On the other hand, she didn't know when she might get another chance to spend time with him. If she didn't strike while she could, Alice might have to wait for weeks.

Expecting to sit there for an hour or two, she was suddenly galvanised by the sight of a man running towards her with one hand holding his hat in place. She knew instantly that it was Keedy. Grabbing her handbag, she let herself out of the room and padded silently downstairs before leaving the house. Alice ran towards him and threw herself into his arms. He kissed and hugged her for minutes then held her away from him so that he could look at her properly.

'I've missed doing that so much, Alice.'

'And I've missed *you*. I've been aching for you to get here.'

'Where shall we go?'

'There's only one place we *can* go, Joe.'

'No, there isn't,' he said, grinning. 'You could always smuggle me into your house. I've always wanted to see that room of yours.'

'My landlady would have a fit,' she protested.

'We could sneak upstairs without making a sound.'

'It's too dangerous.'

'In other words, you don't want me enough.'

'Of course I do. You know that.'

'Then let's take a chance. It will be worth it.'

'Stop teasing,' she said. 'It's just not possible. Do you want me to be thrown out of there altogether?'

'Yes, I do – you can move in with me, then.'

'Joe!'

'I'm the one with the double bed, remember.' He winced as she elbowed him in the stomach. 'That hurt, Alice.'

'It was meant to.'

Laughing together, they walked along arm in arm. They were less than ten minutes from a park where they'd be able to sit and talk. That would be the place to raise the subject of marriage, thought Alice. He was in far too excitable a mood to discuss anything seriously at the moment.

'Has something happened, Joe?'

'Yes, I'm back with the woman I love.'

'I'm talking about this latest case. When you're as lively as this, it usually means you've had a good day.'

'I've had a very good day. Your father actually congratulated me.'

'Why?'

'Because I rang him from the Devonian Hotel to tell him that I might have unmasked the killer.'

'You have?' she said. 'Who is he?'

'I'll tell you when we're absolutely certain.'

'You sound as if you've already reached that point.'

'I have, Alice,' he explained, 'but your Dad still hasn't. You know what he's like. He always insists on rock-solid evidence that will stand up in court.'

'And he's right, Joe.'

'Whose side are you on?' he said in mock fury. 'You should support me.'

'I won't support either of you until I know the full details.'

'Well, you're certainly not going to hear them now. I'm not going to waste precious time alone with you by talking about the case – and I don't want you to talk about what you've been up to at work. Tonight is just for us, Alice. Agreed?'

She kissed him on the cheek. 'Agreed.'

* * *

Gregory Wain had started planning reprisals as soon as he'd been released from hospital. As leader of the Stepney Warriors, he knew that he had to inflict more injury on the Evil Spirits than his gang had received at their hands. They'd been caught napping. It wouldn't happen again. Because there'd been no immediate act of retribution, the Spirits would believe that they'd tamed their rivals and were now in sole control over the territory. In knocking Wain to his knees with a hammer, they felt that they'd disabled the Warriors' leader and frightened his gang into submission. They were about to get a shock.

'They'll be in that shed they took from us,' said Wain to the others. 'I bet they'll still be sniggerin' abaht us.'

'So wor do we do, Greg?' asked someone.

'Stand by till I give the signal.'

There were over a dozen of them, most bearing wounds from the last encounter. Their weapons included knives, razors, clubs, a pitchfork and a hatchet. Wain intended to creep up on the lookout and overpower him, holding a cloth over his mouth so that he couldn't raise the alarm. Gang members would tie him up, insert a gag in his mouth then each kick him in turn. Wain, meanwhile, would sidle up to the shed, hurl a brick through the window and stand beside the door with his pick handle to fell the first person who came out. Still smarting from their defeat, the Warriors intended to give their rivals such a violent beating that they'd never mount a challenge again.

Before they left, Wain roused them with an appeal to their bloodlust. He soon had them pulsing for action. They were about to file out into the darkness when Bruce Kerry came running up to them. He'd been sent out to make sure that the coast was clear. When he got his breath back, he had bad news.

'No good, Greg,' he said. 'Place is crawlin' with bleedin' coppers.'

'Wor you on abaht?' demanded Wain.

'Iss true. They're *everywhere*.'

It was an exaggeration but it had more than a grain of truth. Once he'd established that the shoes had belonged to the murder victim, Marmion drove to Stepney with six uniformed constables, a number that was augmented by the two on the beat in the vicinity. Everitt White had been thorough. He'd not only forced the shopkeeper to name the boy who'd sold him the shoes, he'd gone to the house to speak to the lad. Promising him that he would not be in trouble, he got the boy to take him to the exact spot where the shoes had been found. The letter sent to Marmion had contained the precise location. What Kerry had seen as he lurked near the headquarters of the Evil Spirits was the arrival of two vehicles out of which policemen climbed. It had sent him flying back to the rest of the gang.

Marmion, meanwhile, had led his men down the street to the riverbank. Since the gas lamps shed only poor light, they'd all brought torches. When they got to the place described by White, they saw a figure waiting on the river's edge.

'Who are you?' demanded Marmion.

'I'm Detective Constable Burge, sir,' replied the other, crossing over to him. 'And I suspect that you are Inspector Marmion. This is the exact spot where the shoes were found. Sergeant White told me that you'd be along sooner or later.'

'On good authority, we can say that they *did* belong to Mr Donohoe.'

'But you'd have come even if you didn't know that. Inspector White said that simple curiosity would bring you here.'

'Everitt knows me of old.'

He told his men to spread out to conduct a methodical search. Though he didn't expect them to find anything of value – that would already have been whisked away by the scavengers who haunted the bank – he hoped they'd chance on something else that proved that the murder took place there. If it *was* the scene of the crime, Marmion would have it more thoroughly searched in daylight.

'Burge, did you say? I've heard that name before.'

'They wanted someone to investigate the gangs around here. Superintendent Chatfield was kind enough to put my name forward and here I am.'

'Congratulations on getting the job.'

'I didn't realise it would be linked to a murder case.'

Marmion smiled philosophically. 'Detective work is full of surprises.'

It was just like old times. Keedy and Alice were seated on a bench in the park and savouring the simple joy of being together. It was a warm summer's night and they were completely alone. As they looked up at the stars, his arm was around her and their heads were resting gently against each other. He reached a decision.

'We mustn't let this happen again, Alice.'

'But I love it here.'

'I'm not complaining about the park. It's this job of mine. It keeps us apart far too much and I'm fed up with it.'

'What can we do about it?'

'I could leave Scotland Yard.'

She was so shocked that she sat up and turned to look at him.

'You'd never do that, Joe. You love the work.'

'I love you much more and it's time I started to put you first.'

'It's wonderful to hear that but you don't have to abandon a career that means so much to you. In any case, what else could you do?'

'I could go back to the family business.'

She broke away from him. 'I'm not going to marry an undertaker,' she said, indignantly.

'It's a good profession. I'd never be out of work, I know that. There's always a steady flow of customers. Dying will never go out of fashion.'

'You always said you hated it.'

'What I hated was taking orders from my father all the time. He could be a real tyrant. Then there was the stink – it's not the most fragrant job in the world. But the worst part,' recalled Keedy, 'was having to dress up for funerals and look solemn. It didn't suit me at all.'

'That's why you left. You *belong* in the police, Joe.'

'I don't feel that I do sometimes.'

'Iris thinks you're amazing. If they ever design a recruiting poster, she says, they ought to put you on the front of it. You're her idea of the perfect detective.'

'Is that what you think as well?'

'I don't need to think it,' said Alice, snuggling up to him. 'I *know* it.'

'So I should hope.' He kissed her gently on the lips. 'How

is Iris getting on, anyway? Is she still complaining about being a wallflower?'

'No, she has an admirer.'

'Really?'

'Don't look so surprised. She's a nice woman.'

'But not the kind that men take an interest in, I'm afraid.'

'One man does – Constable Beckett. They went off to the cinema together. Iris was thrilled when he invited her out,' said Alice. 'Honestly, you'd have thought he'd asked her to marry him.'

'That's the trouble with girls like Iris,' he said, jokingly. 'You give them one kiss and they start thinking about their wedding dress. They don't realise that most men just like to have fun.'

'Are you one of them, Joe?'

She hadn't meant it to sound like an accusation.

The search was slow and painstaking but they kept at it. Ignoring the filth and the dog faeces and the rotting food, the policemen moved in a steady line and prodded away. Marmion, meanwhile, was getting to know Clifford Burge a little better.

'So your brother is in the river police, is he?'

'Yes, he rows in Everitt's boat and loves it. The river throws up something different every day. Les says that it's an education.'

'Were you never drawn to it?'

'I'd rather stay on dry land, sir. The Thames can be treacherous.'

'But it has a lot of fascinating stories to tell,' said Marmion, looking at the water. 'We're investigating one of them.'

A policeman picked something up and scrutinised it by

the light of his torch. After a while, he brought it across to Marmion who took it from him.

'I don't know if this is any use, sir,' said the man, 'but it seems a bit out of place here. I don't think many people in these parts get their suits from Bond Street.'

Using his own torch, Marmion looked at the label he'd just been handed. It bore the name of Langley, Hope and Catto and was a vital clue.

'Well done, Constable,' said Marmion. 'Your efforts were rewarded. What you found proves that this is the spot where the murder took place.'

The silence was long and uncomfortable. Neither of them seemed able to break it. They sat there without touching each other, together but apart. Eventually, Alice got up and Keedy followed suit. They started to walk around the perimeter of the park. All the joy had been drained out of them. Alice blamed herself at first then began to feel a sense of justified resentment. If Keedy hadn't been so evasive whenever the subject of their marriage came up, she would not have had to challenge him. On his side, there was a mixture of anger and recrimination. While he was annoyed that she should even ask him such a question, he was honest enough to admit that he had drifted from one girlfriend to another in the past. Alice had put a stop to that. He'd committed himself wholeheartedly to her. Why did she doubt him?

When he eventually broke the silence, he was careful to shift the conversation away from the subject of their future together.

'I wish that Paul would at least get in touch.'

'So do I.'

'It's preying on your father's mind. He hides it very well but I can see the signs. It's wearing him down.'

'Mummy is in the worst position,' she said. 'Daddy and I always have work to do and somewhere to be. She's at home alone most of the time. The irony is that having Paul in the house was a nightmare for her, yet all she can think about now is getting him back there.'

'The longer it goes on, the less chance there is of that.'

'What do you mean?'

'Well, if he manages to survive – and I'm sure he will – Paul will start to build a whole new life somewhere else. No reflection on you and your parents,' said Keedy, 'but he may find it better than the one he left behind.'

'But we're his *family*, Joe.'

'I don't think that matters to him any more.'

'It matters to us.'

They came to a halt and he turned to face her. The tension was tangible.

'Go on,' he said at length. 'Say it.'

'Say what?'

'You're going to remind me what Paul told you.'

'No, I'm not.'

'He said that I'd be a rotten husband – or words to that effect – because of what I was like in the past. I think you're starting to agree with him.'

'That's not true,' she said, earnestly.

'You don't trust me the way you did.'

'All I want is to set a date for the wedding.'

'How many times must I tell you – we'll get married when we can afford it.'

'We could afford it now, Joe.'

'And where would we live?'

'In the short term, we could always move in with my parents.'

'You'd hate that as much as I would,' he said, bitterly. 'And supposing Paul *does* come back. Living under that roof would be murder.'

'Then we'll rent rooms somewhere else.'

'I think we can do better than that, Alice. That's why I've been saving up all this time. I want us to own our own house.'

'And when will that be?' she asked, letting her frustration show. 'This year, next year, the one after, sometime never?' She grabbed hold of him. 'How much longer must I wait?'

Keedy stepped away from her. 'I'll walk you back,' he said.

Claude Chatfield was pleased to hear of the latest development. Having identified the scene of the crime, Marmion had a team of detectives ready to examine it properly not long after dawn. It was a small sign of progress that might get the approval of the press and make the superintendent's dealings with them less of a trial. Marmion's other piece of news was given a more cautious welcome. Like him, Chatfield reserved his judgement on Keedy's theory about the killer.

'It doesn't ring true somehow,' he said. 'Why should Sprake's chauffeur want to murder his employer's business partner?'

'Sprake stands to gain total control of the company.'

'I thought he told you how much he relied on Donohoe's acumen?'

176

'Perhaps he felt he could manage without it now.'

'I'm unconvinced. The description the sergeant gave of this Thomas Day was very nebulous. It could apply to thousands of people – including Keedy himself.'

'They don't all possess a car, sir.'

'I don't understand.'

'Now that we know where the murder took place,' said Marmion, 'we have to explain how Donohoe got there. He'd hardly go to such an unsavoury part of the city of his own volition. We know that he had the use of his partner's chauffeur – Sprake told us that. Donohoe knew and trusted the man. If Peebles had driven him to Stepney late at night, Donohoe wouldn't have realised where they were going.'

'Is this your hypothesis or the sergeant's?'

'It's Sergeant Keedy's, sir. I have my doubts.'

'Why?'

'There'd be no need for Peebles to masquerade as Thomas Day. Why bother to stalk his victim when he already knew Donohoe well and had a perfectly good reason to drive him to and fro? Whoever Thomas Day really was, he couldn't have been the chauffeur.'

'He may just have been a legitimate guest at the hotel.'

'That, too, is possible.'

'Is the sergeant still clinging to his theory?'

'He hasn't arrived yet, sir,' said Marmion. 'Knowing that you'd be at your desk this early, I wanted to discuss the matter with you. It's helped me to see that, in naming the chauffeur as a suspect, we were perhaps being a little hasty.'

'*I* didn't make that mistake,' insisted Chatfield. 'You and the sergeant did.'

Marmion didn't argue with him. He felt sorry for Keedy. When the sergeant had rung him from the Devonian Hotel the previous evening, he was excited at what he thought was a genuine discovery. In spite of his misgivings, Marmion had praised him for his initiative. When they met that morning, he would have to pour cold water over the theory that a guest at the hotel had been Jean-Louis Peebles in disguise.

'The commissioner will be pleased at what you found out last night,' said Chatfield. 'You acted promptly.'

'I've instructed my men to knock on doors in the area of the scene to ask if anyone saw or heard anything on the night of the murder. My expectations are not high,' said Marmion, resignedly. 'Most people there are more used to hindering the police than helping them.'

'Inspector White managed to get some assistance from one of them.'

Marmion smiled. 'He has an unusually persuasive manner.'

'You must thank him for providing such useful information.'

'I've already written to him, sir. By the way,' he went on, 'I had the pleasure of meeting the man you recommended as suitable for looking into juvenile crime in the area – Detective Constable Burge. He was at the scene when we got there.'

'He's a promising young detective.'

'I was like that once.'

'So was I,' said Chatfield. 'We've both come on since then.'

He spoke with a smirk of self-congratulation, reminding Marmion, as he did at regular intervals, that he'd risen to a higher rank. The inspector made no comment. He was keen to get back to his office where Keedy would probably be awaiting him.

'One last thing,' said Chatfield. 'Let's not dismiss the chauffeur out of hand. In your report, you described him as an opportunist.'

'That was the impression I got, sir.'

'Yet his life consists of fetching and carrying for Sprake.'

'He's extremely well paid for doing so and is part of the household.'

'How far would his dedication to Sprake go?'

'Peebles would do whatever he was asked.'

'What if he was asked to assassinate his employer's partner?'

'I don't think he'd turn a hair,' said Marmion.

It was a sad day for Harriet Kane. She was leaving her office in Barnes that morning for the last time. When she'd packed everything up, she went off to say individual farewells to everyone in the building, leaving Peebles to load her things into the car. The chauffeur had been told to drive her to Euston where she'd board a train to Birmingham. Her days in London were definitely over. As he picked up the last bag, Peebles looked covetously around the office.

'It's all mine now,' he said, gleefully. 'Good riddance, you ugly old bitch!'

Iris Goodliffe was glowing. Her night out with a man had clearly been a rewarding experience. She was dying to tell her friend about it. Seeing her from a distance, Alice quailed. The contrast in their positions could not have been greater. One of them was happy and full of hope for the future while the other was depressed and remorseful. It was all too evident to Alice that Iris and her admirer had parted on the best of terms whereas she and Keedy had certainly not. The friends stood side by side as they and the other officers were given instructions before they left. When she'd finished her briefing, Inspector Gale sent them all off with the exception of Alice and Iris. She objected to the broad grin on Iris's face.

'What's so funny?' she snarled.

'Nothing,' replied Iris, 'nothing at all, Inspector.'

'Then I'll do without your impression of a Cheshire cat, thank you very much.' Iris became solemn. 'That's better. Yesterday I had occasion to castigate you for the way you behaved with that dog.'

'We felt it was our duty to do something.'

'What you did was wrong, as I explained. I take nothing back from what I told you but it's only fair to say that your actions met with approval elsewhere. I had a letter from a gentleman praising your courage and your adaptability. He said that you saved the dog from serious injury.'

'We did, Inspector.'

'Having read his more measured account of what happened,' said the older woman, 'I'm inclined to accept his word over that of the dog's owner. You made a brave attempt to rescue the animal.'

Alice said nothing. Though she was glad that someone had spoken up for them, her mind was so firmly fixed on her estrangement from Keedy that she could think of nothing else. Inspector Gale dismissed them and they stepped out into the street. Alice felt duty-bound to uncork the bottle of Iris's joy.

'How did you get on last night?'

'It was magical!' said Iris, giggling. 'I was terribly nervous but Doug put me at my ease straight away. He was so considerate. He was also very honest. He wanted me to know that he had been married but that his wife had died tragically two years ago. Since then, Doug said, he'd never looked at another woman until he saw me.'

'Which film did you see?'

'To be honest, I can't remember. It was enough for me to sit in the dark holding a man's hand. I hardly looked at the screen. Afterwards, Doug took me for a meal. He was so respectful, Alice. I knew that he would be somehow. Some of the policemen we bump into can be . . . well, rather coarse at times, but not him. Doug Beckett is a gentleman.'

Alice soon lost count of the number of times she mentioned his name. Iris was entranced. The evening had ended with a chaste kiss on her doorstep but there had also been a surprise invitation. Beckett had asked to see her again the next day. It was proof positive that he'd enjoyed her company.

'I felt as if I'd known him for ages,' said Iris.

'I'm glad that it went so well.'

'Doug asked after you, by the way.'

Alice was surprised. 'Why did he do that?'

'He was interested in everything I did and everyone I knew. I told him that you were my best friend as well as my partner on the beat. Doug had heard of Sergeant Keedy and of the famous Inspector Marmion. He said I was lucky to have someone as distinguished as you beside me.'

'I'm not distinguished, Iris. I'm still learning how to be a policewoman.'

'Yes, but you've got the right breeding, Doug said.'

'He should have been talking about you and not me. I'd hate to go out with a man and listen to him going on about another woman.'

'They were just remarks he made in passing,' said Iris, tolerantly. 'Most of the time, he went on about noticing me for the first time. He loved my eyes, he said.'

Iris went off into another series of reminiscences. It was ten minutes before she remembered that the person beside her had a private life as well.

'Did you see Joe last night?'

'Yes, I did.'

'How is the murder investigation going?'

'We never discussed it, Iris.'

'Didn't he even give you a hint or two?'

'No, he didn't.'

'So what did you do?'

'We went for a walk in the park.'

'Is that all?'

'There wasn't much else we *could* do at that time of night.'

'So you just . . . walked and talked.'

'We simply enjoyed each other's company,' lied Alice.

'That's what happened with me and Doug. There were times when neither of us said anything for a while. Being together was enough. And we had so many laughs,' said Iris with another giggle. 'I had no idea that Doug would be so funny. You told me once that Joe had a wonderful sense of humour – so does Doug.'

Alice forced a smile. 'I'm very happy for you, Iris.'

'Then why do you look so sad?'

'I'm tired, that's all. I didn't get to bed until late.'

'I was far too excited to sleep. I lay awake thinking about Doug for hours.' She turned to face Alice. 'Are you ever kept awake like that?'

'Yes,' admitted Alice. 'It happened last night. I didn't sleep a wink.'

Keedy was in much the same position, feeling jangled after a sleepless night brooding on what had happened. What made it worse was that he was sitting in an office with Alice's father and was therefore reminded of her every time Marmion spoke. At least he was spared any questions about Alice. Realising that his sergeant was in a sensitive mood, Marmion kept the conversation to operational matters. When he heard the news, Keedy was stung by what seemed to him to be the summary rejection of his theory that the chauffeur might be the killer.

'When I rang you last night, you said it was worth considering.'

'That was before I'd really thought about it. Chat and I talked it through.'

'You might have waited until I got here,' complained Keedy.

'I'm glad that we didn't. If you'd yawned in front of Chat the way you've been doing in here, you'd have been thrown out. Our feeling was this.'

He gave a succinct account of his earlier discussion with the superintendent, stressing that they both approved of the research he'd done with the hotel ledger. Keedy listened impatiently. When it was all over, he jumped in at once.

'I still think it could be the chauffeur. I feel it in my bones.'

'You've never even met the man, Joe.'

'I saw him through *your* eyes and he fitted the description perfectly.'

'Peebles had no reason to stay at the hotel. He lives with Sprake in that house near Richmond Park. I admire your powers of deduction,' said Marmion. 'It may well be that in Thomas Day – if that really is his name – you may have identified the killer but he was certainly not Sprake's chauffeur.'

'That doesn't mean he wasn't involved in the murder,' Keedy contended.

'No, that's true.'

'He might have provided the car that took Donohoe to Stepney where his accomplice, Day, was waiting. Two of them could easily overpower Donohoe.'

'They could have, Joe, but there's no evidence to prove that they did.'

'I'll find it somehow.'

'We have other lines of enquiry.'

'I'd rather stick with this one.'

Keedy refused to concede defeat. Certain that his theory was at least worth exploring, he asked for permission to go to Barnes so that he could meet Peebles, weigh the man up for himself and ask him where he was on the night of the murder.

'It could be a wasted journey.'

'You told me that we should act on intuition sometimes.'

'I agree. I've done it myself often enough. Very well,' decided Marmion. 'I can see that you're like a dog with a bone. You'll keep on gnawing away. If you must, go and meet Peebles yourself. You'll find him a diverting character.'

Having put Harriet Kane on the train at Euston, Peebles drove back to the offices in Barnes. He found Sprake waiting for him in the hallway.

'Has she gone?'

'Yes,' said Peebles. 'The last vestige of Gilbert Donohoe has disappeared.'

'Excellent – this company is all mine now.'

CHAPTER THIRTEEN

She was not alone. Ellen Marmion accepted that. Other parents were in the same position, wondering what had happened to their absent sons. The missing persons were almost invariably young soldiers invalided out of the army. Some came back with horrendous injuries that made their life unbearable. When they disappeared, they were usually found to have gone away to some quiet spot in order to take their own lives. Ellen had read about one soldier who, having lost both legs, felt that he was a burden on his family. He persuaded a friend to take him to the cliffs of Dover where he could hear the sounds of battle on the other side of the English Channel as he flung himself over the edge. The friend, a wounded soldier himself, had been arrested for assisting his suicide.

Deeply affected by the tragedy, Ellen prayed that her son would not seek the same escape. Paul's physical injuries had healed and his eyesight was getting slowly better all the time. There was no reason for him to feel suicidal. Unfortunately, he was no longer a rational person. While living at home, he'd been abusive, obstructive, bloody-minded and selfish. Paul had also taken pleasure from someone else's pain, tormenting a girl, with whom he'd once been at school, out of sheer malice. Ellen could not excuse what he'd done, yet she still cared for him even though he showed no consideration to her and the family. A simple letter to say that he was well would be enough to satisfy her but the chances of his making contact seemed slimmer with each day. They might never know where he was. The ordeal would continue.

Yet she refused to give up. As she cleaned the house that morning, she went into his room and dusted it yet again, even though it was unnecessary. When Paul was there, he'd kept the place tidy. Ellen saw this as a manifestation of his army training and hoped that the habits and skills he'd learnt in uniform would help him in his new life as well. The room was bare now, everything of any significance to him having been taken. Distressingly, the one framed photograph left behind was of the Marmion family on holiday in Devon fifteen years earlier. The fond parents looked on while their children built sandcastles. Paul was laughing happily. Somewhere during the Battle of the Somme, he'd lost that capacity for happiness.

Ellen heard the sound of the letter box opening and

shutting. The postman had been. Though she knew she'd be disappointed, she raced downstairs in the faint hope that their son might just have made contact with them at last. Lying on the doormat was an envelope that she snatched up quickly. It was addressed to Paul.

Admitted to the house in Barnes where the offices were located, Keedy noticed the wheelchair in the hallway. Norris Sprake was clearly there. His handicap didn't deter him from a long day's work. The door had been opened by Jean-Louis Peebles and Keedy had taken a good look at him. When he realised who his visitor was, Peebles gave him a polite welcome.

'Mr Sprake is in his office.'

'Actually,' said Keedy, 'I'd like a chat with you first, sir.'

Peebles laughed. 'It's not often that I get called "sir". I just drive a car and do a little office work. I don't know why you're bothering with me, Sergeant.'

'Oh, I think you underestimate your importance.'

'What makes you say that?'

'It's an observation that Inspector Marmion made and he's very perceptive.'

'I see.' After studying him for a moment, Peebles turned away. 'I'll have to tell Mr Sprake that you're here and wish to talk to me.' He knocked on a door then opened it to enter the office, shutting the door firmly behind him. When he came out of the room, he smiled at his visitor. 'Mr Sprake says that you can talk to me as long as you wish but he'd appreciate a few words with you before you leave.'

'Yes, of course.'

'This way, Sergeant,' said the other, leading the way to the stairs.

When they reached the office, Peebles opened the door with a flourish and gestured for Keedy to enter. He followed the sergeant in and waved at the empty shelves and the bare walls.

'Ignore the state of the place,' he said. 'Hattie Kane moved out earlier today and I haven't had time to settle in yet.'

'This was her office, was it?'

'Yes, she's no longer with us.'

'Why is that?'

'Mr Adrian Donohoe needed her in Birmingham.'

'Did she have to leave so suddenly?' asked Keedy in surprise. 'Having been here for years, she must have a detailed knowledge of how the company works. If you're going to replace her, I'd have thought it would pay you to spend a week or so learning exactly what Miss Kane did. She could have eased you into the job.'

'I was hoping that she'd do just that,' said Peebles, smoothly, 'but she was whisked away. We'll miss her.'

Keedy sat down and Peebles took the chair behind the desk, swelling with pride as he lowered himself into it. He couldn't help looking around his new domain.

'It's been denuded, hasn't it?' he said. 'Hattie brought so many feminine touches to this office. It had colour and personality.'

'I'm sure you'll provide plenty of both, sir.'

Hands clasped, Peebles sat forward. 'What is it you wished to ask me?'

'First of all, have you ever heard of Club Apollo?'

'No, is it a nightclub?'

'Not exactly,' said Keedy. 'So you didn't realise that Mr Donohoe was a member?' Peebles shook his head. 'Was he a secretive man?'

'He could be.'

'Did he confide in Miss Kane?'

'You'll have to ask her. Only she can tell you that.'

'Was she sad to leave here?'

'I don't think so. She was always homesick. Hattie's big regret was that it took Mr Donohoe's death to get her back to Birmingham.'

Keedy was already finding him too glib and self-assured. Though he'd made a point of saying that he held only a minor position in the company, Peebles was behaving otherwise. He was almost luxuriating in his new office.

'Let me take you back to the night of the murder,' said Keedy.

'Oh, you don't need to do that. Mr Sprake and I talk about nothing else. We keep blaming ourselves for not being there at the time to save him.'

'Did you drive Mr Donohoe anywhere that day?'

'No, he was still at the Devonian Hotel, as far as I knew.'

'But you have picked him up from there in the past?'

'Yes, of course,' said Peebles. 'As long as Mr Sprake didn't need me, I was at Mr Donohoe's beck and call. Why pay for a taxi when he could summon me?'

'What did you do that evening?'

'I was at Mr Sprake's house, cleaning the car. Hattie Kane might have known how to brighten up an office but nobody can make a car gleam as much as I can. I spend a couple of hours on it at least twice a week.'

'And that's what you did on the day of the murder?'

'Yes.'

'Is there anyone who can substantiate that claim?'

Peebles stiffened. 'Are you treating me as a suspect?'

'I'd just like to know where you were.'

'Well, I wasn't driving a car I'd just cleaned through the filth of the East End, I can assure you of that. It's not safe, for a start. Some people burn with envy. If they see an expensive vehicle like ours, they want to throw things at it.'

'How did you know that the murder took place in the East End?'

Peebles was halted for a moment. 'The body *was* found near there,' he said, eventually. 'It was in the newspaper.'

'Bodies can be carried a long distance by the tides. It could have been dumped miles upriver.'

'I was just assuming . . .'

'As it happens, your assumption was correct. Last night, we found evidence that the murder occurred in Stepney and that Mr Donohoe's corpse was tipped into the river at a point we identified.'

'There you are,' said Peebles as if he'd just been exonerated.

'The likelihood is that it was in the dead of night. Few people would have been around at that time so your gleaming car wouldn't have been in any danger in the dark. In short, you *could* have been there.'

'I was in Mr Sprake's house all night. Ask him.'

'I intend to, Mr Peebles.'

'To be honest, I find your suspicions of me rather offensive.'

'It's just routine, sir. We have to check all possibilities.'

'Does that mean you have Mr Sprake lined up as a suspect as well?' asked Peebles, sarcastically. 'Perhaps he beat his victim unconscious with his walking sticks. Or what about Hattie Kane – is she on the list as well? Maybe she fell out with Mr Donohoe and lost her temper. I've seen her in a rage. She's quite scary.'

'If it wasn't you,' said Keedy, 'it's more likely to have been Thomas Day.'

The name brought about an instant change. The mocking grin vanished from Peebles' face and he was no longer so irritatingly cocky.

'I've never heard of the man,' he said, slowly. 'Who is he?'

'I thought he might be *you*, sir.'

It was agony for Alice Marmion. Forced to listen to her friend's gushing description of her night out, she was reminded of the split that had opened up between her and Keedy. It would not be easily closed because each was as stubborn as the other. She'd had friends in the past to whom she'd felt she could turn when she had problems in her private life. Iris Goodliffe was not one of them. Besides, it was ludicrous that a woman who'd been engaged for almost two years should rely on the advice of someone with such limited experience of dealing with the opposite sex. One night out with a policeman did not qualify Iris to be a source of constructive sympathy.

Walking beside her friend, Alice was sustained by the wild hope that Keedy would suddenly appear out of the blue, sweep her up in his arms and kiss away the tension between them. Realistically, she knew that it would never happen, and not only because he would have commitments elsewhere. He would deliberately avoid her. As Iris dribbled on, Alice tried to shut out the sound of her voice but there was no way she could ignore the whoop of delight that came from her friend. Douglas Beckett had just come around the corner with his beat partner. Waving to Iris, he gave her such a warm smile that it made Alice's heart constrict. Though she was pleased for Iris, she felt more miserable than ever.

It was mid morning when Marmion got to the Club Apollo. He wanted to be there before luncheon was served and, hopefully, before Jonathan Ulverton turned up. He was keen to look at the place for himself without being supervised by the man who was now its sole owner. What struck him when he was let into the building was the absence of music. The club felt empty without it. Saul Rockwell came out to welcome the inspector and provide an explanation.

'The quartet won't be here until this evening,' he said.

'I didn't come to listen to them.'

'Mr Ulverton is here, if you wish to speak to him. He stayed the night.'

'I'd value a moment with you first,' said Marmion, annoyed that the owner would soon interrupt them. 'I gather that you were in the navy?'

'That's right, sir.'

'Which ship did you sail in?'

'I ended up in HMS *Dreadnought*,' said Rockwell, straightening his shoulders. 'She was a wonderful vessel. When she was launched in 1906, she put all the other battleships in the shade. In terms of speed and firepower, she had no equals.'

'It sounds as if you enjoyed your time aboard her.'

'I've nothing but good memories, Inspector. But those days are gone. I got married and looked for a position that was more suitable. Sergeant Keedy will have explained how I ended up here.'

'You obviously like it.'

'I couldn't wish for a better job.'

'Why do you think you were chosen to be the steward?'

'Who can say?' asked Rockwell with a shrug. 'Mr Donohoe saw something in me and made me an offer. I'd like to claim that my effortless charm won him over but I fancy that he simply wanted someone who wouldn't fiddle the accounts or run off with the silver. My naval experience helped. It proved I was reliable.'

'What's so special about this place, Mr Rockwell?'

The steward chuckled. 'You mean, apart from me?'

'Why are people so keen to become members?'

'They like music and they want somewhere to hide.'

'From what?'

'From whatever it is that they want to escape. One member told me he's in hiding from his wife and another said he was dodging his creditors. It was a third one who had the best answer. He claimed that he just wanted somewhere to stay until the war was over.' He raised a meaningful eyebrow. 'Don't we all?'

'What about the musicians?'

'Oh, they're not actually members.'

'No, but I daresay that Mr Donohoe and Mr Ulverton chose

them with great care. They'd want the best they could get.'

'That's why they employed the Malvern Quartet.'

Marmion was taken aback. 'Do they come all that way just to play here?'

'They don't live in Malvern,' said Rockwell. 'It happens to be where their leader was born. Three of them have been together for donkey's years. When their viola player died, they replaced him with a woman, Dulcie Haddon. Her father is the leader of the quartet, Nigel Haddon.'

'It must be difficult for her,' said Marmion, 'being the only woman in an all-male environment.'

'I doubt if she even notices, Inspector. Musicians like her have only one thing on their mind and that's playing the music properly. I'm a brass band man myself but I have to admit that they make a nice sound.'

Marmion grinned. 'I don't think a brass band would fit in here somehow. It would destroy the atmosphere you try to create.'

'Atmosphere is everything. That was Mr Donohoe's motto.'

'And what's Mr Ulverton's motto?'

'Oh, he has several, sir,' said Rockwell, cheerily. 'I can't remember them all.'

The steward gave Marmion his all-purpose smile, the one he produced for every occasion and behind which he could hide his true feelings. The inspector had seen it on the faces of many people employed in a similar position. Club stewards gave nothing away. Their first duty was to protect their members at all costs, even if that meant being less than cooperative with the police. Marmion didn't blame Rockwell.

He was only doing his job. The inspector came at him from a different angle.

'Sergeant Keedy tells me that certain people who applied for membership were enraged when they were turned down by the committee.'

'That's true.'

'There have even been reprisals.'

'It's nothing we can't handle, Inspector,' said Rockwell.

'Presumably, you keep a list of would-be members.'

'Everybody who shows an interest in Club Apollo goes into the record book.'

'Who keeps it up to date?'

'I do.'

'Can you think of anybody, in recent weeks, who stormed out of here when his application was rejected?'

'I can see what you're getting at, Inspector. Was the killer someone with a grudge against the club? No, I don't think so. Even if there *had* been a person like that, he wouldn't necessarily have picked on Mr Donohoe.'

'Oh?'

'It's because we didn't see him all that often. Mr Ulverton is here more or less all the time. When members think of the Apollo, they think of him. It's Mr Ulverton who goes out looking for new people to join. Mr Donohoe could never do that,' said Rockwell. 'He just didn't have Mr Ulverton's flair.'

'What did he bring to the club, then?'

'He brought a lot, Inspector.'

'Could you be more specific?'

'It's not my place to be.'

The impenetrable smile was back again. Marmion didn't try to remove it. He simply asked a question that had been troubling him for some time.

'Why does Mr Ulverton hate Adrian Donohoe so much?'

'I wasn't aware that he did.'

'He vowed that he'd never let him take over his father's stake in the club.'

'Really?'

'Mr Ulverton was so genial until I mentioned Adrian's name. I know that Mr Donohoe didn't get on very well with his son but why should Mr Ulverton object to him so strongly? He's probably never even met Adrian Donohoe.'

'I wouldn't know about that,' said Rockwell, smile still intact. 'But the person to ask is Mr Ulverton himself and,' he went on, extending a hand, 'here he comes.'

Marmion turned to see the club's owner descending on him, arms spread wide in welcome and features lit up by a broad grin. Hoping to avoid him altogether, Marmion was cornered. The steward, meanwhile, had slipped quietly away.

The Stepney Warriors were no longer the dominant gang in the district. Gregory Wain's triumphant swagger was now a slow trudge. As he walked past a couple of Evil Spirits on a street corner, he kept his head down and tried to block out the sound of their jeers. They were the masters now but, he told himself, it would not be for long. Wain carried on until he came to the river and saw a group of policemen combing the ground for something. They were in the way, just as they had been the previous night. The Warriors would have to wait until they'd disappeared altogether before they could put their plan into action.

Wain swore under his breath, spat on the ground and walked quickly away.

Keedy went back downstairs. Having finished his conversation with Peebles, he knocked on the door of Sprake's office and went in. The older man was seated at his desk, studying a brochure. He gave the sergeant a token smile and motioned him to a chair. Keedy began with the name that had unsettled the chauffeur.

'Do you know someone called Thomas Day, sir?'

Sprake pondered. 'I don't believe that I do,' he said at length.

'I had the feeling that Mr Peebles recognised the name.'

'Jean-Louis has his own circle of friends.'

'He denied knowing the man.'

'Then accept his word, Sergeant. He's very honest. If he wasn't, I wouldn't employ him and I certainly wouldn't have him living in my house.'

'That's a telling point, sir.'

'Who is this Mr Thomas Day?'

'I was hoping that one of you would tell me that.'

'Has the name cropped up in the course of your investigation?'

'Yes,' said Keedy. 'He was staying at the Devonian Hotel on the night that Mr Donohoe was murdered.'

'So did a lot of other people, I daresay.'

'Mr Day caught my eye.'

'Then I'll trust in your judgement,' said Sprake. 'I'm sorry that I can't help you, Sergeant.'

'At first, I thought that this man concealed his real name and chose to call himself Thomas Day. Then I remembered something that Mr Armitage, the manager, told me. He's ordered his staff to take particular care when guests sign in, asking them for two separate proofs of their identity. If they fail to provide them,' said Keedy, 'they're turned away.'

'The manager is only taking wise precautions. In times of war, they're absolutely essential. We don't want German spies pretending to be someone else.'

'I doubt if Thomas Day was a spy, sir. I feel that that's his real name.'

'What makes you think that?'

'There are two reasons. The first is the one I just gave you – the Devonian keeps a close watch on the people they admit as guests.'

'And what's the second reason?'

'He's sitting upstairs in what used to be Miss Kane's office.'

Sprake was roused. 'Jean-Louis is entirely trustworthy,' he said, angrily.

'Then why did he lie to me about Thomas Day?'

'I think you're mistaken, Sergeant.'

'I know how to read people's faces, sir. It's part of my stock-in-trade.'

For a few seconds, Sprake seemed to be on the point of glowering but he quickly adjusted his expression to one of calm inscrutability. Keedy continued to probe away.

'Does the name Club Apollo mean anything to you, sir?'

'No, it doesn't.'

'You've never heard of it in passing?'

'I'm not a clubbable type, Sergeant. As you saw when you visited my home, I'm a family man. I have no interest in belonging to a club of any kind. Why did you mention this one?'

'Your partner, Mr Donohoe, belonged to it.'

Sprake blinked. 'Is that so? He made no mention of it to me.'

'In fact, he was the co-founder of the club. It reflects his passion for music.'

'Well,' said the other, 'there you are. I didn't think there was anything left to learn about Gilbert Donohoe but there was.'

'His partner's name is Jonathan Ulverton.'

'Who?'

'You've never heard of him, I take it.'

'I've never heard of him or of this club, but then I never delved into Gilbert's private life. We worked together as partners and I asked for no more than that. Insofar as I have one, my talent was for lining up potential clients. Gilbert's skill lay in closing a deal. He was an expert at that,' said Sprake. 'Like you, he knew how to read faces. That's a useful asset in business.'

'Why did he and his son fall out?'

'I wasn't aware that they had, Sergeant.'

'Isn't it strange that he excluded his only male heir from key parts of his business activities?'

'Gilbert no doubt had his reasons.'

'You must surely know what they are, Mr Sprake.'

'The only thing I can tell you is that he felt his son lacked the abilities that he himself possessed. To put it bluntly, Gilbert was the master builder while Adrian was only a hod-carrier.'

'That's a rather cruel assessment of him, isn't it?'

'I'm quoting his exact words.'

'This isn't only to do with their respective skills, sir. It goes deeper than that. Mr Donohoe created a whole empire yet his son was confined to the outer limits of it. Was he *punishing* Adrian for some reason?'

'That's something only the son can tell you.'

'He won't even talk about it.'

'Most people in his position just want to be left alone to mourn.'

'We've seen no sign of grief in Adrian Donohoe, sir.'

'He's still reeling from a massive blow, Sergeant. Give him time.'

'We don't *have* time. There's a killer on the loose.'

'Have there been any developments?'

'The most significant is that we've found the scene of the crime,' said Keedy. 'Some shoes belonging to Mr Donohoe were discovered there. His son was able to identify them for us.'

'How was he able to do that?'

'His father's initials were stamped on them.'

'Gilbert Oliver Donohoe . . .'

'That's right, sir – God. Did he really think he was the Almighty?'

Marmion was agreeably surprised. Instead of being as effusive as he had been on the previous meeting at the club, Jonathan Ulverton was much more restrained. He was considerate, softly spoken and serious. His only interest, he promised, was in helping the investigation. He guessed why the inspector had returned.

'You felt that you didn't really explore the Club Apollo properly yesterday because I was at your elbow all the time.' He waved an arm. 'Feel free to have a look around on your own, Inspector. Examine every nook and cranny. We're not trying to hide anything from you.'

'Thank you, sir,' said Marmion, 'but I really came to ask if I could have the names of anyone who resented the fact that they were forbidden to join. Your steward said that you kept a record of everyone who'd applied.'

'That's true and you're welcome to see it.'

'I'd appreciate that.'

'But you're hardly likely to find any killers there. Yes, we have upset people and some have taken umbrage. One of them expressed his disappointment by throwing a brick through one of our windows but that's as far as it went. We've had no death threats, no assaults on our staff and no interlopers.'

'Your steward told me that you were Club Apollo's figurehead.'

'That's very flattering but undeniable. I'm a fixture here. Gilbert was not.'

'Yet his murder could still have its roots here.'

'It's unlikely,' said Ulverton. 'Well, you've seen some of our members. Most of them are slowly heading towards old age. I can't see any of them being capable of strangling to death a big man like Gilbert.'

'They may not be strong enough to do it,' argued Marmion, 'but they're rich enough to hire someone to do it for them. I'm not speaking about your current members. Since he helped to make this club what it is, Mr Donohoe was probably revered by all of them. My interest is in those who, for one reason or another, failed the interview to get in.'

'Did *you* have an interview to join the Metropolitan Police Force?'

'We all did.'

'Some were accepted and others were turned away, I suppose.'

'That's right. The main reason for rejection was that applicants were not judged physically fit enough for the demands of the job. Two of the people in my batch were debarred instantly.'

'Why was that?'

'They had criminal records.'

'That's something *we* take into account as well,' said Ulverton. 'If anyone is found to have a shady background, they get rebuffed.'

'How do you know if they've been on the wrong side of the law?'

'We put them under the microscope, Inspector. One member of our committee is a retired barrister. He more or less cross-examines them.'

'I don't know of any other club with such a rigorous interview process.'

'We have to separate the wheat from the chaff.'

'This record book of yours,' said Marmion, thoughtfully. 'Does it contain the reasons why certain applicants were shown the door?'

'Yes, it does.'

'Then I'd be most interested to see it.'

'Follow me.'

Ulverton led him along a corridor and into an office that was even larger and more luxurious than the one occupied by Norris Sprake. Bookshelves ran the length of one wall. Another was devoted to a series of framed photographs of activities at the Club Apollo. The most prominent of them showed Ulverton and Donohoe shaking hands and beaming to the camera at what looked like the official opening of the club. Some members had been photographed while dining and others while watching a concert. The string quartet, Marmion noticed, comprised four middle-aged men in full fig. Evidently, it was taken before the death of their viola player.

Crossing to the bookshelves, Ulverton indicated two thick ledgers.

'This one contains a list of members,' he said, touching the volume, 'and the smaller one deals with failed applicants. Look at whichever you choose.'

'Thank you, sir.'

Grateful to be given a free hand, Marmion was even more pleased when the other man went out of the office and left him on his own. He was able to take a proper inventory of the place. The furniture was costly and the decor in excellent taste. A faint smell of polish lingered in the air. Intending to look at both ledgers, Marmion first took down the smaller one and went through the names of those who'd been rejected in the previous few months. None were known to him until he turned over the last page and saw a name he recognised. The man had applied for membership less than a month earlier and been turned away on the grounds that he was 'unlikely to uphold the values of the club or to subscribe to its ethos'.

His name was Patrick Armitage.

CHAPTER FOURTEEN

Having heard so much about the manager, Claude Chatfield was pleased to have the opportunity to meet him. The pleasure was momentary because Patrick Armitage was in a foul temper. He'd arrived at Scotland Yard, demanding to see Marmion. When he heard that the inspector was not in the building, he sought out the superintendent instead. Refusing the offer of a seat, he stood in front of the desk to state his case.

'The inspector's behaviour is indefensible,' he began.

'Why – what is he supposed to have done?'

'He sent his sergeant to my hotel to make enquiries behind

my back. I could have told him everything he needed to know. Instead of trusting me, Sergeant Keedy sneaked in there after I'd left for the day.'

'That may have been the only time he *could* call at your hotel,' said Chatfield, evenly. 'Murder investigations make excessive demands on our time. The sergeant was probably tied up during the day and only able to visit the Devonian in the evening. When you're not there, a duty manager is surely in charge?'

'He is,' said Armitage, testily, 'and he was disconcerted at being bombarded by questions last night, especially as some of them were about *me*.'

'I see no reason for complaint there, sir.'

'I see every reason.'

'You're the manager. It's inevitable that you were mentioned.'

'It was more than a mention, Superintendent. I was being checked up on.'

'Then the sergeant was following procedure. We double-check everything.'

'He made it sound as if *I* was under suspicion,' said Armitage. 'That's very damaging. I can't have my staff harbouring the slightest doubts about me.'

'I'm sure that they don't, sir. In their eyes, you're above suspicion.'

'Then why was the sergeant trying to undermine my authority?'

'He was doing nothing of the kind, Mr Armitage.'

'I disagree.'

The manager was simmering. Chatfield was annoyed at the purposeful way the man had come into his office and was now standing over him. He rose to his feet as a means of asserting himself. He'd dealt with irate people many times and knew that their anger was often a smokescreen for their guilt. He didn't believe that was the case here. Armitage was reacting to what he felt was an unacceptable blow to his pride. Chatfield decided to calm him down.

'Do you actually *own* the Devonian Hotel, sir?' asked Chatfield.

'No, of course I don't.'

'So you're simply one of the employees there.'

'I'm the manager. That carries status.'

'Your status was unaffected by Sergeant Keedy's visit yesterday evening.'

'He upset members of my staff. I'm here to defend them.'

'Then we're two of a kind, sir, because I always defend members of *my* staff. Inspector Marmion and Sergeant Keedy are experienced detectives. You should be grateful that they've been assigned to this case. They would never knowingly accuse innocent people,' said Chatfield, 'and that was certainly not what the sergeant was doing when he questioned your staff. He was not trying to link you to the crime, Mr Armitage. He was attempting to wipe the stigma of a murder from your hotel.'

'Why didn't he ask *me* the questions he put to the duty manager and to the receptionist?'

'It's because you were not there, sir.'

'Exactly,' said the other. 'He took advantage of my absence.'

Chatfield sighed. 'You're being unduly sensitive, Mr Armitage.'

'I insist on an apology from your detectives and a promise that they will come to me if they have anything to ask relating to my hotel.'

'Does that mean you'll be there twenty-four hours a day?'

'It means that I want my position to be respected.'

'Then that's another thing we have in common,' said Chatfield, giving his voice more edge. 'I am a detective superintendent in the Metropolitan Police Force and, as a result, I have to deal with a number of serious crimes every day, deploying officers, making tactical decisions, writing reports, facing the press and coping with the sort of groundless protests from members of the public that you've been making for the last few minutes. Lives are at stake in my world. All *you* have to do, Mr Armitage,' he continued before the other could interrupt, 'is to make sure that your hotel is run efficiently. Instead of wasting police time, I suggest that you go back there and do it.'

Walking to the door, Chatfield opened it wide for his visitor to leave. Armitage could see that argument was futile. He would get neither an apology nor a promise from Scotland Yard. After a silent battle of wills with the superintendent, he accepted defeat and marched out. Chatfield closed the door after him and rubbed his hands together in satisfaction. He'd been the decisive winner.

In the short time he'd been there, Clifford Burge had made far more progress in Stepney than he'd have believed possible. Much of the information he'd garnered had come from Everitt

White whose methods were refreshingly direct. He'd not only retrieved Burge's hat for him, he'd got hold of the shoes that had once belonged to Gilbert Donohoe after forcing the boy who'd found them to tell him where he discovered them. In the course of one evening, White had moved the investigation on and given Burge some priceless intelligence in the process. The latter now knew every inch of the territory disputed by the gangs as well as the names of their respective leaders. He also had some useful addresses.

Unless he could intervene, retribution was imminent. The Warriors would be smarting from their defeat and anxious to get their own back and the Spirits, while enjoying their sovereignty, would be ready to defend it in every way. Burge's hope was that he could learn when the battle would take place so that he could have enough officers on hand to nip it in the bud. The only way to make the area safe was to arrest key members of each gang and prosecute them. The older boys could be sent to a borstal institution and the younger ones could be given a taste of incarceration at one of the remand homes run by the police.

Burge's leisurely patrol took him all over the district. Above the general hubbub, he suddenly heard the sound of glass being shattered nearby followed by a howl of pain. He quickened his pace to turn a corner and saw the old man standing forlornly outside his junk shop, the plate-glass window lying in thousands of tiny fragments at his feet. Because he'd helped the police, albeit under duress, a gang had wreaked revenge. Burge found it difficult to find any sympathy for him.

* * *

On his way back to Scotland Yard, Keedy chided himself for showing his hand too soon. Whatever his feelings about Peebles, he should have kept them well hidden. That's what Marmion would have done. Until there was enough evidence to make an arrest, he'd have shown patience and restraint. Keedy had been too impulsive. Because of a description given to him by a hotel receptionist, he'd decided that Norris Sprake's chauffeur had been the killer. His dislike of the man had made him speak too soon. It was foolhardy and unprofessional. The row with Alice was partly to blame for his behaviour. It was a distraction that he couldn't seem to shake off. Desperate to solve the case and have time to spend with her, he'd seized on a possibility without first exploring it. He'd even rung Marmion and told him of his discovery.

As for the argument with Alice, he still couldn't decide if that was his fault or hers. The simple fact was that they'd turned a moment of reconciliation into an excuse to push each other away. Neither of them had wanted an estrangement yet that was what they'd ended up with. When he got back to the office, he was penitent.

'I'm sorry, Harv,' he said. 'I went in too hard too soon.'

'How did Peebles respond?' asked Marmion.

'He was offended.'

'Then you handled it badly, Joe. There was no point in warning him that you had suspicions. He'll be on his guard now.'

'Peebles was so smug and irritating. He's taken over Miss Kane's office as if it was his by right. When he told me that they'd miss her, he was lying through his teeth. He was glad to shunt her out of the way. In short,' said Keedy, 'getting rid of her sounded as if it could be one of the motives behind the murder.'

He went on to describe in detail his interviews with Peebles and Sprake. Though he regretted alerting the chauffeur to his suspicions, he felt that he'd learnt a great deal about the two men during his visit to Barnes.

'Sprake was so calm and collected,' he recalled. 'You'd have thought that his business partner had simply retired and not been brutally murdered. He seemed so *prepared* for the loss of Donohoe.'

'Did you ask him about Club Apollo?'

'Yes – he gave me the same answer as Peebles. He'd never heard of it.'

'Did you believe them?'

'Oh, I'm certain they were both being honest about that. There was a twinge of annoyance in their voices that they weren't aware of the club. Talking of which,' said Keedy, 'how did you get on there?'

'It was a productive visit, Joe. I think that Chat ought to hear about it as well. Let's see if he's alone in his office.'

They walked along the corridor, knocked on the superintendent's door then went into the room. Chatfield was keen to hear what Marmion had to say about the club. Since he'd met both men, Keedy was interested in the exchanges with Saul Rockwell and Jonathan Ulverton. The fact that the string quartet had a female member also intrigued him but it was Marmion's revelation about Patrick Armitage that really startled him. It was the cue for Chatfield to take over.

'It's strange that you should mention him,' he said, 'because he was standing in this very office earlier this morning.'

'What did he want?' asked Marmion.

'He wanted to complain to you, Inspector. Since you weren't here, he came to me instead and gave vent to his spleen.'

When he told them what had happened, the detectives were amused but not surprised. Armitage had done what they'd expected of him. Chatfield assured them that he'd sent his visitor away with his tail between his legs.

'One of you should go to the hotel,' he decided.

'I hope you're not asking us to apologise to him, sir,' said Keedy.

'There's no need for that. Thanks to the inspector, we now have a link between Mr Armitage and Club Apollo. I think he needs to be questioned about that link. It could be instructive.'

'Then I suggest that the sergeant goes to the hotel,' said Marmion.

'Why is that?'

'First of all, he and the manager got on so well together.' Keedy gave a laugh of disbelief. 'Second, I feel it's time for me to go back to Birmingham again. Adrian Donohoe has adjusted to the crisis very quickly and his mother may have got over the initial shock by now. I'd like to talk to them both.'

'Then off you go,' said Chatfield. 'As for you, Sergeant, you can go to the hotel. Since you have such a rapport with the manager, he'll be delighted to see you.'

Keedy looked as if he'd just swallowed a rotting onion.

* * *

Burge waited half an hour before he went back to the shop. By that time, the old man had swept up the shards of glass and shovelled them into a bucket. He was now nailing wooden boards across the window. Burge strolled up to the shop.

'Trouble?'

'It was them bleeding kids,' said the old man, sourly.

'See which ones?'

'Naw, they was too quick.'

'Why pick on you?'

The old man descended from his ladder and closed one eye, studying Burge intently through the other. He lowered his voice.

'Seen you before. You wanted an 'at.'

'Still got it?'

'Naw, someone took if orff me.'

'Why was that?'

'You're a copper, ain't you?' said the old man, suspiciously. 'You arsk too many questions.'

There was no point in denying it now. Hitherto, the shopkeeper would never have dared to cooperate with the police but the situation had changed. He'd been attacked by one of the gangs and their persecution of him might well continue.

'You need help,' said Burge. 'This is only the start.'

'I'll manage.'

'Manage much better if those kids weren't causing mayhem.'

'Nobody can stop 'em.'

'Yes, they can. All we need is ammunition – names, addresses, how they operate. Take them to a juvenile court and they'll be locked away. Windows would be safe then. People round here could breathe easier. Think about it.'

After lengthy consideration, the old man grunted. 'Come inside.'

Back in his natural milieu, Patrick Armitage cruised around the hotel with accustomed aplomb. There was no sign of the anger he'd displayed at Scotland Yard. He was relaxed, vigilant and in control. When he saw Keedy enter, he gave him a polite welcome. Only when they'd adjourned to his office did the manager's mood change.

'I spoke to Superintendent Chatfield earlier on,' he said, sharply.

'So I'm told, sir.'

'You had no right to question my staff while I wasn't here.'

'The duty manager raised no objection.'

'He resented being grilled.'

'If that's how he wishes to describe our brief conversation,' said Keedy, 'then so be it. He was very obliging at the time.'

'You've cast a shadow over the Devonian.'

'I would've thought that Mr Donohoe's murder had already done that, sir. Be grateful that the crime didn't actually take place here. If it had, then you'd have had guests pouring in with morbid interest. That wouldn't have been good for the sedate image of the Devonian, would it? Don't you agree, sir?'

'Yes, I do,' conceded the other. 'It's a great relief.'

'At least, there's something we agree on.'

Armitage eyed him warily. 'Why have you come back here?'

'I was wondering if you might be able to throw light on a couple of things, sir. When I looked through the list of guests staying here on the night of the murder, I came across a name that interested me.'

'And what was it?'

'Thomas Day,' said Keedy. 'Do you recall the gentleman?'

'I'm afraid that I don't, Sergeant.'

'That's a pity. Your receptionist led me to believe that you had an almost encyclopaedic knowledge of your guest list.'

'He was overstating my ability.'

'So you've never heard of a Thomas Day?'

'I've already told you that,' said the other, petulantly.

'Then I'll move on to another name and I know for a fact that you'll recognise it this time.'

'Who is the person?'

'It's not a person,' said Keedy, 'it's a place – the Club Apollo.'

'What about it?'

'You applied to join it, sir.'

Armitage bristled. 'How do you know that?'

'The inspector was there this morning and given permission to look through the list of people who were turned away. You were one of them.'

'My face didn't fit, that's all.'

'It wasn't your face that let you down, sir, it was the feeling that you might not be committed enough to the values of the club.'

'That's arrant nonsense!'

'I'm only repeating what it said in the record book.'

'What does it matter, anyway?' said Armitage, recovering instantly. 'It's water under the bridge now.'

'How did you first hear about the club?'

'I don't see that that has any relevance to your investigation.'

'It might do, sir, if Mr Donohoe had mentioned it to you.'

'Well, he didn't.'

'But he must have been chairman of the panel that interviewed you.'

'Yes, he was.'

'So who did try to recruit you? Was it Mr Ulverton?'

'That's a private matter, Sergeant.'

'And what happened afterwards?'

'I'm not prepared to discuss it.'

'I sympathise with your position, sir,' said Keedy. 'You're eager to join an exclusive club yet you're barred by no less a person than Gilbert Donohoe, one of your regular guests at the hotel. You'd have expected him to have spoken up for you out of friendship. Yet he didn't. Why was that, do you think?'

'The matter is closed, Sergeant.'

'I'm very impressed that you could afford to join the Club Apollo. I know what the annual membership fee is. You have deeper pockets than I imagined, sir.'

'My financial situation is of no concern to you,' said Armitage, peevishly.

'Let's go back to Mr Donohoe. If I'd developed a friendship with him over the years and was then rejected by the club of which he was a co-founder, relations between us would have been very strained. Didn't that happen in your case?' asked Keedy. 'Didn't you wince every time you saw him?'

'No, Sergeant, we carried on amicably as before. I've learnt to rise above any mild setbacks and carry on as if they never existed. It makes for a quieter life.'

Keedy realised that he would get no further with this line of questioning. Being refused membership of a club would certainly have needled Armitage but, in itself, it was unlikely to have provided him with an urge to commit murder. He'd need a much stronger reason to hate Gilbert Donohoe.

'Is that all?' asked the manager, anxious to get rid of him.

'Not quite, sir,' said Keedy. 'Let's return to Thomas Day . . .'

As he boarded the train at Euston, Marmion was looking forward to reviewing the case in depth on the journey to Birmingham. In the event, he found himself thinking about Keedy instead. Something was amiss with his relationship with Alice. Marmion was too finely attuned to the sergeant's moods to be unaware that a rift had occurred. It had clearly affected Keedy's judgement. Had his private life been as happy as it usually was, he would never have made the mistake of bungling his interview with Peebles. His mind had been on Alice. As her father, Marmion was bound to worry. Both she and Keedy were strong characters. Dissension between them was never easily resolved. The longer their dispute lasted, the more their stances would harden.

The train was steaming over the border into Warwickshire before he was able to give the murder his full concentration. They needed help. While they'd identified possible suspects, they'd failed to build a convincing case against any of them. London accounted for only a small part of the victim's life.

It was in the Midlands that he'd made his name and where he spent the bulk of his time. Marmion was hoping that he could gather more evidence about Donohoe on his home turf. The crime might have taken place in London but it was not impossible that the killer hailed from Birmingham. Marmion might be heading towards him at that moment.

As on the previous occasion, he took a taxi from the station to the Donohoe residence. Though the victim's son was not there, his wife was and for once she was not playing the piano. Marmion found her in the lounge, reading from the Bible. When he apologised for disturbing her, she raised a forgiving hand.

'I've been hoping you'd come sooner or later, Inspector,' she said. 'I'd like to know what's going on.'

'Your son could have told you that, Mrs Donohoe.'

'Adrian is too busy trying to cope with the upheaval this has caused. My husband was a pillar of strength in every sense. When he disappeared, his whole empire tottered a little.'

'Do you think that your son will be able to make it more stable?'

'He'll do his best,' she said in a voice that was devoid of any optimism. 'He lacks his father's drive but – God willing – this may be the making of him.'

'May I ask some questions about the family?'

'I assumed that you did that with Adrian.'

'He was not as helpful as we'd hoped, Mrs Donohoe. When he was asked about the Club Apollo, for instance, he didn't wish to talk about it.'

'I'm quite happy to do so, Inspector. I liked the place.'

'You attended concerts there, I believe.'

'Oh, I did more than that,' she said, getting as close to a smile as she could. 'I actually commissioned some of them. That's to say, my husband sought my advice about which musicians we should book and what music we should request. As a result, I was able to listen to bespoke concerts.'

'That must have been a delight for you.'

'Oh, it was. My only regret was that there weren't enough of them.'

'In essence, it is a gentlemen's club.'

'Yet I never felt we were there on sufferance.'

'How did you get on with Mr Ulverton?'

'Oh, he's charming and so is his wife. They act as hosts on Ladies' Nights at the club. That's not a role Gilbert and I would have relished.'

'What about your son?'

'Adrian didn't have the slightest interest in the club. He's the wrong age, for a start, and preoccupied with other things.'

'Mr Ulverton was rather critical of him.'

'Well, he's no reason to be,' said Clara with maternal defensiveness. 'Adrian is a wonderful son and a good businessman. How can Jonathan Ulverton be so critical of him when he's never even met him?'

'He didn't explain that, Mrs Donohoe.'

She was doing her best to exert self-control but Marmion could see that she was quite fragile. He questioned her as gently as he could.

'Have you ever played a part in your husband's business activities?'

220

'None at all, I'm pleased to say. That's probably why they flourished.'

'Did your husband ever discuss his ambitions with you?'

'Naturally,' she replied. 'When he got to know Jonathan Ulverton, he asked me what I thought about a club that offered its members classical music. And I was the only person in whom he confided his political ambitions.'

Marmion started. 'I didn't know that he had any.'

'He was approached more than once to stand for Parliament and the idea seemed to grow on him. He told me once that he'd love to be Lord Mayor of Birmingham. Gilbert said that it would be a businessman's dream.'

It was yet another side to the murder victim and Marmion was duly impressed by the man's versatility. He wondered if Ulverton knew that his friend was nurturing ambitions for a political career later in life.

'Did your husband ever talk about retirement?'

She gave a brittle laugh. 'He didn't know the meaning of the word.'

'But there must have been a point when he planned to hand over to his son.'

'Gilbert thought he would live for ever, and he will – in our hearts.'

'How are your daughters coping with their loss?'

'They're both married. They have someone to help them through it. And they, in turn, have been so kind and considerate to me. What's happened has been truly dreadful but it's brought us all closer together.'

'Does that include your son?'

Marmion saw her eyelids flutter and feared that his question had offended her.

'Yes,' she said at length. 'I suppose that it does.'

Since he had the luxury of a car at his disposal, Keedy asked the driver to take him to the site in Stepney where the murder had occurred. Uniformed policemen were still keeping people away from the area. Detectives had just finished their detailed search. They'd found evidence of a struggle and a few tiny items – ignored by riverside scavengers – which could conceivably have belonged to the victim. Keedy chatted for a few minutes with the leader of the team, then broke off when he saw Clifford Burge walking towards him. They exchanged greetings.

'How are you getting on?' asked Keedy.

'Enjoy being back on my old stamping ground.'

'It's a pity it's been overrun by gangs.'

'They won't terrorise the place for long.'

'That sounds promising.'

'I've made headway – thanks to Everitt White.'

'Yes, he's the reason this search has been taking place. He discovered that this is where the murder victim's shoes were found. How do you know Inspector White?'

'My brother, Les, works with him.'

Burge went on to give a full account of how much White had assisted him. When he admitted that his hat had been stolen by gang members, he made Keedy laugh. Burge pointed out that he not only had his hat back, he had the old man in the junk shop on his side at last.

'He wants this neighbourhood cleaned up as much as anyone.'

'It sounds to me as if he got what he deserved. He was happy enough to work with the gangs when they sold him things they'd stolen. Can you trust him?'

'I think so,' said Burge, confidently. 'He's been sobered by the attack on his shop. He's promised to keep his ear to the ground for us.'

'I wish that we had someone like that.'

'How is the investigation going?'

'Slowly,' replied Keedy. 'It's going very slowly.'

Since she knew how eager he was to speak to her son, Clara Donohoe insisted on putting the car at his disposal. During the drive to the Northfield factory, Marmion tried to pump the chauffeur for information about the family but the man gave little away. When they reached the factory, they parked by the impressive entrance. The chauffeur opened the door of the car to let him get out and Marmion went into the building. He was startled to see Harriet Kane coming down the corridor towards him.

'What are you doing here, Miss Kane?' he asked.

'This is where I work from now on.'

'Didn't your boss give you time to . . . adjust to the situation?'

'He believes that the best way to keep grief at bay is to lose oneself in work and I agree with him. If I was at home, I'd be bursting into tears all the time.'

'You were obviously fond of Mr Donohoe.'

'I worshipped him, Inspector.' She glanced at the door to her left. 'Things will be different now. This is his son's office,'

223

she went on, a hand on the doorknob. 'I'll just see if he's free to talk to you.'

She tapped on the door before entering the office and closing the door behind her. Marmion was left to reflect on the way that a murder had transformed her career. After being secretary to a highly successful property developer and enjoying the kudos of being employed in London, she was now occupying a more lowly position and was controlled by a man she neither liked nor respected to the same degree. Loyalty to the family kept her there. In time, it might begin to wear thin.

She reappeared and kept the door open so that he could enter the office. She shut it gently behind him. Adrian Donohoe rose to his feet behind his desk and reached across to offer a reluctant handshake. Marmion sat opposite him.

'I've just been speaking to your mother,' he said.

'You shouldn't have bothered her, Inspector. She's quite frail.'

'Mrs Donohoe was desperate for news of the investigation. You told her very little, I gather.'

'I'm trying to protect her from the unpleasantness of it all.'

'The full facts will come out in due course, sir. You can't hide them from your mother. While we're on the subject of facts, there is a macabre detail I've been keeping from you.'

'Why have you done that?'

'I didn't wish to shock you, Mr Donohoe.'

'And what is this detail?'

'Your father was not just murdered. His tongue was cut out.' The younger man reacted with alarm and disgust. 'What sort of person would do that to him?'

Adrian needed a moment to recover. 'I've no idea,' he whispered.

'Had he betrayed someone? Was the killer signalling that he'd been silenced for ever? There's usually something symbolic in such an act.'

'Well, I can't see what it was.'

'Your mother told me something interesting. Mrs Donohoe said that your father nurtured political ambitions. To achieve those, he'd have to make lots of speeches. Is that why his tongue was removed – to shut him up completely? Does he have political enemies?'

'I've told you before. My father had rivals but no real enemies.'

'I'm afraid you're wrong on that score.'

'The murder must have been a case of mistaken identity.'

'Nobody would ever confuse Mr Donohoe with someone else, sir. From all the evidence we've gathered, one thing is clear. He was unique.'

'Yes, he was,' said the other with sudden urgency. 'My father was a genius in some ways. You'll never meet anyone quite like him. He could do *anything*.'

'Is that why he believed that he was God?' asked Marmion. 'That was the name inside his shoes. Two initials would have been enough to identify them as his but he used all three.'

'It was a joke, Inspector.'

'Then it's a rather weird one.'

'He could be eccentric.'

'The last time we met, you were unwilling to talk about the Club Apollo.'

'What was I supposed to say?'

'Well, you might have told me why you resented Mr Ulverton, for a start.'

'He's nothing to me,' said Adrian with a contemptuous wave of his hand. 'He belonged to a part of my father's life that I knew very little about – and that's all I'm prepared to say.'

'Then let me turn to someone else, sir.'

'Who is it?'

'It's a man by the name of Thomas Day. Have you ever heard of him?'

Adrian fell silent and averted his gaze.

Ellen had spent the whole day on tenterhooks. The letter addressed to her son had raised all kinds of hopes. According to the postmark, it had been sent from Warwickshire. Was that where Paul had been all this time? Had someone discovered his home address and tried to get in touch with him? Inside the envelope, she came to believe, there was vital information yet something held her back from finding out what it was. Ellen needed someone to tell her that she had a perfect right to open any correspondence to their missing son. Ideally, that person would be her husband but she knew that she wasn't allowed to ring him at work unless it was an emergency. In her mind, news about Paul qualified as an emergency and she lifted the receiver three times, only to put it back down again. When she plucked up the courage to pick it up a fourth time, she got in contact with Scotland Yard, only to be told by a voice she didn't recognise that Inspector Marmion had gone to Birmingham.

Sitting down again, she examined the envelope once more. It was obviously not an official communication. The handwriting was little more than a scrawl and there was a smudge. As the day wore on, she became more and more frantic. Every time she decided to tear open the envelope, however, something made her draw back. Ellen couldn't stand the suspense any longer. Since her husband wasn't able to help her, she caught a bus to central London and turned to another member of the family.

'Mummy!' exclaimed Alice. 'I never expected to see you here.'

'I just had to come.'

'Why – what's happened?'

'This letter came for Paul,' said Ellen, taking it from her handbag. 'I've been in agony, not knowing whether to open it or not.'

'It's private.'

'But it might be able to give us a clue as to where he is.'

Alice had just finished work and was leaving the building with the other policewomen. She could see how agitated her mother was. With an arm around her shoulders, Alice led her along the street and around a corner. They found a quiet spot where they could talk without interruption. Taking the letter, Alice inspected it.

'It's very sloppy writing.'

'That doesn't matter. It's been sent by someone who knows Paul's address.'

'What do you want me to do, Mummy?'

'I only came to you because I couldn't get in touch with your father. I know this is a feeble excuse,' said Ellen, 'but I just need someone to give me permission to read this letter.'

Alice made the decision for her. 'Open the envelope,' she said.

Her mother tore it open and took out the letter.

'Thank God!' she cried. 'Paul is still alive!'

CHAPTER FIFTEEN

Marmion had finally got him at a disadvantage. Ironically, it was in a place where Adrian Donohoe would be expected to have maximum defence against intrusive questioning. He occupied an impressive office in a large engineering factory employing a substantial number of people. He was also the main beneficiary of his father's death and would soon take control of Gilbert Donohoe's empire. In doing so, he'd acquire a higher status, untold wealth and almost unlimited power. An already arrogant man would thereby take on new layers of self-importance. He should be unreachable yet he'd suddenly been flustered by the mention of a name. Marmion was bent on finding out why.

'You haven't answered my question, sir,' he said.

'The name is . . . vaguely familiar. That's all I can tell you.'

'Oh, I think you can tell me a lot more than that. From the moment you first heard about your father's murder, you've been singularly unhelpful. Since you're the person in the best position to help us, we find that very frustrating. Don't you *want* us to catch the killer?'

'Of course I do.'

'Then why don't you cooperate with us?'

'That's what I've been trying to do, Inspector.'

'Well, you haven't been trying very hard, sir. There are two areas of great interest to us. One is the property company set up by your father and the other is the club that he helped to found. You dismissed the first with a sentence or two and won't even discuss the second. It's not what we'd call cooperation.'

'Then what would you call it?'

'It's a case of wilful obstruction.'

Adrian was stung. 'Nobody has a stronger reason to want the murder solved,' he said, vehemently. 'While you're dealing with the crime, however, I'm trying to cope with the consequences of it. You don't appreciate how complicated and time-consuming that is. My father's empire has lost his guiding hand. I have to speak to everyone in senior management and make major decisions about the future. Do you know how long that will take?'

'That's your problem, sir.'

'I'm letting you get on with *your* job,' said Adrian, jabbing a finger. 'Please let me get on with mine.'

'I'll do so on one condition.'

230

'And what's that?'

'Tell me why you're afraid to talk about Thomas Day.'

'I hardly know the man.'

'That's not true,' said Marmion, quietly, 'and we both know it.'

He met the other's gaze with steely determination. However long it took, Marmion was not moving until he got an honest reply. After resorting in vain to an attempt at browbeating, Adrian Donohoe realised that he'd lost the battle.

'Tom Day was a business associate of my father,' he admitted, finally.

'Go on.'

'He's an estate agent and property developer.'

'Where is he based?'

'Right here in Birmingham – but he has branch offices elsewhere.'

'Did he work closely with your father?'

'He did until they fell out.'

'When did that happen? Was it when your father set up a property company?'

'Yes, it was. Tom felt . . . excluded.'

'Did he expect to be a partner in the new enterprise?'

'I don't know the full details,' said the other. 'All I can tell you is that the relationship turned sour. I can't say that I was sorry. Tom was a prickly character. My sister found that out.'

'Oh?'

'Before she was married, Doreen made the mistake of letting him court her. I think she still bears the scars. Tom Day is no gentleman.'

'Right,' said Marmion, summarising the situation. 'Thomas Day was an associate of your father's and a friend of your sister's. In short, he was closely involved with your family – so much for the name being vaguely familiar to you.'

'We've put him out of our minds, Inspector.'

'Why?'

'My father had a strict policy. When someone let him down, he flushed them out of his life as if they'd never been there. That's what happened to Tom Day.'

'So you've had no contact with him since then?'

'None at all – we treat him like a pariah.'

'And what was Mr Day's attitude to your father?'

'Tom hated him. He kept well clear of our entire family.'

'That's a myth, I'm afraid,' said Marmion. 'It may interest you to know that, on the night of your father's murder, Thomas Day was staying at the Devonian Hotel. Now why do you think he did that?'

Their elation was fringed with alarm. Such as it was, the letter seemed to confirm that Paul Marmion was alive but it was not sent by a friend. Three words had been written in spidery capitals on flimsy lined paper – DON'T COME BACK. Two pound notes had been enclosed. Ellen and Alice were befuddled.

'It doesn't make sense,' said Ellen. 'The message is hostile yet there's money for Paul. I don't understand.'

'There's the explanation, Mummy,' said her daughter, pointing to the address at the top of the letter. 'Paul must have been working at Corley Hall Farm. This is money he earned there.'

'Then why wasn't he given it at the time he left?'

'Judging by the tone of this message, I think he might have been thrown off the farm by someone in a temper. It was instant dismissal. Maybe the farmer felt guilty at not paying him. That's why he sent the unpaid wages.'

'What on earth could Paul have done?'

'There's only one way to find out. Someone must go to the farm.'

'Well, it won't be your father,' said Ellen, sadly. 'He's had all the leave he was due and is deep in his latest investigation.'

'That settles it, then.'

'What do you mean, Alice?'

'Since Daddy is tied up, one of us will have to go instead.'

Arriving back at Scotland Yard, he went straight to the superintendent's office. As well as reporting on his visit to the Devonian Hotel, Keedy was able to pass on the encouraging news from Clifford Burge. Chatfield was pleased.

'He was my recommendation,' he said.

'Constable Burge was a good choice, sir. He blends in.'

'Had you not already been involved in a case, you'd have been a possibility for the assignment. On balance, however, Burge was the better man.'

Keedy shrugged off the put-down. 'I'm sure you're right, sir. As for the Devonian,' he continued, 'I had a long chat with the manager.'

'Was he still in a truculent mood?'

'No, he seemed to have calmed somewhat.'

'That's my doing,' said Chatfield. 'I had to slap him down.'

Having been slapped down by the superintendent many times, Keedy had a fleeting sympathy for Patrick Armitage. It soon disappeared. He went on to recall his conversation with the manager and told how the latter had finally conceded that he did remember the name of Thomas Day, after all.

'Why didn't he tell you that in the first place?'

'He was anxious to get rid of me.'

'It's to your credit that you hung on until you squeezed the truth out of him.'

'Unfortunately,' said Keedy, 'it wasn't the *whole* truth. What I got was only a partial confession. What he told me was just enough to qualify as a reasonable answer but he was definitely holding something back. The Devonian offers such excellent service that the bulk of its guests are regular patrons. They come back time and again. When a new face appears, Mr Armitage makes a point of speaking to the person.'

'Well, I hope he adopts a more friendly tone than the one I had to endure.'

'That's how he came to meet Thomas Day.'

'So the fellow was staying there for the first time, was he?'

'Yes, sir.'

'How did Armitage describe him?'

'He said that Day was a pleasant, affable man in his late thirties with a trace of a Midland accent. In some ways, he claimed, Day looked a little like me.'

'That means he was fit, healthy and therefore capable of murder.'

'I haven't murdered anyone so far,' said Keedy with a

234

grin, 'but I take your point. He sounds as if he was physically powerful enough to strangle Mr Donohoe.'

'Did the manager ask him what he was doing in London?'

'Mr Day said he was there on business. He's often in the capital, it seems.'

'There you are,' said Chatfield, pouncing on the information. 'A regular visitor would have a regular place to stay. If he singled out the Devonian Hotel for this particular trip, there had to be a reason.'

'That was my immediate thought.'

'So what have we got here? Thomas Day is a fit, able businessman with a Midland accent that could link him to Birmingham. He chooses to stay for the first and only time at a hotel where one of the guests is murdered. I think that takes us beyond coincidence.'

'So do I, Superintendent,' said Keedy, glad that his theory was at last being given credence. 'He has to be regarded as a suspect.'

'I agree,' said Chatfield. 'Where the devil *is* the man?'

Marmion was asking the same question in a more polite way. He'd called at the offices in New Street from which Thomas Day ran his business. The estate agent was clearly successful. The premises had been recently refurbished and all of the properties on display in the shop window were at the more expensive end of the market. Day, he noticed from a large poster, was also responsible for building some luxurious houses in the city suburbs. While not in the same league as Gilbert Donohoe, the man was a definite presence on the Birmingham business scene. Day's secretary was a tall, shapely woman in her thirties with an educated voice and a welcoming smile. Marmion was bound to contrast her with Harriet Kane. The two women were worlds apart. Thomas Day and Gilbert Donohoe looked for very different things in a secretary.

When he asked to see Day, the woman explained that her employer was away on business, viewing some land in Surrey with a view to purchasing it. His secretary had no means of contacting him. She had to wait for Day to ring her when he was ready to return to Birmingham.

'When he does telephone you,' said Marmion, 'I'd be grateful if you could ask him to get in touch with me as a matter of urgency.' Taking out a card, he gave it to her. 'I can usually be reached at that number.'

'I didn't realise you were a detective,' she said, reading the details on the card. 'May I know why you're so keen to speak to Mr Day?'

'I'd like to discuss his relationship with Mr Donohoe – the *late* Mr Donohoe.'

'Oh, yes, of course. We read about it in the newspaper. It's very distressing.'

'Does that mean Mr Day will be distressed?'

'Yes, of course,' she replied, smoothly. 'He always had great respect for Mr Donohoe. The whole business community here is shaken by what happened.'

Marmion looked around. 'Do you like working here?'

'I like it very much. Mr Day is a very considerate employer, if that's what you want to know. I've known far worse, Inspector.'

Since she was prepared to talk so freely about the estate

236

agent, Marmion exploited her willingness. He learnt a great deal about Thomas Day and discovered aspects of the man's character that Adrian Donohoe had deliberately suppressed. For instance, Day had been heavily engaged in charity work among deprived children.

'That's very creditable,' said Marmion. 'Does he have a family of his own?'

'Mr Day is not married.'

'Is that by choice?'

'*Everything* he does is by choice,' she said, firmly. 'That's the sort of person he is. You'll find that out, Inspector.'

'I look forward to doing so.'

Back at home, Ellen and her daughter pored over an atlas that was open at the page displaying a map of Warwickshire and its adjacent counties. It was ages before one of them spotted the name they sought. Alice's finger marked the spot.

'There it is – Corley. Do you see? It's close to Fillongley.'

'Where's the nearest railway station?'

'It must be Coventry, by the look of it.'

Ellen lifted her head. 'What was Paul doing on a farm, I wonder?'

'He was working there, Mummy. That much is clear and we ought to be glad. It shows that he's alive, well and able to make some sort of living.'

'But he'd only be a labourer, wouldn't he?'

'There's no shame in that. Farmers are crying out for help on the land. That's why so many young women have gone to work on farms. Paul's big and strong. He'd be a real asset.'

'Then why was he told not to come back?'

'We could speculate endlessly about that,' said Alice, closing the map book. 'The first thing we must do is to tell Daddy. He deserves to know that our worst fears were quite unnecessary.'

'They've been replaced by others now.'

'But Paul is alive. That's what you were so desperate to know.'

'Yes, but he obviously upset this man he worked for, the farmer who didn't even bother to sign his name. He sounds as if he's very cross with Paul.'

'Yet he sent money for him. How did he know the address?'

'I can't answer that.'

'Paul wouldn't have given it to him. He cut himself off from this house. To all intents and purposes, we don't exist.'

'Alice!'

'It's the truth, Mummy.'

'I can't let myself believe that. Deep down, he's still one of the family.'

'That's not what Paul thinks. Oh, it's so difficult, isn't it?' said Alice, embracing her mother. 'One day we want him back and the next day we don't. Though I'm relieved that we know he's able to hold down a job for a certain length of time, part of me wishes that we didn't.'

'Would you rather go on torturing yourself about him?'

'No, I wouldn't.'

'Then be glad that we know something positive at last.'

'I am.'

Alice broke away and her mother saw the tears in her

eyes. Ellen realised that her daughter's mind was not entirely focussed on her brother.

'Forget Paul,' she said, softly. 'Tell me about Joe instead.'

Keedy kept going over and over the evidence in his mind. Alone in Marmion's office, he opened his notebook and flicked through it. Four names stood out in the current inquiry – Patrick Armitage, Jean-Louis Peebles, Norris Sprake and Thomas Day. All but Sprake had the ability to garrotte someone but it was more difficult to equip each of the quartet with a strong enough motive to do so. Keedy resisted the impulse to add Adrian Donohoe's name to the list. Though there was patently bad blood between him and his father, he did not seem capable of murder or of hiring an assassin to kill on his behalf. Jonathan Ulverton was another contender to be eliminated. Though he stood to gain control of Club Apollo from his partner, he had no apparent reason to get rid of Donohoe. The two men had mutual interests. There was no sense of rivalry between them. They were natural friends.

Following the advice Marmion gave in every investigation, Keedy looked for connections between the suspects. Peebles was employed by Sprake but neither of them were regular visitors to the Devonian. On the other hand, there was some link, as yet unidentified, between Peebles and Thomas Day. The chauffeur had hotly denied knowing the man but Keedy was certain that he was lying. That was why he believed the two of them might have worked together. Though he was probably not in league with anyone else, the hotel manager could not be crossed off the list. His rejection by the Club Apollo would have infuriated him and one of the men who personified the place was an habitué of the Devonian. Armitage must have seen Donohoe many times since he'd been rebuffed. His urge for revenge would have kept bubbling away.

Keedy was still trying to decide which of the four men should be the prime suspect in the case when Alice dismissed everything else from his whirring brain. The rift between them worried him. While he understood her desire to name a day for the wedding, he held to his belief that they needed to build up their savings first. He'd known friends who'd begun their married life under the roof of the bride's home and, to a man, they complained about being embarrassed and inhibited. A home of his own was an essential in Keedy's view. He baulked at the notion of moving in with Alice's parents and he felt that Marmion would object to it as well. Keedy was in a cleft stick, desperately wanting to appease Alice yet quite unable to do so. The impasse between them could not be allowed to go on. The sooner the murder was solved, the sooner he and Alice could apologise to each other and sit down for a proper discussion.

He turned back to the four suspects with increased urgency.

Marmion didn't even consider interviewing Mrs Doreen Pinnick, as she now was. The murder victim's younger daughter could tell him little about her brief relationship with Thomas Day. Indeed, she might well prefer to tell him nothing at all. Unwilling to dredge up unpleasant memories from the past, she would be of no real use to the inspector. When she knew Day, she was a single woman. Doreen was now married with

240

two children and still grieving for her father. It was the worst time to approach her. Marmion therefore contented himself with what he'd learnt from his time with Clara Donohoe, her son and Thomas Day's secretary. Some mysteries had now been solved. Others remained.

With so much new information to collate in his mind, he hardly noticed the noise and discomfort of the train journey to London. It seemed a matter of minutes before he was stepping on to the platform at Euston. Taking a taxi to Scotland Yard, he first reported to the superintendent. Chatfield seized on the news.

'So the sergeant may be right, after all. Thomas Day could be our man.'

'He's certainly someone we need to track down, sir,' said Marmion. 'His secretary told me that he usually stayed at a hotel in Knightsbridge whenever he was in London. That's some way from the Devonian.'

'And where is he at the moment?'

Marmion explained that Day was somewhere in Surrey but that, when he spoke to his secretary, he'd be asked to get in touch with the inspector immediately.

'If he doesn't make contact,' said Chatfield, 'we'll both know why.'

'It doesn't necessarily mean that he's the killer, sir.'

'What other interpretation could you place on his behaviour?'

'I'm going on what his secretary told me about him. He's not the villain we're starting to paint him as. To begin with, he's revered by his staff. That's in his favour.'

'I'd prefer to rely on Adrian Donohoe's estimate of him. Thomas Day is a business rival with an axe to grind. Why else would he stay at the Devonian if he didn't have designs on Gilbert Donohoe?'

'I don't know, sir.'

'Then sit by the telephone until he calls – *if* he calls, that is.'

'Oh, I've no doubts on that score. Mr Day is not going to take to his heels and give himself away. In my view, he may yet have no reason to do so. Until we have more evidence,' Marmion reminded him, 'he must still be presumed innocent.'

'I'm the last person who needs to be told that,' said Chatfield, prissily.

'Of course, sir.'

Taking his leave, Marmion went along the corridor to his office. No sooner had he sunk into his chair than the telephone rang. Had his message got through to Thomas Day already? Hoping that it had, he snatched up the receiver excitedly.

'Inspector Marmion here . . .'

'Thanks heavens!' exclaimed a familiar voice.

'Is that you, Ellen?'

'Yes, it is. Something's happened.'

'Is it to do with Paul?'

'He's been working on a farm in Warwickshire.'

There would not be long to wait. Burge sensed it. The Stepney Warriors had gone ominously quiet but it was not because they'd been routed. They were ready to strike back at the most propitious moment. He needed to find out when that moment was. His informer was the old man from the junk shop, fearful of repercussions but putting his trust in the police.

'What have you heard?' asked Burge.

'Very little.'

'Seen anything of their leader?'

'Greg's keeping his head down. It's still heavily bandaged after the attack.'

'Won't stop him fighting.'

'Nothing'll do that, Constable.'

'Meanwhile, the Evil Spirits are lording it over them. I've watched the cheeky bastards marching down the streets as if they own them.'

'They're really nasty. I done business with 'em so I know.'

'Have you had any more threats?'

'I've had stares,' said the old man, worriedly. 'That's enough.'

'Your troubles may soon be over,' said Burge. 'If we catch them in the act, we can put them away and get rid of the terrible fear that's in the air. You know these kids better than anyone. Keep listening.'

When he entered the room, Keedy was pleased to see that Marmion had returned. The inspector was just about to come to the end of a telephone call and, from the pained expression on his face, it looked as if he'd heard bad news. Keedy waited until he put the receiver down.

'Trouble?'

'Yes and no.'

'Who were you talking to?'

'Ellen.'

'She'd only ring if it was serious.'

'It is, Joe.'

Marmion told him about the letter addressed to Paul and how his wife had agonised over whether or not to open it. Unable to get advice from her husband, Ellen had accosted her daughter and been encouraged to tear open the envelope. Keedy was astonished to hear what it contained.

'Paul's alive and someone was employing him?'

'That's the good news. The bad news is that he's been sacked, by the look of it. We know where he used to work but we have no idea where he is now.'

'Someone has to go to the farm.'

'That's why Ellen rang. It will be her or Alice.'

'Then it will have to be Ellen. I can't see Gale Force showing any sympathy. That woman has a heart of stone.'

'You're being too harsh on her, Joe.'

'How did Ellen sound?'

'She was pleased and worried at the same time,' said Marmion. 'And she was still feeling guilty about opening Paul's letter.'

'Thank goodness she did! At least, we know he's not dead. Ellen shouldn't have any qualms about what she did. It was her right as a mother. I'm sorry that it caused her so much anxiety.'

'That's not the only thing that's upset her, Joe.'

'Oh – what else was there?' Marmion gave him a look. 'Ah, yes – that. Every couple goes through a bad patch from time to time,' he went on, uncomfortably. 'It's nothing serious.'

'Alice obviously thinks that it is.' Getting no response from Keedy, he set the subject aside. 'Let's get down to business. What happened at the Devonian?'

'I finally got Armitage to admit that he remembered Thomas Day, after all.'

'Did you learn anything valuable about the man?'

'Not really.'

'Then I'm way ahead of you.'

Marmion told him about the visit to Birmingham and how Adrian Donohoe, under pressure, had talked at length about Thomas Day. He was no longer an anonymous guest at the Devonian Hotel but a sworn enemy of the Donohoe family. Set against that was the image of Day that was supplied by his secretary. Keedy ignored that in favour of what he'd heard from Adrian Donohoe.

'That's fairly conclusive,' he said. 'Knowing where his target routinely stays when he's in London, Day books into the same hotel and lies in wait. Once the murder is committed, he makes a hasty exit.'

'But there's no proof that he *committed* the murder, Joe.'

'He was party to it somehow.'

'Who was the killer?'

'If it wasn't him, it was Peebles. He and Day are in this together.'

'That seems an unlikely partnership. Day is in competition with the property company for which Peebles works. His chauffeur is dog-loyal to Mr Sprake. Why would Peebles team up with a rival like Thomas Day?'

'Look at it another way, Harv. The facts are undeniable.

Donohoe is murdered and Day immediately vanishes. I fancy that he's gone to ground somewhere.'

'He could equally well be closing a deal in Surrey.'

'What was he doing at the Devonian on that fatal night?'

'I hope to put that question to him before long,' said Marmion. 'Meanwhile, we must not forget the Club Apollo. That was an important element in Donohoe's life and I'd like to know a little more about it. We've only seen the place during the daytime. I think it's time we found out what happens there of an evening.'

'Do you want me to find out?'

'Yes, I do. It could prove instructive.'

'What will you be doing?'

'If I had the choice,' said Marmion, seriously, 'I'd be on my way to that farm in Warwickshire, but this case has the first call on my time. Paul will have to wait.'

Ellen was suffering the pangs of motherhood. The son of whom she'd once been so proud had disowned her and her daughter was moping about her private life. Inclined by nature to worry, Ellen had much to bemoan. She and Alice sat either side of the kitchen table, each with an untouched cup of tea in front of them.

'I'm so sorry to spring up in front of you like that,' she said.

'Don't be silly, Mummy. I was pleased to see you.'

'But you might have had plans for the evening.'

'All I was going to do was to sit in my room and pine for the days when Joe and I were happy together.'

'You still *are* happy, Alice, but it's a different kind of

happiness now. You can't expect those early feelings of joy to last for ever. You have to make adjustments. I'll always believe that you and Joe Keedy were made for each other.'

'Then why do we have different ideas about our future?'

'He'll come round to your point of view in the end.'

'I'm not sure that I *have* a point of view any more,' said Alice, forlornly. 'Until now, Joe and I have always done everything together – but we're miles apart now. As for jumping on me when I finished work,' she continued, 'I couldn't have been more grateful.'

'Why – has Inspector Gale been giving you a hard time?'

'She always does that.'

'So why were you glad to see me?'

'It's because you saved me from further persecution. Iris has been badgering me for hour after hour, going on about this new friend of hers as if it's the romance of the century. They've only been out together once but she's been talking non-stop about it. Was *I* like that after my first ever date?'

'No – you told me very little.'

'Iris is telling me far too much. I don't think Doug would like it at all.'

'Doug?'

'PC Doug Beckett is, in her words, the man of her dreams, even though he's almost fifteen years older and has this sinister moustache. I don't begrudge Iris any pleasure. I just wish she'd attracted someone else. Doug is too experienced – he was married but his wife died. On the strength of one night out, Iris is hoping to replace her,' said Alice, pursing her lips. 'She could be in for a big disappointment.'

'She has unreal expectations, poor dear!'

'Maybe that's *my* trouble as well.'

'No, Alice,' said her mother, 'you're far too level-headed. What you and Joe Keedy have is built on solid rock. Iris, on the other hand, is living in a sort of fairy-tale world. It sounds to me as if she's heading for a fall. She'll need a friend like you to be on hand to catch her.'

Iris Goodliffe had spent over an hour in front of the mirror, making constant mistakes and repeatedly chiding herself for being so inexperienced in the use of cosmetics. When she'd finally finished her make-up, she turned to the next problem. What should she wear? Though her wardrobe was limited, she felt that she had to put on a different dress from the one she'd worn the night before. Trying everything on in turn, she paraded in front of the mirror. Iris then reminded herself that Douglas Beckett had taken an interest in her when she was wearing an unattractive police uniform. What she had on was not that important to him. His focus was on her personality.

On the previous night, she'd been kept waiting. Beckett was already there this time, standing on the corner where they'd agreed to meet. He raised his hat politely and gave her a toothy smile. Iris beamed.

'You look wonderful,' he said.

'Thank you, Doug.'

'But, then, you always look wonderful to me.'

Iris simpered. 'What are we going to do?'

'Well, I thought we'd start off with a walk. It's such a beautiful evening and the park is only five minutes away. We can work up an appetite for a meal. Does that suit you, Iris?'

'Yes, it does.'

'Then let's go.'

He offered his arm and Iris took it, her whole body suffused with a warm glow. As they headed for the park, she didn't hear the rumble of traffic or feel the pavement slabs under her feet. With the sound of church bells in her ears, she was walking down the aisle with her husband.

CHAPTER SIXTEEN

Though he'd turned up unexpectedly, Keedy was given a welcome at Club Apollo. Saul Rockwell shook his hand warmly and asked how the investigation was going.

'It's too soon to say,' replied Keedy.

'The members are all hoping for an early arrest. They talk of nothing else.'

'Mr Donohoe's death must have rocked them.'

'This is a small, well-knit club, Sergeant. When one of its founders is killed, it sends jitters through the whole lot of us.'

'You don't look like a man who suffers from jitters.'

Rockwell grinned. 'I'm an exception to the rule.'

'Working as a steward must be a huge change from being in the navy.'

'There are pluses and minuses.'

'What's the biggest bonus of being here?'

'I get to see my wife a lot more often,' said Rockwell. 'Navy wives have to put up with the fact that their husbands are at sea for months on end. Only a very special woman will accept that. My wife decided she wasn't one of them – though she's very special in other ways, of course.'

'Has she ever been here?'

'No, it's not a place for her.'

'Doesn't she like music?'

'Not that kind of music. What about the future Mrs Keedy? Does she like string quartets?'

'We never go to concerts,' said the other. 'In fact, when I'm involved in a case like this, we never go anywhere.'

'That must be hard on her.'

'It's hard on me as well.'

There was a rueful note in his voice. Instead of visiting the Club Apollo, he'd have preferred to be spending time with Alice, trying to resolve their differences. If it ever came, their reconciliation would have to wait. Before he could question the steward further, he saw Jonathan Ulverton swooping down on him.

'Good evening, Sergeant,' he said, offering his hand. 'Am I foolish to hope that you've come bearing good tidings?'

'I'm afraid that you are,' said Keedy, shaking his hand. 'Since it featured so much in Mr Donohoe's life, Inspector Marmion felt that we should know a little more about Club Apollo.'

'And he's quite right.' He turned to Rockwell. 'Thank you, Saul – I'll look after the sergeant now.'

'Very good, sir,' said the steward, melting away.

'He's a chirpy character, isn't he?' observed Keedy.

'This place would fall to pieces without Saul Rockwell.'

'Is he that important to you?'

'He's irreplaceable,' said Ulverton. 'Now, then, what can we show you? I'd love you to join me for a meal in the restaurant but it's strictly for members only and, in any case, I expect that you're forbidden to indulge yourself when on duty.'

'If I did, the superintendent would flay me alive.'

'Then let me introduce you to the real luminaries of the Club Apollo – the Malvern Quartet. Before long, you'll be able to hear them in action. They're going to give us a taste of Boccherini, I believe. Do you like classical music?'

'I can't say that I do.'

'You may change your mind when you meet them – especially Miss Haddon.'

'Why is that, Mr Ulverton?'

'You'll see.'

After handling another lively press conference, Claude Chatfield made his way to Marmion's office. Glad to find the inspector there, he sank into a seat opposite him.

'How did it go, sir?' asked Marmion.

'It was like a bear pit in there. Where do newspapers get people like that? It was like being in front of the Spanish Inquisition.'

'The public has a right to be informed.'

'And we have a right to tailor information carefully.'

'I agree, sir. It's vital. The killer will read tomorrow's papers. We must keep him guessing as to how much we know.'

'Quite so,' said Chatfield. 'No word from Thomas Day, I suppose?'

'Not yet, sir.'

'He won't ring.'

'I still believe that he might,' said Marmion with a weary smile. 'And if he doesn't, it simply means that he hasn't been in touch with his secretary yet.'

'What's the sergeant doing?'

'I sent him back to Club Apollo.'

'Good idea – we need to find out a lot more about that place.'

'The only way we can do that properly is to become a member.'

'Well, don't look at me,' said Chatfield, huffily. 'I can't afford those exorbitant fees and I'd much rather spend time with Mrs Chatfield than with a group of men whose twin aims in life are to eat heartily and listen to classical music.'

'I feel the same about the place, sir.'

Chatfield eyed him shrewdly. 'Are you all right, Inspector?'

'Yes, I'm fine.'

'You look as if you're preoccupied with something.'

'This case is proving to be a real test for us.'

'There's something else, isn't there?'

'Yes,' conceded Marmion, 'there is. We've had some news about our son.'

He told Chatfield about the letter from a Warwickshire farm and how it had lifted their spirits. The only way that the farmer could have known his home address was that Paul was carrying some sort of identification with him. It was a hopeful sign. He hadn't entirely written off his family. While he listened sympathetically, the superintendent made one thing clear.

'I hope you're not going to ask for more leave,' he said, warningly.

'There's no question of that.'

'Good.'

'Somebody else will have to go. It looks as if it will have to be my wife.'

'What about your daughter?'

'Alice doesn't believe she'd get permission from Inspector Gale.'

'Has she *asked* her?'

'There's not much point in doing so, sir. The inspector has a reputation.'

'And it's a good one, from what I've heard,' said Chatfield. 'I can't believe that she's that hard-hearted. Look, it's very presumptuous of me but would you like me to have a word with Inspector Gale?'

Marmion was surprised. 'Would you really do that, sir?'

'If it would help, I'll do it gladly.'

'Thank you – thank you very much.'

'There's no guarantee that I'll get the desired result, of course, but one can but ask. I'm sure that Mrs Marmion would much rather go to Warwickshire with someone else. She'll have a trained policewoman with her.'

'That's true.'

Chatfield got up. 'I'll see if Inspector Gale has a home telephone number.'

254

'I can't tell you how grateful we'd be, sir.'

'You son is missing. He needs to be found.'

Without another word, the superintendent went out of the office, leaving Marmion to realise yet again that Chatfield, for all his well-known defects, did have hidden reserves of kindness. He felt that it would have been quite wrong to intervene himself on Alice's behalf. Coming from a senior officer, however, the appeal would have more weight. Even though the Women's Police Service was a separate entity, Inspector Gale was bound to respect the opinion of a superintendent in the Metropolitan Police Force. On her visit to Warwickshire, it was highly unlikely that Ellen would find their son. Alice's presence at her elbow would therefore be critical.

Marmion was musing on the possibilities of what they'd discover at the farm when the telephone rang. The noise brought him out of his reverie.

'Inspector Marmion,' he said in to the receiver.

'I was told to get in touch with you.'

'Who is this, please?'

'Tom Day.'

Working on the supposition that she'd have to travel alone, Ellen rehearsed what she was going to say when she reached the farm. She relied heavily on Alice's advice.

'What if they refuse to speak to me?' she asked.

'They *have* to speak to you, Mummy. You must insist.'

'I'm not very good at arguing.'

Alice laughed. 'That's not what Daddy says.'

'Don't listen to him.'

'You usually get your way in the end. You're very persuasive.'

'I'm not cajoling your father this time, Alice. I'm up against someone who may be very angry.'

'But he's not angry at *you*,' said Alice, 'only at Paul.'

'I can't think why.'

'There are lots of reasons. If it's a dairy farm, perhaps Paul left a gate open by mistake and some of the cows got out. Or maybe he damaged something by accident. It may even be something as simple as a row. After the way the army treated him, Paul won't be pushed around by anybody. That's the most probable explanation,' decided Alice. 'He stood up to the farmer and got himself sacked.'

'I keep wondering if he did something worse than that.'

'Such as?'

'Well, he might have stolen something from the farm or had too much to drink and got into a fight.'

'You can forget the first one, Mummy. If Paul had stolen money, the farmer is unlikely to send two pounds to him through the post. Having too much to drink is more likely. That's what he did when he first came back home,' she recalled. 'You could always smell the beer on his breath. That's what made him so aggressive.'

'I know, Alice. I was at the receiving end.'

'You'll find out the truth tomorrow.'

'That's what worries me,' said Ellen with a shiver. 'I'm frightened.'

'Why?'

'I'm afraid I'll discover Paul did something really horrible.'

* * *

Forewarned as he had been, Keedy was nevertheless unprepared to meet Dulcie Haddon. She was a dazzlingly pretty young woman in her twenties who seemed wholly unaware of her charms. He'd never met anyone so unselfconscious. The viola player's large, blue eyes sparkled and she seemed to radiate intelligence. When he joined the musicians in the room set aside for them, Keedy was introduced to each of them in turn. Nigel Haddon, leader of the Malvern Quartet, was a big, adipose, flat-faced man with a goatee beard. Evidently, his daughter had not inherited her good looks from him. Once they'd asked him about the investigation, the men fell to a discussion of the pieces they'd planned to play that evening, allowing Keedy to have a word with Dulcie. She was plainly obsessed with her art.

The quartet relied heavily on Haydn and Mozart, she explained, because they'd written masses of string quartets between them, though never one together. The two Austrian composers were dominant. It was the turn of an Italian master that evening and she talked excitedly about Boccherini's special qualities. All of it wafted into Keedy's ears and straight out again like so much smoke. The sheer detail of her musical commentary was bewildering to him. She was talking a foreign language. When it was time for them to start playing, he managed to ask her something that puzzled him. Waiting until the other three musicians had left the room, he touched her arm.

'Excuse me, Miss Haddon,' he said. 'What does it feel like to be the only woman in a building full of men?'

She blenched. 'I hate it, Sergeant.'

Then she rushed off to catch up with the others.

* * *

Marmion couldn't believe that he was talking on the telephone to a murder suspect. Thomas Day was chatting familiarly to him as if they were old friends. He claimed to be shocked at the death of his rival and pointed out, with a laugh, that there was a time when he thought he'd end up as Donohoe's son-in-law.

'His son mentioned that.'

'Then Adrian will have told you I behaved abominably. That's what happens when friendship turns to competition. Everything I ever did with regard to that family was suddenly seen in a darker light. The truth of it was,' he said, confidingly, 'that I broke off the relationship with Doreen and not the other way around. She was as meek as a lamb and would never have rustled up the courage.'

'I'm not really interested in that, Mr Day,' said Marmion. 'I simply wish to know why you chose to stay at the Devonian Hotel on the very night of the murder.'

'How was I to know that someone was lying in wait for Gilbert?'

'Did you speak to him at all?'

'Of course I didn't. I had no idea he was under the same roof.'

'I can't believe that, sir. You and Mr Donohoe were very close at one time. You must have known it was his favourite hotel.'

'I did,' confessed the other, 'but I had no idea that he was a guest at the same time as me. I never set eyes on him, I swear it.'

'What made you pick the Devonian?'

'I didn't pick it,' replied Day. 'The decision was made for me. The man with whom I've been negotiating a deal suggested that we meet there before going on to view the property the following day. I can give you his name, if you wish. He's one of the biggest landowners in Surrey. He'll vouch for me.'

'We need to speak to each other properly, Mr Day.'

Day laughed. 'Isn't that what we're doing now?'

'I like to see the person I'm talking to, sir.'

'Then you'll have to wait until tomorrow, I'm afraid. I've promised to dine with a friend and his wife tonight. They'll be very upset if I tell them I'm being hauled off to Scotland Yard because I'm a suspect in a murder enquiry. And don't worry,' he added, jovially, 'you won't have to block the ports to stop me escaping abroad. I'll be banging on the door of your office at 9 a.m. tomorrow. Is that good enough for you?'

Marmion reached a quick decision. If Day was involved in the murder, he might not even have bothered to make contact. Yet he had done so and he sounded very plausible. The possibility of his taking flight could easily be dismissed. Day had far too much to lose by doing that. He'd never desert a staff that idolised him.

'Let's make it 8 a.m.,' said Marmion. 'I like an early start.'

Keedy had long experience of feeling out of place. During an investigation into a murder at a stately home when he was a young constable, he'd tiptoed furtively around as if, at any moment, he was about to be thrown out by the butler. There had also been crimes associated with the other end of the social spectrum, giving him a glimpse into a world of such squalor and degradation that it had made his stomach heave. No human beings, he always felt, should be forced to live in such inhumane conditions. The Club Apollo made him feel out of place at three levels. The first concerned age. He was too young to be a member. Balding heads and silver manes predominated. They were allied to wealth, the second reason he could never feel at ease there. Keedy could neither afford to join the Apollo nor enjoy a privileged existence where leisure was taken for granted.

Music was the third barrier. Its strange intricacies were quite alien to Keedy. Apart from him and the steward, everyone else in the building knew and loved the concept of a string quartet. While he got pleasure from watching Dulcie Haddon play, he realised that she inhabited a wholly separate world. She fitted seamlessly into a quartet that made the music fill the air with magical precision. While he was strongly attracted to her, he knew that he could never get anywhere near such a woman. Her viola would always be in the way. Besides, he'd already made his choice and – in spite of the tiff with Alice – had no intention of changing it.

Ulverton was an attentive host, answering his questions, introducing him to members of the committee and encouraging him to explore the building at will. A murder had given Keedy rights that cost anyone else a large amount of money.

When it was time for him to leave, Ulverton showed him to the door.

'What did you think of Dulcie Haddon?' asked the older man. 'Isn't she the most wonderful musician?'

'Yes,' said Keedy, savouring the memory of her sparkling eyes.

'String quartets are so interdependent. Harmony is vital in every sense.'

'I'm sure that it is.'

'Dulcie is happy to be working for her father – unlike some people. They find the family connection rather oppressive.'

'I was one of them.'

'She's both a musical and decorative asset.'

'I was glad of the opportunity to meet her and the others.'

'Will we be seeing you again?' said Ulverton, opening the main door for him.

'Who knows, sir?'

'Give my regards to the inspector, won't you?'

'I will.'

Ulverton chuckled. 'I daresay you'd like me to give your regards to Dulcie Haddon, wouldn't you? She has that effect on everyone.'

Ellen came back into the living room in something of a daze. She'd just had a telephone call from Marmion and couldn't quite believe what he'd told her. Alice saw the look on her face.

'Is everything all right, Mummy?' she asked.

'Yes, it is.'

'Who was on the phone?'

'It was your father. He had some wonderful news to pass on.'

'Have they made an arrest?'

'It wasn't about the investigation, Alice. It was about us. When your father explained our situation to the superintendent, he offered to help. He rang Inspector Gale at home and got permission for you to have a day's leave.'

Alice was amazed. 'He actually got a *concession* from Gale Force?'

'Yes, he did. It means that we can go together tomorrow.'

'If *I'd* asked her, my request would certainly have been turned down.'

'Superintendent Chatfield managed to win her over.'

'He's not known for his charm, according to Daddy. Who cares? The main thing is that you'll have company tomorrow and I won't be anxiously walking the beat, wondering how you're getting on. And there's an additional bonus.'

'Is there?'

'Yes,' said Alice, 'I've been set free. I won't have to listen to Iris droning on about her second night out with PC Beckett.'

After a long walk around the park, they adjourned to a small restaurant for dinner. It was a fairly modest establishment with a limited menu but Iris didn't mind. With her admirer smiling at her from the other side of the table, she'd have been happy to eat anything. Doug Beckett was a police constable earning only a moderate wage. In her eyes, the very fact that he was prepared to spend his money on her was proof of his interest. The romance was still in its early stages but Iris felt that it already had a feel of permanence. She asked him about his ambitions.

'I'd like to pass the sergeant's exams,' he said.

'Are they difficult?'

'So I'm told,'

'You'll pass them with flying colours, Doug.'

'I'm not so sure. I was never the brightest pupil at school.'

'You'd make a good sergeant.'

'I'll have to get through the exams first and the truth is I'm not very good at studying. I get easily distracted.'

'Could I help you?' she volunteered.

'How would you do that?'

'Well, I know that you'll be asked about particular laws. I could read out the questions to you until you get the answers off by heart.'

He was delighted. 'Would you really do that for me, Iris?'

'Yes, I would.'

'It might make all the difference.'

'Two heads are better than one.'

'Thank you,' he said. 'I appreciate it, Constable Goodliffe.'

'Call on me any time, Sergeant Beckett.'

When they shared a laugh, he reached out to squeeze her hand.

Marmion was going through his notes about the case when Keedy returned with news of his visit to Club Apollo. The inspector was interested to hear about the impact that a female viola player had had on him.

'This young lady obviously impressed you, Joe.'

'Oh, she did. It's very brave of her to play with three older musicians who each have a lot more experience.'

'Her father obviously thought that she was good enough.'

'Yes,' said Keedy, 'he kept glancing across at her with approval. Miss Haddon only ever lifted her eyes from the music to look at him.'

'What about the members? I suppose they stared at her throughout.'

'Oddly enough, some of them didn't. They just got on quietly with their meal. Some even had muted conversations. They were definitely listening, though. When the quartet came to the end of a piece, there was always a lot of applause.'

'Were they playing Haydn again?'

'No, it was someone called Boccherini. Miss Haddon told me that he wrote many string quartets. If she'd had the time, I think she'd have given me his entire life story. Anyway,' he concluded, 'what have you been up to while I was away?'

Marmion told him that Chatfield had not only offered to try to arrange some leave for Alice on the following day, he'd actually succeeded. Somehow he'd managed to persuade Inspector Gale that it was important for her to release one of her policewomen. Keedy was pleasantly surprised.

'I didn't know that Chat was a ladykiller.'

'He talked her round, somehow. Ellen was overjoyed and I feel much happier about her trip, knowing that Alice will be beside her. The Warwickshire countryside will be very different to living in the biggest city in Britain. If she was on her own, Ellen could find it intimidating.'

'Thanks to Chat, she won't be on her own. What about Thomas Day?'

'He's popping in to see us first thing tomorrow.'

Keedy blinked. 'How do you know?'

'I had a long chat with him on the phone.'

'So he did ring you, after all.'

Marmion gave him an edited account of the conversation he'd had with the businessman, stressing how ready to help the man had sounded. He asked Keedy to be there early in the morning so that he could form his own opinion of Day. Intrigued by what he'd heard of the man, the sergeant was happy to do so.

'Did you ask him about Jean-Louis Peebles?' he said.

'No, I didn't.'

'Why not? I'm convinced there's some link between them.'

'On the basis of what you found out, so am I. But I didn't want to challenge him on the subject of Peebles. It's so much easier to lie during a phone call. I'd rather put the question to him when he is least expecting it and when I can look him in the eye.'

'Good thinking.'

'He'll have the two of us watching him like hawks.'

'What do you think his answer will be?'

'All I can tell you is that there will *be* an answer. Tom Day can talk the hind leg off a donkey. Whatever we ask him, he's not going to be lost for words. How many of them we choose to believe, of course, is another matter.'

It had been a perfect evening so far. Mindful of the fact that she tended to lose all her inhibitions if she had too much to drink, Iris Goodliffe drank very little alcohol. What had been a rather ordinary meal had tasted like a feast to her. The more she knew of Beckett, the more she liked him. She wasn't blind to his defects. He was far from handsome and his moustache didn't really suit him. There was also a morose streak in him. He lapsed too easily into reminiscences of his wife and talked about the pain of being made a widower at a relatively young age. Yet she was ready to forgive all his imperfections. Having asked her out once, he'd done so again. It meant an enormous amount to someone who was accustomed to being ignored by men as a matter of routine. Her confidence steadily grew.

'I never thought you'd even notice me, Doug.'

'Why not?'

'Well, you'd only seen me when I was on the beat with Alice Marmion. She's much prettier than me. When I'm beside her, I'm invisible.'

'Not to me, Iris.'

'Do you really mean that?'

'You're the one I asked out – not your partner.'

'She's spoken for, Doug. You'd have been wasting your time.'

'I got the woman I wanted,' he said with awkward gallantry.

'Thank you.'

Iris came close to blushing. To prolong their time in the restaurant, they ordered a second cup of coffee. She now had a good idea of the sort of man he was and the type of life he led. One detail was missing, however.

'Where do you live, Doug?'

'Less than fifteen minutes from here.'

'Is it a house or a flat?'

'Oh, it's a nice little house,' he said, proudly. 'My parents bought it forty years ago. Dad died first. When I got married, we moved in with my mother but she was very poorly and needed a lot of looking after. Bertha, my wife, helped to nurse her. It was not long before my mother passed away, then Bertha became ill herself. We never really had the time to enjoy the sense of freedom.'

'What a pity!'

'We were hoping for children but . . . well, they never came.'

'It might have been just as well, Doug.'

'I've come round to thinking that. Suppose that I'd been left with a couple of toddlers to look after on my own. I don't think I could have managed and I certainly don't think I'd have been able to stay in the police force.'

'Ideally, children need both parents.'

'No, Iris, they need two parents and four healthy grandparents. Children can't have enough people who love and look out for them.'

'My two grannies were the making of me. They looked after me in turns when my mother was working in one of our shops. And there's one big advantage of having a father who's a pharmacist. As soon as there's the slightest sign of illness, he knows what to prescribe for you. No wonder I was the healthiest girl in my class.'

'You still are glowing with health, Iris.'

'That may just be the drink we had.' They giggled. 'So you've got a nice little house of your own, have you?'

'Yes, it's more than enough for me. You must see it sometime.'

Eager to agree, Iris managed to hold back her reply. The simple truth was that she'd only known Beckett for a very short time and still had a lot to learn. When she'd been about to go on her first date with him, she'd sought advice from Alice and been warned to stay in public areas. Until she'd learnt to trust him, Alice had said, she had to exercise caution. If she went too readily into a house or a flat with him, Iris might be giving him the wrong signal. As a result of the advice, she kept him waiting for her reply.

'I'd like that, Doug,' she said at length, 'but there's no hurry, is there?'

* * *

When he got to the Mermaid Tavern, he found Everitt White ensconced at a table with a half-empty beer tankard in front of him. For once, White was not in uniform. Clifford Burge bought himself and his friend a pint, then went over to sit at the table.

'Hello, Cliff,' said the other. 'Made any arrests yet?'

'No, but it won't be long before we do. There's a big fight coming between the gangs. We'll be ready to break it up.'

'Make sure you hold on to your hat.'

'I'll be wearing this old cap, Ev. Losing my hat once was enough. You not only got it back for me, you found me someone who knows those gangs inside out. They've kept that old man supplied with stuff for years.'

'Is he being helpful?'

'He's being very helpful since I leant on him. I told him it was a choice between helping us or having his shop burnt down by the Evil Spirits.'

'That must have forced a decision out of him.'

'It did. He's on our side of the law now.'

'Good.'

'Where's Les this evening?'

'Sitting at home with the missus, I expect.'

'How is my brother doing?'

'He's one of the best men I've ever had, Cliff. Rowing any boat in the Thames is not for weaklings and ours is particularly difficult. You need the strength of an ox. Les not only has that,' he said with a grin, 'he actually looks like an ox.'

'Even as a kid, he always loved messing about on the river.'

'We don't mess about. It's serious business. The Thames is the lifeblood of the capital. Unfortunately, it's also been the cesspool. When people wanted to get rid of something nasty, that's where it would go. Luckily,' said White, 'we've got a proper sewage system now but we still get lots of filth in the water. I've fished out more dead cats than I could count.'

'Les always talks about a dead horse you saw floating past.'

'Yes, that doesn't happen every day – thank God!'

'How did it get in the water in the first place?'

'I don't think the owner threw it in there. It was still quite young. I fancy that it fell in accidentally and didn't have the strength or the skill to swim with the tide. On the other hand,' he added, winking, 'it may have deliberately committed suicide.'

Burge laughed. 'Why – did it leave a suicide note?'

'It never had the time to write it, Cliff.'

As they drank their beer, they began to talk about the differences between the Thames River Police and the Metropolitan Police. White conceded that the latter had far more territory to cover and a huge population to police. On the other hand, he argued, the river told more beguiling tales, spewing up bodies that invariably had a mysterious history.

'Look at the latest one, for instance,' he pointed out. 'He's baffled everyone at Scotland Yard. They still haven't worked out who killed him, why they cut out his tongue and how he ended up in the Thames without any shoes on. When the full story comes out, it will be fascinating. Les will tell you the same thing,' he went on, sipping his beer. 'The river is the biggest and best crime scene in London.'

Caught up in a piece of driftwood, the body was largely immersed in the water. Every time a passing vessel created a bow wave, it bobbed up and down in the darkness.

CHAPTER SEVENTEEN

Excited by the possibility of learning where Paul had been living, his mother and sister slept fitfully and rose early. When the police car came to pick Marmion up, he was able to give them a lift to Euston Station.

'Don't expect too much,' he warned from the front passenger seat.

'We won't,' said Alice. 'We'd just like to *know*.'

'For a start, we've no idea when Paul actually left the farm. That letter might have been sent a week or more after he'd been turned out of the place. Or maybe he went of his own volition,' said Marmion, thoughtfully. 'That could be the explanation.

It's a busy time of the year on a farm. If Paul walked away and left the farmer in the lurch, he'd every right to be angry.'

'We'll be realistic,' said Ellen. 'Paul has obviously caused real trouble. It's been someone else's turn to suffer at his hands this time.'

When they reached the station, the women thanked the driver and started to get out of the car. Marmion turned to his daughter.

'Is there any message for Joe?'

'Give him my love,' she muttered.

'And you can give mine to the superintendent,' added her mother. 'But for him, I'd be making this journey on my own and shaking in my shoes.'

Marmion wished them both well before being driven off. When they'd bought their tickets, they went to the appropriate platform and waited. They could see that the train was going to be full.

'I hope we get seats,' said Ellen.

'We'll make sure we do, Mummy.'

'I wonder if your father was right.'

'What about – Paul walking out on his job?'

'Yes, Alice, that could be the answer. There's a mean streak in him since he was invalided out of the army. He seemed to enjoy letting people down.'

'That's not what happened this time.'

'How do you know?'

'If Paul had just left of his own accord, the farmer would have been livid. He wouldn't have sent money after him. He'd have docked Paul's wages.'

'I never thought of that.'

'I spent half the night thinking about it,' said Alice. 'The money is critical. How was it earned and why was it sent? I know that Paul had some savings when he left but they wouldn't have kept him going for ever. He needed food and shelter. How could he buy those without money?'

'He couldn't.'

'And there's another thing to remember. His real name was on that envelope. He hadn't disowned us, after all. Whoever employed him knew him as Paul Marmion. He kept the family name. That's encouraging.'

Ellen was sceptical. 'I wonder.'

'Let's do what Daddy always advised me to do whenever I took an exam.'

'What was that?'

'Fear the worst and hope for the best.'

'I'm afraid that we may have to settle for the worst.'

'Don't feel like that. Try to see this as an adventure. We're having a nice day out in the country and we may learn something of Paul's whereabouts. For my part, it's like having an unexpected holiday.'

'How will Iris react when she realises you're not there?'

Alice sighed. 'She's going to be very, very upset.'

Bursting with joy and keen to tell her friend about the latest instalment in her private life, Iris Goodliffe stood with the other policewomen as they were given a briefing by Inspector Gale before being sent off on their respective beats. Iris was dismayed by the absence of Alice. It was unlike her to be late.

'Excuse me, Inspector,' said Iris. 'What's happened to Alice?'

'She's indisposed,' replied the other.

Iris was worried. 'She's not ill, is she?'

'You heard me. She's indisposed. Look up the word in a dictionary.'

'Who am I going to walk the beat with today?'

'Me,' said a voice.

Iris turned to see a tubby woman standing beside her with an apologetic smile. It was Jennifer Jerrold, a rather plain, dull, insignificant policewoman with thick eyebrows that met in the middle like a pair of friendly caterpillars. There was no way that Iris could confide in her. The tingling delight would have to stay bottled up inside her for another day. It would be agony.

As befitted a man whose life consisted of dashing from one appointment to another, Thomas Day arrived punctually at Scotland Yard. Marmion and Keedy were there to greet him. After introductions had been made, they all sat down and the detectives were able to make their initial assessment of their visitor. Day was a well-built man of arresting appearance, well dressed, well featured and with a full head of naturally wavy brown hair. He wore self-confidence like a halo.

'Right, gentlemen,' he began as if chairing a meeting, 'bring me up to date with the progress of your investigation.'

'If you don't mind, sir,' said Marmion, forcefully, 'we'll ask the questions.'

'I've no argument with that, Inspector.'

'Let's start with the Devonian Hotel.'

'Please do.'

'Knowing, as you did, that it was Mr Donohoe's favourite hotel, why did you agree to stay there? Weren't you afraid there might be a chance meeting?'

'I think you're misinterpreting our rivalry,' said Day. 'Just because Gilbert and I came to the parting of the ways, it didn't mean that we loathed each other. We simply had conflicting agendas. Neither of us feared bumping into each other because the times we'd had together were exceptionally good times.'

'Adrian Donohoe said that you and his father were sworn enemies.'

'How would he know? He was never party to our discussions.'

'You don't sound as if you have a high opinion of him,' said Keedy.

'I don't have any opinion of Adrian. He's an irrelevance.'

'Not any more, Mr Day. He's taking over his father's mantle. That must make him one of the most important figures in the Midlands.'

Day was unimpressed. 'So?'

'I'm sorry to take you back to the hotel,' said Marmion, 'but you didn't really answer my question. London is full of hotels. We think it's an amazing coincidence that you agreed to stay in the same one as your former partner.'

'I explained to you last night,' said Day, patiently, 'that the booking was made by someone else. I was picked up by car at Euston and driven to the Devonian to meet the client of mine who'd made all the arrangements. Of course, I was surprised at the coincidence – surprised and amused. Out of all the hotels in London, he had to pick that one.'

'You didn't have to stay there.'

'I can see that you're not in business, Inspector. You never upset a client.'

'We'll need his name.'

'I have it all ready for you,' said Day, taking a card from his wallet and handing it over. 'You can reach him at that address. He's expecting a call.'

Marmion was silenced for a moment. Day's explanation was starting to have an unwelcome ring of truth to it. Keedy took over the questioning.

'Have you ever met Mr Jean-Louis Peebles?'

'I don't believe that I have, Sergeant.'

'He works for Mr Sprake,' said Keedy, 'and you've certainly heard of him.'

'Oh, yes, I've met Norris Sprake. He's an interesting man.'

'Among other things, Mr Peebles is his chauffeur.'

'Then it's conceivable I have met him – though I can't recall ever hearing his name. And what an odd name it is, by the way. Jean-Louis Peebles. Does he come from a Franco-Scottish family?'

'Yes, he does. So you're quite sure you've never spoken to him?'

'You heard my answer, Sergeant. Why do you keep asking me about him?'

'Peebles knows you.'

Day was at last brought to a halt. After a few moments' consideration, he said that he met hundreds of different people in the course of his business activities and couldn't be expected to remember the names of secretaries, chauffeurs and other minor figures. What he could say categorically was that Peebles was no friend.

'I've never talked to him,' he claimed, 'in English or French.'

Marmion found his voice. 'You shouldn't dismiss secretaries and chauffeurs so easily,' he said. 'They are often key individuals. Take your own secretary, for example. Because she knows everything about your commercial activities, she was extremely helpful to me.'

'Mary Paige organises my entire life.'

'Then you're in excellent hands, sir.'

'She keeps a record of all my business contacts. If you search through it, the one name you won't find is Jean-Louis Peebles. Well,' he said, slapping his knees and standing up, 'if that's all you brought me here for, I'll be on my way.'

'Not so fast, Mr Day.'

'We've only just started,' said Keedy.

'Why don't you sit down again, sir?'

Day frowned and lowered himself slowly back down on to the chair.

They managed to get seats on the train but their compartment was full and left them no opportunity for a private conversation. Ellen and Alice were glad to reach their destination. Their first impression of Coventry was that it was a quaint medieval town with a lot of church spires visible. Horse-drawn vehicles mingled with the motorised traffic. They waited in the taxi queue until it was their turn. Getting out of his cab, the driver, a wizened old man with a lighted cigarette in his mouth, realised they were strangers to the area.

'Where d'you ladies want to go?' he asked, cigarette trembling on his lips.

'Corley,' replied Alice. 'How far away is it?'

'Must be around five miles, miss.'

'Then please take us there.'

'D'you have an address?'

'Yes,' said Ellen, 'it's Corley Hall Farm.'

The old man chortled. 'Then you're both in luck.'

'Are we – why is that?'

'Corley Hall is the big house.'

His manner had annoyed Marmion from the very start. Thomas Day had talked to both of them as if they were old acquaintances sharing a drink in a bar. There was no vestige of interest in the murder itself or of any concern for the Donohoe family. Marmion's second trip to Birmingham now paid dividends. He pressed the suspect about his record as an estate agent, using ammunition that had been supplied by Adrian Donohoe and that made Day look at the inspector with more respect. He had to accept that neither Marmion nor Keedy were going to be easily shaken off.

'So, in fact,' said Marmion, 'it was only when Mr Donohoe turned his attention to property development that you got interested in branching out.'

'Not really – it had been at the back of my mind for some time.'

'You were described to me as more of a follower than a pioneer.'

Day was nettled. 'Is that what Adrian said about me?'

'He's not one of your admirers, sir.'

'Well, he used to be. There was a time when it looked as if I might end up as his brother-in-law. I don't remember him sneering at me then. He was only too happy to agree with his father's assessment of me. As a future member of the family, I was viewed as a sound investment.'

'Did they always see things in commercial terms?' asked Keedy.

'They did – but I didn't. I saw it in terms of flesh and blood. Doreen was an attractive, desirable young woman. Unfortunately, it soon became clear that we were incompatible. That was the point at which Adrian decided that I'd tried to molest his sister.'

'He was only quoting her,' said Marmion.

'No, Inspector, he was deliberately misquoting her. I was working closely with her father. If I'd so much as put a hand on her thigh, he'd have been at me like a terrier. The Donohoes are a Roman Catholic family. They stick to the rules.'

'Do you have any religious affiliation, Mr Day?'

'Yes, I do, though I'm very far from being devout.'

'What did you think of the Devonian Hotel?' asked Keedy.

'Oh, we're back to that, are we?'

'The manager remembers you well.'

'I like to leave my mark on a place. Mr Armitage had a chat with me and hoped that I'd stay there again. Given what later happened, there's no possibility of that happening. Besides, I prefer to stay in Knightsbridge.'

'Is that where you'll be going on to now?'

'No, Sergeant,' replied the other, 'when you finally run out of unnecessary questions, I'll be heading for home. If you need me again, ring my secretary. Mary will know where to find me.'

'What's your opinion of the Club Apollo?'

Day shrugged. 'I've never heard of the place.'

'Your former business partner was one of the founders.'

'That's news to me.'

'Didn't he ever talk about it?'

'Not to me, he didn't. Gilbert was a deep man with a variety of interests. He divided his life up into little compartments. I only got access to the main ones. He chose to keep this club a secret from me.'

'Do you belong to *any* London club, sir?'

'No, I don't – on principle.'

After a few more questions, Marmion accepted that they'd get no further. He'd rattled Day a few times but hadn't come close to piercing his guard. He decided that it was better to send him off believing that his involvement with the police was over.

'Thank you, Mr Day,' he said. 'The interview is finished.'

'Then I bid you good day.' He rose to his feet. 'And thank you.'

'For what?'

'Your lenience towards me – I was expecting to be stretched on the rack before you got busy with the hot poker. Isn't that how you question suspects?'

'We've been discussing the murder of a man who used to be your friend. I find your comments in the worst possible taste.'

'So do I,' said Keedy.

'I didn't mean to cause offence,' claimed Day with contrition in his voice and all over his face. 'I do apologise. It was both stupid and insensitive of me. Believe me, gentlemen, I'm as anxious to see the killer caught as you are.'

'Then try being more honest the next time we speak, sir. That will help.'

Keedy was pleased to see him wince.

The journey from the station took them through the suburbs of Radford and Keresley. Neither passenger paid much attention to the little communities because their minds were fixed on what lay ahead. Alice was getting increasingly impatient to reach the farm and discover what had happened to her brother. Ellen, by contrast, was starting to regret the decision to come, certain that they were going to hear something detrimental to Paul and, by extension, to his family. She was not even sure that the farmer would deign to speak to them and braced herself against the possibility that he might send them on their way with a few harsh words. Hope was balanced by despair. While Alice felt that a great weight might be lifted from them, her mother feared that it would be replaced by a far heavier one.

When they reached a sign for Corley, they discovered that it was not really a village but a series of scattered dwellings. There was no real centre to it and no village green. They caught a glimpse of an ancient church off to their left before the vehicle swung sharply to the right and plunged down Rock Lane. The long steep hill took them past some looming red sandstone. It was not long before Corley Hall reared up on the left. To people who lived in a small house, it looked massive. It was partly obscured by the high front wall. Through the iron gates, they saw it fleetingly in its entirety. Alice noticed the carved stone gryphons on the gateposts. Centuries old, the house had a weathered look. The facade had been rendered at some stage then painted liberally with whitewash. Though time had blotched and peeled it somewhat, it still shone in the morning sunshine.

All around were rolling fields and they could see a herd of Friesian cattle chewing the cud contentedly. To the right of the house was the farm itself, a higgledy-piggledy collection of buildings and barns. A line of churns stood outside the milking parlour. Other animals were quickly in evidence. The noise of their taxi made the chickens flee but the geese held their ground. From a large shed at the rear, they could hear the grunting of pigs. But it was the dog who took charge. Racing towards them, it barked fiercely and circled the vehicle. The two women were frightened. They were very relieved when someone shouted and the dog stopped barking. Wearing old trousers, a tatty shirt with the sleeves rolled up and a pair of Wellington boots, a huge man emerged from one of the barns and strode towards them. His hands were filthy and his face grimed. When he got to the taxi, he put his hands on his hips.

'Lost your way?' he asked.

'This is where they asked to come,' said the driver.

He gazed in at them. 'Never set eyes on 'em before.'

While Ellen shrunk back in her seat, Alice was brave enough to get out of the taxi and take a step towards the man. She waved the envelope at him.

'We've come about the money you sent,' she explained.

'Who are *you*?'

'I'm Paul's sister. We're hoping you can help us.'

'Oh, yes,' said the farmer, scowling, 'I'll help you all right. Get back in that thing and go straight home. We don't want you anywhere near us.'

Iris Goodliffe was aching with frustration. Instead of being with her best friend, she was landed with a complete stranger. She felt like a child who rushes off to school to show the other pupils her wonderful new toy only to find the place utterly deserted. As she plodded along beside Jennifer Jerrold, she was pining. After walking in silence for some time, her nervous companion finally spoke.

'You're always on duty with Alice Marmion, aren't you?'

'That's right.'

'I'd love to be like her. She's so clever.'

'I know.'

'Where is she?'

'I've no idea.'

'Her father is that famous inspector who solves murders. Alice must have learnt so much from him. I wish I had a father like that.'

'We all do, Jennifer.'

'Jenny,' corrected the other. 'You can call me Jenny, if you like.'

But the hand of friendship was extended in vain. All that Iris wanted to do was ignore her partner and keep going. Without Alice there, she was lost.

During the interview, Keedy had kept notes and he now referred to them as they discussed the claims made by Thomas Day.

'I still think there's a connection with Peebles,' he argued.

'Then you'll have to find out what it is from Peebles himself because I don't think Day is going to oblige you. Listening to him, I realised why I could never go into business. All that false geniality would drive me mad.'

'It obviously works, Harv. It's made him very rich.'

'I don't care. What was your general feeling?'

'He was lying through his teeth.'

'No, I think there were one or two fairly straight answers stuck in there. And,' he went on, picking up the card Day had given him, 'there's this chap, Reginald Brimscombe. He's got letters after his name so he could be legitimate.'

'Are you going to contact him?'

'I'm not sure there's much point. Day will have him well primed.'

'If you don't want to check on him,' said Keedy, 'then I will. It will give me another excuse to call on Patrick Armitage again. Day claimed that he and his friend stayed at the hotel together. I'd like to confirm that.'

'Then he's all yours, Joe.'

When he took the card from him, Keedy glanced at it before slipping it into his pocket. He looked at his notebook again.

'I find it hard to believe he'd never heard of the Club Apollo,' he said.

'I disagree. He gave one of his few straight answers about that.'

'You can't keep something like that hidden from a business associate.'

'It was hidden from Mr Sprake, remember.'

'That's true.'

'Neither he nor Thomas Day were considered as potential members.'

'Why not, I wonder?'

The conversation was cut dead by the sudden arrival of Claude Chatfield, who opened the door and came into the room. Keedy stood up and turned round.

'Ah,' said Marmion, 'you're just in time, sir. We're discussing the interview with Thomas Day. It was quite revealing.'

'Forget him,' said Chatfield.

'Why?'

'Something more important has come up.'

'But we still feel that Day may be implicated in the murder.'

'You're talking about *this* murder. I'm interested in the other one.'

'What other one?' asked Keedy.

'A second body was fished out of the river this morning. I'm certain it's a related crime because the modus operandi is identical. The victim was garrotted and the tongue was cut out.'

'Do you have any idea who the man is?' asked Marmion.

'It's not a man,' replied Chatfield. 'It's a woman this time.'

They were saved at the last moment. As Alice was getting back into the taxi again, a tall, round-shouldered woman in her fifties came scurrying towards them. It was the farmer's wife. Having been roused by the barking of the dog, she'd come to see what was going on. Her husband still glared aggressively at the visitors but his wife was more compassionate. When she heard who the women were and why they'd come, she ignored her husband's protest and invited them into the house. The farmer stalked off with his dog yapping at his heels. Alice paid the taxi driver, who was in the act of lighting another cigarette.

'Do you want me to wait?' he asked.

'No,' said the woman. 'You can go.'

'How will we get back to the station?' asked Ellen.

'We'll find a way.'

The woman introduced herself as Binnie Vout. Big-boned, red-faced and with unkempt hair, she was wearing a smock over her faded floral dress and had on a pair of boots. There were no handshakes. She could read the question in their eyes.

'Yes, I know it's a big house but we don't live here like lords and ladies. Everyone has to work on the farm, including me and Henry – that's my husband. None of us is afraid to get dirt on our hands and mud on our boots. You'll have to take us as you find us.'

'Thank you, Mrs Vout,' said Alice. 'Having come all this way, it would have been dreadful to be sent straight back.'

'My husband's a hard man. You have to be sometimes.'

'How long was Paul here?'

'The first thing is that he didn't use that name.'

'What name did he use?' asked Ellen, confused.

'Colin Fryatt.'

'Colin was a friend of his who died in action.'

'That's what he told us to call him.'

'When did you know his real name?'

'It was only when my husband searched his belongings.' She looked upwards. 'He had a room in the attic next to the servants. It was how we got to know his real name. We were shocked. Henry didn't like being lied to and neither did I.'

'It was very kind of your husband to send the money,' said Alice, trying to strike a note of appeasement. 'When exactly did Paul – or Colin – leave the farm?'

Binnie Vout sniffed. 'It must be the best part of a month ago.'

They arrived at the morgue and were given the pathologist's initial report. While Keedy went in to view the body, Marmion read the comments. The woman was in her thirties and had been in the water for two weeks or more. Her body was hideously bloated and distorted. The cause of death was given as asphyxiation. Her tongue was missing and there was evidence of sexual interference. There would be no chance of identifying her by her clothing. The victim had been tossed naked into the Thames.

When Keedy rejoined him, Marmion was filled with sympathy for the deceased and fury at her killer. His feelings were mirrored by the sergeant.

'Her own family wouldn't recognise her in that state,' he said.

'Was there anything at all to go on, Joe?'

'No, I'm afraid not. There were no effects.'

'What about rings on her fingers or tattoos on the body?'

'There was nothing.'

'The report mentions a final indignity,' said Marmion, handing it to him. 'It looks as if the killer had some fun with her.'

'Was that before or after she was dead?'

'To a monster like that, it probably didn't make any difference. Donohoe goes into the water fully clothed while she doesn't have a stitch on her. Apart from the obvious answer, what do you deduce from that?'

'Donohoe was murdered in a hurry,' suggested Keedy, 'then tossed quickly into the river with his shoes off. The woman's death was more leisurely so the suffering was more intense. The killer took his pleasure before dumping her in the Thames. That's my guess, anyway – not that it helps us very much.'

'We have the same killer for two very different people. What's the connection between them?'

'Lord knows! I'm just relieved that I'm not in the river police. I'd hate to have hauled someone like that aboard. It's such a grotesque sight.'

'If she'd been missing that long, someone must have reported it.'

'I'll check when we get back to the Yard.'

'She can't have been employed by Donohoe or her disappearance would already have been noted. And I don't think she has any link with the Club Apollo because there are no women there.'

'You're forgetting Dulcie Haddon.'

'I was thinking of the staff there – all men.'

'That takes us on to the property company. Was she working in some way for Donohoe and Sprake? No,' he went on, answering his own question, 'or Sprake would have told us that she'd gone missing.'

'Not if he'd been instrumental in her death.'

'That would make Peebles the likely assassin.'

'I wouldn't find it difficult to believe in that, Joe.'

'Neither would I,' said Keedy. 'There's something about that man that's just not right. I still fancy that there's a link between him and Thomas Day.'

Jean-Louis Peebles had transformed his new office. Out went all the individual touches put there by his predecessor and in came some photographs of Peebles on a yacht and a painting of Edinburgh Castle. It was a much more masculine environment now and it gave him a sense of having been promoted. When the telephone rang, he picked it up with a lordly hand.

'Peebles here . . .'

'I need to see you,' said a voice.

'Yes, yes, of course,' replied Peebles, suddenly more subservient.

'Did you tell that sergeant that you knew me?'

'No, no, Mr Day, I denied it.'

'Then you didn't do it convincingly enough. He didn't believe you.'

Entering Corley Hall had been like stepping back in time. The floors were paved with stone and the walls were half-timbered. Sloping ceilings showed that there'd been a degree of subsidence over the years. Right angles were in very short supply but cobwebs were plentiful in the dark corners. The air was musty. Binnie Vout took them into the kitchen, a large room at the rear of the house with an undulating paved floor. As they sat at the table, the visitors noticed a piece of wood under one of the legs to keep it level. Through the window they could see cattle grazing in the field beyond. Ellen and Alice were already crestfallen. The news that Paul had left as much as a month ago meant that the trail had gone decisively cold.

While she made a pot of tea, their hostess told them what had happened. Her manner was brisk rather than friendly.

'Colin, as we knew him, came to us three months ago,' she recalled. 'He was looking for work and desperate enough to take almost anything. He hadn't eaten for days. Henry had his doubts but we certainly needed help so he took Colin on.'

'What sort of work did he do?' asked Alice.

'This is a dairy farm. That means a very early start. He'd be up at four in the morning to do his chores, then he'd take the dog with him and bring in the herd. When he'd got them into the standing pen, he wheeled the churns into place. They're very heavy when they're full so a pair of strong hands came in useful.'

'Did he tell you about his time in the army?'

'Yes, he was injured at the Somme, he said.'

'He was covered in shrapnel wounds and blinded completely for a while.'

'That bit was true then, was it?'

'Oh, yes.'

Binnie went on to talk about the way that their new labourer had taken on a variety of jobs. They were surprised to hear that he took the churns to the station to be loaded on to the milk train. The idea of Paul handling a horse and cart seemed incongruous. Life on the farm involved hard physical labour but it also provided him with food, shelter and the feeling of doing something useful.

'He liked it here,' said Binnie, 'and we grew to trust him.'

'Did he talk about where he'd been before coming here?' said Ellen.

'Not to me, he didn't.'

'What about your husband?'

'Henry's not a talking man. He judges people by what they do, not what they say. And Colin did well for a while.'

She broke off to make the tea then set the teapot in the middle of the table before crossing to the Welsh dresser to get three cups and saucers. Opening a drawer, she took out three teaspoons. Milk and sugar were already standing on the table. Ellen and her daughter waited patiently, ready to let the conversation go at the pace set by the farmer's wife. Conscious that Paul had left under a cloud, they didn't want to say anything out of turn. While she was pouring the tea, Binnie took up the story.

'Henry's a good man,' she said, defensively. 'He was angry when it happened, that was understandable, but it preyed on his mind that Colin left with money owing to him. In the end, he felt he had to send it after him.'

'That's how we come to be here, Mrs Vout,' said Alice. 'We've lost track of my brother completely. It's the first time we had any idea where he was so we came here straight away.'

'Well, I can't say I was pleased to see you both but you can't be to blame for what he did. The least we could show was a little hospitality.'

'We're very grateful.'

Ellen put milk and sugar into her tea and stirred it. She ventured a question.

'We still don't know why he was dismissed from here. Did he steal anything?'

'He tried to,' said Binnie. 'He tried to steal the most precious

291

thing we have. That's why Henry grabbed him by the scruff of the neck and threw him out. Don't ask for details,' she went on, voice hardening, 'because I'm not going to talk about it. The truth is, Mrs Marmion, we're sorry we ever met your son.'

CHAPTER EIGHTEEN

Claude Chatfield reacted to the latest development with commendable speed. He drafted in more detective constables and briefed them at a meeting attended by Marmion and Keedy. They admired his grasp of detail and the way he used diagrams to illustrate the points he was making. When he'd finished, he handed over to Marmion who began to deploy the new men accordingly. He reinforced a point that the superintendent had made: newspapers would give them a bumpy ride. They'd been criticised heavily in the press over one unsolved murder. A second one – related to the first – would only increase the severity of their reproaches. When the meeting broke up, Chatfield called the two of them over.

'How many more bodies are we likely to find?' he asked, ominously.

'Let's just worry about the two we have, sir,' said Marmion. 'At least we've made headway on the first investigation. Once we identify the second victim, we can look closely into her background.'

'What if she doesn't have a background?' asked Keedy.

'Everybody has a family and friends, Sergeant.'

'Then why have none of them come forward to report her missing? Any family or group of friends would worry if someone vanished for a fortnight. If most people go missing for twenty-four hours, someone will contact the police, yet they didn't do so here. When we checked the list of missing persons, nobody fitting the victim's description was on it. That's telling.'

'And what does it tell you?' asked Chatfield.

'I believe she could be a displaced person, sir. War has created hundreds of thousands of them. We have so many Belgian refugees that they outnumber our own citizens in some districts. Then we have French, Dutch and other nationalities. If some of them had fled their country entirely on their own, who is to raise the alarm if they disappear?'

'That's a sound argument, Sergeant.'

'Thank you, sir.'

'We should contact foreign communities in London,' said Marmion. 'Nobody lives in isolation. Even those who came here on their own tend to make friends. Why didn't this woman do so?'

'It's exasperating,' said Chatfield. 'We know far too much about one victim and nothing whatsoever about the other.'

'We have one key detail,' Marmion reminded him. 'The same man killed them, so they have to be connected in some way.'

'What about the obvious one?'

'We thought of that, sir. From what we know of him, it's very unlikely that Mr Donohoe had a mistress. He was a family man and, like you, a Roman Catholic. His wife is especially devout. If you'd met his secretary, Miss Kane,' said Marmion, 'you'd have realised that he was not exactly a ladies' man. Those who are,' he added, thinking of Thomas Day's secretary, 'tend to like pretty faces around them.'

'I bow to your superior knowledge on the subject,' said Chatfield, drolly. 'Where do you and the sergeant propose to go next?'

'We'll have to split up and go over old ground, sir. One of the people we've already met, I suspect, knows who that woman in the morgue is and they have a good reason for keeping the information from us.'

'Give me some names.'

'Jean-Louis Peebles is the first that comes to mind. If the victim is indeed a French refugee, she might have turned to him for help.'

'I'll bear that in mind when I speak to him,' said Keedy.

'Thomas Day would be my second contender. To speak to him, I may well have to go to Birmingham once again. That will enable me to question Donohoe's family as well. There's a lot more I need to shake out of his son.'

'Are you naming Adrian Donohoe as a suspect?' said Chatfield.

'I wouldn't put it quite like that, sir.'

'Who's next?'

'Jonathan Ulverton. He's too good to be true.'

'I'd never accuse him of being involved in two murders,' said Keedy. 'He's Mr Pickwick to the life – honest, generous, a little eccentric and the soul of decency.'

'But he's not a fictional character, Sergeant. He's real and real people are sometimes capable of the most alarming behaviour. Our prisons are full of them.'

'Peebles, Day, Donohoe's son and this fellow Ulverton,' said Chatfield, counting them off. 'Have we forgotten anyone?'

'If there was a supplementary list,' said Marmion, 'I might put the manager of the Devonian Hotel on it. That has an important place in the story. When the sergeant has finished in Richmond, I'd like him to go and see Mr Armitage again.'

Keedy grinned. 'He'll like that.'

The ordeal had continued and the pattern was repeated hour after hour. Iris Goodliffe and Jennifer Jerrold walked side by side and kept their eyes peeled. Every so often, Jennifer would ask what her partner considered to be an inane question. Iris would give her a brusque answer and ensure silence for a while. There were few incidents to distract them. From Iris's point of view, it was simply a question of walk, talk and suffer the endless boredom. Then her gloom finally lifted. Douglas Beckett stepped out of a side street to have a quick word with her. Iris was so thrilled that she hardly heard what he said. In less than a minute he was gone, hurrying to get back to his prescribed beat. Jennifer was stupefied.

'Who was that?' she asked.

'That was my gentleman friend.'

The words tasted like the finest honey.

All they could do was to sit in the kitchen, drink their tea and listen to the problems of running a dairy farm. Binnie Vout refused to say anything more about Paul, leaving her visitors feeling that their journey had been in vain. Ellen was wishing they hadn't come and Alice felt that they should first have written to the farmer instead of turning up unannounced. As it was, hours had been wasted on the enterprise. Draining her second cup, Binnie sat up.

'We'll need to get you back into Coventry,' she said.

'Is there a bus?' asked Alice.

'It only comes once in a blue moon and you'd have to walk half a mile to catch it. No, I said I'd get you back and I will. If you'd like to wait outside, I'll get my younger son to harness the horse and take you in the trap.'

'Thank you very much, Mrs Vout.'

'We can't leave you stranded.'

She took them out through the back door and led them around to the stables. They waited while she went off in search of their driver. Surrounded by noise and inhaling pungent country odours, they felt thoroughly out of place and wondered how Paul had adapted to life there. Accustomed to the populous streets of London, they felt they'd been marooned on an island. Everything was foreign to them. It was then that a figure came out of the barn and strolled towards them. She was a pretty, fair-haired girl of eighteen with the bloom of youth on her. When she first saw them, she managed a smile then she slowly seemed to work out who they might be. It brought her to a sudden halt. Alice was the first to realise that she was looking at the reason for Paul's sudden ejection from the place. He had got too close to the girl. The most precious thing that the farmer and his wife had was their daughter.

She'd been caught with Paul Marmion.

The mood in Stepney remained uneasy. People went about their business as usual and the rubble had now been cleared from the houses destroyed in the bombing. Yet there was an underlying apprehension, especially among old people. While the gangs held sway, they were all potential targets. The Evil Spirits reinforced their control over the area by patrolling it in numbers. Clifford Burge saw evidence of their determination to remain in control. Spotting a member of the Warriors daring to walk on the same side of the street as them, a group of Spirits gave chase, hurling whatever missiles they could find and hitting the youth more than once. Though he managed to outrun them, he'd be going home with bruises to remind him of his folly. Burge saw a large stone that had been hurled with vicious force at the boy. Sooner or later, he feared, the gangs would start killing each other.

'Come in, Sergeant Keedy.'

'Thank you, sir.'

'It's nice to see you once again.'

'I'm sorry to disturb you, Mr Sprake.'

'Dare I hope that you've brought us good news?'

'Unfortunately, I haven't, as it happens.'

When he called at the offices in Barnes, Keedy was given a cordial welcome. Norris Sprake was his usual mixture of charm and watchfulness. Assured at first that progress was being made, he was disturbed to hear of the second murder.

'Are you *certain* that it's linked to Gilbert's death?' he asked.

'Yes, sir, we're absolutely certain.'

'Who was the woman?'

'I was hoping that you might be able to hazard a guess or two.'

'If you're suggesting that Gilbert was involved with this person,' said Sprake, stoutly, 'then you are on the wrong track. He was a man who honoured his marriage vows. In short, the killer was not a jealous husband who murdered his wife because of her liaisons with Gilbert Donohoe.'

'How do you know that, sir?'

'We were partners, Sergeant. We worked closely together.'

'Yet you'd never heard of his association with Club Apollo.'

'That's true,' admitted the other.

'And you did say that your respective lives were not intertwined.'

'Save yourself the trouble of searching for evidence of his adultery,' said Sprake with asperity, 'because it doesn't exist.'

'We're not suggesting it does. Our question is this – since the formation of your company, have you or Mr Donohoe ever employed a woman who might fit the description of the victim?'

'I don't employ *any* women, Sergeant.'

'Yet Miss Kane worked here for years.'

'She was Gilbert's secretary, not mine. Besides, we never regarded Hattie as a typical woman. Worthy as she undoubtedly was, she always seemed part of an intermediate species.'

'That's very unkind, sir.'

'I'm not saying I didn't like her. In fact, I grew to like Hattie very much. But she'd settled for life as a spinster and it told.'

'Adrian Donohoe is more appreciative of her talents. He not only took her back to Birmingham, he's employing her in his own office.'

'That's his prerogative.'

'Indeed, it is,' said Keedy. 'Well, since you can't suggest who the latest victim might be, I'd like to speak to Mr Peebles.'

Sprake huffed. 'He won't be able to help you.'

'Your chauffeur is single, affable, very handsome and he has French blood in his veins. Please don't try to tell me there are no women in *his* life.'

Marmion was relieved to discover that Jonathan Ulverton was not as yet at the club. He'd gone home the previous evening and would be staying in Rochester that morning so that he and his committee could go through the final details of the Dickens Festival. It allowed Marmion to have a conversation with Saul Rockwell in the certain knowledge that they wouldn't be interrupted by one of the founders of the Club Apollo. The steward was shocked to hear of the second murder but failed to see what connection it might have had with Donohoe.

'The killer doesn't strike at random,' explained Marmion. 'He chooses his targets with care. We believe that there has to be a link between the two victims.'

'Well, you won't find it here, Inspector. It's a haven for the male sex. The only woman ever seen on these premises is Miss Haddon, who plays in the quartet, and she is always watched over protectively by her father.'

'What about the occasional Ladies' Night?'

'Yes, we do have women here then, but only for a couple of hours.'

'And they all tend to be music-lovers, I assume?'

'They are,' said Rockwell, 'and they're also well above the age of the murder victim. You've seen our membership, sir. Their wives are all equally mature.'

'Have you never employed female secretaries, cooks or waitresses?'

'It's against club policy.'

'Why is the Apollo so defiantly masculine?'

Rockwell smiled. 'The only way to find that out is to join us.'

'No, thanks,' said Marmion. 'I like action. This place is altogether too subdued and passive for me.'

'It does have its livelier moments, sir.'

'But they don't involve women.'

'I'm afraid not.'

Marmion appraised him. 'Did you ever meet Mrs Donohoe?'

'I had the good fortune to meet her a number of times,' said Rockwell with enthusiasm. 'She was – and still is – a very gracious lady. Whenever she came, she always spent a long time talking to the musicians.'

'How did they seem together – Mr and Mrs Donohoe, I mean?'

'They were exactly as a husband and wife should be, Inspector.'

'Could you be more exact?'

'They were *together*. That doesn't mean they spent every moment in each other's company, because they didn't. But they were a couple in a way that some of the members and their wives were not. That's no criticism,' he added, quickly. 'It's not my place to pass judgements. All I will say is that marriage means different things to different people.'

Marmion immediately thought of his own wife, a loyal, loving woman who saw very little of him and with whom he'd spent even less leisure time as the years passed. Neither of them had envisaged that kind of life when they'd first married. He'd had a job in the Civil Service that entailed regular hours. Police work had pushed them apart. He counted himself fortunate that their love had survived the changes imposed on them. Clara Donohoe was not unlike Ellen in one respect. As his business activities mushroomed, she and her husband spent most of their time apart. Yet he always knew that he could rely on her.

'What sort of a person is Mrs Ulverton?' asked Marmion.

'She's a remarkable lady,' said Rockwell. 'She has to be to keep up with her husband. Mr Ulverton is like a force of nature. Once he sets his mind on a project, there's no stopping him.'

'Mrs Donohoe told me that she had the highest opinion of him.'

'Everyone does.'

'How will the Club Apollo manage without Gilbert Donohoe?'

'Oh, it will thrive,' said the steward, proudly. 'Mr Ulverton will see to that.'

It was not until they were clear of the hubbub at Euston Station that they were able to talk without being overheard. A full compartment on the return journey had limited them to the briefest of exchanges. Ellen and Alice could now exchange thoughts.

'We came back empty-handed,' said Ellen, sadly.

'No, we didn't, Mummy. We now know for certain where Paul's been living and how he came to leave there. We ought to be pleased that he was able to hold down a demanding job on the farm.'

'It was only until he was sacked.'

'I'd like to have spoken to that girl. She backed away when she guessed we might be something to do with Paul. If he got close to the farmer's daughter, he'll have told her about how he came to be there in the first place. She'd know things that could have given us some reassurance.'

'I don't think I'd be reassured, Alice. I keep remembering what happened in Gillingham with Colin Fryatt's girlfriend. Paul molested her in a church. If he'd treated the daughter like that, the farmer would have thrashed him.'

'Stop expecting the worst of Paul,' said Alice.

'I didn't hear anything good about him today – did you?'

'No, but I'm ready to give him the benefit of the doubt.'

'He had a job with a place to live and he threw it all away.'

'Mrs Vout only told us one side of the story.'

'He let himself down, Alice. I feel ashamed of him.'

'Well, I don't,' said her daughter, 'because I don't know if he was entirely to blame for what happened. That girl might well have encouraged his interest. Don't forget the two pounds. No father would pay wages like that to someone who'd assaulted his daughter. So, I disagree with you,' she went on. 'We didn't come back empty-handed at all. We learnt that Paul is able to survive on his own. Discovering that has made the effort of going all the way to the farm well worth it.'

Jean-Louis Peebles spent the first few minutes pointing out the changes he'd made to the office so that it reflected his character rather than that of Harriet Kane. He'd grown very quickly into his new and more important role there. Keedy was happy to let him do all the talking at first. Once they settled down in their seats, he took over, telling him about the second murder and gauging his reaction. Peebles was startled.

'When was this, Sergeant?' he asked.

'We believe that she was killed at least a fortnight ago.'

'Then it was well before Mr Donohoe's murder.'

'Yes, it was. The lady stayed in the river much longer than him and it showed. I know that because I had to view the body.'

'And you have no idea at all who the victim might be?'

'We believe there's a link with Mr Donohoe. That's why I came here – to see if you or Mr Sprake could suggest the name of any woman with whom he came into contact during his time here.'

'There are none that I know of, Sergeant – apart from Hattie, that is.'

'You ferried him around London in the car a great deal,' said Keedy. 'Did you ever take him to meet a younger lady?'

'His business appointments were solely with other men.'

'Where did they usually take place?'

'It was either here or at the Devonian Hotel.'

Keedy fixed him with a long, penetrating stare and it was met with an unwavering half-smile. Peebles seemed to be telling the truth. The sergeant moved the conversation to a question where the man's veracity was in doubt.

'I asked you once before if you knew a Mr Thomas Day.'

'My answer remains the same – I don't.'

'Yet you saw a lot of Mr Donohoe when he was in London. There was a time when he and Mr Day were partners. I can't believe that his name didn't slip out occasionally. Mr Sprake would certainly have heard of him because he's one of your rivals in the property market. Did *he* never mention Thomas Day?'

'No, he didn't.'

'Would you swear to that?'

'Bring me a Bible and I'll do it instantly,' said Peebles. His brow furrowed. 'Are you telling me that this Mr Day is a *suspect*?'

'We'd just like to know who his associates in London are.'

'Well, I'm not one of them, Sergeant, and neither is Mr Sprake.'

The half-smile had a slight tinge of defiance now. However much he pressed Peebles, he decided, he wouldn't get an honest answer. Backing off, he changed his line of questioning.

'By the way,' he said, 'when I was talking to Mr Sprake just now, I thought he was looking rather strained.'

'He's not in the best of health, Sergeant.' He opened a drawer and took out a couple of bottles of pills. 'He needs regular medication.'

'Are they all painkillers?'

'By no means,' said Peebles. 'He always carries a supply of them himself because his legs are a constant problem. But he also suffers from diabetes and from a number of other conditions. Nurse Peebles has to be on hand all the time.'

'There are very few chauffeurs who could do what you do, Mr Peebles.'

'I've had to develop all kinds of skills as I go along.'

'You must be very adaptable.'

'I do my best.'

After shadow-boxing with him for a few more minutes, Keedy saw that he wouldn't be able to break down the man's defences so he took his leave. Peebles went straight to the window and watched as the detective left the building and got into the waiting police car. As soon as it drove off, Peebles grabbed the telephone, anxious to pass on a warning to Thomas Day.

Arriving back at Scotland Yard, the first thing that Marmion did was to report to the superintendent. Chatfield, he discovered, was in conference with the commissioner so he went back to his own office. He'd scarcely had time to sit down when there was a tap on the door and, when it opened, the face of Everitt White peeped around it. Marmion beckoned him in and got up to shake his hand. Though he was in uniform, White explained that it was his day off and he'd come in the hope of hearing the identity of the second body he'd hauled out of the river that week.

'We haven't a clue who she is, Everitt,' confessed Marmion.

'Somebody must be missing her.'

'Well, they haven't told us about it.'

'Have you made an appeal to the public?'

'The superintendent did that. It will be in all the papers but it may be in vain. If someone was going to come forward, they'd have done so long before now.'

'The press will give you some rough treatment over this, Harvey. It was bad enough when the victim was a wealthy businessman. Now that we've found a naked body in the Thames, they'll be saying that no woman in London is safe.'

'We'll find the killer,' said Marmion, evenly.

'Do you have much to go on?'

'We have precious little – beyond the fact that one man killed both victims.'

'He must be a sadistic bastard. I saw the bruises on that woman. She really suffered before he put her out of her misery.'

'I'm grateful that you found her and not me. Joe Keedy told me what she looked like. How do you cope with terrible sights like that?'

'The first time is the worst,' said White. 'In my case, it was when I was in the merchant navy. When we spotted the body of a man floating in the sea we didn't realise it had been there for a long time. A boat was lowered and two of us were sent to recover him. I'll never forget it.'

'Why?'

'When I reached out to grab his arm, it came apart from the

body and more or less dissolved. I threw up straight away. We got the rest of him in a net but bits of him kept breaking away. After that experience,' he concluded, 'I reckoned I could put up with anything. That's why I joined the river police. Nothing could scare me.'

'Why have you taken a special interest in this latest one?'

'It was because she didn't stand a chance. Joe Keedy will have told you about the marks on her wrists and ankles. She was tied up and defenceless. When he'd had his money's worth out of her, he killed her. People like that don't belong in a civilised society. Catch him, Harvey.'

'We'll get him in the end.'

'Let me know when you do. I'd like a quiet word with him.'

'It won't be allowed, Everitt, and you know it. I appreciate how you feel but the law must take its course. He'll finish up at the end of a rope.'

White glowered. 'Then at least let me pull the bleeding lever.'

The manager was busy when Keedy arrived at the Devonian Hotel so he had to wait for some time until Armitage finally emerged from his office. When he saw the sergeant, he gave him a reflex smile. It soon disappeared when Keedy told him about the second murder and its apparent connection with Gilbert Donohoe's death. Armitage appeared to be distressed that the latest victim was a woman.

'Do you know who she was?' he asked.

'Her identity is still unknown, sir.'

'So why have you come to the Devonian? I hope you're

not going to suggest that the woman might also have been a guest here?'

'That's highly unlikely, Mr Armitage.'

'I'm glad to hear it.'

'I came to tell you that Thomas Day is no longer a phantom figure. Inspector Marmion tracked him down and we both interviewed him.' Taking out his wallet, he extracted the card and handed it over. 'He claims that he stayed here for one night with this gentleman, Mr Brimscombe. Could you please confirm that?'

'I thought you'd been carefully through our records when I was off duty,' said Armitage, sullenly. 'You must have seen his name.'

'I can't remember doing so.'

'Then let's go and check, shall we?'

He led Keedy to reception and went behind the counter. Flicking the pages of the ledger, he went through the list of guests on the relevant day. After a glance at the business card, he gave a nod.

'Mr Brimscombe did stay here that night. He and Mr Day had rooms next to each other.' He handed the card back to Keedy. 'Is that any help to you?'

'Yes, it is. It would also be helpful if you could tell me whether he's stayed here before. Brimscombe is an unusual name. Is he a regular guest?'

'Not as far as I know.'

'That was the impression Mr Day gave us. Brimscombe made the booking and that's how they both came to stay here.'

'That may well be so, Sergeant, but this is the first time I've ever heard of the gentleman. As a rule, I try to speak to any new guests but Mr Brimscombe eluded me somehow – though I did have a chat with Mr Day.'

'We had a long conversation with him and you just proved that he told us at least one lie. My feeling is that it was Day who made the booking because he was keen to be here at a time Mr Donohoe was a guest.'

'Oh, there's no doubt about that,' said Armitage.

'How do you know?'

Stepping out from behind the counter, he took Keedy into the lounge.

'When you questioned my staff in my absence,' said Armitage, resentfully, 'you missed out the most important person.'

'And who's that, sir?'

'It's Vincent, our barman.' He indicated the diminutive figure behind the bar. 'He sees everything and forgets nothing. When *I* asked him about Mr Day, he came out with an intriguing piece of information.'

'What was that?'

'On the night that he was killed, Mr Donohoe was having a drink in here with a man who was almost certainly Thomas Day. Vincent gave a detailed description of him. Mr Day ordered a single malt whisky.'

'That can't be right,' said Keedy, confused. 'Donohoe fell out with him. The two men hated each other.'

'Then they must have kissed and made up. My barman's eyesight is as good as his hearing. What Vincent saw and heard when he brought their drinks across was two friends chatting happily about old times. In other words . . .'

Keedy completed the sentence. '. . . they *arranged* to meet here.'

Sir Edward Henry was alarmed to hear details of the second murder and to be told that they had no idea who the victim might be. The consequences were clear.

'The newspapers will use this as a stick to beat us with,' he complained.

'It was ever thus, Sir Edward,' said Chatfield.

'Isn't there something with which we could appease them?'

'Reporters are wild animals. The more you feed them, the more they want.'

'I'm glad to hear that you've put more men at Inspector Marmion's disposal.'

'It isn't just a question of resources, Sir Edward. What we need is help from the public. Until someone comes forward to tell us who that poor woman is, the investigation can't really move forward.'

'So we'll remain under attack.'

'Yes – unless we can deflect press interest.'

'And how do you suggest that we do that, Superintendent?'

'You've already set it in train,' said Chatfield. 'Your decision to tackle delinquent gangs in Stepney was both wise and necessary. If we can make an example of some of them, it will send out a message to the others. Sergeant Keedy met the man you appointed for the task – Detective Constable Burge. What he heard from him sounded promising. Burge was an inspired choice.'

311

'You were the one who recommended him.'

'I always keep my eyes open for signs of talent.'

'It's paid off in this case,' said the commissioner. 'Burge's reports have been very detailed. He's already gathered more intelligence than anyone else managed to do. According to him, a major confrontation is imminent.'

'Then I hope we're prepared to deal with it.'

'We have a unit on standby. All we need is a word from Constable Burge.'

'But how will he know when gang warfare is about to erupt?'

'He has someone advising him who knows most of the little thugs involved.'

Chatfield nodded grimly. 'That should be a great help.'

He had to be careful. All of the gangs had spies, sharp-eyed lads whose job was to monitor the activities of their rivals and warn of any police activity in the area. If he was seen too often in the same place, Clifford Burge knew that he'd arouse suspicion so he made sure that he didn't visit the junk shop very often. As it was, the old man who ran it was already in trouble with some of the youths who'd done business with him. Having seen him earlier that morning, Burge walked casually past the place hours later. When he saw that nobody was watching, he stepped smartly into the shop. The old man curled a lip.

'Thought you'd be back sooner or later,' he said.

'Any news?'

'There might be.' He held out a hand. 'It comes expensive.'

Burge grabbed him by the throat and pushed him against the wall.

'You have a simple choice, old man. Help us or be arrested. Which is it?'

'I can't speak,' spluttered the other.

Burge released his grip. 'What's your answer?'

'Don't I get *anything*?' wailed the old man.

'Yes, you get a safe place to live in and a guarantee that those lads won't be in a position to get their revenge. That's a pretty good reward, I'd say.'

'I'd prefer money.'

'What have you heard?'

'It's today,' said the other, sourly. 'The Warriors attack at midnight.'

Marmion was known for the speed with which he could make important decisions. The moment Keedy told him about what he'd learnt at the Devonian Hotel, the inspector led him out of the building and ordered the waiting police car to take them straight to Euston Station.

'Going to Birmingham is getting to be a habit,' said Keedy.

'I'm hoping that this may be the last visit, Joe.'

'Third time lucky?'

'Why not?' asked Marmion. 'We're due a bit of good fortune.'

'Who would have thought that Donohoe and Thomas Day were friends again?'

'We don't know that they are.'

'But the barman at the Devonian saw the pair of them drinking together.'

'I've been known to have a pint with Chat before now,' said Marmion, 'but that doesn't mean he and I are friends. Appearances can be deceptive. It may be that Day somehow convinced Donohoe that he'd buried the hatchet when, all the time, he was setting him up for execution.'

'Do you really think Day was the killer?'

'Oh, he'd never actually commit the crime. He doesn't have enough courage for that. He'd make sure he was somewhere else at the time with a cast-iron alibi.'

'What are you going to say to him?'

'Nothing at all, Joe – he's all yours.'

'Why are you leaving him to me?'

'You were the one who found out what he was really doing at the Devonian. That information has given the whole investigation a fillip. He did say he'd be going back to Birmingham so you should be able to corner him in his office.'

'I look forward to it.'

'If in doubt, threaten him with arrest. That usually loosens tongues.'

'He's a slippery customer, Harv. I'll need my wits about me.'

'You have my complete confidence,' said Marmion, slapping him on the knee. 'Tell him that we have a low opinion of people who tell us lies.'

'What will you be doing?'

'I'll be carrying out interviews of my own.'

'Who will you start with – Donohoe's son?'

'No, there's a more important person than him.'

'His mother?'

'His secretary, Joe,' said the other. 'We've been overlooking a valuable source in Harriet Kane. She's seen the drama unfold from the inside. I know that she was hired for her discretion but, in the interests of justice, I believe it's time for her to be indiscreet.'

CHAPTER NINETEEN

After their visit to the Warwickshire countryside, they were relieved to be back in the urban sprawl of London. They belonged there. When they got back to the house that afternoon, Ellen kicked off her shoes and put them aside to be cleaned. As well as picking up mud stains, they were giving off a faintly unpleasant smell. Once she'd put her slippers on, she made a pot of tea and sat down to drink it with Alice.

'Aren't you going back to work?' she asked.

'No, thank you. Gale Force gave me the day off and I'm going to take every last minute of it.'

'Iris will be missing you.'

'She's the main reason I'm staying here, Mummy. I'm not in the mood to listen to memories of a night out with PC Beckett. It's cruel, I know, but I can only take so much of it.'

'You're only saying that because you and Joe are . . . having difficulties.'

'That's probably true,' conceded Alice. 'Am I being selfish?'

'Iris will have you back tomorrow. Make the most of your time off.'

'That's what I intend to do, Mummy.' She spooned sugar into her cup and stirred her tea. 'Why did Paul do it?'

'Do what?'

'Why did he call himself Colin Fryatt? It's such a strange thing to do. Colin was a pale shadow of Paul. He could never compete with my brother. The funny thing is that it was the other way round in reality.'

'I don't understand.'

'It was Colin who wanted to be Paul. He aped him in every way but could never actually match him. The only thing he ever did better than Paul was to play that mouth organ. Otherwise, he was just a copycat.'

'Paul didn't want the farmer to know his real name.'

'I can't see why.'

'He wanted to start a new life with a new identity.'

'But why pick that one?' asked Alice. 'It's weird. And it was so unfair on the farmer's daughter. She'd have believed that he really was Colin Fryatt.'

'So?'

'She'd befriended a dead man.'

'That never occurred to me,' said Ellen in dismay. 'That's an awful thing to do to the girl. I just hope she never finds out the truth.'

'My hope is that he doesn't go back for her.'

'Do you think that Paul would do anything as dangerous as that?'

'In the state he's in, he could do anything. It all depends on how close they got. If it was just a friendship, he'll forget all about her. But if Paul was in love with her – and if she felt the same about him – he might try to rescue her.'

'That's her home, Alice. She's not in prison.'

'It may seem like it to her.'

'I can't believe Paul would do such a thing,' decided Ellen. 'His judgement may be unreliable but even he would realise there was no future in being on the run with a girl of that age. They'd set the police on to him.'

'That idea might excite him.'

'Where could they go and how could they eat?'

'They'd manage somehow.'

'You've got me worried now, Alice. I'd rather talk about something else.'

'Very well,' said the other. 'The simple truth is that we'll never guess what Paul is really going to do because we don't understand how his mind works.'

'I used to when he was younger,' said Ellen, plaintively, 'but not any more.' She looked quizzically at her daughter. 'What are you going to do about Joe? That's the other thing preying on my mind.'

'You worry far too much.'

'Then stop giving me cause for anxiety. This . . . estrangement has upset me.'

'It's not an estrangement, Mummy.'

'Then what would you call it?'

'I'd call it stupidity on both our parts. We each want our own way.'

'Your father and I were the same at your age. We had our rows but we made sure they never pushed us into opposite corners.'

'I desperately *want* a compromise,' said Alice, earnestly, 'but something is holding me back from suggesting it.'

'Joe has the same problem, I fancy.'

'So what do we do?'

'Nothing at all,' said Ellen. 'You wait for the dust to settle, then you carry on where you left off. Above all else, forget about a date for the wedding.'

As the train steamed through Warwickshire, Marmion glanced out of the window and wondered how his wife and daughter had got on at the farm. It grieved him that something as important as Paul's sudden reappearance had to be set aside in favour of the murder investigations. News of where Paul had been working made him want to down everything and get to Corley Hall Farm as fast as he could. He chided himself for being unable to trace him there during his ten-day search. It was pure luck that a letter was sent to his son. Chance had contrived what he could not.

For his part, Keedy was thinking about Alice, but not because she'd been on the trail of her brother. He wished that their compartment was empty and that he'd be able to talk to Marmion in the same way that Alice talked to her mother. But it was impossible. Too many things got in the way. Besides, he believed, men never shared their emotional woes. They preferred to keep them hidden. He'd find it much too embarrassing to wear his heart on his sleeve. All he could do was to brood on his folly in falling out with the woman he loved and hope that they'd soon be together again.

As the train began to slow, he realised that they were approaching their destination. Marmion leant across to give him some advice.

'Don't let him talk his way out of it, Joe. Put him under pressure.'

'I'll do my best.'

'You've got the advantage of surprise. Use it to the full.'

Jean-Louis Peebles was reading some correspondence when the telephone rang. It was a summons from his employer. Putting the letters aside, he hurried downstairs and went into Sprake's office. The old man looked pale and drawn.

'I don't feel very well,' he explained. 'Take me home, Jean-Louis.'

'What about your tablets, sir?'

'I've had two of those.'

'Did they have no effect?'

'None at all – get me out of here, please. And don't worry about me,' said Sprake, struggling to his feet, 'after a couple of hours in bed, I'll be as right as rain.'

Peebles steadied him. 'Sergeant Keedy noticed how unwell you seemed.'

'As you know, I have good days and bad days. This is one of the latter.'

'Lean on me, sir. We'll soon get you out of here.'

He helped Sprake out of the room and into the wheelchair waiting in the corridor. Once the old man was seated in that, he could be wheeled out to the car then lifted into the back seat. Peebles put a blanket over his legs. When he got into the driving seat, he reached for the peaked cap beside him and put it on.

'What did the sergeant say to you?' asked Sprake.

'It was nothing important, sir. To be frank, I don't know why he bothered to speak to me. It was a waste of his time.'

Starting the engine, he drove slowly away from the building.

Thomas Day was taken aback by the unheralded arrival of Keedy. For once in his life, he was lost for words. He invited his visitor in, offered him refreshment and tried to buy time to compose himself. Keedy looked around the office. Patently, it belonged to a prosperous man and had his character imprinted all over it. Declining the offer of a cup of tea, Keedy hurled his first accusation.

'Why did you lie to us, Mr Day?'

'I wasn't aware that I did.'

'You told us that you never even met Mr Donohoe when you stayed at the Devonian Hotel. You were only there at the behest of Mr Brimscombe.'

'That's right. Reggie Brimscombe will corroborate that.'

'And will he corroborate the fact that you were seen drinking with Gilbert Donohoe in the lounge?' Day's lip twitched involuntarily. 'Thanks to the manager, I discovered the truth. The barman remembered you well. I spoke to him. You drank a single malt whisky. Mr Donohoe preferred a brandy.'

'Where is all this leading, Sergeant?'

'Unless you can start telling the truth, it could lead to your arrest. How would your staff react if they saw me taking you out of here in a pair of handcuffs?'

'There's no need for that, surely?'

'That's up to you, sir.'

Day lapsed into silence. Caught off balance, he was trying to regain his equilibrium. He realised that Keedy was more intelligent than he appeared. When he'd been questioned by the two detectives, it was the inspector who'd asked the more searching questions. He now learnt that the sergeant also had the power to unnerve him.

'You don't understand the situation,' said Day.

'That's because you concealed it from us, sir.'

'I was forced to do so.'

'Were you? I didn't see anyone twisting your arm.'

'The business world is vicious, Sergeant. It's a case of dog eat dog.'

'Oh, I think the dinner menu at the Devonian runs to something a lot tastier than dog.'

'I was speaking figuratively.'

'You mean that you're telling me a lie by means of a metaphor?'

'I'm not going to bandy words with you. What happened was this . . .'

The explanation came out so smoothly that it was almost as

if Day had been rehearsing it before Keedy arrived. There had recently been a truce between him and Donohoe, the estate agent said. Since they were operating largely in the same city, it was foolish of them to maintain their earlier stance of hostility. When he heard that Donohoe was going to London for a few days, Day stayed at the same hotel so that they could patch up their differences. It was not something either of them wanted to broadcast to the wider business community. In any case, they didn't intend to go into partnership again. They simply wanted to put their relationship on a better footing because they were each in a position to do the other favours. In the course of his speech, Day gathered momentum. His voice became more assured and his gestures more expressive.

'So you see, Sergeant,' he said in conclusion, 'your journey was in vain.'

'All you've done is to substitute one pack of lies for another.'

'I dispute that.'

'Why go all the way to London for a meeting with Mr Donohoe that could much more easily have taken place here in Birmingham?'

'I preferred to meet him on neutral ground.'

'You originally said you had no idea Mr Donohoe was actually staying at the hotel.'

'That bit wasn't quite true.'

'Ah, you've made a concession at last.'

'There's no need to be sarcastic.'

'Then don't give me the opportunity, sir,' said Keedy, 'and don't start waving your friend Mr Brimscombe at me either. I think that you went to the Devonian for one reason and that was to meet Mr Donohoe. What isn't so clear is what part you played in his murder.'

'I played none at all,' shouted Day, leaping to his feet.

'We can do without a display of righteous indignation.'

'I'll be reporting you to your superintendent after this.'

'He's looking forward to meeting you, Mr Day. Ever since your name came to our attention, he's wanted to know more about you. So have we. You fascinate us. If you want to get us off your back, all you have to do is tell us the truth. I know it will be painful for someone so accustomed to dishonesty as you but, for your own sake, I suggest that you make the effort.'

Day retreated into silence and looked like an animal at bay.

Marmion arrived at the factory in Northfield to discover that Adrian Donohoe was not there. Instead of having to ask his permission to speak to Harriet Kane, he found her conveniently alone in the office.

'Mr Donohoe is at home,' she told him. 'He's had word that the body will soon be released for burial so he's discussing funeral arrangements with his mother.'

'I see.'

'It's not the ideal time to approach him, Inspector.'

'Actually, I came to see *you*, Miss Kane.'

She was astounded. 'Me?'

'Yes,' he said, 'and I'm pleased to see that you're alone for once. We're unlikely to be interrupted.'

'There's nothing I can tell you.'

'I suspect that there's a great deal. Before I ask any questions, however, I should tell you that we've recovered a second body from the Thames. It's that of a woman who was killed in exactly the same way as Mr Donohoe.'

She goggled. 'Who was she?'

'We don't as yet know but there's clearly a link with the murder of your former employer.'

He gave her an outline description of the woman and asked if she had any idea who it might possibly be. Harriet insisted that she did not, adding that Donohoe had very few women in his circle and none who could possibly be the deceased. Marmion began to probe into her background.

'Your family must be pleased to have you back here.'

'They are, Inspector.'

'Did they imagine that you'd ever finish up working directly for one of the city's most celebrated businessmen?'

'No, they didn't. The most they hoped was that I'd get a job I liked that would give me a regular income.'

'Until the move to London, did you always live at home?'

'Yes, I did.'

'How did you keep in touch with your parents?'

'We corresponded. Since they don't have a telephone, it was the only way.'

'You must have exceptional commercial skills.'

'Mr Donohoe thought so.'

'So does his son, by the look of it. As soon as you became available, he snapped you up for himself.' She looked uneasy. 'Am I simplifying the situation?'

'I just do what I'm told.'

'How does your predecessor feel about it? Until you came here, another secretary must have occupied this office. Without warning, you supplanted her. That must have come as a shock.'

'I suppose that it did.'

'So why was Adrian Donohoe so keen to have you?'

'That's something you'll have to raise with Mr Donohoe himself.'

'I could hazard a guess, Miss Kane.'

'Could you?'

'Yes,' said Marmion. 'I get the strong feeling that he wants you here so that he can keep an eye on you.' He saw her swallow hard. 'Now why should he do that?'

Claude Chatfield was preparing his notes for the next press conference when the commissioner tapped on his door and came into his office. Sir Edward Henry was anxious to know if the second murder victim had been identified yet. When he heard that she was still without a name, he was irritated.

'The killer is not making it easier for us, is he?'

'No, Sir Edward.'

'He did the same thing with his first victim.'

'In that case,' Chatfield pointed out, 'we overcame the handicaps he gave us. By dint of visiting the man's tailor, Inspector Marmion soon identified him. This second victim – the first one, chronologically – will be a more difficult proposition.'

'Sergeant Keedy felt that she might be a foreigner.'

'That's a possibility.'

'I think that it's worth mentioning to the press.'

'I agree.'

'We may know nothing about the victim but this other murder has given us some additional information about the killer. Donohoe's death showed that the man was ruthlessly efficient. We've learnt that he took a perverted delight in killing that poor woman.'

The commissioner bunched a fist and struck the palm of his other hand.

'He must be taken off the streets of London, Superintendent.'

'He will be, in due course.'

'You'll have to edit the post-mortem report very carefully.'

'That's exactly what I've been doing, Sir Edward,' said Chatfield, indicating the paper in front of him. 'The first detail I excised from it was that – as in Donohoe's case – her tongue had been cut out.'

'Does the killer have some weird fetish regarding tongues?'

'I don't know, but the two victims have suffered more than enough indignity as it is. I'm not having a full account of what they endured splashed across the front pages of the newspapers. It would be indecent.'

'Your judgement in these matters is impeccable.'

'Thank you, Sir Edward.'

The commissioner was on the verge of leaving when he recalled something.

'When we spoke earlier, we talked about my initiative in Stepney.'

'That's right – is their further news?'

'There is, indeed. We've received word from Detective Constable Burge.'

'What did he say?'

'Battle will be joined tonight.'

* * *

Thomas Day had always flattered himself that he had the gift of the gab. Combined with his appearance, his articulacy was a potent weapon. He had talked many clients into deals they wouldn't otherwise have even considered. Faced by Keedy, however, his silver tongue proved ineffective. Every time Day came up with what he thought was a convincing explanation, the sergeant shot it down with ease.

'Facts are facts, Mr Day. You were seen in the bar at the Devonian, chatting amicably to Mr Donohoe.'

'Yes, I admit it freely. Gilbert and I did meet up in the bar. What's wrong with that? Have you never had a drink with a friend, Sergeant?'

'Of course, but none of them went off to be murdered soon afterwards.'

'What's the point of me telling you the truth if you don't believe it?' said Day, angrily. 'You really are the most exasperating man.'

Keedy was irritatingly calm. 'Why don't we wipe the slate clean of all your lies and start again?' he asked.

'I've nothing else to say.'

'Then it's my turn. You've never been involved in a murder investigation before so let me tell you what always happens. We interview suspects and get the most extraordinary claims from them. At the end of it all,' Keedy stressed, 'the facts eventually come out and the people, like you, who thought they could pull the wool over our eyes end up with red faces.' He smiled. 'Can you understand what I'm telling you, Mr Day?'

'I think so.'

'If you're not completely honest now, you'll be made to look a fool when we have the full picture. That will hardly be good for business, will it? Do you wish to be quoted in national newspapers telling us brazen lies?'

Day was worried. 'My name won't be in the papers, will it?'

'We might even arrange for a photograph.'

'That could be damaging for me.'

'It's self-inflicted damage, sir.'

'Listen, Sergeant,' said Day, getting to his feet, 'I will swear on the Holy Bible that I didn't kill Gilbert Donohoe and was not party to his murder in any way. What could I possibly stand to gain from it?'

'You'd gain a lucrative partnership with Norris Sprake.'

Day gasped. 'That's absurd.'

'You've been in contact with his right-hand man, Mr Peebles, haven't you?'

'Why on earth should I do that?'

'I'd be obliged if you'd tell me.'

'Peebles is only a chauffeur. I've no reason to talk to him.'

'Oh, I suspect that you have, Mr Day. It may interest you to know that I called on him earlier today. Peebles is a clever man but he doesn't have your talent for deception. When I mentioned your name, he gave himself away. You know each other well.' He raised his eyebrows. 'Am I right?'

Day sank back into his chair with an air of defeat.

When he questioned a woman, Marmion didn't like putting her under any real pressure. It felt wrong to him. In the present case, however, he believed that it was necessary. Harriet Kane knew things that were relevant to the investigation so they had to be drawn out of her one way or the other. He'd always felt that his daughter would be good at interviewing women. Alice had the patience, persistence and mental clarity that was essential. She might well be able to get things out of another woman that a man could not. Unfortunately, there were no female detectives as yet and policewomen, with their limited roles, were not involved in murder cases. Scotland Yard was a male bastion. Harriet Kane could only be interrogated by a man.

'I think that Mr Donohoe is hiding something from me,' said Marmion.

'Then you ought to speak to him, Inspector.'

'I need to learn a few things from you first.'

'There's nothing more I can tell you.'

'There are lots of things, Miss Kane. You may regard them as useless bits of information but they could be valuable to us. Let's start with a name you're bound to recognise – Thomas Day.'

'What about him?'

'He and Gilbert Donohoe broke up their partnership but we've reason to believe that it was about to be renewed. Is that true?'

'Yes, it is.'

'Did Mr Day ever ring your former employer?'

'Yes, Inspector.'

'And did he ring him when you were both at the offices in Barnes?'

'Now and then.'

'Was Mr Sprake aware of those phone calls?'

'They were private.'

'Did Mr Donohoe deliberately conceal them from him?'

'He saw no reason to mention them,' she said, cagily. 'I daresay that Mr Sprake had private calls of his own that he didn't discuss with Mr Donohoe. They each had separate contacts. Most of Mr Donohoe's calls were to his wife. He hardly needed to give Mr Sprake details of those.'

'What about his son? When he was in London, was he in touch with Adrian?'

'No, Inspector.'

'Why was that?'

'There was no need.'

'Could you enlarge on that?'

'Adrian had a job to do and he did it well. His father preferred to let him get on with it quietly.'

'Did they spend any time at all together?'

'Only when there was a special event in the family,' she replied.

'So Adrian had to wait for birthdays and anniversaries before he actually got to see his father – is that what you're saying?'

'They were both extremely busy.'

'Do you know what I think?'

'No, Inspector.'

'I think that Mr Donohoe arranged his life in such a way that he barely set eyes on his son. He certainly didn't promote him in the way you'd expect. Instead of being a major figure with a full range of responsibilities, Adrian is a factory manager with a grudge against his father.'

'Running this factory is an important job,' she said, chin jutting out.

'It's a small, offshore island in an international empire.'

'Adrian doesn't quite have his father's flair.'

331

'That's because he's not encouraged to have it,' argued Marmion. 'He's been held back on purpose and I'd like to know why. What was Adrian's crime? What did he do – or not do – to upset his father?'

'I can't tell you that, Inspector.'

'Does that mean you don't know – or are you holding something back?'

'Speak to Adrian.'

'I'm speaking to you, Miss Kane, because I was hoping for a measure of honesty. I can't get that out of Adrian. It's almost as if he's afraid of the truth.' He put his face closer to hers. 'Are you afraid of it as well?'

'I don't know what you're talking about,' she murmured.

'Family secrets.'

'You'll have to look somewhere else for those.'

'I'd rather concentrate on you because you're not part of the family.'

'My loyalty is to them, Inspector.'

'Why did Adrian make you his secretary?'

'You've asked me that already.'

'I'm hoping for a better answer this time.'

'It will be the same as before.'

'Then I'll have to provide my own answer, won't I?' said Marmion. 'On the day when I informed him of his father's murder, Adrian Donohoe jumped on a train to London to sort various things out. Your position was one of them. You were told to clear your office so that you could return to Birmingham with him and take up a post as his secretary. And why did he make that decision?'

'He valued my experience.'

'He wanted to keep you quiet, Miss Kane.'

'I didn't have to take the job.'

'Oh, I think you did. If you'd refused, he could have made it very difficult for you to get another job with the same status. The Donohoe name packs a big punch around here. Where else could you expect to work alongside someone with such enormous power in the business world?'

'I like it here.'

'You have no choice.'

'It's not fair of you to question me like this, Inspector,' she said, voice cracking. 'I've done nothing wrong. I can't see why you're doing it.'

'You *know* something, Miss Kane. Because of that, Adrian Donohoe took you from that office in Barnes and brought you straight here. I'm sure you're well paid and that may be a consolation to you.'

'I didn't accept the post because of the money.'

'No,' said Marmion, looking deep into her eyes, 'you accepted it because you had no choice. There's only one reason why he wanted you here: Adrian needs to ensure that you keep your mouth shut.'

Harriet Kane promptly burst into tears.

Alice Marmion sat opposite her mother and read the paper they'd bought at Euston. It contained an article on the murder of Gilbert Donohoe and criticised the apparent inability of the police to solve the crime. Her mother had been reading a novel but, when Alice lowered the paper, she saw that Ellen had fallen fast asleep. In repose, her face looked old and anguished. The book lay open in her lap. Sympathy welled up inside Alice. Her mother was having a hard time of it. She was married to a man she rarely saw and was the mother of a son who'd brought her untold grief. Whether he was at home or in some unknown part of the country, Paul was causing her pain and heartache. Alice, too, made a contribution. Having come home ostensibly to support her mother, she'd only added to her general distress by moping about Joe Keedy.

Was she looking at her own future? The thought made Alice sit up in alarm. If she married a detective, would she have to stay at home for interminable hours while he was involved in a complex case? If they had children, would she have to cope with a fractious son and a daughter whose relationships with the opposite sex were never untroubled? It was a daunting prospect.

Having achieved what he thought was a minor triumph against the estate agent, Keedy caught a taxi and gave the driver the Edgbaston address of the Donohoe family. He and Marmion had arranged to meet there. As luck would have it, Keedy arrived in time to see the inspector paying the driver of his own taxi. The detectives were able to have a brief discussion about what they'd learnt from their respective visits. Both felt that they'd made progress. They approached the house. Knowing that the family was preoccupied with the funeral arrangements, they felt that it was a bad time to call but their arrival was, in fact, welcomed by Clara Donohoe. She was keen to speak to Marmion, so Keedy was left to talk to her son.

Adrian Donohoe was in the office, studying the preliminary draft they'd made of the order of service for the funeral. Until he was told about the second murder, he was rather offhand. The news concentrated his mind.

'And you're *certain* it's the work of the same killer?'

'The pathologist had no doubt about that, sir.'

'Where was the body found?'

'It was over a mile upriver from where your father was discovered. Had she not been entangled in some driftwood, she might have stayed underwater even longer. I just wish that we had a name to go with the body.'

'Yes, I'd be interested to know who she was.'

'I'm more interested to know who the killer might be,' said Keedy. 'That's why we're following every possible line of enquiry.'

Adrian frowned. 'Is that what I am – a line of enquiry?'

'The inspector feels you have valuable information to give us.'

'I've already told you everything I know, Sergeant.'

'That's not strictly true. I've just spent a testing hour or so with Thomas Day. He pretended that he'd told us everything as well. It was only when I pointed out that he'd simply given us a tissue of lies that he provided some real help. And no,' he added, quashing the other man's attempt at interrupting him, 'I'm not saying that *you* told us any lies, sir. Because your father was a murder victim, it was in your interest to tell the truth. We just feel that we didn't hear enough of it.'

'What is it you wish to know?'

'Well, it would help if we knew why there was such tension between you and your father. There's no denying it, Mr Donohoe. It's too blatant.'

Adrian looked at him with mingled resentment and curiosity, annoyed to be questioned about something he regarded as a private matter yet wondering how far the sergeant could be trusted. Keedy could see that he was being weighed up.

'We're not here to pry into family affairs, sir. Our only interest is in finding the brutal killer of two victims. You can help us and, as we've said before, we treat everything you tell us in confidence with respect.'

'You won't pass it on to the papers?'

'I give you my word.'

'What proof do I have that you'll keep it?'

'Your father's death was, mercifully, quite swift. That's not the case with the other victim. She was stripped naked, tied up and raped.'

Adrian grimaced. 'That's disgusting!'

'Before she was tossed into the river, her tongue was cut out. Open a newspaper tomorrow and you won't find a single one of those details there because we've kept them back. In other words, we exercise discretion, Mr Donohoe. That's what I'll do with whatever you tell me,' promised Keedy. 'I'll protect you and your family from embarrassment.'

Adrian looked at him for a long time before he made his decision.

'I could do with a cup of tea,' he said, pressing a button in the wall. 'Would you care to join me, Sergeant?'

Keedy grinned. 'Is there any chance of a biscuit, sir? I'm hungry.'

* * *

In preparation for the battle between the two gangs, Clifford was making a final tour of the area. He'd already picked out a number of houses where he felt he could hide the men who'd be detailed to help him. Since it would be close to the centre of the action, the junk shop was another place where his reinforcements could lie in wait. Pausing on a corner, he was surprised to see Everitt White strolling towards him. The older man was not in uniform.

'Why aren't you at work, Ev?' asked Burge.

'I'm always at work. Coppers never rest.'

'Is it your day off?'

'Yes, I was on duty through most of the night so they signed me off until tomorrow. Have you heard that we found another body?'

'No – who was he?'

'*He* was a naked woman who'd been in the water far too long.'

White told him about the discovery and how he'd gone to Scotland Yard to see if they had any idea of the victim's identity. Burge was intrigued to hear that she'd been killed by the same man who dispatched Donohoe. The case had now become even more intriguing. Burge's desire to be part of a murder enquiry was strengthened. Meanwhile, there was another problem to address. He told White about the Warriors' plan to reassert their authority over the Evil Spirits.

'Where will you be, Cliff?'

'I'll be lurking in the junk shop with four men.'

'Make it five men. I'll join you sometime after eleven.'

'It's not your fight, Ev.'

'Oh, yes it is,' said White with a throaty chuckle. 'I was born here so I've got a stake in this part of the East End. It needs cleaning up and I'm not going to miss out on any of the action.'

Alone in the music room with the inspector, Clara talked about her favourite sonatas and how she'd loved to play them for her husband in his rare moments of relaxation. When she'd finished, she sat down on the stool in front of the grand piano. Marmion gazed at the magnificent instrument with admiration. He'd bought an upright piano when, as a child, Alice had shown an interest in learning to play, but it was tiny compared to this one. The grand piano would fill the entire living room at the Marmion house. He could see that Clara didn't really want to talk about music. She wanted to be in the room where she felt most at home and was getting herself gently into a mood to answer his questions. At length, he sat opposite her.

'I feel ready to talk now, Inspector.'

'First of all, I have to tell you something, Mrs Donohoe, and it's not very pleasant. However, I'd rather you heard it from me than saw it in tomorrow's newspaper. It would give you a shock.'

'Why – what's happened?'

Minimising the detail, he told her about the second murder and she brought a hand up to her mouth. The fact that the crime was connected to her husband's death was like a physical blow to her. Marmion gave her time to recover.

'That's terrible news,' she said at length. 'Tragedy strikes another family.'

'We don't yet know who that family is, alas.'

'Thank you so much for telling me, Inspector. You were quite right. Had I seen the story in a newspaper, it would have upset me greatly.'

Marmion sought to calm her down a little by changing the subject.

'By the way,' he said, 'your husband knew a good string quartet when he saw one. Sergeant Keedy heard them playing and said they were wonderful.'

'The Malvern Quartet has four quite brilliant musicians.'

'The sergeant kept talking about the viola player.'

'That would be Dulcie Haddon,' she said. 'She plays the instrument superbly. The viola's role is largely supportive, of course, but no less important for that.'

Marmion let her talk on until she seemed to be back on a more even keel.

'Before I came here,' he began, 'I spoke to Miss Kane at the factory.'

'What on earth is she doing there?' exclaimed Clara. 'Harriet shouldn't be working at all. She needs time to mourn just as the rest of us do.'

'It was your son's decision, Mrs Donohoe, and I fancy that Miss Kane was happy to agree to it. While she's at work, she has no time to brood on the horror of what happened.'

'But she's known my husband for so long. His death will have wounded her.'

'She seems to have recovered from the initial shock. Being back in the place where she was born has been a big help to her.' He paused for a few seconds. 'What will happen to the Club Apollo?'

'It will go on as before, Inspector. That's what Gilbert would have wanted.'

'I was thinking about *your* involvement.'

'Oh, I'll stay away for a while until things . . . settle down. In time, I hope, I'll return on Ladies' Night to hear the Malvern Quartet play. It won't be the same without my husband, of course, but he'll be there in spirit.'

'How much time did he devote to the club?'

'As much as he could – Gilbert adored his music.'

'Mr Ulverton told me that he and your husband made a large investment in it.'

'Well, it will bear fruit, Inspector. The initial outlay has more or less been repaid and there's a waiting list to join. I don't know the details but I'm told that the Club Apollo will soon start turning a profit. It's such a shame, isn't it?' she went on. 'At the very moment when Gilbert was about to get the last of his money back, he was killed. Isn't that an appalling coincidence?'

Marmion said nothing.

Keedy had the feeling that he was at last getting through to Adrian Donohoe. The man was no longer treating him with complete disdain. A measure of trust had been established between them. It was gratifying. Keedy didn't rush. He waited until he'd drunk his tea and finished eating his biscuit.

'I finally got some truth out of Thomas Day,' he said.

'That was an achievement.'

'In view of what you told the inspector about him, it may surprise you to know that Mr Day was about to go back into business with your father.'

Adrian was aghast. 'Tom Day is a crook.'

'I'm only telling you what he said. Since he became a property developer, he's been very successful. Your father judged him on that success and not on his moral standards. They met at the Devonian Hotel to discuss plans for a merger. Later that night, Mr Donohoe was murdered.'

'Then you need to arrest Tom Day at once.'

'He's not involved, sir. I'm certain of that. Our attention is now turning to Mr Sprake. What your father was discussing with Mr Day was how to ease Mr Sprake out of the company. They had an ally in a man who worked closely with Sprake.'

'Are you talking about Peebles?'

'He's been in contact with Mr Day for weeks. Sprake, as you know, is not in the best of health. He doesn't have the strength to fight off a takeover. What he might have, however, is the strength to hire a killer,' said Keedy. 'Your father was staying in the background and letting Day keep in touch with Peebles. It looks as if Sprake discovered the plot to get rid of him and struck back at your father.'

'Then why don't you take him into custody?'

'We need more evidence to do that, sir.'

'I never trusted Sprake. He's too cunning.'

'Thomas Day and your father had their share of cunning. They were trying to take advantage of a disabled old man in poor health. Peebles would have given them bulletins about him so that they could move in when he was at his weakest.' He paused to let Adrian take the information in. 'I'm sorry if this shows your father in a bad light, Mr Donohoe.'

'What upsets me is his lack of judgement. Going into

business with Tom Day once more was a grave error.'

'What about the plot to seize the company from Mr Sprake?'

'Business is business, Sergeant. The weakest go to the wall.'

'In other words, you're not shocked by your father's takeover bid?'

'Nothing shocks me about my father,' said Adrian, quietly.

'He baffles us, sir. We've never met anyone who had a variety of interests. How did he manage to keep abreast of all of his business activities? He must have had the most enormous energy.'

'He did.'

'Now that we're talking properly at last,' said Keedy, 'perhaps you could explain something that's been troubling us from the start. Every so often, your father seems to have vanished for a couple of days. He'd simply walk out of the Devonian Hotel without saying a word. Where did he go? We know that he didn't go to Sprake's house or to their offices in Barnes or to the Club Apollo. Have you any idea where he *did* go?'

Adrian bit his lip and fell silent. He stared at Keedy for a long time, trying to decide if he could be trusted with information that he'd kept to himself and never expected to share. The circumstances had made his decision untenable now and he realised that the police needed all the help they could get. The more they knew about Gilbert Donohoe, the more likely they were able to identify his killer.

Keedy prompted him. 'I think you know the answer, sir.'

'As a matter of fact,' replied Adrian, 'I don't, though I did make the effort to find it. My father did disappear for days on end. It's true. There were lots of other things about his behaviour that worried me. The worst of it was that I couldn't discuss it with anyone else in the family. I had to cope with it on my own.'

'What did you do?'

'I did something you may regard as shameful, Sergeant. I hired a private detective. Isn't that a terrible thing to do – paying someone to spy on your father?'

'You obviously expected him to find something.'

'I did. However bad, I had to know the truth.'

'Yet you didn't get it. The man you hired let you down.'

'No,' said Adrian, taking a deep breath. 'He was good at his job. He picked up a trail and followed it. What he didn't realise was that he himself was being followed. He was beaten up so badly that he was in hospital for six weeks. I had to pay for him to have major surgery.'

'Did you hire someone else?'

'No – I'd learnt my lesson.'

'So your father *knew* what you'd done?'

'As a result, he froze me out in every way. On the rare occasions when we actually met, he hardly said a word to me. He just gave me a warning look. That was enough for me.'

'You've just made a lot of things clear, sir.'

'I'm relying on your discretion.'

'You're also telling me that we're likely to find something out about your father that may be very unpleasant.'

'I'm certain of it, Sergeant.'

'It's going to come as a real blow to your mother and your sisters.'

'They'll be shattered. They worshipped him.'

'What about you, sir?'

'I loathed the sight of him,' said Adrian, almost snarling. 'When I heard that someone had murdered my father, I was delighted.'

CHAPTER TWENTY

While her mother was cooking the meal, Alice Marmion was wondering whether she should spend the night at home or return to her lodging in case Keedy tried to call on her there. If she stayed at the house, she'd at least have company and might even still be awake when her father returned. There was, she knew, a third alternative. Instead of going back to her own room, she could wait outside the house where Keedy lived and surprise him. What she didn't know was how late he'd be and if he'd welcome the sight of her lurking outside the front door. Going to the window, she glanced out and saw that it was raining steadily. The idea of keeping vigil outside Keedy's house suddenly lost its appeal. There was another strike against it. Because it was cheaper to do so, he lived in a comparatively rough area. If a woman was seen loitering in the street after dark, she could easily be mistaken for a prostitute. That decided it. Alice had only two real choices.

'I'm not sure whether to go or stay, Mummy,' she said.

'You know what *I'd* like you to do.'

'Yes, you'd like me to come back home for good.'

'Until you get married, anyway,' said Ellen.

'I'm not sure that I *will* get married now.'

'What a ridiculous thing to say!'

'Attractive men are few and far between. All the best ones have gone off to war. If I fall out with Joe, he'd be snapped up by another woman in a jiffy. I've seen the way they look at him. It annoys me.'

'I don't think *you'd* be short of suitors, Alice.'

'I don't want them. I already have the man I want – at least, I did.'

'You still do. Be patient.'

'If only I had the chance to speak to him!'

'That chance will come.'

'How many years do I have to wait until it comes?' Ellen laughed. 'It's no joke, Mummy.'

'Then stop being silly. You and Joe are both sensible adults. This spot of bother will soon blow over and you'll wonder why you took it so seriously.' She used a fork to prong the potatoes in the saucepan. 'These will need a few more minutes.'

'It was clever of you to get so many potatoes. They're like gold dust.'

'Everything is getting scarce. The Germans are starving us out.'

'This war can't go on for ever.'

'I'm beginning to believe that it can, Alice.' She put the fork down. 'I keep wondering how your father will react when we tell him about that farm.'

'He'll be angry that he wasn't able to track Paul to Warwickshire.'

'We should have asked what he looked like.'

'What do you mean?'

'Well, has Paul grown a beard? Does he wear his hair long? If he's changed his appearance, it will make it more difficult to find him.'

'Do you want to go back to the farm?'

'No, thank you,' said Ellen, pulling a face. 'I felt so uncomfortable there.'

'I worry about that girl. What happened between her and my brother?'

'We'll never know.'

'Seeing him thrown out must have been upsetting for her. I remember how impressionable I was at that age. Things that I can shrug off now used to torment me.'

'They still do, Alice.'

'Being with Joe has helped me to grow up.'

'I agree,' said Ellen. 'Being without him is your problem.'

'That's horribly true,' said Alice with a hollow laugh. 'I've been thinking about Mrs Fryatt.'

347

'You hardly know the woman.'

'I've been wondering what she'd say if she knew that Paul was calling himself Colin Fryatt. I've got a feeling she'd be very upset.'

'*I'm* very upset as well. It's unsettling.'

'Are you going to mention it to Mrs Fryatt?'

'No, I'm not letting Paul upset *her* as well.'

On the way back to London, the detectives had the luxury of an empty compartment for part of the way and were therefore able to discuss at length what they'd each found out. The visit to Birmingham had been a revelation to them. It was as if a veil had been lifted from the Donohoe family.

'I knew that Adrian was hiding something,' said Marmion.

'Hiring a private detective like that was a very big decision. He must have nursed suspicions about his father for some time before he was forced to act.'

'Where does he think Donohoe was during those disappearances?'

'He still doesn't know,' said Keedy. 'He told me that he'd rather not find out now. He hopes that we can solve the murder without having to show the world what his father has been up to. I warned him that was impossible.'

'When you lift the lid of a sewer, you can't prevent the stink.'

'I put it more gently than that, Harv.'

'That makes a change.'

'What about Thomas Day?'

348

'He might unwittingly have done us a favour,' said Marmion. 'If Sprake found out that Day and Donohoe were plotting against him, he'd be tempted to get his revenge on his former partner. We need to tackle him about it.'

'He obviously didn't know that Peebles was helping the plotters.'

'No, the chauffeur is a sly devil, Joe. They picked the right man. Since he was with Sprake every day, he made a good spy.'

'Peebles was playing with fire, betraying his employer like that.'

'They must have dangled a huge reward in front of him.'

'If Sprake did hire someone to kill Donohoe,' said Keedy, 'he couldn't have been acting alone. He'd need help. For a start, he'd have to know when Donohoe was leaving the Devonian Hotel.'

'Perhaps he was in league with the ideal person.'

'Armitage?'

'Nobody was better placed than the manager to watch Donohoe and he'd probably have been delighted to assist. Don't forget that Donohoe rejected his application to join the Club Apollo.'

'I can't understand why he'd want to join in the first place. Armitage still has some life in him. Why should he want to spend an evening listening to music with a lot of tired old men?'

'There's no accounting for taste, Joe. Take our beloved superintendent, for example. He's mad about growing marrows. Who'd have thought that a man like him would be a passionate gardener?'

The train thundered on before finally starting to slow down. Since they were likely to have other passengers joining them very soon, Marmion came to a decision.

'I suggest that we report to Chat before going on to see Sprake.'

'Are we going to arrest him?'

'In the first instance, we'll just rattle his cage.'

'What about Peebles?'

'Tell him you questioned Day. That will scare the daylights out of him.'

'I'd love to know how they bribed him.'

'In my opinion,' said Marmion, 'they offered him security of tenure. In other words, he'd keep his job with the company. Peebles must be fed up with driving Sprake everywhere and making sure that he takes his pills every day. He wants to spread his wings. Wouldn't you in his position?'

He was taking no chances. To avoid the possibility of arousing too much interest, Clifford Burge abandoned his patrol and went to ground for a few hours. Plans had been put in place to bring a lot of officers to the area after dark. He hoped that they wouldn't come in vain or he'd get the blame. His informer, the old man in the junk shop, had overheard two members of the Stepney Warriors talking about the plan to batter their rivals into submission. The boys had come into the shop in search of weapons. Pretending to go off into the back room, the old man had heard every word. Reluctantly, he'd passed on the details to Burge.

His main worry was that the old man would lose his nerve and warn the Warriors to abort the attack. If that were the case, a large number of policemen would have been deployed to Stepney in vain. Everitt White would be furious. Hoping for the chance to kick a few adolescent backsides, he'd feel cheated. There'd be no free pints in the Mermaid for Burge after that. He'd have to avoid the river policeman for a while. With so much hanging on the success of the operation, Burge started to have doubts. How reliable was the old man's information? Was the attack really timed for midnight? How could all the gang members possibly be there then?

For the other policemen, it would be a routine operation; for Burge, it would be much more. Success would make his promotion more likely while failure would delay it by years. His future at Scotland Yard lay in the hands of two feral gangs who were fuelled by hatred and bent on violence. What if they let him down?

The commissioner was pleased to hear that something positive was being done at last. Having heard the report from his detectives, Chatfield had gone to Sir Edward Henry's office to tell him about the visit to Birmingham made by Marmion and Keedy. The superintendent was confident that they'd taken strides forward.

'What about the second victim?' asked the commissioner.

'Her identity still remains a secret, alas.'

'Editors always get excited when naked females are found dead. Two of them have rung me already and pressed for details. If an old woman in a fur coat had been dredged out of the river, they wouldn't have shown anything like the same interest.'

'The sexual element is always titillating,' said Chatfield. 'It's deplorable.'

'But it sells newspapers.'

'Sadly, it does.'

'Marmion and his sergeant have done well today. I hope you told them so.'

'They had sufficient praise, Sir Edward. Too much applause tends to give them inflated ideas of their abilities. I always guard against that.'

'Is an arrest in the offing?'

'As a first step, they're simply going to bring Mr Sprake here. If he's interviewed at home, he has a degree of comfort. When he's hauled in here, however, he's in more hostile surroundings.'

'From what you've told me, he sounds like a devious individual.'

'He won't be quite so devious when we've finished with him,' said Chatfield. 'I'll interview him myself and drag the truth out of him somehow.'

During the drive to Richmond, they were acutely conscious that they hadn't eaten for several hours. When Keedy suggested that they might stop at a cafe for a snack, he was overruled by Marmion.

'Duty comes first, Joe.'

'I have a duty to stop my stomach rumbling.'

'Do it afterwards.'

'Chat will never know that we had a quick meal.'

'When we've delivered Sprake to him, we can have a real feast.'

'You're a hard taskmaster, do you know that?'

'I just want to get the job done.'

When they arrived at the house in Richmond, they saw the car standing outside. Evidently, the chauffeur was there. In fact, in response to the ringing of the bell, it was Peebles who opened the door.

'What are you doing here?' he asked, eyes widening.

'We've brought you regards from Thomas Day,' said Marmion. 'Sergeant Keedy had a long chat with him this afternoon and he's told us about the way you've been spying on Mr Sprake for him.'

'I've been doing nothing of the kind.'

'You betrayed your employer. It's high time he knew about it.'

'Let us in so that we can talk to Mr Sprake,' said Keedy.

Peebles raised his palms. 'He's not here.'

'Don't play tricks with us.'

'It's true. He was taken ill at work and asked me to bring him back here. His condition deteriorated so much that I called the doctor. He had him moved out of here at once. Mr Sprake is in hospital.'

They'd finished the meal and done the washing-up so they were relaxing in the living room. The idea of staying there overnight was beginning to exert a seductive appeal. Alice was not looking forward to a journey across London to the house where she had a small and rather cheerless room. She shared the bathroom with other female lodgers and had no real privacy. Being at home again was refreshing.

'If you don't mind,' she said, 'I'll stay the night.'

'You don't have to ask permission, Alice. Stay whenever you wish.'

'I feel so weary. I need an early night.'

'You might want to change your mind about that.'

'Why?'

'What if your father brings Joe back with him and you're snoring in bed?'

'There's a fat chance of Joe turning up tonight.'

'Is there?'

Alice saw the smile on her mother's face and realised that she'd asked for Keedy to be brought back in the police car. In her own way, Ellen was trying to help. She wanted her daughter to have the opportunity to speak to Keedy again before their relative positions began to harden.

'He doesn't know that you'll be here, of course,' said Ellen, 'and I wasn't going to force you to stay. It had to be your decision – and it was the right one.'

'Thank you, Mummy.'

'The rest is up to you and Joe.'

'And there was me thinking I'd be in bed by nine-thirty.'

'That's far too early.'

'It is now,' said Alice.

'And you won't have to worry about facing Iris Goodliffe

354

in the morning. When she starts telling you about this police constable of hers, you'll be able to tell her about your detective sergeant.'

The disappointment of hearing that Alice was indisposed had now been forgotten. Iris Goodliffe was in a buoyant mood again. When she'd had a fleeting moment at work with Douglas Beckett, he'd asked her if she was free to go out with him that evening. It was a mark of how much he'd enjoyed their two earlier dates. Iris was cock-a-hoop. She'd have even more to boast about when she met Alice the following day. After being overlooked by men for years, she'd now attracted someone who found her company so enjoyable that he couldn't get enough of it. The third invitation in a row from Beckett had moved their relationship on even more.

Looking at herself in the mirror, she brushed her hair up at the back and anchored it with a large slide. Then she applied a little make-up and studied her features with new interest. Iris had always accepted that she was plain and unappealing. Beckett disagreed. Whatever he saw in her, he obviously wanted more of it. Her confidence soared. She'd made an even greater effort to look smart and desirable for him this time. After the pleasure he'd brought into her life, he deserved it. Having turned up early for their first date, she kept him waiting this time and arrived ten minutes late. He waved away her apologies and fell in beside her. Arm in arm, they walked a few blocks and went into a pub. The slight nervousness between them vanished with the first drink. After a second one, her inhibitions began to dissolve away completely.

'Let's go for a walk,' said Beckett, slipping an arm around her waist.

'Yes, I could do with some fresh air.'

'Thank you so much for coming out with me again.'

'I should be thanking you, Doug,' she said.

'Are you happy with the way things are going?'

'I'm very happy.'

As they came out of the pub, they linked arms again and strolled along almost jauntily. Beckett was grinning and Iris felt as if she were floating on air. They turned down a side street and stopped outside a house. Detaching himself from her, he took out a key and unlocked the front door.

'Where are we?' she asked.

'I've got something to show you, Iris.'

'What is it?'

'Come on in and you'll see. It's a surprise.'

Doubts began to arise for the first time but she was unable to respond to them. Taking her hand, he drew her into the house and shut the door behind them. Her nice, quiet, respectful friend then disappeared to be replaced by a wild man with a single objective. Rushing her into the living room, he pushed her down on to the sofa and stopped her protests by kissing her fiercely and pushing his tongue down her throat. His hands were everywhere, squeezing her buttocks, feeling her breasts and lifting her legs so that she swung to one side and lay horizontal on the sofa. Holding her down by his weight, he got on top of her and began to kiss her even more desperately. Iris was in a panic. All she could think about was escaping. There was no chance of appealing to him because she couldn't speak with his mouth clamped to hers. She tried to shove him away but he was too heavy. When he moved sideways so that he could get his hand up her skirt, she realised that he was determined to get what he wanted. It was terrifying. Iris was a virgin at the mercy of a strong man. She was raw, inexperienced and unready. Still with his lips pressed hard against hers, he got a hand on her knickers and began to pull them down.

Iris reacted by reflex. Grabbing the slide in her hair, she swung her arm and jabbed the side of his face hard enough to draw blood. Beckett howled in pain and released her, pulling out a handkerchief and holding it against his cheek. Iris took advantage of the moment to push him off, roll to the floor then haul herself up. Before he could stop her, she scampered out of the house as fast as she could. She didn't stop running until she reached the safety of her home.

Her romance was over.

'We're sorry to intrude at such a time, sir,' said Marmion.

'You have your job to do, Inspector.'

'Our evidence is starting to point in your direction.'

'I'll be interested to hear it.'

Norris Sprake was propped up in a hospital bed. His face was a strange colour and he looked as if he could barely keep his eyes open. The detectives felt embarrassed at having to level their accusations against him when he was in such a poor state of health.

'I would ask one favour,' said Sprake. 'If you mean to arrest me, please wait until *after* the operation. I've been admitted as an emergency, you see. They're going to try to keep me alive for a little longer.'

He told them that he had a number of medical problems but that it was the angina that had finally struck him down. Though he'd obeyed all of the doctor's advice, he couldn't prevent himself from developing complications that might yet prove fatal. That depended on the skill of the surgeons.

'What makes you think that I sanctioned Gilbert's murder?' he asked.

'Thomas Day told me about their plan,' said Keedy. 'He and Mr Donohoe were plotting to take over the property company and push you out. When you learnt of their scheme, you must have been enraged.'

'I was upset rather than enraged. I thought Gilbert was a friend.'

'Day had enlisted the aid of your chauffeur, Jean-Louis Peebles. He told them how feeble your health really was.'

'Yes,' added Marmion, 'the man you trusted most turned against you.'

'What arrant nonsense!' said Sprake.

'We have Day's word for it, sir.'

'Don't listen to him. He's too stupid to realise that Peebles was acting on my orders. I sensed that Gilbert was getting restive and looking for someone to replace me so I asked Jean-Louis to do a little spying on my behalf.'

'You *knew* about the plot all along?'

'I not only knew, Inspector, I'd taken steps to circumvent it. Gilbert and that slimy partner of his, Tom Day, were heading for a huge disappointment. Before that happened, however, Gilbert managed to get himself garrotted.'

'We believe the killer was in your pay,' said Keedy.

'No, he wasn't. I'd have much preferred to keep him alive. I'd have loved to have seen his face when he realised that I'd outflanked him. Instead of seizing the company from me, Gilbert would have been booted out himself.'

'So Peebles was on *your* side all the time?'

'He owes a lot to me, Sergeant.'

Keedy traded a glance with Marmion. What they'd just heard had proved that Sprake was not a party to the murder. The old man had no reason to lie. He was about to have a major operation from which he might never recover. They knew that people tended to speak honestly at such a time. Sprake was innocent.

As the evening wore on, Stepney was blanketed by darkness. The men moved silently into position, forming a circle around the area where the hostilities were expected to break out. Burge supervised the placement of the various officers with care. When he'd finished, he withdrew to the junk shop with four of the men. White was already there, determined not to be left out.

'This is going to be a real achievement for you, Cliff,' he said.

'Only if the information I had was correct.'

'What if it isn't?'

'Then I'll be in serious trouble, Ev.'

'How far can you trust the old man?'

'He won't dare double-cross me after my warning.'

'What warning was that?'

'I took a leaf out of *your* book,' said Burge, 'and tried some old-fashioned policing. If he let me down, I told him, I'd put his head between the rollers of that mangle over there and keep turning the handle until I'd squeezed every last drop of blood out of him.'

It was late when the police car dropped them off outside the house. They were tired and jaded. Certain that Sprake was somehow implicated in the murder, they'd misread the evidence. Marmion was ready to stay up half the night with Keedy to discuss the case until they both fell asleep. They felt they were on the verge of finding the solution to the crime. All it would take was some intensive discussion. As they walked to the house, the front door opened for them.

'I thought I heard the car,' said Ellen.

'I've brought Joe back with me,' said Marmion. 'He can sleep on the sofa.'

'You're very welcome, Joe.'

'Thanks,' said Keedy.

'How did you get on at the farm?' asked Marmion.

'Come into the kitchen and I'll tell you.'

'I'd like to hear the story as well,' said Keedy.

'Then someone else will have to tell it to you,' she said. 'Alice is in the living room. Why not ask her?'

She whisked her husband off to the kitchen and shut the door behind them. Keedy was nonplussed at first. He hadn't expected Alice to be there and wasn't at all sure what to say to her. A full minute passed as he dithered. In the end, the door to the living room opened and Alice looked out.

'Are you coming in or aren't you?' she asked.

'Hello, Alice.'

'Hello.'

'How are you?'

'I'm waiting for you to make a decision.'

'Oh, I'm sorry,' he said.

He followed her into the room and they stood facing each other.

'This is a real surprise, Alice.'

'Is it a good surprise or a nasty surprise?'

'It's a good one – a very good one, in fact.'

'That's all right, then.'

There was a long pause as their eyes locked and their feelings took over.

'What happened at the farm?' he asked.

'We believe that Paul got too friendly with the farmer's daughter.'

'So where is he now?'

'We've no idea. He was sacked almost a month ago.'

'Then why didn't they get in touch with you earlier?'

She moved closer. 'Do you *really* want to talk about my brother, Joe?'

'No, I don't.'

'What *do* you want to talk about?'

'I'm not sure. What about you?'

'I'll go along with whatever you suggest.'

He grinned. 'This is not the right place for the suggestion I have in mind.'

'They'll be in the kitchen for quite a while.' She stepped into his arms and kissed him. When she pulled away, there were tears in her eyes. 'Don't let's argue like that again. It was all my fault.'

'No, it was mine.'

'You're arguing already!'

Laughing together, they hugged each other and rocked happily to and fro.

'Did I hear Daddy say that you'd sleep on the sofa?'

'I'd be ready to sleep on the floor if I can be near you, Alice.'

'I've got a much better idea,' she said. 'You can have Paul's room.' She kissed him gently on the lips. 'It's next to mine.'

The Evil Spirits had no trouble getting together for the midnight celebration. Those with watchful parents sneaked out unseen. Those who simply did what they liked walked brazenly out of the front door, confident that no member of the family would dare to challenge them when they got back. Days earlier, some of them had broken into a pub cellar and stolen crates of beer. The fact that they were too young to drink legally only added to the excitement. They were the masters now. It was time to have a party. The venue was the ramshackle shed that had once belonged to the Stepney Warriors. When they asserted their dominance over their rivals, they'd seized the shed and turned it into their headquarters. There was no electric light so they brought plenty of candles. Bottles of beer were passed around. It wasn't long before they were giggling, singing and boasting about their triumph. Since they outnumbered the Warriors, they believed they could be in power indefinitely.

Their rivals, however, had other ideas. After gathering together in the darkness, they crept slowly towards what they still thought of as their shed. The Spirits had left a sentry outside but he was swigging from a bottle and showed more interest in what was happening inside the shed than outside. Greg Wain soon disposed of him. Leaping on the lookout unexpectedly, he put a hand over his mouth to stop him raising the alarm. It was the signal his gang had been waiting for. Weapons ready, they moved into position near the door of the shed. Bruce Kerry lit the rag protruding from a bottle of paraffin and hurled the home-made bomb through the single window of the shed. After a sudden explosion, there was pandemonium.

Yelling obscenities, the Spirits came out to punish whoever had tried to ruin their celebrations, only to find themselves having to defend themselves against a frontal attack from the Warriors. Since some of the Spirits were unarmed, they used beer bottles as their weapons, smashing them against the wall to get a jagged edge with which to flail and jab. But the Warriors had the upper hand this time and Wain had the satisfaction of felling the leader of his rivals with the flat of a spade. It was his only victim. A police whistle sounded and the street was suddenly alive with officers wielding truncheons. They waded into the melee and dragged out the combatants one by one, hurling them into the waiting Black Marias then going back for more. A few escaped but the vast majority were quickly rounded up.

Though he'd picked up a few bruises, Everitt White was delighted.

'I'm so glad I didn't miss all the fun,' he said.

'There'll be some very unhappy families around here tomorrow,' said Burge, 'but they'll be in the minority. Most of the people will give us three cheers for taking these wild animals off the streets.'

'Yes, Cliff. There are so many offences they can be charged with that the courts won't know which ones to pick. You did well – congratulations!'

'Thanks, Ev. I hope the commissioner will be pleased.'

'Pleased!' repeated White. 'He'll give you a bleeding medal.'

Keedy was thrilled. Having gone to bed thinking about Alice Marmion, he'd woken up thinking about a different woman altogether. On the drive to Scotland Yard, he confided in Marmion.

'We've been looking in the wrong direction,' he said.

'Have we?'

'Yes. Instead of chasing after Mr Sprake, we should have been talking to Dulcie Haddon.'

'Isn't she part of the string quartet?'

'She's a lot more than that. She's often the only woman in that entire building and she told me something I never expected to hear.'

'I think I can guess Joe. She said that she hated playing at the club.'

'Yet her father doesn't and neither do the other two men in the quartet. Why? It's because they have regular, well-paid work in congenial surroundings. They have a captive audience that loves their performances. Most musicians would give their eye-teeth to have that.'

'I agree. Many of them are out of work most of the time.'

'So why is Dulcie Haddon the odd one out? She should have been overjoyed to be part of a distinguished quartet like the Malvern.'

'Perhaps she feels uneasy in front of a male audience.'

'It's more than feeling uneasy,' said Keedy. 'She *detests* it.'

'She's out of place there, that's all.'

'It's much more serious than that and I'm annoyed with myself for not realising it before. When she's playing with the quartet, Dulcie Haddon only ever looks at her father or at the music. Her gaze never wanders to the audience. I didn't understand why until now.'

'What's the answer?'

'She's afraid to see the way some of those men are looking at her.'

'And what way is that?'

'It's the way they'd look at a naked woman.'

Saul Rockwell enjoyed the days when neither of the club founders was on the premises. It meant that he was in charge. He could take all the decisions himself, bully the staff and welcome the members as they began to dribble in. Club Apollo, he believed, was really his. Nobody had made such a huge contribution to the running of the place. Nobody did as much to safeguard its future. By mid morning that day, he was in the foyer, shaking hands with new arrivals, then noting their names in the book. One cabinet minister and two senior politicians had already arrived. Wearing his clerical garb, an archdeacon had also been signed in. While he was not expecting the next two people who came in through the door, Rockwell beamed at Marmion and Keedy. They exchanged niceties.

'If you've come to see Mr Ulverton,' said the steward, 'then you're out of luck. It's the first day of the Dickens Festival. He's in Rochester.'

'We've come to see you, actually,' said Marmion.

'How can I help you, Inspector?'

'I'd like to see some of the club records. Mr Ulverton said that I was to have access to anything I wanted. Shall we go to the office?'

'Yes, yes, of course.'

They followed him into the back room. Taking out a key, he unlocked a cupboard and took out two ledgers. Marmion shook his head.

'No, Mr Rockwell,' he said, 'I've already seen those. What I'd like is a list of your entire staff. It's probably in one of the other cupboards.'

'I can't let you see that, Inspector.'

'Why not?'

'It's confidential. You'd need Mr Ulverton's permission.'

'In essence, he's already given it. He said that I should have a free hand here.'

'I can't allow that, I'm afraid.'

'Who's in charge here?' asked Keedy. 'Is it you or Jonathan Ulverton?'

'When Mr Ulverton isn't here, I have full authority.'

'Then I suggest you use that full authority to give us what we want.' Rockwell looked uneasily from one to the other. 'Don't make us go through the rigmarole of getting a search warrant. If you've nothing to hide, do as the inspector says.'

'You have no grounds for a search warrant,' said the steward, puffing out his chest. 'We have excellent lawyers among our members. They'd challenge your right to burst in here, making demands.'

'We didn't burst in at all,' argued Keedy.

'And we didn't make demands,' said Marmion. 'I made a polite request and you refused it. In my view, you're trying to cover something up.'

'I'm simply trying to do my job.'

'A major part of it is concealing the truth about this place.'

'The Club Apollo is a perfectly legal establishment, catering for professional men with a passion for music.' He saw both the detectives smile. 'What's so amusing about that?'

'Their passions do not stop at music, Mr Rockwell.'

'They expect rather more for their exorbitant fees than that,' said Keedy. 'We've just paid a visit to one of your musicians, a young lady named Dulcie Haddon. You know her well, of course. She arrives with the quartet and does exactly what she and the others are engaged to do.'

'Miss Haddon is very popular here,' said Rockwell.

'But it's not only because of the way she plays the viola, is it?'

'What are you trying to say, Sergeant?'

'Coming here is something of an ordeal for her.'

'That's a ludicrous suggestion!'

'Miss Haddon doesn't think so. Before she can play with the quartet, she has to grit her teeth. Does that sound like someone who's happy at what she's doing?'

'Where is all this leading?' demanded Rockwell.

'Eventually, it will lead to you showing us the employment records,' said Marmion. 'When the sergeant mentioned a search warrant, it was no idle boast. We've never had our application for one turned down yet. What's it to be? Do you cooperate with us or do we have to take a different route?'

Rockwell's eyes were darting. 'I'll need to speak to Mr Ulverton.'

'Mr Pickwick is not available.'

'I could ring his home. Someone could get a message to him.'

'Why spoil his fun? He loves the Dickens Festival.'

'In fact,' said Marmion, 'he loves being somebody that he's not. Mr Donohoe was the same. He showed one face to the world but it was only when he was here that he could really be himself. That's what drew them together, isn't it? Ulverton and Donohoe were two of a kind. It was the perfect partnership – until they fell out.'

'We're still waiting to see those employment records,' said Keedy.

Rockwell was torn between anger and fear. They'd cornered him at a time when Ulverton was away and they posed a real threat. Unable to keep them at bay, he eventually agreed to show them what they requested. He unlocked a second cupboard and took out a folder that contained a sheaf of papers.

'If you must poke your nose into our affairs,' he said, testily, 'then here's the list, though why you wish to check on our waiters, chefs and maintenance staff, I haven't a clue.'

Taking the folder from him, Marmion opened it and took out the first page. After running his eye down a long list, he showed it to Keedy. Both were struck by the number of female names, one of which had a line drawn through it.

'I thought you didn't employ women here,' said Marmion.

'They're only cleaners,' said Rockwell.

'Did you have to import them from Europe? Some of these names are either French or Belgian. There's no shortage of British cleaners. Why not employ them?'

'Unless they do more than simply clean the place,' said Keedy.

'We do nothing illegal,' said Rockwell. 'We follow the letter of the law.' He took the folder back. 'Is that all?' he asked, pointedly.

'Not quite,' replied the inspector, 'we'd like a tour of the building.'

'You've already had that with Mr Ulverton.'

'He missed something out.'

'These are large properties,' said Keedy. 'They all have basements. That's what we'd like to see, Mr Rockwell. It's the part of the house that Mr Ulverton deliberately kept us away from.'

'There's nothing down there to interest you,' insisted Rockwell.

'All the same, we'd like to see it.'

'It's out of bounds.'

'Nothing is out of bounds to us.'

'It would be a waste of your time,' said Rockwell, starting to gibber. 'It's used for storage. It's full of empty crates and piles of cartons.'

'Show us.'

'Why bother?'

'Show us, Mr Rockwell,' said Marmion, reinforcing his demand with a hand on the man's shoulder. 'We want to see the basement.'

'It's locked up.'

'Then find the key and take us down there.'

'No,' said Rockwell, squaring up to them. 'I can't do that.'

'Are you daring to obstruct us?'

'It's what Mr Ulverton would expect me to do.'

Tossing the folder on to the desk, Rockwell folded his arms in a show of defiance. When he saw their expressions harden, he knew he'd lose the confrontation. The detectives had found out too much. They were too determined to get the full truth. Since there was no way of stopping them, Rockwell put self-preservation first and decided to make a run for it. Leaping across the room, he pulled open the desk drawer and thrust his hand in but Keedy was too fast for him. He kicked the drawer hard so that it jammed the steward's fingers. Before Rockwell, screaming in pain, could take anything out, Keedy grappled with him and pulled him away from the desk. The steward, however, was strong and resourceful. He fought back with the ferocity of a man in a desperate situation. He punched, kicked, spat and even tried to bite. Keedy had to take a lot of blows before he finally pinioned Rockwell long enough for Marmion to handcuff the man. Blood was streaming from the steward's nose and he was snarling like an animal.

'You met your match this time,' said Marmion. 'The sergeant didn't turn his back on you like Mr Donohoe and he wasn't easily overpowered like your second victim. I daresay her name is on that list we saw, isn't it? Then there was the private detective hired by Mr Donohoe's son. He came sniffing around the Apollo. Were you the one who beat him up?'

'I'm saying nothing,' growled Rockwell.

Keedy opened the drawer and saw the revolver hidden away inside it. He took the weapon out and held it up for examination.

'Well,' he said, 'I suppose it's one way to keep the members in order.'

Chatfield got to the commissioner's office as Clifford Burge was being shown out.

'You're just in time to add your congratulations,' said Sir Edward. 'Last night's operation was a complete success. Thanks to Detective Constable Burge, Stepney will be a much safer place from now on.'

'Well done!' said Chatfield, shaking Burge's hand.

'Thank you, sir,' said Burge.

'I had great faith in you.'

'It's been handsomely repaid,' said the commissioner.

He put a gentle hand on Burge's shoulder to help him on his way and the younger man walked off happily down the corridor. He'd been praised so highly for the work he'd done that he could dare to think of promotion, or, at the very least, of being assigned to work on homicide investigations. Gratified that the officer he recommended had been an unqualified success, Chatfield watched him go. He then turned back to the commissioner.

'There may be good news on another front,' he said.

'We're talking about Inspector Marmion, I assume?'

'He and Sergeant Keedy called in earlier. They told me they were going on to meet someone who could help them to identify the killer.'

'That sounds promising. Who is this person?'

'She plays the viola, Sir Edward.'

Before the steward was dragged off by Keedy to the police car, Marmion divested him of his keys. He then went down the steps to the basement and tried a succession of keys until he found the right one. Of one thing he felt certain. In spite of what he'd been told, the basement wouldn't be filled with empty crates and cartons. What he did find made him stare in amazement. Earlier in his career, Marmion had taken part in many raids on brothels and they'd always been rather squalid places. This one was very different. There was a faint smell of perfume in the air. Off the main corridor were a number of bedrooms that were nothing short of luxurious. Each had a wall that consisted of a large mirror. The rooms were equipped with ropes, masks, whips and a range of harnesses.

But the real discovery was yet to come. It was only when Marmion got to the end of the corridor that he saw there was a subterranean tunnel to the adjoining property. Well lit and with a thick carpet on the floor, it went under the extensive garden between the two houses. Reaching the other basement, he saw that it had a series of bedrooms furnished exactly like the others. Marmion went on until he came to a flight of steps. At the top of them was a locked door but one of Rockwell's keys soon opened it. He emerged into the corridor of a house identical in design to the one he'd just left. Hearing voices from the lounge, he walked on till he came to the room and stood in the doorway. A short, stout, scantily dressed middle-aged woman glided across to him with a broad smile. Her face was heavily powdered, her lipstick bright scarlet. With a wave of her arm, she indicated the various prostitutes, most of them in silk gowns or revealing underwear.

'What's your pleasure, sir?' she asked. 'Choose any girl you wish or, of course, you may prefer a young man to do your bidding.'

Four slim youths, wearing black leather trousers and black leather waistcoats over their naked torsos, stood up and preened for Marmion's benefit.

'Well,' said the woman, 'which will you take?'

'I'll take all of them,' he said, producing his warrant card. 'I'm Inspector Marmion of Scotland Yard and I have a number of policemen outside waiting for orders from me.'

She was horrified. 'However did you get in here?'

'Mr Rockwell loaned me his keys.'

'We've done nothing wrong. We're here at the invitation of the Club Apollo. You can't prosecute us for being guests at a party.'

'Oh, yes we can. When they've each been questioned, these people will be released. It's obvious to me that they're all here against their will.' There was a loud murmur of agreement from the prostitutes. 'One of them tried to escape from here and she was murdered as a punishment. They're not guests at a party. They're prisoners at the mercy of the whims of the members.' He turned to the others. 'I'm pleased to tell you that the Club Apollo is closed for business.'

There was a loud cheer.

Alice Marmion couldn't understand it. She'd been walking beside Iris Goodliffe for well over an hour yet there'd been no mention of Douglas Beckett. Iris was gloomy and preoccupied. Alice could see that she was in distress.

'What's happened, Iris?'

'Nothing,' said the other.

'Are you feeling unwell?'

'I'm fine, honestly.'

'Have I said something to upset you?'

'No, Alice.'

'Then what's going on?'

'I'd rather not talk about it.'

They continued on their beat in silence.

When they got to Rochester, the police car couldn't park in the main street because it was thronged with people dressed up as characters from the novels of Charles Dickens. Many of them clustered around the cathedral, which had featured as Cloisterham in the author's last and unfinished book, *The Mystery of Edwin Drood*.

Oliver Twists were there in profusion and there were a number of Fagins as well. The noise was deafening, the mood joyous. Everyone had taken pains to get the correct period costume. Many went a stage further, declaiming speeches by their characters taken wholesale from the books.

Marmion and Keedy had a problem. Looking for one Samuel Pickwick, they were confronted by several others, all of them remarkably lifelike. Indeed, they came close to arresting the wrong man on three occasions. They eventually found Jonathan Ulverton in the shadow of the castle. With his back to the river, he was holding court to a group of friends that included three Scrooges, two Mrs Gamps and a rather fearsome-looking Joe Gargery, the blacksmith from *Great Expectations*. When he saw the detectives pushing their way through the crowd, Ulverton detached himself from his friends. He spread his arms wide.

'Welcome to the Dickens Festival,' he said, grandly.

'It's a case of hail and farewell, I'm afraid,' explained Marmion. 'We're here to arrest you and take you back to London with us.'

'You can't do that, Inspector! This is *my* festival. I'm needed here.'

'It will have to manage without you, sir.'

'Saul Rockwell is already in custody,' said Keedy, 'and the Madam of your brothel has given us the name of the prostitute who was murdered when she tried to escape. Rockwell will hang alongside you.'

'There must be some mistake,' said Ulverton, blustering. 'I know nothing of a murder.'

'There were two, sir. The second victim was Gilbert Donohoe. His death was sanctioned by you. Rockwell garrotted him.'

'According to your Madam,' said Marmion, taking over, 'your steward was given extra privileges. He could have any of the women he chose. As it happened, he preferred young men. That was his reward for the special services he provided for the club, like murdering one of its founders.'

'Gilbert betrayed me,' said Ulverton, shaking with fury. 'He had the gall to try to take over the club and ease me out. I couldn't let him do that. *I* was the real power behind the Apollo. When he started arguing with me, we shut him up for good. I've kept his tongue in a jar in the safe.'

Marmion took his arm. 'You'll have to come with us, sir.'

'Take your hands off me! I'm Samuel Pickwick.'

'No, Mr Ulverton, you're not. From what I recall, Pickwick was a benign, warm-hearted character who wouldn't hurt a flea. That disguise doesn't fool us. We know the truth about you.'

Ulverton was breathing heavily and starting to sweat. If they had Rockwell in custody and knew about the brothel he'd established, then he was done for. He was destined to hang. Until the detectives had arrived, he'd been the toast of Rochester. What would they think of him now? Ulverton simply couldn't face the trial and the accompanying disgrace. There had to be a way out. With a sudden push, he shoved

Marmion aside and ran to the nearby bank, jumping into the River Medway and landing with a splash.

'It's a suicide bid, Joe,' said Marmion. 'He can't hope to get away like that.'

'Should we just let him drown?'

'No, if we don't go in after him, someone else will.'

'That means me,' said Keedy, starting to take off his coat.

'You stay here, Joe. It's my turn for the heroics and I don't mind getting wet.' He peeled off his coat, handed it to Keedy with his hat, then took his shoes off. 'You deserve the plaudits for remembering Dulcie Haddon. What she told you changed everything.' He walked gingerly to the bank through the gathering crowd. 'See if you can rustle up a couple of towels. We'll need them.' He gazed down at the spluttering figure of Ulverton. 'Don't worry, Mr Pickwick,' he shouted. 'I'm coming!'

To the accompaniment of loud cheers, Marmion jumped into the river.

When she bought the newspaper the following morning, Ellen was pleased to see a photograph of her husband on the front page. He and Joe Keedy were credited with solving two murders, arresting the killer and exposing the truth about the Club Apollo, thereby causing its former members acute embarrassment. Scotland Yard was no longer under attack for its perceived shortcomings. With its strategy against the gang culture in Stepney as an additional success, it was lauded. At the end of a fraught week for the family, Ellen had the satisfaction of seeing her husband's reputation vindicated and her daughter's rift with Keedy well and truly healed. Paul was still missing but at least she knew he could survive on his own. He had no wish to come home again. Ellen decided that perhaps that was best for all of them.

EDWARD MARSTON has written well over a hundred books, including some non-fiction. He is best known for his hugely successful Railway Detective series and he also writes the Bow Street Rivals series featuring twin detectives set during the Regency, as well as the Home Front Detective series, of which *Under Attack* is the seventh book.

edwardmarston.com

ALSO BY EDWARD MARSTON

THE RAILWAY DETECTIVE SERIES

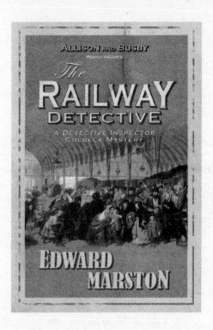

London, 1851. The London to Birmingham mail train is robbed and derailed, injuring the driver and others aboard. With the opening of the Great Exhibition at hand, interest is mounting in the engineering triumphs of the railways, but not everyone feels like celebrating. Planned with military precision, this crime challenges the new Police Force to its limits and leads Detective Inspector Robert Colbeck to discover a tangled web of murder, blackmail and destruction.

The Bow Street Rivals series

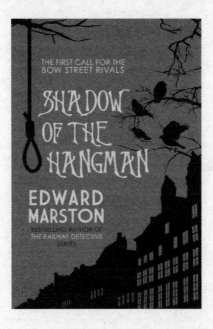

1815. Peter and Paul Skillen, identical twins and fearless thief-takers, help police the dangerous streets of London. When they catch a notorious burglar, they infuriate the Bow Street Runners, who believe they have a monopoly on policing in the capital.

During a massacre of American prisoners of war at Dartmoor, two escape and come to London in search of retribution. If their demands are not met, Home Secretary Viscount Sidmouth will be killed. The Skillen brothers are hired to catch the fugitives and must compete with the Runners to bring the villains to justice.

The Bracewell Mysteries

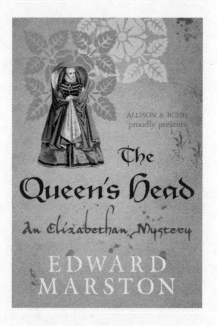

ALLISON & BUSBY
proudly presents

The
Queen's Head

An Elizabethan Mystery

EDWARD
MARSTON

Will Fowler was egotistical, verbose, and hot-headed to a fault. But he did not deserve to die. Fresh from a performance on stage at the Queen's Head theatre, the actor met his end in a bar-room brawl – but not before he gasped for Nicholas Bracewell to find his fast-fleeting, red-bearded murderer and administer a just revenge. Yet finding Will's murderer in London's dark, crowded streets is seemingly impossible with Lord Westfield's Men commanded to appear at the court of Elizabeth I – an honour one dare not refuse.

To discover more great books and to
place an order visit our website at
allisonandbusby.com

Don't forget to sign up to our free newsletter at
allisonandbusby.com/newsletter
for latest releases, events and exclusive offers

Allison & Busby Books
@AllisonandBusby

You can also call us on
020 7580 1080
for orders, queries
and reading recommendations